The Case of the Floating Corpse

By

James Michael Walker

A Sherlock Holmes Mystery

Library of Congress and Printing Information.

First Printing December, 2019

Printed in the United States of America

Author's Tribute to

Gillette's Castle 100 Year Anniversary

'The Case of the Floating Corpse', commemorates the 100th year anniversary of William Gillette taking up residence in the castle he designed and built in East Haddam, Connecticut in 1919.

William Gillette was a leading stage actor, screen writer, and special effects creator from 1890 to 1915. He is most famous for bringing to America, and portraying, the famous sleuth of Sir Conan Doyle - Sherlock Holmes.

Sherlock Holmes, to this day, remains one of the most recognized fictional detectives and continues to intrigue mystery lovers as strongly as ever. Most of the visualizations of Sherlock Holmes were created by William Gillette's portrayal of him, such as the deerstalker hat, the Macintosh coat, and even his best known line, "Elementary, my dear Watson!"

Gillette Castle still stands today, as it has for over 100 years, sitting atop a series of hills known as the Seven Sisters, that overlook the Connecticut River. As a Connecticut state park, it is now host to thousands of visitors each year from all across the globe. The castle itself is a testament to the creative genius of William Gillette.

Enjoy this mystery which takes place at Gillette Castle and the surrounding towns and along the Connecticut River. If you have visited the Castle you will recognize the many descriptive passages and be inspired to visit William Gillette's home once again. Enjoy!

The Case of the Floating Corpse

1

"Chester! Five minutes to Chester! Please gather all your belongings and wait until the train is completely stopped before disembarking! Chester!

I waited until I felt the rush of air and heard the noise of the train increase for a moment, and then I grabbed my saddlebags and made my way off in the opposite direction of the Conductor. I was impressed that he hadn't even glanced at me.

I made my way to the back of the passenger car and went out the rear door. It was a bit dicey, carrying my loaded bags and crossing over the platform to the next car.

This one was crowded, second class, and the passageway was filed with people gathering up their children, baggage, and whatnot. I had to rather bully my way through, jostling many with my leather bags draped across my shoulder. Folks glared at me then looked away confused. Not many guys wear fifty-dollar suits and tote cowpoke luggage around this part of New England. I had just made it through the throng as I felt the train begin to slow.

In any case, a few bucks slipped earlier to the conductor gave me a key to the cargo car. I let myself in then locked the door behind me and hung the key on a nail in the wall, as the conductor instructed me to. Now, I could get ready to make a grand departure from the train. By the time the train had begun to walking pace, I had secured my saddle bags and donned my riding boots, jacket, helmet and googles. I had just pulled on my gloves and straddled my motorcycle when the train lurched to a stop. Luckily, the kick stand was still down, or I might have gone over.

It was a few long moments before the side doors were pulled back and a wide board was propped up against the floor. Quickly I kicked started the engine and eased over to the ramp. When my front tire went over the edge of the ramp, I realized it was too steep for my bike to clear without bottoming out. I gave it a burst of throttle and pulled back on the handlebars.

The front end went up so smoothly that when my rear tire cleared the lip, I kept the front tire in the air and rode the ramp down. Gaping passengers milled about on either side of the ramp. After I was on level ground, I had to keep the wheel up for show and give it another goose.

I ran out of platform quickly and found myself facing a short set of stairs that went down to the train stations drive. In the air I went, to the sounds of gasps and short screams from the crowd. Thankfully, I kept my balance and landed smoothly, letting the front tire touch the gravel like a leaf that falls from a tree. I heard a few cheers but I didn't have time to bask in their delight, as I had to hit the brakes hard.

Standing not twenty feet in front of me was a burly man in a uniform, pointing a nightstick at me and shouting angrily, words I couldn't hear over the roar of my engine.

I probably could have just gone around him and been on my way, but his meaning was clear, and I didn't want to be a fugitive minutes after I arrived in Chester, Connecticut. I managed to lurch to a stop, just inches from his future children.

With impudent slowness, I reached over and shut down my engine to catch the copper in front of me in mid rant.

"What do you think you're doing tossing that contraption through the air and scaring folk half to death! Lucky you didn't hit anyone or you'd find yourself in cuffs Bucko!" He jabbed me hard in the chest with the end of his stick. "You'll be lucky if'n I don't run you in right now for disturbing the peace!"

I might have been contrite but for the jab, I just grinned and said, "I feel truly blessed, Officer."

The copper tilted his head and started slapping his club in the palm of his other hand. "Oh, a clever one. And what brings you to our sleepy little town? You're not from around here, that much I know."

"I'm here to visit my uncle." I replied curtly. I noticed a small crowd was watching this proceeding with interest.

He was getting annoyed as he laid the club on his shoulder, poised to smack me. "And just who might that be?"

I wasn't particularly scared of the club or the uniform, but I didn't want to embarrass my uncle, so I tried to put a little respect in my tone.

"Gillette. William Gillette. Makes his home somewhere around here, I think. Big stone place? Near the river? Perhaps you could give me directions and we could both get about our day."

I could see the copper's demeanor change instantly when he heard the name 'Gillette', just as I thought it would. After all, William Gillette was the most famous actor of our times and his portrayal of Sherlock Holmes was known worldwide. He was most likely the richest man in this county to boot and I was counting on his name to get this flatfoot off my back.

The Copper lowered his stick, but he wasn't done with me yet. "Yes, you have the right place, but you still haven't told me what they call you when your home."

"Frohman. Collin Frohman."

His eyebrows went up at that. "Any relations to a Charles Frohman?"

"My father."

His features softened, and he stepped off to the side of the wheel, putting his nightstick back in a loop on his belt. "How long are you planning to stay?"

"A few weeks, more or less."

He sighed and smiled. "I suppose we'll have the two of you racing about on those things for a while. Mr. Gillette is always tearing about on his."

I grinned, "I'll be the one out front."

He laughed, "Just use some caution, is all we ask. Take a left out of here and go up a few miles until you hit the Ferry road. Follow that and you'll come to the ferry. You'll find it from there." He smiled at me slyly. "Big stone place on a hill overlooking the river. You can't miss it."

"Thank you, Officer." I said as I rose up and kicked the machine into life.

Over the roar, he leaned in and said, loud enough to hear, "A good man, your father!"

I nodded and dropped into gear, a lot of my cockiness knocked out of me as I sped off.

It was a fun ride, if a bit short. The road was pleasantly windy and hilly, and my new motorcycle made it feel as if I was riding on the back of an eagle, soaring and diving in the wind. The trees thinned out and some homes began to dot the roadside. I had to reduce my speed as I came up on the outskirts of a town and traffic began to thicken. There were still a good amount of horse and buggies, and I did see a smattering of automobiles and trucks along the way. I got a lot of glares from the former, especially those whose horses sidestepped away when I passed by, and a lot of waves from the latter. Before I knew it, a fairly good- sized river ended the road. Fortunately, there was a ferry at the end of the road, and I made it just as it was preparing to depart. I sped over to the ticket booth, but the woman inside just smiled and waved me on. I wondered why there was no charge, but I didn't have time to ask questions and lunged forward onto the deck of the ferry just before they hung the chain railing up and the boat began to pull away.

I was still confused by the no fee, but happy I didn't have to wait until the ferry made its circuit before I could cross the river. I killed the engine and put down the kick stand. I remained in my seat, planting my feet on the deck, not sure about the bike's balance on rolling waters. I didn't want any scratches on her until my Uncle saw her.

As I was pulling my helmet off, a man about my age and two girls came up alongside. All were clutching paper and pencils and looking at me in adoration. I had to laugh at their looks of sudden disappointment. One girl even began to pout. More strangeness. What was going on? Leave it to Uncle Will to settle in the land of crazies.

"Am I that ugly?" I asked hoping to keep their attention.

Ignoring me, the guy turned to the girl next to him. "That's not him! I told you he was too short!"

"Well, how many people wear nice suits and ride one of those things around here!" She demanded in return. "And I already knew it wasn't him-he's too young!"

With that, she spun and stalked away, the other two in tow.

9

"Rats!" I heard the second girl say. "I would have loved his autograph!"

That made me laugh! Those chumps thought I was William Gillette! Nice suit and a motorcycle! Uncle Will should get a kick out of this.

I looked around to see if I had any more admirers, but nobody was paying any attention. In fact, all I saw were backsides. Each and every one of the passengers and some of the crew, including the three that approached me, were lining the railings and pointing out over the water from time to time. I wondered what they were looking for or at. Another enigma. That made three in less than a half hour.

The first one was also quickly solved when a deckhand came over to me and asked, "Excuse me, sir. Do you have a ticket?"

A bit embarrassed, I replied, "No. I never got one. I went to the ticket booth, but the girl just smiled and waved me on."

He nodded slowly. "Yes sir. I see. The thing is…she thought you were another person, who has a permanent pass."

"William Gillette?" I ventured.

"Err…yes, sir. We all thought you were him, with the motorcycle and all."

He seemed a bit skittish, so I decided to pull his leg a little. "My God, Man! How could you make that mistake? William Gillette owns an Indian Chief and this magnificent machine I straddle" I put my hands together in a V and thrust them between my legs, "is a Harley-Davidson!"

He was not amused, and his eyes narrowed. "You're still not him! You need to pay for your passage!"

I held up a hand to placate him and put my other in my pocket. "How much I owe you?" I was going to insist on half price because we were well on our way across but decided to save my humor for someone who would appreciate it.

He told me the fare and I pulled a bill out of my clip. His eyes widened, and he said, "I'll have to see if we have change for this, Mister."

Just as he spoke, I looked up over his shoulder and saw it for the first time. My jaw dropped down to the gas tank and I waved the man away,

"Keep it."

Squatting there, not a half-mile away atop the biggest hill, was a great stone edifice that seemed to reach the clouds. The sunlight made the stonework glow and multitude of pinpoints of light reflected off the windows that dotted the structure. It looked like something torn from King Arthur's kingdom and set down in New England.

Uncle Will had outdone himself.

For a guy who spent most of my life living on his boat and occasionally renting a place, this was a real swing in the other direction!

Though, I suppose, for the most successful actor of our times and the man who started this whole money making, mad craze for Sherlock Holmes in America- I guess I shouldn't have been so awed. But, even with my father's description and the love I knew my uncle had for dramatics, it was hard not to be daunted!

I sat on my bike, studying the lines of the castle and seeing more of the detail as we readied to dock. I saw a roadway that led directly up to the castle from the ferry landing, so I knew how to get there once we tied up, which happened very quickly. I'd like to say I was being courteous, but the truth was-I didn't trust the drivers of a few of the automobiles. They looked a little green with their machinery and I had no intention of getting run over or even worse, having my bike getting banged up before I could show it off.

Soon enough, the coast was clear, and I roared off the deck and onto dry land. I went to the left on the road I had seen earlier, but only made it as far as a newly built foundation for a house, with yet another oddity. There was a donkey tied to a stake in what would someday be the front yard. The animal didn't even notice the noise of my engine, and just kept nibbling away at the grass.

In truth, I was just stalling for a moment. As much as I wanted to see the castle and my uncle, I had butterflies in my stomach. The misery heaped upon my family, in just six months' time, had turned my life upside down. Now I had but one chance to get the life I wanted so desperately. Uncle Will was my only hope. Heaving a great sigh, I dropped the bike into gear and dashed up the hill. The ride was fast and before I knew it, and without a chance to really look at the castle as I came up, I found myself at one end of a short bridge that spanned a crevasse between the road and the castle. Even then, I hardly notice the castle as my whole being was focused on a little man who stood in the center of the other side.

Dressed in a black suit, slender, short, and Asian, Ozaki looked almost the same as he had since my first memories.

William's manservant, confidant, and companion had been with my Uncle as long as my father and Wiliam had been friends -- long before I was even thought of. Consequentially, Ozaki has been a big part of my life, teacher, caretaker, and always a friend. Where William was more of an uncle than anyone could want, Ozaki was that special cousin. Older, wiser, and the one that would tell you the things about life nobody else would.

He just stood perfectly still, hands folded at his waist as I settled my bike and walked over to him. His stoic face tore at my heart and the rents widened as I neared and saw the worn look to his features. He looked like he had aged five years in the last nine months. I tried to smile as I stepped up to him, but before I could catch myself, I sank to one knee and threw my arms around his waist. I buried my head in his chest and cried like a little girl.

Ozaki said nothing, just held me for a moment or two then he suddenly thrust me to arms' length and gave me a little shake.

"*BAKA!*"

I had to smile at the Japanese obscenity, and I rose to me feet. I stepped back and gave him a low bow.

"Please forgive my weakness, Sensei. It is good to see you."

He just smiled and patted my arm. "There is no shame. Sometimes grief is a sneeze."

I didn't have time to process that, as he turned and began to slowly walk towards the side of the castle. I stepped up alongside him, but we walked very slowly. Usually, that meant he had something to say to me.

"I must take you to your Uncle right away! He has been looking forward to seeing you."

"How is he?"

Ozaki took a moment to think that over. "Better. He was like a warking dead man for months after, but putting the finar touches on this monstrosity." He gestured to the castle that loomed over us like a sculpted cliff face, "has brought some life back to him. He has been more rike his old self after you wrote to say you were coming." He cast an eye on me, "Why you wait so rong?"

13

"Me?" I protested. "I've asked to come see the place at least three times since the funeral. Uncle Will kept putting me off! I figured I disappointed him in some way. I…I guess I can understand…"

Ozaki stopped dead in his tracks and glared at me. "You understand nothing!"

I didn't want to start my trip with an argument. "How are you, Ozaki? You look tired." I said to deflect the question.

He smiled slyly at me. "Your Uncre has been a hard man to rive with these past months."

By then we had reached some steps that led up to a patio area. I went up the steps quickly and there, on the other side of the stone courtyard, standing by the railing that faced the river was my Uncle, William Hooker Gillette, actor, playwright, inventor, and much more to me, stood stiff backed, one leg bent, and chin held high. I smiled to myself. Always posing for effect! We saw each other at the same time, each of us putting on a brave smile as we closed the distance between us. Not trusting myself to speak, in case the water works started anew, I ignored his outstretched hand and threw my arms around him. "Uncle Will, I'm so glad to see you."

I broke away and looked up at his face. Tears were streaming down his cheeks.

"It's so very good to see you, Collin. You must forgive me, it's just…well, I miss your father so very much." Then he added softly, "I'm sure I always will."

There it was, out in the open. My father was gone.

Charles Frohman was dead.

2

Uncle Will quickly dried his eyes on his sleeves and gave me another quick hug. With a genuine smile on his face, he said, "Come. Come, Collin. Let's have a seat. We have so much catching up to do!" Taking me by the arm, he led me towards a set of stone benches and a small café table, which overlooked the river. "I'm sure Ozaki will be out shortly with refreshments."

It was only then, I realized Ozaki had slipped away. He was as quiet and devious as a cat at times. We settled into our seats and William took out some cigarettes and offered me one, which I gratefully accepted. After lighting up, we both sat back and Uncle Will smiled at me. "My word, Collin, but it's good to see you! I'm so glad you came for a visit. I haven't seen nor heard from you since…"

"the funeral." I finished for him. "I know. I'm sorry I couldn't spend more time with you then, but there were so many people coming and going."

"Your father had a lot of friends."

"But you were his very best friend." I pointed out. "I guess I was just numb at the time."

"We all were," he said as he reached over and patted my arm, "I was in a fog for months. Nearly drove Ozaki to drink!"

"Ah!" he said, "Speak of the devil!" I swiveled my head to see Ozaki walk up to us, bearing a tray with beverages and a covered plate.

Ozaki, bless his heart -- put a ice-cold ale in front of me and a glass of some dark fizzy drink in front of William. The plate held a few crackers, along with some cheese and sliced fruit. After he laid everything out, he picked up a mug of what I knew was tea and sat down with us. Ozaki then put the palms of his hands together in front of his face and bowed from his waist, "I cannot tell you how sorry I am for the death of your father, Master Corrin. My English isn't good enough to convey the respect and admiration I had for Charles. It was a senseress act."

"A senseless act of mayhem!" William said with a vehement tone. "One that will drag our country into war."

"Do you really think so?" I asked. I wasn't so sure about that. A lot of folk were talking about keeping out of this conflict. I hated to think about the consequences of that. I had already lost two family members to this war and America was still sitting on the sidelines.

"Absolutely! I have it on good authority we will declare war on Germany before the month is out. Next month by the latest!" His eyes narrowed. "I won't say I'm not happy about it either! The Huns need to pay for their butchery!"

On that, we agreed.

My father was on a trip to check on his investments in England and Europe aboard the *HMS Lusitania*, when it was sunk by a German U-boat on May seventh of last year. He was among the nearly twelve hundred passengers and crew that lost their lives in the Celtic sea off the coast of Ireland. The Lusitania was my father's favorite passenger ship and his usual mode of transportation when he went to England.

As if he were reading my mind, Wiliam said. "I'm so sorry he was on that particular voyage. I tortured myself for months for encouraging him to take that trip."

"You shouldn't beat yourself over it, Uncle." I said firmly. "Dad had that trip planned for months. I'm just glad you weren't on board with him. I couldn't have survived losing both of you."

"And what word do we have of your brother. Is there any news? I know your mother and sister have gone to see him."

I nodded. "Yeah, they left a few days ago, but we haven't heard anything more from the doctors. Charlie's still in a bad way."

My brother, Charlie was lying in a hospital bed somewhere in London, half burnt and without the use of his arms and legs. He was the oldest of us siblings and the heir apparent to our father's theater business, a burden that now rested on my shoulders and half the reason I had come to see my Uncle.

After my father's memorial service last June, Charlie's grief turned to anger and a thirst for revenge. He hated the Huns for murdering innocents and vowed to 'fix their wagon'. As fate would have it, Charlies Frat brother at Harvard- Norman Prince- had formed an American squadron in France, called the Lafayette Escadrille. Really just a few pilots that wanted to fight the Germans in the sky. Before any of the family knew what was happening, Charlie had bought his own aero plane and learned how to fly. He joined the squadron just last month and on his first patrol was shot down by a German Ace. Charlie managed to bring the plane down, but the wings collapsed, and the plane crashed into a vineyard and burst into flames. Luckily, some workers pulled him from the burning wreckage, but he was scorched over half his body and his neck was broken. The last telegram we received from the hospital was less than hopeful for his recovery. William and Ozaki already

17

knew all this, as they kept in regular correspondence with my mother and sister.

As for myself, I was torn between being devastated for the brother I loved and angry that he left me in this position.

"Damn fool lost his head!" I groused. "Thinking he could bring he Kaiser to his knees with a plane. He was mad as a hatter!"

"Baka!" Ozaki said, swatting me on the forearm closest to him. "He acted with honor! Do not be angry that your brother fought against injustice."

I was about to snap back at him but caught myself. As when I was a boy, I was still cowed by that stern expression on his face.

"What I think Collin is trying to say, Ozaki, is that Charlie might have gone off to war with some false assumptions."

That piqued my interest. "Have you heard some of the same rumors as I have, Uncle Will?"

He shrugged, "I have heard it…bandied about, that munitions were smuggled on board in mislabeled barrels. That is why the U-boat targeted the *Lusitania*."

I leaned forward, "This is straight from the horse's mouth, a guy I know who runs a loading crew on the docks. Over twelve THOUSAND barrels of 'pork' and 'Cheese' were loaded into the holds of the Lusitania just before they let the passengers check in. That's a lot of bangers and mash wouldn't you say?"

"Indeed", he replied. "and if true, someone should be held accountable for that act of irresponsibility."

I sat back and sighed. "Yes, they should. But it still doesn't change the outcome."

With that, we all fell into a remorseful silence. William looked out over the river for a long minute then slowly turned his head to face me. "Collin, before you arrived, I had debated to myself whether I should tell you this story. I do not wish to open any wounds, yet you will probably hear it at one point or another and I wish you to hear an accurate version."

"Go ahead, Uncle Will," I replied. "I can take it."

He smiled sadly and spoke,

"A few weeks ago, I had a visit from an actress. A Miss Rita Joviet. She was a passenger on the Lusitania that trip and one of the few survivors. She was with your father when he …was lost."

Ozaki saw the look on my face and swore, "BAKA! Don't say it like that", he hissed.

"I won't dignify that by responding," Uncle said sternly to his man, "Now get your mind out of the gutter!" Ozaki stuck his tongue out at him and that broke the tension.

"Back to the story: When the ship was struck and began to go down, your father went up to the promenade deck. When someone asked him what was happening, he replied 'This is going to be a close call.' But while others tried to jump to the lifeboats and others abandoned ship, your father and some nobler men stayed back to wrap as many of the smaller children as they could in life jackets. He showed them how to tie two together and secure the toddler in it, so they would float upright."

"Moses baskets!" I cut in, "I remember Pop-Pop talking about them once."

William nodded, "When they had finished, the ship was almost completely under. Your father was left on deck with a millionaire, a Captain Scott, and the woman who told me this story, Rita Joivet. She said your father was calm and seemed at

19

peace with his fate. He lit a cigar, took a swig from his flask and passed it on, saying, 'What is death-but the greatest adventure life gives us!'. Then the final wave broke over the deck and they were separated. Only the woman survived."

I smiled. "Peter Pan. Dad loved that play." Then I grabbed his hand, "Thank you, Uncle William. I'm glad you told me. I've…well…I've had a hard time with Dad's death."

"Of course!" Ozaki said. "You should be proud of your father. He died with great honor."

Uncle Will gave him a side look and added, "Yes, Collin. You should be happy to know your father kept his wits about him and helped others before himself."

"It's not that. I am just happy he got a last drink and a smoke in!"

Ozaki spit out his tea and nearly choked.

Uncle laughed like a loon. "You're absolutely right, Collin. We've been missing the big picture!"

We sat for a moment then Uncle Will tapped the table with his finger, "I do confess to one enigma that occurred to me after Miss Joviet left us."

"What's that," I asked.

He shrugged, "I don't mean to be crass, but I wondered why Miss Joviet managed to survive, while your father did not. She confessed that she wasn't a particularly good swimmer, but the wave that swept them from the deck carried them past the suction of the ship sinking and she was quickly assisted by a lifeboat. Your father, on the other hand, spent his whole life by the sea and I knew him to be an excellent swimmer. Strange that she survived, and he did not."

I really didn't want to rehash it any further and I had never shared this fact with anyone-even my family- but Uncle Will had a special relationship with my dad, so I let him in on a little-known fact.

"I can solve that riddle for you, Uncle. I read the coroner's report on my father and he didn't actually drown. The back of his head was crushed. Probably he hit it when he was swept off the deck. It read that he likely died instantly."

William took that in then slowly nodded his head. "Thank you for sharing that, Collin. I...I have often prayed he didn't suffer."

He shook his head and smiled brightly. "Gentlemen! That is enough maudlin talk for the time being." He pulled out his pocket watch and murmured, "If I'm not mistaken..."

A dinner bell rang from somewhere inside the castle. "AH! Lunch is served!"

We all stood and Uncle Will announced, "First we shall eat, then you get the nickel tour! How does that sound.

"Grand," I assured him, as we headed into the Castle.

3

My first impression of the great room was that it looked less like a castle hall and more like a fine hotel lobby. I was surprised how cozy it was, nothing as large as the outside would suggest. Unless you happened to look up. The ceiling rose far above the second floor and was high enough to fly a kite under.

One wall was dominated by a massive fieldstone fireplace, its top disappearing into the darkness of the upper floors. It was flanked by entryways on the right and the left to what I assumed was a conservatory, considering the moisture beading on the inside of the glass panes. The French doors we came in, a set of windows, and a player piano took up another side of the room.

Across from the fireplace were two sets of circular couches set into the walls, spaced apart, and a door that led to another room. Above that was an open hallway with a railing that ran the length. I could see a few more doors up there.

The side directly across from where we came in had more hallways running off from it and a set of stairs that led to the second floor. Wherever there was open wall space, William had hung rattan mats or tapestries, mostly depicting cats. More of these also hung from the massive wood beams that ran from one end of the room to the other,

There were a few couches, easy chairs, and lamps, making a snug sitting area near the fireplace, but the feature that stood out was a massive carved oaken round table that had chairs around it. It was so ostentatious I wanted to ask my Uncle if Sir Galahad was coming to lunch also.

Uncle Will gave me a few moments to drink it all in and asked, "Well, Collin, what do you think of my humble abode?"

I smiled, "Humble, Uncle Will? It may be humble for the Tsar of Russia, but I think it suits you perfectly. Majestic, yet warm and inviting."

He beamed with joy. "That is precisely why you are my favorite godson."

I gave him a sideways look, "I'm your ONLY godson, Uncle Will."

"Ha!!" He chortled. "Never dissect a compliment, Collin. They are all sarcasm on one level or another."

I shook my head in bewilderment. "You have been spending too much time with Ozaki."

He laughed. "And speak of the devil," as he pointed to the staircase where Ozaki stood at the top. "Why don't you let Ozaki show you to your room and you can freshen up before lunch. I'm sure the girls will have the table set by the time you return."

I didn't really need to freshen up, but Uncle Will was a stickler for formalities and I did need to empty my bladder. I thanked him, then crossed the room and went up the stairs. Ozaki led the way down the open hallway. As I followed him, I looked down into the great room and thought it would be a bully place to watch people if William had a party, which certainly he would in the future. He cherished his privacy, but every now and then, he crammed his entire social life into hosting some very fancy parties. In the past, they were usually held on the *Aunt Polly*, his yacht, or he might rent a place, but I was sure he would be anxious to show off his new home to an elite group of friends. A hiss from Ozaki, who was far ahead of me now, broke my daydreaming, and I hustled past a few doors to catch up with him. He opened the door he was standing next to and stepped aside.

The room I entered was modest. The stone was covered by wood and rattan and it was sparely furnished. There was comfortable bed, an armoire, and a desk like table with a chair. Nothing too lavish, but it had its own fireplace and a window, with a magnificent view of the river and woodlands.

My luggage hadn't arrived from the train station, but the clothes I had in my saddle bags were neatly hung, with a fresh shirt and pants laid out on the bed. I don't see how he could have found the time to go out to my motorcycle, empty the saddle bags, and bring them up, since we were together almost the entire time. But I had given up trying to figure him out a long time ago. He had been amazing to me and my family for all the time we had known him.

"Next door is a guest bathroom," he informed me. "Do your business before you wet yourserf and wash up for runch. After you change, come down. Do not rorry- gag! We are hungry." With that, he slid out of the doorway and disappeared, leaving me shaking my head in amusement. Seven or twenty-seven years old, Ozaki would always treat me the same.

I was shipshape in no time, so I headed down to join the gang, but when I peeked over the railing, the only one at the table was Uncle Will. Ozaki and the girls were still putting the food together, so I walked slowly and took in the surroundings. There were some more doors that led away from the staircase.

The door closest to the staircase happened to be open and I glanced in. It was nearly an exact duplicate of my room. Neat as a pin and free of clutter, the only way I knew it was occupied was by a pair of slippers by the bed, a portrait of a beautiful young woman that hung over the bed, and the combs, brushes, lotions and oils that were neatly lined up on the dressing table.

I suddenly realized that it was my Uncle's room! I had seen other pictures of the woman that was in the portrait. She was Helen, Uncle Will's wife who left him a widower a long time ago. It kind of turned my brain sideways when I thought about him, living like a monk. Here was a man prone to flamboyancy, professionally and personally, and yet he spent most of his alone time, in such a spartan existence. I suppose, from what I had read of my father's stories, a man of his intellect is his own best stimuli.

Uncle Will was reading a small newspaper and was so absorbed he didn't notice me coming up alongside him. It wasn't until I greeted him, did he fold the paper and put it on the table.

"Well, Collin, how do you like your accommodations?"

"Fine, Uncle Will, I'll be quite comfortable."

"Excellent! The room is yours, stay as long as you like, whenever you like." He smiled at me with a glint of mirth in his eyes, "Consider it a part of your inheritance!"

Before I could thank him, Ozaki burst out of a hallway carrying a large round wooden object and spitting Japanese over his shoulder. A tall, matronly woman came, the object of his tirade, came right on his heels, pushing a serving cart that was loaded with dishes.

"Don't you take that tone with me Ozaki!" She chided him, as she came to a stop. She put her hands on her hips and took a deep breath, "And I've told you time and again- I do not appreciate you talking that gibberish at me! You're embarrassing us in front of our guest!"

Ozaki set the lazy susan on the table with a grunt and winked at me before he turned back to the woman and really let loose with the jappo talk. She stood her ground, shaking her finger in his face until William stepped in.

"Ozaki! Behave yourself! Why must you provoke her? What will Collin think of us? I…"

The rest of his words were lost to me when a skirt came out of the hallway, carrying a basket of bread and a handful of serving utensils. She was a pretty girl, not in an exotic way, or even as glamourous as the women I had met in the theater. She was fairly average with all American features, creamy white skin, deep blue eyes and her hair pulled back in a pony tail. Still, I had to warn myself not to ogle her, for she had a striking figure, with a slim waist and ample bosom. She seemed about my age. What made her truly beautiful was her smile. She was grinning from ear to ear and she just rolled her eyes at me as she stepped around the other two to put her load on the table. She wiped her hands on her apron and beamed at me, holding out her hand.

"Hi! You must be Mr. Frohman. Mister Gillette has been talking about you for weeks now! Pleased to meet you."

I stood and took her hand, but before I could respond, William stepped over. "Collin Frohman, this is Catherine. She keeps the order amidst the chaos in my home."

She laughed like an angel. "What he means is I do the cleaning and laundry."

William smiled and turned to gesture at the older woman. "And this is our epicurean master- Mrs. Woods."

"He means cook and dishwasher." She said with a smile.

"Don't let them fool you, Collin. We couldn't manage this place without either of them. "He looked at me and said, in a heartfelt voice. "They make this house a home."

Mrs. Woods kept the smile glued to her face, but I could see she was forcing it when she spoke again. "Catty and I…well, we just want you to know how sorry we are for your loss. We didn't know him long, but the few times we spent with him…well, he was kind and gracious. He was a special man."

I was touched to see the two of them had tears welling in their eyes and I was afraid I was going to spring another leak, but Uncle Will saved the moment.

"Now, now, Dana, no more tears," he said kindly to his cook, "That's enough said about it. We shall always keep him in our hearts, so, let's just give our mouths a rest on the subject for a while. Lets' eat instead," he cried out, rubbing his hands in anticipation.

Everyone seemed more comfortable in action, so, as Mrs. Woods took the assortment of plates and bowls off the cart, Ozaki arranged them on the lazy susan and we all sat. I was pleased that Catherine took the seat next to me, especially when she took off her work apron and pulled the tie out of her pony tail and let her hair cascade across her shoulders.

Lunch was quite a spread. As the susan turned lazily, stopping when someone picked out an item they wanted, I saw plates of meats and cheeses, salads and slaws, preserves, and every kind of condiment I knew of. Uncle Will took two slabs of the fresh baked bread and began building quite a sandwich, spearing pickles and olives to go with it as they went by. I took a little of nearly everything and started on my own.

When everyone had taken what they wanted to start with, I turned to Catherine.

"Catty? Is that what people call you?"

She laughed that magical way again, "It used to be Katie when I was a little girl, but my younger brothers never said it right, calling me Catty and it stuck." Then she grinned and

27

added, "And they still talk like they have marbles in their mouths."

We all laughed at that and went back to our plates. I took a few bites of my sandwich, and then started looking around for something to wash it down with. I realized there were no liquids at all on the table. I saw William smirking at me from the corner of my eyes and realized everyone else at the table looked amused.

William made a great show of craning his neck to search the table over and spin the lazy susan around. "My word!" he exclaimed in a stage voice. "I do believe we have forgotten something! Refreshments!" He turned to his man, who was obviously waiting for a signal. "Ozaki?"

Ozaki jumped right up and walked over to the serving cart. He pulled the curtain back on the lowest shelf, to reveal what looked like a milk pail, only it was oval and twice as long. I could hear bottles sloshing in ice as he lifted it onto the top shelf and pulled away the cloth draped over it. Eight to ten bottle tops stuck up and Ozaki put three between the fingers of one hand and two in the other. Carrying them over, he deftly set a bottle in front of each of us. It was a strange looking bottle. About a third to a half the size of a wine bottle but instead of straight sides, they were curved, almost an hour-glass shape, and filled with a dark amber liquid. I turned the label and saw it was that new drink that caught on a few years back in the soda fountains across the country-Coca-Cola.

"Have you ever had this before," William asked. When I told him that I hadn't tried the drink yet, he waggled his eyebrows at me as he leaned over and took the cap off my bottle. "Then you are in for a treat. Try some. It's best straight from the bottle."

When I picked up the bottle, I was impressed. The curvature made it easier to hold, even with condensation making the outside slick. I tilted the bottle up and filled my mouth. It was an incredible sensation; ice cold, bubbly, and a sweet robust flavor that scoured out your palette, leaving a refreshing aftertaste. I was an instant Coca-Cola fanatic. I took another drink, then another. I nearly had half the bottle before Uncle Will spoke.

"Well? What do you think?"

"Aside from one of Ozaki's Sloe Gin Fizzes," I assured him, "it's the best thing I ever drank in my life."

"That is good," Ozaki said. "It may be your rast drink if prohibition is passed. I hear there was a big march in Boston yesterday!"

"Ha! I knew you'd like it! I have made it a staple in my diet as of late." William pronounced.

"Staple?" Mrs. Woods exclaimed, "You'd drink our whole stock up in a day -if I let you!"

William looked a bit abashed at that, so, I said quickly, "I can see why! I would too! But when did they start putting it in bottles? And these curved bottles? I think they're the cat's meow." I took another swig.

"They only just begun to bottle it in the last year and these bottles are not yet availible to the general public." He looked at me and winked. "We have an 'in' as it were -, even so, I can only procure six cases per delivery. I'll let Catherine explain, for she is our connection to this nectar."

She rolled her eyes at his theatrics and said, "It's my brother, Marquis, really. He's been bringing us the Coca-Cola for a few months now. Mystery recipe however the name says most of what you need to know. Its cola with a tiny bit of cocaine."

I was surprised at that. "He's a distributor?" I turned to my Uncle, "I thought I heard that the company gave the rights to the distributer licenses to just two fellows."

"That's right", Catty answered for him. "Marquis met one of them in Hartford last year and talked him into having the river from Hartford to the sound and one mile on either side as his territory."

I was impressed. I knew of some men with real money who couldn't get a slice of that pie. I gave a low whistle, "He must be one glib so and so. I imagine he's made a fortune off it by now."

Catty shrugged. "Oh yes, he's got a silver tongue, my brother. Father says he could talk a seagull off a fishing boat."

"Or the occasional pretty young girl onto his boat for a river cruise." Mrs. Woods put in. I gathered from her tone she didn't approve.

Catty ignored her and went on, "As far as making a fortune-that's yet to come, like a lot of his schemes. He can only get six cases at a time for now, and the occasional one for the family, so he just supplies Mr. Gillette. Lucky for us, Marquis can't stand the taste, so Mr. Gillette gets all six."

"Still, he sounds like a hustler!" I said.

"Oh, yes, he is that-and more! He bought himself an old fishing schooner a few years back and started a company he calls, the 'Connecticut River Express'. He started plying the river, buying seafood and taking it up to Hartford to sell it and picking up fruits and vegetables from the farms up north and then selling it here in town. He also delivers whatever folks want taken from here to there and sometimes even people book passage." She laughed a little. "He's the ambitious one of the family. He says that someday he'll use boats, the railroads, and trucks to deliver things all across the country."

"That's not such a bad idea," I said, thinking out loud. "Folks will always pay more for something- somewhere else. In Denver Colorado people pay a sinful amount of money for a lobster that we could pick out of a tidal pool at low tide for nothing." I turned to Catty, "Your brother sounds like he's on the right tracks."

"And it doesn't hurt that he's extremely handsome and has a silver tongue. That dark, wavy hair and steel blue eyes has caught many a young girls' fancy!" Mrs. Woods murmured, and then looked embarrassed when we turned our attention on her.

"Mother says he has the devil's tongue in his head." Catty leaned towards me and said in a mock conspirator's voice, "He's broken a few hearts around town and ruined a few reputations too. I always tease him that he stays on the water because there's always a father or brother waiting on shore with an axe handle!"

We all laughed, and William said, "Now, Catherine! Every young man wants to sow some wild oat-though I will admit Marquis isn't too choosy about who's field it is". He smiled and added, "He is a reliable and resourceful young man! Quite a few times he procured certain items I needed to make a window latch or door lock and he has come through for me- in a timely fashion and a reasonable rate."

"Well, he'd better!" Catty declared, "Or I'll feed him to that river monster he's always going on about!"

Uncle Will rolled his eyes and sighed, "Don't you start up about that, young lady. I am sick to death of hearing about the 'River Monster'! I got a haircut last week and had to sit through a series of tall tales, superstitions, and downright lies- all centered around that fable. There is no mythical creature lurking in the river!"

31

Catty smiled and shrugged, "I'm sure you are right, sir," She agreed, sounding like she really didn't, "but Marquis is quite insistent about what he's seen."

"There are more things under this heaven and earth than your phirosophies arrow, Horatio!" Ozaki said with smug look on his face. He did love to give my uncle a good dig from time to time.

"Bah! It's not worth the breath it takes to discuss it."

Everyone at the table looked like they were having fun, tweaking my uncle, so I decided to join the fun. "It sure sounds interesting, Uncle Will. I, for one, would like to hear all about it." I turned to Catty, "What kind of river monster are we talking here?"

I could see that Catty was chomping at the bit to answer me, but she looked to William first, who rolled his eyes before he gestured for her to go ahead with the story.

"No one knows what it is really. It started a few months ago, when folks that lived or worked near the river told of a great amount of bubbles that surfaced on the river from time to time. Nobody knew what could cause such an underwater release of air. Even Gordon, our town dockmaster, who thinks he knows everything, saw a bubble patch, that he says could only have come from something the size of a very large fish!"

"Well, there you have it then," I said. "You may just have a lost whale swimming around."

Catty wiggled her eyebrows, "That's exactly what the sceptics said." She cast a playful eye on my Uncle, "But there's more to it. Last week, Mr. Hauer, our town storekeeper, was out scooping bait fish for the shad run, when he said a bubble patch came up right under his boat, scaring him so badly he nearly lost his balance. He said he was so mad he grabbed a rifle and started shooting into the water all around him, trying to wound or kill the beast. But he only got off a few shots before something hit his boat so hard, he was flung into the water. He claims something brushed his legs hard, but he managed to climb back into the boat before it got him!"

Uncle Will snorted. "Carlton was probably a few sheets to the wind and just fell out of his boat! The 'Monster' was just a convenient way to save embarrassment." He turned to me, "mind you, the man will tell you about the time he was confronted by Blackbeard's ghost, every time you need a bag of sugar, if you let him."

Catty just shrugged, but Mrs. Woods took up the mantle, "I will admit that Carlton will stretch the truth quite some ways to tell a good yarn, but that doesn't explain the bait boxes!" She paused her story for a moment to tell me what a bait box was, but I assured her I was familiar with the objects. I didn't bother explaining that I had grown up around people who made their living by the tides and seasons. Satisfied, she went on, "You see, around here, folk put out their bait boxes a few weeks before the shad starts running. They trap minnows and other bait fish. That way they are ready when the run starts. Every year they hang them off the docks around town, but this year, half the folk that pulled up their traps to check them, found them crushed or torn apart." She steely eyed her employer, "And these are honest working folks, not gossipers or tellers of tall tales.

I've seen a few of the damaged ones for myself, my Son's included. I tell you honestly that I don't think a man in a rage with an axe couldn't have crushed them better!"

William just gave her a smile that said, 'Well, there you have it then', but she just rode over him,

"Oh no, Mr. Great Detective, there were no clean edges or straight cuts! This wasn't done with human tools!"

Everyone looked to William for his reaction. He shook his head and put his sandwich down. Forming his fingertips into a steeple before him, he sighed and asked, "Dana, you are a sensible woman. You can't really believe there is some mythical diabolical sea creature, swimming about the river, can you! The idea is absurd! Let me ask you this, why has it shown up now? I have lived here for six years-and you both have lived here your whole lives! So, why would this plague strike us now? Where did it come from and why? With half the town looking for signs of it, has no one actually laid eyes on the thing? If I had to venture a guess, I'd say it's a wayward shark, which swam up the river by mistake."

"A shark doesn't blow air bubbles, "I pointed out. "And if it came close enough to capsize a boat or bite a bait box, someone would have seen a fin or a tail."

"Exactly, Collin," William said, as if I proved his point, "There is no devil fish that could live up to that reputation for mayhem!"

Catty had a sudden thought, "What if it were one of those dinosaurs? I read in a magazine that men are digging up huge bones from strange animals all the time?"

I had to stifle a laugh. "They are not really bone, Catty. They have turned to stone and are called fossils. Those animals have been dead for hundreds and hundreds of years. Maybe even a thousand."

"Right again! It's good to see you learned more than sass at University!" William chortled, "More than likely this is no more than someone's idea of a bad jest."

Mrs. Woods went back to her lunch, obviously disagreeing with her boss, and Catty simply smiled and shrugged, "You'll never convince Marquis of that. He's been talking on and on about it for weeks."

William laughed, "Knowing the entrepreneur in your brother, I wouldn't be surprised if he was whipping the town into a state of hysteria, just so he could double his rates!"

Catty smiled and picked up her bottle of soda pop and held it like a toast. "As long as he keeps bringing us these at a fair price."

"Here, Here." William answered, and we all took a slug. That ended the great 'River Monster' debate for the day.

The rest of the lunch was pleasant. Uncle Will relaxed and told us some great stories about my father and we talked about the town, the country, and even of the Great War. We were all surprised when Ozaki finally got up and announced he had things to do before the sun went down. We had frittered away a good part of the afternoon.

4

William jumped to his feet and hastily helped me out of my chair in his enthusiasm to tell me all about the castle. After a few minutes, I could see why Ozaki retreated. Uncle Will had more facts and figures than a city tax assessor and he delivered in a style that rivaled P.T. Barnum himself.

He told me of the tonnage and gage of the steel girders that made the frame and the many thousand stones that covered it. I was a bit concerned as he described that some of the castle didn't even have mortar, just rocks carefully stacked, one on another! I began to see why my father described it as a 'great stone heap'. He droned on about the walkways and their pitches to keep water from pooling. He pointed out the windows and the doors, the balconies and how they were all blended into the style of castle he wanted.

I'll admit, I only listened with half an ear. I was already in awe of the place without the statistics and couldn't help looking up and down each side as we walked around the building. He showed me the outside of the conservatory then we went down a few steps and past what he called his workshop. A few more steps up and we came to the massive carved wood front doors and then we went up some more steps onto a veranda that overlooked the courtyard, which lead us right back to where we had our drink earlier. It was an easy walk around the perimeter, giving the illusion it wasn't as big as it looked from the drive but when I looked around, the shear tonnage of stone and the work it took to place it was awe inspiring.

He must have seen something on my face, because he suddenly stopped and said, "I'm boring you to tears, aren't I Collin. I'm sorry, I just get carried away. This project has been my life for the past six years."

"No, no, Uncle Will. It's fascinating. I'm just overwhelmed. I love the place!"

"Why, thank you."

"Not that I wouldn't have minded staying on the *Polly* with you either! I loved the time we spent on her. She was like a second home to me growing up. Where is she, anyways?" I asked, looking out over the river.

He walked over to the other side of the veranda and pointed. I stepped up and looked down to see the old girl sitting pretty at a dock with eight pilings. She was roped off to the pylons in what looked like a big cat's cradle. Then I noticed the platform that jutted out from the side of the bluff.

"Ah! The notorious tramway! Is that still in operation? Can we take a ride on it?"

Uncle Will made a wincing face. "It's been a bit dicey of late. The engines are about burned out and the bolts that keep it together have loosened to a state that has kept us from letting anyone ride on it."

"I am surprised it lasted this long, as it has hauled many, many tons of material since I put it up six years ago. I have one more project I wish to complete then I will most likely dis-" A quizzical look came across his face and he looked at me sharply. "Why did you say 'notorious'?"

"What do you mean?"

"You said the 'notorious Tramway'. Why did you refer to it like that?"

Mentally, I slapped myself on the forehead. I knew better than to make a slip like that in front of my Uncle. He was the sharpest tool in the shed! I had one secret I meant to keep, lest it change our relationship, so I shrugged and thought up a story Johnny on the spot.

"No reason, really," I sputtered. "Dad told me about how scared he was to ride it. He said it was 'harrowing', I believe."

He gave me a look that said he didn't quite believe me, but he was too polite to say so. I didn't trust my wits enough to say anymore, so I just stared out over the river and found a distraction.

"Look, Uncle Will!" I pointed to two shapes floating in the wind. "I think those are eagles!"

William smiled indulgently, "You are absolutely correct, my boy! There is a mated pair that nests near here."

The eagle's flight brought them much closer to the castle. It was incredible to see them fly by. At this height, we were level with them as they soared high above the river. Suddenly, one of them screeched then began a long- angled dive towards the water. I thought the bird was going to plunge right into the river when it suddenly flared its wings and stopped as its talons went into the water. With a few powerful flaps, it began to rise again, with something wiggling on the end of its talons. For a city boy, watching an eagle hunt was a real treat!

William nodded. "The shad run has begun."

Surprised, I asked, "You can tell what kind of fish that was from here?" It was at least a hundred yards away and below us.

He winked at me, "I have always been blessed with excellent eyesight. I can see farther than most."

'And you see everything!' I thought to myself. My esteem for him went up another notch.

He clapped me on the shoulder. "Come along, Collin. Let me show you some of the inside. Perhaps you're ready for a cocktail."

"Lead on, Mac Duff!"

We went in the same doors we had originally and Wiliam led me across the room and into the formal dining area. He gestured to a huge cupboard that filled on wall and said, "Help yourself." Then he took a seat at the edge of a horseshoe shaped booth that surrounded the dining room table. He looked as smug as any of the cats that wandered around. William picked one up and set it in his lap, looking at me as if to say, 'Get on with it'.

The cupboard had a large mirrored back with and drawers and cabinets below. The shelf was alcohol free, so I checked the cabinets and drawers. Searching high and low as best I could without emptying the contents onto the floor, I couldn't find any booze. There were no signs of liquor and I began to fear my uncle had joined the teetotalers. Though I had never known him to take more than a sip of wine or champagne, he was never opposed to spirits.

I turned to him in confusion, and he waggled his eyebrows before setting the cat down and stepping over to the cupboard. He pushed in a spot and I heard a soft click and one of the panels on the mirrored back popped open. William slid it back to reveal rows of liquor and side racks of glasses.

"Geez Louise Uncle Will! I thought you'd become a holy roller for prohibition or something!" I joked.

"Quite the opposite, Collin. I'm a 'holy roller' for choice! But the day will come soon; mark my words, prohibition will pass!" He struck a noble pose, "And I, for one, shall never deny my guests their rightful pleasures!"

Then he winked at me and touched the side of his nose, "That is why we must keep this little secret in the family."

I never felt closer to him than I did right then. I learned that sometimes respect and understanding were as thick as blood.

Fortified with a Maker's Mark, neat, we continued the tour of the inside. We went around the side of the staircase and down a hallway that led to a back room, which I would describe as an everyday dining room. There was an oblong table that could seat six, with two of the chairs tucked into the corners near the row of windows. The view wasn't as spectacular as the one from the front of the house, but it was pleasant enough, with rolling hills that led to an estuary. There was an abundance of waterfowl that I pointed out to my Uncle.

"Oh, yes. I've spent many a breakfast and lunch watching their antics. But you must come in the fall when the sparrows migrate. That is a sight to see!"

'Oh, goody, goody!' I thought to myself sarcastically. If I wanted to see a bunch of birds, I'd go to Central Park and feed the pigeons. From there we passed through an open room that had sideboards, filled with glass and china, and food locker, plus an enormous ice box. Then we entered the domain of Mrs. Woods. I was surprised at how small the kitchen was in relation to the Castle. It looked no bigger than one you'd find in a more modest home. I think it was even smaller than the galley on the Aunt Polly. Yet it had everything it needed to be functional and highly efficient, and even a small counter by the window with two stools. I could imagine, Mrs. Woods and Catty shelling peas or having a cup of coffee there.

William pulled open a door on one side, to reveal a staircase going down into darkness. At the bottom, William flipped a switch and I got my first glimpse into his workshop. It was darker down here and a bit danker, giving it an eerie ambiance.

The only natural light came from under a door that led to another room.

A long wooden table, set against the stone foundation, dominated one wall. Upon it sat hundreds of small parts, wooden and metal, that were strewn across the top like the aftermath of an explosion. I couldn't make heads or tails of what he was trying to put together.

"What is all this stuff, Uncle Will?" I asked. "Are you trying to emulate Dr. Frankenstein down here?" I joked, referencing the book by Mary Shelly we both loved.

He laughed. "Nothing so grandiose, my boy. It's just the remains and failures of the window and door hardware manufacturing. You sometimes can only succeed by persevering many failures". He laughed again, "It adds up when each door and window have their own unique, lock, latch, and closer."

"Each one is different?" I asked, awed by the amount of time he must have spent.

He nodded, "I carved all the light switches also."

The more I thought about it and the size and scope of this place, the crazier it seemed. Most sane folk would have simply picked out a style and had a carpenter install them. It seemed like such a mundane thing to spend what must have been months on.

"Jeepers!" was all I trusted myself to say.

He shrugged. "A bit obsessive, I'll grant you that, but it did help keep my mind off things this past year."

That, I could understand. I clicked my tongue, "Pop always said you were a whiz at set design."

41

The next room we went into was more of a storage area that sat below the main entrance. There I found my motorcycle, lined up next to William's Indian Chief. I had forgotten I had left it out front.

I shook my head. "Ozaki shouldn't have gone to the trouble. He could have just told me to park it here."

"I must confess" William said, "It was me. I was afraid Ozaki would try to walk it down and spill it, so I hopped on and coasted in. I hope you don't mind."

"Not at all, Uncle. The key was in it, you should have taken her for a spin."

"Ha!", He said with a grin as he pulled open the bay door to the outside, "Have someone see me on a Harley? Not on your Nellie!"

We went up the little incline and went back into the Castle by way of the massive front doors. I was prepared to help William swing back one of the massive, carved oaken doors, but it was so well balance that he pulled it open with little effort.

Once inside, he gave me the official tour of the library and study and we whiled away the rest of the afternoon as William pointed out various playbills he had mounted and told me funny stories about the cast and my father's role in the productions. We hadn't even noticed the sky darkening with the dusk until Ozaki showed up and announced that dinner would be served in an hour.

William, surprised, took out his pocket watch and gave a low whistle. "By Jove, where has the time gone? Well, Collin, I guess we'll have to cut the tour short for today. I wanted to take you to the upper reaches, but that would be better suited for the daytime."

"What about the conservatory? Do we have time to see that?" After reading my father's description, it was the room I was most curious about.

William clapped me on the shoulder. "How about we save that for after dinner? We could have our brandy and cigars in there."

My Uncle neither drank brandy nor smoked cigars, but I was up for the double duty.

When I met him at the dining room table, precisely at eight, I was confused to see two place settings, at the other end of the table, deep into the booth where there was little room. Uncle Will was looking quite smug, so, I decided it was a good time to act confused.

"Is Ozaki going to slide the food down to us?" I asked.

William waggled his eyebrows then pulled the table out with one hand. It slid smoothly out on tracks, leaving us plenty of room to take our seats in the rear. We walked in and he gestured for me to sit in a spot across from him, and then slid the table back into place, putting the settings directly in front of us.

I grinned, "That is the cat's meow, Uncle."

He smiled. "It will be quite handy when I have a dinner party. Yet, tonight, let's slide down to the head. That way Ozaki can serve us easier."

We each slid our settings down and Ozaki appeared, bearing our soup and a bottle of wine. William had just a splash in his glass, but Ozaki poured me a full measure.

William didn't touch his soup right away and I feared we might have to pray before we ate, but he raised his glass in salute and said, "Here's to friends. Old and new."

"Hear, Hear" I replied.

The meal was wonderful, both Uncle Will and I digging in with gusto. Aside from us, we were joined by eight or nine cats that materialized out of thin air. I had to laugh as Uncle Will fed them tid-bits off his plate then chided them for being gluttons. As far as I could tell, it was every cat for himself as he tossed the food onto the floor. Ozaki would shoo them away between courses, but they came right back after he returned to the kitchen.

After dessert, William led me to the conservatory and opened the glass doors. With a flourish, he bowed me into the room. My excitement at seeing this spot-so aptly described by my father-made me grateful to still have my Uncle Will. It was like stepping into the tropics. The air was thick with moisture and I could see steam rising from vents on the floor. The waterfall cascaded in the corner, with a soothing sound of running water, collecting in a pool at its base. The room was filled with large and exotic plants, but I was only interested in one thing. Something my father had written about.

I bee-lined it over to the edge of the pool and began talking loudly to my Uncle, who was shutting the door behind us. I kept my eyes on the stone shelf that surrounded the pool, but I still nearly jumped out of my skin when two frogs hopped out of the water-right in front of me, croaking to beat the band.

I spied a small sugar bowl on a small café table next to me and I lifted the lid to find what I expected. It was half full of dead flies. I took a little pinch and sprinkled it over the frogs, which lapped them out of the air with their long tongues. I crowed with delight, feeling like I was six years old.

44

"What are you doing, Collin?" I heard my Uncle ask behind me.

"Just feeding the guard frogs", I answered. I winced to myself as soon as I said it.

"Have a seat Collin," William said firmly.

Feeling like I had gotten caught with my hand in the cookie jar, I stood and turned to see Ozaki, holding a bottle of brandy, a glass, and a cigar on a tray, standing next to my Uncle and looking suspiciously at me. I took a seat and the frogs began their chorus of croaks again. William bent over, pointed at each one, and then waved his hand.

"Mike! Lena! That is enough, you little water pigs! Back in the water." To my utter amazement and delight, they each did a twisting leap and dove back into the pool.

William gave me a stern look, as Ozaki poured me a drink. "How much did your father record of his last visit?"

I took a large swallow of the brandy. I didn't want to lie, but I was leery of what his reaction might be to the truth.

"What do you mean…record?" I asked, trying to sound innocent.

He sighed and looked knowingly at his valet. Ozaki crossed his arms and gave me the evil eye. "None of your mealy mouth comments! Answer the question."

When I covered my lips with my glass to my lips, in another vain attempt to stall, William shook his head.

"Collin, you were away at University between the time your father ended his visit with me and he boarded the Lusitania. Yet, you knew Mike and Lena were here and earlier today, you called it the 'notorious Tramway'. Aside from those two slips, you were obviously underwhelmed by much of what you saw

45

today-as if you knew about it already. Now, knowing your father, and his propensity to write down his experiences, I have to believe he left some account of his visit- which you have read! All I want to know is how much he described in his narrative."

I poured myself another drink and took my time lighting the cigar. I was stalling to try and decide how much I wanted to reveal but decided to throw caution to the wind. "All of it, I guess. From when you picked him up in New London until your last talk on the telephone before he left for England."

William groaned and slapped his forehead, but Ozaki laughed out loud. William gave him a sharp look and barked, "This is no laughing matter, Ozaki! Charles gave his word he would never speak of it."

Ozaki looked at him like he was the village idiot. "Correct! That he would never SPEAK of it!"

William stared at him for a moment, and then half smiled. "I should have known better. He was the master of wording contracts." He sighed theatrically, "Never did he promise not to write it down."

He looked down at me. "You must burn those papers as soon as you return home, young man. There will be dire consequences if that story ever comes to light."

I took a big pull on my stogie and blew it out in a long steady stream. I loved my Uncle dearly and didn't want to go against his wishes, but he took one look in my eyes and knew that wasn't going to happen.

"You would never willingly destroy them. I suppose, if I were in your shoes, I would never do so. But you must understand the consequences, if the story ever got out."

"I'm not sure of your reasoning, Uncle Will. Surely, with all the people involved, not to mention a very public murder, the story is bound to come out one day, regardless of my silence."

"Ah!" He put a finger in the air, "You are making assumptions. Yes, there are many people who know parts of the story, but only a handful are in possession of ALL the facts. Aside from various government officials, only Rowan, myself, and your father knew the whole story."

"Besides the mastermind," I reminded him, "who got away."

To my surprise, William poured himself a jot of brandy and took the seat across from me. Even Ozaki took a glass and sat on the stone ledge of the pond, next to his employer! They each took a small sip, and then William set his down and gave me a stern look. "I sincerely hope, now that you're a major player in the theater business, that you haven't entertained the thought of publishing the story or turning it into a play!"

The thought had crossed my mind, but it wasn't the direction I wanted my life to go in. It occurred to me that, I might use it as leverage to that end, the last thing I wanted to do was black mail my Uncle! In the end, perhaps because of the strong drink, I plowed ahead with the real reason I came to see him."

"Well, Uncle Will, there is a way you could be sure that didn't happen."

"How so?"

Well…if you were to take over as president to the syndicate, you'd have control of all my father's journals and ledgers. I'm willing to step aside, right here and now."

William and Ozaki looked at each other in shock that turned their attention to me- and burst out laughing.

I wasn't about to let that put me off. "What's so funny? You'd be the perfect man for the job! You say you're retired from the stage, but you still know the business from side to side and top to bottom, have more contacts than I'll probably ever meet, and everyone loves you. You could build it into a business to rival the railroad people! In a few years, you could make enough money to build ten of these places-anywhere in the world!"

William blinked and took another sip, "You are serious, aren't you?"

"Yes! Doggone it, Uncle Will. I'm only twenty-five years old. I don't want to be chained to a desk the rest of my life. Reading reviews and shuffling papers is not my idea of a life! Maybe in ten years or so, when you retire for good, I can step up."

William smiled at me warmly and replied. "You blithering saphead! Do you think I built my home, out here in the boondocks of Connecticut, just so I could step back into the limelight? I have spent a good part of my life in the public eye and have seen every side of humanity. Aside from a select few persons, I prefer the company of my cats! And I have all the money I need."

"Excuse me, master saphead" Ozaki spoke up, "But when did you ever see your father chained to his desk?"

Taken aback, I asked, "What do you mean?"

William leaned forward and stared at me intently, "Listen to what he's asking, Collin! You father was never chained anywhere! He went where he wished, whenever he wanted! Sure, he went to his office, but he didn't HAVE to! Most days he spent the mornings there trying to decide where he was going to have lunch. Then he took the rest of the afternoon off! He had, and now, you have, an army of employees. Administrative, accountants, producers, directors, a bevy of actors under contract, stage managers, call boys and roustabouts. Everyone knows their job and do it because they respected your father and the company. All he really did theses last five years or so, was made a few decisions and let his presence be known. The rest will run itself. Who's running things now, with your mother on route to England and you sitting across from me and drinking my brandy?"

I shrugged and poured myself another bracer. "Aunt Rae-Rae is keeping an eye on the office. Hell, she knows more about the business that I ever will!"

He nodded, "For which Miss Geisling is handsomely compensated. Simply continue to pay her well and she'll run things the same way for you as she did for your father. All your employees will. Besides, you've been around the business your entire life."

"Yeah, maybe, but I never really paid that much attention to the business end. How will I know which plays to run and which ones to scrap? Or what actor or actress to fill the bill? Or where to start a new venture and how much to spend."

William just smiled broader. "You'll learn Collin. You are smart as a whip and twice as quick."

"Or you wirr die penniless and unroved," Ozaki put in, grinning over the rim of his snifter.

"Thanks, Ozaki, you're a cheery bugger!"

"I am an honest bugger," He replied. "Karma, neh?"

I had to laugh, and somehow a lot of my trepidation drained away. My one chance to walk away was taken, but once I knew my path, I was determined to stride it with pride.

"Well, that's that, then. I guess you're both looking at the new president of the syndicate."

William beamed, "Excellent! I know you'll do just fine. Now, back to our original subject. What are your plans for your father's journal, now that your black mail scheme failed?"

"Don't say that, Uncle Will. I would never do anything to harm or embarrass you! Of course, if it's your wishes, I shall keep them hidden away. I promise I will share them with no one -- at least until you are gone -- then all bets are off!"

William thought that over then nodded. "I can live with that. Upon my death, feel free to do what you want with it." He raised his snifter and Ozaki and I joined in clinking them together, before we all took another sip. I emptied mine and poured another.

William raised an eyebrow at me, "Before you drink that, there is another matter we need to discuss."

5

William and Ozaki grew serious and the room seemed to darken. The cozy, warm ambiance of the conservatory turned ominous and I left my brandy untouched, feeling a need to stay sharp for whatever was coming from my Uncle.

William sat back in his chair and his demeanor totally changed. He crossed his legs and steepled his fingers in front of his chest as if he were about to pray. His face looked thinner and his eyes more streamlined. I could swear his nose grew longer and thinner. Looking somewhere over my shoulder, with unblinking eyes, he began to speak as if he weren't talking to me but rather an audience only he could see.

"In many ways, having you read the story makes this easier for all of us. What do you recall of Captain Roy?"

I thought about what I'd read before I answered. "He was the mastermind behind the hullabaloo last year when my father came to visit. I know he was going to kill you and Dad before Ozaki stepped in, and that you had alerted the police beforehand. I know he had been captured but escaped on his way to federal court. And I know you were worried he may come back..." It hit me like a ton of bricks.

"Is that why you've put me off all these months? Do you really think he'll come back after you?"

"I believe he is a man of his word. Unfortunately, I do not know his time-table." He turned his head and looked me dead in the eye, "I believe he is a formidable threat. Do you know the circumstances of his escape?"

"No, should I?"

"Not at all. It was kept very quiet on orders from Washington. When the train stopped at a station, just outside of Baltimore, to take on coal and water, no less than eight men stormed the train at the station to free Roy. Four soldiers and three federal Marshals were gunned down along with several innocent bystanders. He is extremely important to someone. Of course, I knew he had a brilliant mind and he was a fine actor in his own right. Though I saw through his 'salty dog sea captain' façade immediately, I thought it a harmless quirk and I failed to see the evil lurking beneath it. He was a more than able seaman and the work that he and Nicholas did to the Aunt Polly was impeccable. He made a complete fool out of me!"

"Uncle Will", I protested. "You can't blame yourself! From what I read those plans had been in the works for months. No one could have seen that coming!" I looked down at Ozaki and shrugged, "Karma, neh?"

Ozaki looked at William pointedly, "That is what I have been saying for months! Risten to your nephew!"

Somewhat mollified, William said, "I suppose the two of you are right. Who could have seen the vast resources that Roy had! Did you know, Collin, that there were many parts of that submarine that could not have been manufactured in this country, let alone in my boathouse? A high-ranking Officer at the submarine base in Groton, just up the coast, came to interview me when they made the discoveries, after, of course, they confiscated my submarine. Roy must have had the specialized submarine items smuggled in."

I nodded slowly, seeing an answer to an enigma that had struck me in my father's story. "That makes sense. I mean, they built a submarine, restored your launch, and kept the *Aunt*

Polly ship shape in Bristol fashion all at the same time. He must have smuggled some manpower in also."

William looked like the cat that got the canary. "Excellent, young Frohman. There is great hope for you, yet."

He sat up suddenly and leaned forward towards me. "And so, with these new insights, I decided that I needed more assistance than I would get from the local constabulary. I engaged the Pinkerton agency, in an attempt to locate Roy and recapture him. They thought they had him cornered in Washington DC, but again, he eluded them. He remains unaccounted for and at large…Now you know why I haven't asked you to visit before now. I could not bear it if you were hurt from retribution directed at me!"

I patted his arm then glared at him, "If I had known all this-I would have been here sooner! You don't need to worry about me, I can protect myself and you could use someone to watch your back!" I nodded in Ozaki's direction. "I doubt much could get past me and Ozaki!"

William smiled and placed his hand on Ozaki's shoulder. "I have no doubt about that, Collin. Ozaki already bested Roy easily when they went one on one."

"What if he brings help? Could you both stop six or eight men? You will have to remember to carry extra bullets, Uncle Will."

He laughed. "I hope your skill has grown with your bravado, although I know you to be an excellent shot. Are you armed now?"

"No, not at the moment, but my new 45 and a docker's rig is in my saddlebags and I brought ammo. I was hoping to practice a little while I was here."

"Excellent. Please wear it while you're here."

The rest of the evening passed pleasantly. We talked of family and friends, with a fair amount of good advice from my Uncle about the duties of my new position. I'm not sure if his calm reassuring talk, or the half a bottle of brandy I drank, but I felt much better about my life when I finally climbed the stairs and retired for the night.

The morning was another matter altogether. I was comfortable tucked between the sheets when I awoke suddenly, with a strange feeling I was being watched. When I rolled over and opened my eyes, bright sunlight stabbed me in the eyeballs, igniting a firestorm in my head. When I could focus, I found myself looking at Ozaki, staring down at me, with a bundle of white cloth in his arms.

He was dressed in a judo gi, which was a sort of Japanese short bathrobe with long shorts under it. In his hands he held another gi and I knew exactly what that meant.

I groaned at him. "Jimminies Ozaki, I'm on vacation. Can't a fella sleep in?" Truth was, I had partaken of a good amount of the excellent gin and brandy Uncle Will had provided after dinner last night and I was a bit groggy to be training in the martial arts so early in the morning. Ozaki had trained me my whole life and his training sessions could be brutal.

His face grew hard, "*Baka* on your vacation!" he dropped the clothes on my chest. "You Frohman's are arr arike – you rike your father - drink, drink, drink! Ret us see how much you have forgotten, *Vertora saku!*"

Vetora saku meant little monkey in Japanese, a name Ozaki had dubbed me the first lesson he gave me at age seven. My head throbbed and that made me just annoyed enough to jump out of bed. Since I always slept naked, I quickly pulled on the pants and wrapped the judo gi around me.

54

Ozaki smiled and handed me a red belt. I smiled back at him and walked over to my saddle bags hanging off a chair and rummaged around until I found my own belt. I held one end and let it unroll to the floor. It was black! Little did Ozaki know that I had found another teacher while I was at college and had continued my studies under him.

"OH KO!", Ozaki exclaimed, eyes wide. Then his eyes narrowed. "So, the student has been training and seeks to be a master. Prease join me in the courtyard -- NOW!"

Shaking my head to clear the fuzz off my eyes, I snarled, "Mind if I water my pony first?"

"Five minutes", he snapped back and said over his shoulder as he was leaving, "Do not make me come back."

The art of karate is an ancient Japanese fighting technique. Literally it meant, empty hands, or something like that. Ozaki explained to me that since only the Samurai class could have weapons, the peasants developed this method of fighting using only their hands and feet. Ozaki had taught me since I was old enough to lift one leg and not fall over. I will be eternally grateful to him for that, because I had never lost a fight in my life growing up. Well, once, a few years back, I lost one but only because I lost my head and my father stepped in and threw me overboard on the Aunt Polly.

In Ozaki's absence at school, I found another Sensei, or teacher, to study under. I found him in Chinatown and, obviously, he was a Chinaman not Japanese. He too was willing to teach me the martial arts, for a stiff fee, but his style was 'Kung Fu', and many of its movements and names were based on various animals. I was nearly giggling with the thought of surprising Ozaki with my new found knowledge, as we faced each other on the courtyard overlooking the river.

I was grateful to see that he had dragged some large rattan squares outside to cover the stone patio in a ten by ten foot space. Though I was confident I might catch Ozaki off guard, the look on his face told me I might hit the deck a few times before it was over.

I was amazed at the shape he was in. More than fit, every muscle rippled on his diminutive frame. Though he was small, he was strong as a bull and fast as a snake. Without a word, he stepped onto the mat opposite me, put his hands to his sides, and bowed. I did the same on my end and as soon as we straightened up, we each struck a fighting stance. Ozaki took the tradition pose, while I chose a crouching tiger stance to throw him off.

Not that it worked. He launched himself at me and I found myself hard pressed to keep his hands and feet away from me. I managed to deflect most strikes, except for a few minor glancing blows, and touch him a few times myself. We went on for what seemed like hours, twisting, kicking, and punching. Striking out with our hands and feet in an attempt to knock each other down. My limbs were growing numb with the strikes, but Ozaki showed no signs of slowing down.

His strategy, I knew, was to move in close where the advantage of my size and reach would be negated. Suddenly, I was dealing with his knees and elbows too! In a desperate attempt to pull him in to close to strike, I foolishly reached out to grab him.

He grabbed my arm with both hands, and I found myself ass over teakettle to land hard on my back. Not only was the wind knocked out of me, a searing pain went up my arm as he kept hold of it. Before I could even try to kick out of it, his legs were around my neck in a pincer and my air supply was cut off. I squirmed and wiggled, but the longer I went without oxygen, the harder it was to remember my training. I started seeing spots in front of my eyes and I knew that Ozaki was punishing me for taking a black belt from another teacher. Things began to grow dim and I was seriously considering biting him in the crotch, when a woman's voice cut through the still morning air.

"Ozaki! What the devil do you think you're doing? Release him this instant!"

Mrs. Woods, with Catty in tow, came charging up the steps. She was brandishing her umbrella like a sword. She must have looked like a charging bull because Ozaki slipped his legs off me and rolled over backwards to jump to his feet. He even took a few steps back.

I was sucking in great gasp of air and trying to get up on my elbows when Catty knelt down and cradled my head until I caught my breath. Mrs. Woods, however, had the bit between her teeth and she stepped right over me to confront Ozaki.

"What do you think you're doing, you yellow devil?" She screeched. "And why are you going about it in your bed clothes?"

Catty, thinking I was hurt, fussed while I slowly got to my feet. I was sore from head to toe, but unscathed. She held arms around me to keep me steady and I didn't let on I was alright, and we stood together looking at each other and trying not to laugh, while the other two had at each other.

Mrs. Woods, who saw that I had gotten to my feet and wasn't spurting blood everywhere, seemed relieved, but she didn't cut any slack with Ozaki over it. "What were you thinking, you little heathen? Hopping around in your underclothes and trying to choke the life out of young Frohman! What in the name of heaven is ailing you?"

"The only probrem we have", Ozaki spat back, "is woman who do not mind their own business. Now, get in the house and go about your duties!"

Catty rolled her eyes and whistled softly, and I grew a little scared of the rage that poured out of Mrs. Woods. She seemed to grow two inches and her eyes blazed as she let him have it with both barrels.

"How dare you, you little pipsqueak! I don't work for you and you'll not be ordering me around! If it weren't for William, I'd throw you off this patio and into the river. Then let you swim back to wherever you came from! William just might beat me to it when he hears how you tried to kill his nephew! Never in all my days have I seen such..."

The rest of her tirade was drowned out when Ozaki started yelling back at her. Only he was yelling in Japanese and loud enough to wake the dead. I had no idea what he was saying, but I picked out a few uncomplimentary words I had learned from him over the years. Neither one gave an inch and the hollering went on.

"Maybe we'd better break this up", Catty said softly. "I've never seen Dana this mad and I don't want to end up doing all the work myself today."

I had to agree and was trying to find a way to separate them without losing my head, when a voice called out from the heavens.

Uncle Will was standing on the second story balcony in his nightclothes and a robe, looking irritated that he was awake. Both Ozaki and Mrs. Woods shut right up and looked up at him.

"Ozaki! That's enough! In the future, if you wish to whomp the tar out of Collin, or spar or whatever you call it, please do us the courtesy of doing it out of sight and of hearing. That din would raise the dead and one of us needs our beauty sleep!"

"Would you be liking your coffee now, William? "Mrs. Woods called up to ask, as if she wasn't just threating to castrate Ozaki. "I think Mr. Frohman would like a cup, once he's recovered."

"I may as well, Dana. I doubt I'll be getting back to sleep now."

Dana Woods nodded, "It will be ready when you are dressed. Come along, Catty. We may as well get started before any more mayhem sets in around here!" She cast an evil eye on Ozaki, sniffed, and walked towards the house.

"Can you make it on your own Collin?" Catty asked. I was touched by her genuine concern.

"I'm fine." I assured her, though my throat was on fire and my back and shoulders ached from hitting the ground. "I'll get dressed and join Uncle Will for coffee."

"Too bad you have to change", she said with a wink, "You look very cute in those pajamas." Then she went to join Mrs. Woods in the kitchen, leaving me to blush like a schoolboy.

Just then a truck pulled up, near the structure between the house and the embankment. Six or so men jumped off, some carrying saws, shovels, and axes and they headed for the woods.

"What have you got going now, Uncle?" I called up to my Uncle, who was waving at the crew.

"Get yourself cleaned up and dressed, Collin, and I shall reveal my next project. That is, if you can walk a few miles. We need to take a short hike, if you're to get the whole picture. Think you can do that?' He grinned, "Ozaki seems to have given you a rather sharp lesson this morning."

It was more pride than sense that made me say, "Bull dinkers! Osaki was lucky the women showed up when they did!"

Even though I was half kidding, Ozaki smoothly retook his formal fighting stance and bowed toward me.

Uncle Will just put a hand up in his direction. He looked down at me with a smirk, "While it is true that I did not witness this bout, I would point out one thing, Collin. You are limping and Ozaki seems unscathed." As with all martial art lessons I responded to Osaki with a formal stance and a deep bow to end the match. Standing upright I again I addressed Osaki. "He's right, Ozaki, I didn't mean what I said. You beat me fair and square and I will always be grateful for your lessons."

Osaki looked at me with a mixture of pride and sadness. Then he said some words I thought I would never hear. "No, *Vetora Saku*, I can teach you no more. Only experience and practice will make you more proficient. I am proud of the warrior you have become."

All I could do was to bow deeply to him again.

I hobbled up to my room, took a French bath and dressed quickly. Remembering what my Uncle said, I slung my docker's rig on and put on a sturdy pair of boots. My interest was piqued, wondering what the 'latest project' was as Uncle Will always had the most imaginative ideas.

Catty was pouring the coffee when I entered the conservatory. Looking up, holding a sugar cube with a set of small tongs, she asked. "One lump or two?" William was trying to stifle a laugh, when she went on, "Oh! I forgot! Maybe just some cream? You already got your lumps this morning."

Laughter burst from Uncle Will, but I couldn't be mad at the remark, because she looked so great this morning. Her hair was swept off to one side and cascaded down her right, leaving the left side of her face exposed. She had pretty ears. Her dress was just snug enough to show all her curves and open enough at the top to give a peek of cleavage. The apron she wore around her waist simply accented the whole package, and the perfume she wore made me want to bury my face in her neck and breath deep.

Instead, I replied sarcastically, "HAR! HAR! HA! Very funny!"

She cast her eyes down and gave me a little pout that was anything but sincerely apologetic. "I'm sorry, Mr. Frohman. I didn't mean to offend you."

"Oh no! You didn't", I said quickly, not wanting her to think I was a stiff board. "I was just joshing. I got so many lumps; I guess a few more won't hurt. I'll take three in my coffee. I like it sweet with lots of cream. And please, always call me Collin."

She fixed me a mug of coffee and handed it to me, saying, "Here you are, Collin. You may call me Catty if you like."

I took a sip and gave her a confused look, "But, I already do."

"Yes", She deadpanned, "but now it's alright."

With that, she patted me on the shoulder and glided out of the room.

I looked at William and shook my head. He, of course, was looking like the cat who caught the canary. "You had better watch yourself, young man, or soon you may have to decide whether to fish or cut bait!"

I was thinking along those same lines myself, but he just was so smug, I replied. "Oh, what would you know about it? You've been out of the game a long time, Uncle!"

Really? Well, I know she has never worn her hair like that before, she has never worn perfume while on duty, and her dress is usually a bit more utilitarian. Since she is here until well after dark today, I doubt, very much, she is trying to get Ozaki's or my attention!" I didn't know how to respond to that, but I didn't have to, because William went on, "Out of the

61

game, you say? Wherever did you get that absurd notion?" He gestured to the chair next to him.

I sat down and said in all seriousness, because women and Uncle Will is what I wanted to broach with him for a long time but didn't know how to get past his aloofness. "Well, gee, Uncle Will. I've never seen you with a woman and Pop never mentioned one in his journals I've read so far. Heck, even the gossip columns never put you with one starlet or another. But you really should think about it", I went on in a rush, "I know Aunt Helen was a fantastic woman, but life goes on. You don't have to be alone, Uncle Will. You should have someone to share all this with." I waved my arms in a big circle over my head. "You have the right to be happy."

He laughed, but I could see he was touched by my concern, "Collin, you could not be more wrong. Though it is true that I will not remarry; once a man has had true love, it cannot be replaced. Not for me, at any rate. I have always, and still do in my advanced age, cherished the company of a woman from time to time. Some are and were fleeting, some I still partake with. As far as the ignorance, as to my private affairs, you must realize I am not like Paul or E.L., whose conquests are prolific but mine are hard sought. I learned a long time ago to keep my dealings with the fairer sex out of the lime light and I will give you my last word on the subject. Once women get the word that you are truly discreet – the opportunities presented are endless."

I'm not bashful about saying I was dumbfounded to say the least. After all those years I wanted to give him my advice and he turns it around and drops an epiphany in my lap. I was so stunned, I had to sip at my coffee to hide the slackness in my jaw.

"As far as Catherine goes…well, I know you were raised better than to dally with the help." He gave me the steely eye, "not that I consider Catherine a mere servant. I am quite fond of her."

I could have protested. I could have assured him the thought had never crossed my mind, but I decided that there was no time like the present to practice his advice. I smiled at him over the rim of my mug and said, "I'm glad we had this little talk."

He laughed, and I was glad I didn't say more when Catty came to the door and asked if we'd like some breakfast to go with our coffee. Will looked to me and I shrugged. The coffee was fighting the remnant of what I drank last night, so I was not all that hungry.

Wiliam rose to his feet. "I think we shall forgo a sit- down meal, Catherine. Instead, wrap a couple of those fresh blueberry muffins up in a napkin and we'll eat them as we walk."

She just looked at him and rolled her eyes. "How did you know she made muffins?"

I knew he was about to show off a bit and I wanted to be in on it.

"He must have smelled them." I offered, "Or he peeked in the kitchen."

"I do not smell anything more than the foliage and my coffee in this room, young Frohman- especially with the doors closed! And I assure you I haven't been near the kitchen this morning. I came straight here from my room and the kitchen is on the other side of the house."

I looked Catty up and down, but she didn't look or smell any different than she did when she poured the coffee, except that she had put her hair back in the usual bun and was alternating rubbing her hands. I was stumped.

"Then how did you know?" Catty asked. "I've got no batter on my apron and I hope I don't smell like a muffin!"

William smirked, "While I was on the balcony this morning, refereeing the match, I notice the cold storage was unlocked. Since Ozaki was occupied with Collin, I surmised that it was Mrs. Woods who had retrieved something out of it on her way in to work this morning. At such an early hour, she would hardly bother unless she needed it for breakfast. Also, there is a small smudge of baking powder on your right cuff. Since you are left- handed, you would hold the measuring cup in your right and pour with your left. You came back from the kitchen just now, with your hair piled in a bun, as is your custom when you work the oven, to keep it from being singed. Yet my usual breakfast comes out of a pan. Then too, there are tiny burn lines on the balls of your thumbs that you get half the time you take something out of the ovens."

"Usually the muffins", she agreed. "Dana likes to put them on that skinny middle shelf."

"So I have noticed over time", he quipped. "Frohman and I will stop for a take-out when we finish our coffee."

"No need, Sir", Catty said with a quick curtsy, "Drink up and I'll bring you back a few. Then you can be on your way."

"Thank you, Catherine." William said, "And could you please cut mine in half, butter and grill it?"

"Planned on it!" she replied with a big grin. She looked to me, "Yours too?"

"I think I'll have mine au natural," I replied, just to tease her. I doubted, very much, a girl from Chester, Connecticut, knew any French. It was a bit naughty of me as the phrase could mean either without accompaniment or 'in the nude'.

"Fine," she said, with a sparkle in her eye, "But don't expect anyone to watch you eat it naked."

64

She was out the door before I could reply. William sighed and rolled his eyes in mock despair.

Good as her word, she brought us a couple of fat warm muffins, wrapped in paper, for our walk.

Going out the French doors to the courtyard we headed towards the bluff. Soon I found myself standing in a long, stone building that was lined on all sides with large window like openings. It made me think of a large lawn tent only made of granite.

William unwrapped his muffin slowly and took a bite as I looked around. I wondered why he might have had this large granite structure built. It was too open to afford any protection from the weather and the floor had a large raised circle in its center.

Of course, Uncle Will just savored his muffin until I asked, "Just what is this place for, Uncle Will?"

He broke off another piece of the muffin top and popped it in his mouth. Chewing slowly, he rewrapped his breakfast and put it on the ledge next to him. He swallowed, then threw his arms out wide, dramatically and announced, "This is Grand Central Station! He laughed at the quizzical look on my mug and explained. "Or so it shall be, abet on a smaller scale."

I shook my head. "Stop joshing, Uncle Will. What is it really?"

He scoffed at my query. "I assure you, Collin, this is where my railroad shall start."

Now I know he was joking. Though a man carrying another on his shoulders could walk through the entrance, it was nowhere big enough for a locomotive engine. I just stared at him, waiting for him to get serious. He raised an eyebrow at me, "Oh Ye of little faith. I am being earnest, Collin. It is my intention to build a railroad line and run a train from here to a point a few miles or so along the riverbank. There I will construct another station, with a turn around to run back to this point. Of course, as I said, it will be on a smaller scale. The engine, cars and tracks will all be gauged to about a third of a regular train."

"Where are you going to find a train that small," I asked, my mind not yet grasping the concept.

"I'm having them built, even as we speak. A company down in New Haven should have them ready for the tracks in a few months." He pointed out the front to a large swath of vegetation that was cleared for a road. "The land is being cleared for the tracks by Ollie and his gang now. It will be easier for them this time of year-before the summer growth."

He stepped over to me, and placed an arm around my shoulder, gently turning me to face outwards. He put his face level with mine and stretched out an arm in the direction of the path.

"Imagine, Collin, if you will, a scaled down, yet absolutely genuine engine, pulling two or three cars and a caboose. Imagine the vistas, with the river on one side and the pristine forest and meadows on the other. The route will hug the Connecticut River below and be as real as a regular train. I'm even building a trestle over a fissure in the embankment at one point. It will be the sight to behold in any season. Imagine the cool spring air and the budding flowers you'll see, the hot air of summer, being cooled in the rush of air under the bright summer sun, the crisp clean autumn air with the vibrant colors of the changing leaf. Even bundled up, dashing through the snow, will be an experience you won't soon forget." He looked at me and I thought of a little boy on Christmas Eve. "What have you to say about that?"

It finally clicked in that he was not pulling my leg. I realized that a man of his talent and wealth could very well build his own miniature railroad if he wished. If it was only partially as grand as his home, I knew it would be a sight to see. I promised myself to be sure I was on hand for her maiden run. His excitement was infectious and I had a million questions, but I said simply," I think it's going to be a hoot!"

He laughed and clapped me on the back. "To say the least Collin! Now, let us take a walk down the track route. You need to see the view to really appreciate it."

We wolfed down our muffins and headed down the path. The growth was sparse at first, although you could see a definite track where the crew had cleared and leveled the ground. The further we walked, the cut brush began to pile up on either side and soon we saw fallen trees lining the path as the forest grew thicker.

Uncle Will was droning on about track gauges, horsepower, speed, and other minutia, but I only listened with half an ear. I wasn't really interested in the details; I just wanted to take a ride someday…and maybe blow the whistle.

Suddenly, William came to a dead stop and peered forward in concern. As soon as he stopped talking, I could hear frantic movement up ahead of us. A man suddenly appeared, running pell-mell towards us and shouting!

6

I went for the pistol I had in a docker's rig, but William put a hand over mine and shook his head. "That is one of Ollie's men."

Still almost a hundred yards away, I stared in fascination at this man, about my age and height as he came barreling at us hollering at the top of his lungs, 'Mr. Gillette', over and over. Arms flailing, knees bobbing to his chest, it was no wonder that, when he finally came close, and he tried to stop, his feet got tangled and he pitched forward-right at us! William and I each took hold of an arm to bring him to his feet since all that wild energy was gone out of him. William dusted him off, telling him in a soothing tone to breathe deeply, while I held him steady. Soon enough he got his wits about him enough to find his vocal cords. When he opened his mouth, it was like a windmill in a hurricane.

"Mr. Gillette! Thank God! You have to come! I mean, Sir! Mr. Ollie sent me! You have to come, Sir!"

"Steady, Andrew", William replied to the outburst. "Come where?"

"The man pointed in the direction he came from. "There! Down a way! Mr. Ollie sent me to find you. He wants you to come!" He was trembling like a mouse under the paw of a cat.

"Is there a problem? Do we need the authorities?"

This really put him in a tizzy. He shook his head violently, "No! No! Nobody else! Only you! Mr. Ollie! Find you! Only you!"

He looked like he was on the verge of a total breakdown, so William quickly assured him. "That's fine, Andrew. We were on our way to see Ollie, as a matter of fact."

That seemed to snap him out of it. He actually saluted and barked. "I'll report to Mr. Ollie!" Then he bolted back down the path before William could question him further.

"Jeez Louise", I muttered as I watched him hightail it away as if the devil was in his shadow. I turned to William, "Five will get you fifteen he knocks himself out before he gets where he's going."

William chuckled. "Yes, Andrew can get quite excited when he is under stress. But don't be too hard on him, Collin. He spent last year in France and rode with the American Ambulance Corps. He's a good worker and a steady enough man until he gets excited. The war has left a mark on him."

Like my brother I thought to myself. "Well, whatever got him going is up ahead. You want me to chase after him?"

"That won't be necessary, I think, whatever lies ahead is no doubt important, but it's not imminent." With that, he walked briskly and I stepped quick to catch up.

"How do you see that?"

"Because Collin, if it were an injury or even a death, Andrew is the last person Ollie would have sent. He is the only one on the crew with any medical training. The fact that Ollie told him to find only me and yet he was hesitant to tell me what the issue was, tells me that Ollie told him not to speak with anyone else about the matter. Since you were present, and Andrew will follow an order to the fullest, he was at a loss if he should tell

69

me or not. So, as I said, I believe it to be important-not imminent."

"Maybe they found Blackbeard's treasure", I teased him, knowing that my father and he had a go at pirate treasure years ago. I read it in one of Dad's journals. He gave me a sharp look then went to staring ahead in concentration.

"I have reservations that it will be as pleasant as that, Frohman."

Walking as quickly as we could over the uneven terrain, it took us another ten minutes till we rounded a slight curve and came upon a slightly wider clearing. Andrew was standing on the edge of the path waving us on. The shadows created by the budding leaves made it hard to see too far, but I could make out the silhouettes of men. None of them were speaking and the silence lent an eerie feel to the cool breeze that came from across the river and over the back of my neck. Not knowing what we were walking into, I was tempted to put my colt in hand, but Uncle Will didn't seemed concerned and I didn't want to look like a nervous nelly. I was watching my feet as I stepped over fallen logs and stumps when an old man popped out of the trees in front of us.

William stopped and planted his feet. Putting his cane out in front of him and leaning on it with both hands, he asked. "What's this all about, Ollie?"

Ollie looked up at him, a sad look in his eyes. "You better see for yourself, Mr. Gillette."

I thought that Uncle Will might demand an answer, but he simply nodded and gestured forward with his cane. His foreman turned and led us into the grove. As my eyes adjusted, I saw seven men, standing in a loose semi-circle around a large tree. I don't know why, but I looked up and thought I was seeing things.

A man sat on the crook of a large branch that was at least twenty feet in the air. He was really lounging with his ankles crossed, as he twirled a knife between his fingers. When he saw his employer, the knife slapped into his palm and he sat still, looking straight down at us. By the time I looked over for my Uncle's reaction, he was already looking up at him.

"What is it, Frank?" He called up.

The man said nothing in reply but pointed with the knife to his right. It was difficult to see what he was pointing at through the dense foliage. Uncle Will and I stepped closer to the trunk and scanned the tree tops, but it was hard to focus on the upper branches with the sun shining directly down at us. After a few moments, my eyes adjusted, and a rather ethereal image came into focus.

Hanging from a branch was a round object, bright white with a halo of light around it. Wispy streamers wafted away from the core, dancing about as the breeze struck them through the leaves. I was mesmerized by the floating orb. It looked like a piece of cloud that had caught in the trees. I also wondered what all the hullabaloo was about. Why was everyone so disconcerted by such an object of beauty? I turned to ask my Uncle that very question, but it died on my lips when I saw his expression.

He had taken off his hat and stuck it on his cane, which he leaned against the trunk of the tree. Using both hands, he shielded his eyes from the sun's glare. He slowly lowered his eyes and then his shoulders sagged and his face grew long.

"Is it empty?" He barked out, without looking up.

"No"

"Please bring it down", still not looking up, he grabbed his hat and cane and turned to walk a few steps away.

I was surprised that my uncle would risk one of his men so cavalierly. The branches that led to the orb were much thinner than the one the man stood on. When I really looked, the object was actually in the next tree, a large pine.

Without hesitation, the man swung himself around the trunk and inched out towards his goal. When it was obvious that the branch had thinned too much to bear his weight, he simply whipped off his belt and used it to catch the top of the tree and draw it near. Putting the belt end between his teeth, he took hold of the bundle with one hand and used the knife to cut it free. As soon as he had it, he began to clamber down the tree, cradling the white bundle in his arm.

I stepped back to join my uncle and gave Frank room to jump down. He was more than halfway now. "Do you know what that is?" I asked.

He looked down at me with sad eyes, "I fear it is swaddling, Frohman."

I had little time to process that statement as the man jumped down from the lowest branch, landing lightly on his feet. He held the bundle out in both arms towards my Uncle like he was offering a sacrifice in a pagan ceremony.

If I were going to put this scene in a play, Frank, was exactly who I would cast in the role. He was medium sized with dark eyes, jet black hair, and dark weathered skin. He wasn't a negro -- as his hair was straight, nor was he Spanish, European, or Asian. I realized he was must be an Indian.

Uncle Will looked around and spied a flat boulder, about waist high, to our left and pointed with his cane. Frank took the bundle over and laid it gently, almost reverently, on the flat top. Uncle Will stepped over to it and the other men gathered

72

around in a loose circle. Up close, I saw it was a white cloth, wound around something that was still hidden in the folds. The wispy tendrils I saw floating in the wind were tattered ends, like you would find on a flag that had flown in the elements for a long while. Leaning his cane against the rock, William gently tugged at the folds of cloth until he revealed a sight that made my heart leap into my throat.

Nestled deep within the cloth, was the tiny round face of a baby. Or at least, what was once a child. The face was nearly black from exposure, the eyes squeezed tightly shut, tiny nose sunken in, and the mouth was stretched wide open over rotting gums in a rictus of pain. I could feel that muffin I just ate flip over in my stomach.

Uncle Will looked sick at first, but he kept his composure as he turned to Ollie, standing next to him. "Send someone to the house. Use the telephone to call the Chief Inspector and ask him to come as quickly as possible." In a quieter voice he added, "Not Andrew. He needs time to get his breath back."

Ollie nodded and looked around. He fixed his look on a younger, lanky man. "Go, Matt. Ask for Chief Inspector Rowan and tell him Mr. Gillette needs him here."

Matt didn't look happy with the assignment, but he handed his shovel to the man next to him and started towards the path back to the castle, until William called to him.

"Matt, please tell Inspector Rowan that there has been a murder and ask him to bring the doctor if he is availible."

"New doc or the old?" Matt asked in return.

"Dr. Blum. He is still the medical examiner for the county, if I am not mistaken."

Without another word, Matt turned and headed down the path and was quickly out of sight. Uncle Will said nothing more for the moment; he just stared up at the tree-top with a

73

pensive air about him. I took a look around the circle of men, who were waiting for my Uncle to speak again and then I asked the question that was on everyone's mind.

"Murder? Where do you get murder from?" Trying not to sound callous, I added, "Babies get abandoned all the time, Uncle Will."

"Not on my property, they certainly do not!" He snapped, irritated. Then he gave me a half smile to take the sting out of his tone. "Besides, the Inspector needs a little incentive from time to time." Before I could ask, he added. "I want the doctor to see the child before we disturb the scene any further."

That made sense. If the doctor determined the child was already dead before it was put in the tree…well…it was just a piss poor way to treat the deceased, but leaving a live baby would be a different story altogether. That led to my next question.

"How the hell did it get up in that tree anyways?" I addressed the question to my Uncle, but I looked around at all the men. They either shook their heads or mumbled thier ignorance. Uncle Will looked to his foreman.

Ollie shook his head sadly. "I haven't the foggiest, Mr. Gillette. I doubt we would have even seen it, since our line runs that way." He pointed in a direction that ran about thirty yards perpendicularly to the tree the where child floated. "Frank found it."

Everyone turned to look at Frank, who had drifted away from the circle and found a seat on a fallen tree. He got up and walked back over. Without preamble, he said, "We cut a tree down over there this morning." He pointed to a spot about five yards before the cleared path ended. The stump was still visible. "There was a Magpie nest in it and I saw many of these cotton threads woven into it. These birds will use whatever they can find in the area to build their nests and I wondered

74

how they came across cotton threads when no one ever came out here. The nearest people are those at the castle and that is too far for a magpie to rummage." he shrugged. "When Mr. Ollie told us to take a break, I took a look around and found the cloth high in the tree."

"Do you have a theory how the babe was placed there?" William asked.

Frank shook his head. "I have thought hard about it but can see no way. But I have not searched the area. This much I know-anyone big enough to carry that weight to the top of the tree could not get through the branches-and they wouldn't support them if they did. I suppose they could have put it there the same way as I took it down, but I keep asking myself why?" He smiled slyly, "Except that white men are crazy!"

Some of the men acted as if they didn't like the remark, though it had the feel of an old joke amongst them to me. No one took offence, at least. Frank certainly had respect with the crew. Frank looked sadly at the bundle and then he spoke, "I didn't know what it was until I climbed the tree next to it. At first, when I saw it blocking the sun with its ghostly tatters, I thought it was one of the tree spirits like my grandmother used to tell me stories about when I was young.

William nodded sagely. "Perhaps it was a spirit that led you to the child."

"Perhaps" was the only reply he got.

I had no desire to see this turn into a revival, so I asked the questions. "So, setting aside how the child got up there for now, just where did the person who brought it come from? Why leave a baby out in the middle of this God-forsaken wilderness? I mean not to be crude, but why not just sink it in the river? That's just a few hundred yards from here."

William gave me a long look and replied. "The last question will have to wait for more data, but I believe we can look into the first two, while we await the authorities."

He turned to Frank, "If you would please do me the service of looking for any sign of where our abandoners came from?"

Frank shrugged, "Sure. There's really only one way they could have come from." Without further ado, he headed across the cleared path and towards the river.

"Why only one direction?" I asked my Uncle as the Indian headed down the slope.

William stepped up next to me and pointed with his cane to the densely wooded area between his castle and the main road off in the distance.

"This whole area is thick with briars and prickers." He saw the confusion on my face and explained. "Prickers are what the locals call low growing vines that sport long razor- sharp thorns. Think of them as angry brambles. There are acres out there that would rip a man to shreds if he tried to cross them."

He stepped in front of me and pointed to a direction that was mostly in line with the cleared path. "Approximately fifty yards in that direction is a large chasm that is too big to cross. That leaves only access from the river or my home-and I assure that was not the route."   William turned to his foreman. "Ollie, you may take the men back. I fear work is done for the day. By the time the police have come and gone, I doubt there will be time to resume." He looked over to his crew and announced. "You may all have the rest of the day off." The men looked a bit disappointed, until he added, "With pay-of course."

The men thanked him in a jumbled chorus, some even adding condolences. They wasted no time getting their things and before you could blink, my Uncle and I were alone.

76

He looked around for a minute then declared, "We will begin to investigate your first question while we wait for Frank and or the Inspector. Whoever comes first!" With that, he started over to the tree the child was found in. I followed behind and was even more confused as I stood at the base of the pine and looked up. I could barely see the remainder of the cloth which was attached to a high branch. Uncle Will started to walk around the tree slowly, fighting his way through the thick foliage. He stopped when he reached the opposite side and scanned the area around him. He looked my way and waved me over to join him.

Strangely, the branches on the back of the tree were not nearly as full as the side we came up on. It was like the Christmas tree that you put close to a wall. From about halfway up the tree, the branches were sparse and broken. Only the smaller limbs and new growth remained. There was even some scarring on the trunk itself. In fact, the area looked as if an angry giant had stomped his way through here, leaving crushed brush and a huge tree toppled. Uncle Will bent over to examine the felled tree and looked back at the object of our attention. He stood and nodded to me in a satisfied way as he headed back to where we left the child. There is your first question answered, young Frohman. We can make a reasonable deduction as to how the babe was placed so high in the tree."

"Come again?" I challenged him.

He stopped and looked at me as if I were a dolt. Then a light seemed to go off in his head and he smiled. "Ah! You would not know about the snow. That's what made it all possible."

"What snow? What does snow have to do with anything?" I was afraid the discovery was starting to unhinge him a bit.

He continued walking through the foliage and I followed him until we came to the rock where we left the child. "Six weeks ago, we had a freak nor'easter come through here and it dumped almost a foot of snow. Fortunately, the weather began to warm up shortly afterwards and the thick blanket disappeared within a week. Think about what you observed back there and add the factoring weight of wet snow and I am sure the solution will reveal itself to you."

I mulled it over a moment and disagreed. "Um…no it won't."

He laughed and shook his head. "So like your father! You see all the parts, yet you refuse to put them together. In any case," he went on before I could object, "I think I hear Frank coming. Now we shall get the answer to your second question. Where did the culprits come from?"

A little miffed, I said petulantly, "What makes you think he found anything? Snow or no snow!"

"Frank is a full-blooded Mohegan. He belongs to a local tribe that makes their home in a town up the road called Uncasville. The town was named for their chief.

"Frank is also one of the best trackers around. Someone once told me that 'Frank can track a fly back to where it hatched'. He will know something. He has never failed me in the past."

I had to grin when a thought popped into my head. "So, what is he? One of your Baker Street Irregulars?"

William laughed at that. "Hardly, but it's good to have a competent woodsman around when you live out in the country."

Frank suddenly appeared in the cleared path and he walked directly over to William. Handing him a fist sized round stone with red markings, he said, "One man. Came by boat. Slow in, fast out."

I guess I was expecting more, but my Uncle was satisfied. Still, I had to pipe up. "That's it? What the hell does that mean?"

Frank swiveled his head to give me a flinty stare, but Uncle Will just ignored my outburst.

He crossed his hands over his chest and raised one hand to tap a finger against his lips slowly. Finally, he said, "January tenth was the storm, so he must have left the child sometime between the eleventh and the thirteenth or fourteenth."

Frank grinned from ear to ear. "Excellent, Mr. Gillette. You know about the tree." He laughed, "We'll make an Indian tracker of you yet."

Now I was just getting frustrated with these two and their crazy talk. "How could he tell all that if there was snow on the ground and what is going on with the tree?" I demanded of my Uncle.

William just sighed heavily and addressed Frank. "If you would care to explain the first, I will handle the second part."

Frank shrugged and said, "There was keel paint on the river rocks a few feet from shore where he grounded the boat. Then I found boot prints in the mud along the bank and marks on a tree where he tied up. Two parallel groves, horizontal. Probably from ropes for a light anchor around the trunk. Nearby, a few feet into the river, there were two sets of prints; solid even prints towards the land and messy and uneven coming back. Thus, a boat landed here, and one man carried the child to the tree and returned empty-handed."

That shut me up and Uncle Will put another stitch in my lip. "As for the tree and how the child ended up at the top- Remember I told you we had a fierce Nor'easter. The strong winds must have toppled that elm tree at an angle that landed it on the pine. The pine is slender and more supple, so, it bent under the weight of the elm until its top was close to the ground. The snow and freezing temperatures kept the elm in place- until the rapid thaw. Then it slid down the trunk, tearing off the lower branches, allowing the pine to straighten up and raise the child skyward."

I kept my mouth shut as they discussed what type of boat it could be. Uncle Will was estimating the draft from how close to the shore the rock was found.

"I believe we should be on the lookout for something between twenty and thirty feet. Engine, not sail, I should think. A small working boat with substantial weight."

"Why's that?" I blurted.

The angle of the paint marks. Frank said it came straight into shore. There were high winds all that week and it would have been near impossible to tack in on a sail boat. Then there would be the ice factor."

"Ice?"

"Of course. Though we had a mild winter the only time the river was safe to traverse was during the holiday season however there was still a thick sheath of ice built up along the shoreline. A vessel would have to be sturdy and heavy, to break through the ice and scrape along the river bed." With that, he tossed me the rock Frank had handed to him.

I looked at it carefully and he was right. There was no mistaking the sheen of marine paint. I had seen plenty of it, scraping barnacles and repainting the bottom of boats under my Grandfather's critical eye. It was thick and ground into the smooth surface of the rock, so I had to believe Uncle Will was on the right track.

"Well," I mused, "If it was a working boat, I would guess it was a fisherman. That means…"

"Nothing!" my Uncle cut me off. "Idle speculation without data will only lead to erroneous conclusions! Kindly limit your observations to facts Collin!"

His tone alone was rude enough to start a bar fight and talking down to me like I was a child still rankled me. I had to grit my teeth, so as to not stick my tongue out at him.

'La di da!' I thought to myself. Though I had seen glimpses of this side of him, years ago, I didn't realize just how obnoxious he could be when he was in this mode. Just to be petulant, I was about to crack wise, but again, he cut me off.

"Please, Frohman. Spare me the inane conversation and let me think! I want to have the facts in order before the authorities arrive!"

Frank took his former seat on the fallen tree and said nothing. Miffed, I stomped over to a nearby stump and took a seat, fuming at being rebuffed.

In a kinder tone, William called out softly. "Don't pout, Frohman. It's unbecoming in a business tycoon." The corners of his lips twitched, and then he went back to his silent contemplation.

7

After a few minutes, I cooled off and settled in for the wait. I glanced over at Frank, but he looked to be in a trance deeper than my Uncle's. In my mind, I could see someone grounding his boat on the shore then carrying the babe up the path. I could envision a shadowy figure, struggling through the deep snow and howling winds to thrust the child into snow covered branches. I could follow Uncle Will's explanation of how the pine tree righted itself and carried the bundle aloft. What I could not grasp was why.

Why come out all this way to nowhere to tie a baby to a tree branch? I jumped up to tell William what had occurred, but he wasn't in his place. I looked around and the Indian was gone too. I heard rustling in the trees and my eyes went upwards to see Frank back in the branches and climbing like a squirrel. Uncle Will was at the base of the tree watching, and I had the feeling I was lagging sadly behind.

"I suppose you sent him up to check out the knot?"

He smiled, "Actually, I sent him to retrieve it, but I am glad the thought finally occurred to you. There is hope for you yet, Collin."

Before I could reply, I heard the faint sound of an engine. William heard it too.

"Ah! That should be the inspector and the doctor." William turned and called up to Frank, who was just starting to cut the branch. "The authorities have arrived. Frohman and I will wait for them; hang on to that for now." Frank acknowledged with a simple nod, and we pushed out way back into the clearing.

We had just managed to brush off and straighten our clothes as the police car came into view. I could tell by the sound of the motor it was a Ford.

Sitting on extra wide tires was an elongated Model T chassis with the biggest engine Ford had made to date. There were two seats, front and back and a large metal box behind the rear seat. Black, with white highlights, the side was emblazoned with POLICE.

I gave a low whistle. "Gee, Uncle Will, for a one-horse town, that's quite the machine.

William raised his brows. "I had it built and donated it to the town in honor of Rowan's ascension to Chief Inspector."

I thought that a mighty big gift to the town. My Uncle was a kind and generous man, but he had a reputation for deep pockets. I began to see just how much my uncle respected the danger regarding Captain Roy.

I shrugged and grinned up at him. "It's always good to have the coppers in your corner."

The wagon finally jolted to a stop some forty-feet from us, and all four doors were flung open. Two men in uniform headed around the front of the car to join the other two. The man from the front seat was tall and thin, with a head of dark hair. He dressed like an official, in a dark suit with a long coat over it. His eyes swept over the area around him and I could tell he took it all in. He pulled a small notebook from his jacket pocket. He, most assuredly, was Chief Inspector Rowan.

The man from the back seat was obviously Dr. Blum, as he was older and toted a large black bag. He smiled grimly and waved when he saw us.

Rowan was far more intent. He ignored us for the moment and began barking orders to his men.

"Sargent get the kit out of the back. Fenn, you set up the camera."

"Set it up where, Sir?" the younger blonde policeman asked.

"Just fetch it out of the back!" Rowan snapped. "I'll let you know in a minute."

Without acknowledging their salutes, he turned his eyes on us and strode over to us like he meant business. The doctor rolled his eyes and followed on his heels. The inspector slowed, swiveling his head to take in the surroundings, and the doctor passed him and stuck out a hand to my uncle.

"William, it's been too long."

William took his hand briefly, but before he could reply, Inspector Rowan stepped in front of us and his two men came barreling up behind. The one he called Sargent had large leather satchel and the other carried a box camera on a tripod. When the men reached his side and stood at semi-attention, waiting orders, he turned to my Uncle.

"William." He said and nodded like he was Caesar come to conquer.

"Chief Inspector, what is all this?" He waggled his cane at the two officers.

Rowan beamed like a new father. "The Sargent here has our crime scene kit. Everything one needs to measure, record, and collect evidence, including talc powder, blotting paper, and magnifiers to identify fingerprints.

"Fenn here is trained to photograph the scene to allow us to study the clues for as long as we need back at the office. I told

84

you I was going to bring this department into the twentieth century! Now, where's the victim?"

William pointed over to the bundle, still sitting on top of the flat rock. The doctor was the first to recognize the bundle for what it was, and he hot footed it over, while the Inspector and his men simply gaped in confusion. By the time Rowan ambled over, the doctor had already peeled back the layers of cloth to reveal the child's face completely. Rowan was staring at it mutely as we joined the circle around the child.

Without looking up, the Chief Inspector growled in a low voice. "Your cook told me there was a murder." He turned his head to look at my uncle with undisguised distain, "How does this constitute a murder?"

William's face tightened, and I could see his eyes begin to smolder. "If ever there was a victim, it is that infant who lies there! My men discovered the babe, tied to an upper branch of that pine." He paused to turn and pointed at the tree and added, "While they were clearing this patch."

The Inspector looked up, then grunted and slapped his forehead. "Ugh! Another flying corpse?"

I could see William was about to erupt, but the doctor forestalled any rebuke when he looked up from his examination and asked, "Just why are you clearing this land, William?"

Uncle turned to the sawbones and barked, "Irrelevant!" Then he looked Rowan square in the eye, "Someone brought the child by boat to the nearby riverbank, then trudged up to these woods and tied the child's swaddling to a tree branch that ended twenty feet in the air!"

Rowan mulled that over for a second then exploded. "You don't even know if it was alive or dead when it was left here! If it was the latter-how can you call it murder?"

"Alive or deceased-the question still stands, Inspector."
Uncle Will had his dander up now.

Rowan mulled it over some more as we all looked at him
expectantly. Suddenly he nodded and went into a tirade. "I can
tell you this much, there are no missing babies in my district!
Even if there were, why go to all this trouble? No Sir! This was
the work of some outsiders! Gypsies or Redskins."

"Or WHAT?" Frank growled from my side. I jumped, as I
never even heard him join us.

"Don't get your feathers in a ruffle, Chief" Rowan warned,
when he saw the anger on Frank's face. He pulled back his
jacket to reveal a small thirty-two caliber tucked into a waist
holster. I was pleased to see that mine was bigger. "Besides,
don't Indians bury their dead up in the air?"

"That is the mid-western plain Indians custom, Chief
Rowan!" Frank snapped back. "I assure you that we don't hang
our children alive or dead -- out like laundry to dry!"

"And I'd watch that Gypsy talk too! We're not exactly sure
where Ma hails from." I put in, just because I never liked a
bully who hid behind their gun.

Rowan snapped his head towards me and suddenly I was the
center of attention. I tried to look bored as he eyed me up and
down. "And just who might you be?" he asked

William, looking irritated by the interruption, stepped up.
"Forgive me. Chief Inspector Kevin Rowan, this is Collin
Frohman."

The inspector recoiled as if he was slapped, but he quickly
recovered and stuck out a hand, which I took briefly.
"Pleased." He mumbled.

If his greeting was a bit subdued, the doctor more than made
up for a welcome. His eyebrows shot up, and his mouth formed

an O. Breaking into a big grin, he stepped up and thrust out his hand.

"Frohman? Charlie's son?" I nodded, and he pulled me into a near hug. "Tom Blum. I admired your father greatly." He took my hand in both of his and stared at my face. "You have your father's eyes." Then he winked and added, "And his mouth!"

"Now that we have dispensed with the socials, may we please return to the matter at hand?" William said loudly in exasperation. Doctor Blum rolled his eyes and winked at me again, but he released my hand and went back to examining the child.

The younger officer, sagging under the weight of the camera, asked tentatively. "Take it back to the car, Paul!" he snapped, and then added, "Go with him Sargent. Stow the kit and get the car started. We're leaving soon."

Uncle Will was not happy with that decision. "Is that all the effort you are willing to expend? You intend to disregard your resources and rely on felonious conjecture? Certainly, I know you for a better investigator than that!"

Rowan straightened up to his full height and placed his hands on his hips. He was looking pretty steamed. "Damn it, William! I can't be responsible for what some outsiders left in your yard!"

When William just glared back at him, Rowan plowed on, pointing at the child,   "Look at the coloring of its face! Be it negro or Indian…"

"NO!", The Doctor said sharply, straightening up and turning to face us.

Rowan glared at him and asked, "What do you mean, no?"

"The child is Caucasian. The coloring is due to exposure and decomposition. The baby is white." He avoided the Inspector's glare and said to Wiliam. "Blue eyes."

William looked almost triumphant. "I already knew that, Doctor. Only a progeny of both a white mother and father can have blue eyes."

He turned his head back to Rowan and added, sarcastically, "Imagine what we might glean if there was some actual police work done!"

Rowan went beet red in the face and snarled, "There is no need for sarcasm, Gillette!"

"The fact is--there are still no missing babies in my jurisdiction!"

Blum held up a hand to stop William's retort. "He's right about that, William. There have been only two births this winter, and I attended them both. Mothers and children are doing fine. I saw them all last week, in fact."

That set my Uncle back a pace. I could see why. It was just another piece of this strange puzzle that didn't fit. While he mulled the possibilities over, Rowan took the bit between his teeth.

"And it doesn't change the fact that you lured me out here, under false pretenses, and in the process pulled me away from a matter of paramount importance that needs my personal attention.

And all for what? For a case that most likely wouldn't amount to more than trespassing and perhaps the illegal disposal of human remains; we even have a statue on the books to cover that! Calling it a murder is nothing more than dramatics."

Uncle Will took some umbrage I can tell you. His eyes went dead cold as he barked back. "If someone bringing a child by boat, then grounding his vessel on the bank and trudging up the hillside in deep snow to leave a human being in the snow covered branches of a pine tree, is not worthy of your talents, perhaps you should have brought a junior detective along and dumped it in his lap." Then strangely, William smiled viciously and added. "Well, perhaps not. Look how that ended with your predecessor."

It took everything within me not to wince at that barb myself. Rowan looked like he had been backhanded, but to his credit, he didn't wince either.

"That is as unfair as it is rude, Gillette!" he said in a loud hard voice. "There is absolutely no sign of foul play here! It's all in your head -- and your ego!"

"Can you be so blind as to not see the incongruities here? If so, your promotion had quickly dulled your skills -- and your wits."

"Now you listen here, Gillette..."

"Cease fire!" Blum yelled at the top of his lungs, causing all of us to jump. When he had our complete attention, he said calmly. "Perhaps you gentlemen can continue this conversation AFTER I have made an examination back at my office. If I can determine whether the poor babe was left alive or dead- then you may at least resume your debate."

Uncle Will looked like he was going to go on, but I held up my hand to stop him. "He's right. Perhaps more hard facts are needed before we proceed."

William gave me a surprised look, nodded, and was calming down. "You are correct, Frohman. Let us see what the good Doctor can glean from his examination." He turned to the Chief, "Agreed?" Rowan nodded, and William turned back to the Doctor. "Do you need assistance on getting the child to the car?"

Blum had already covered the child back up and gathered it in his arms. "I can manage, William. Thankfully, the smell is gone by.

"Ride back to the castle with us. There is plenty of room."

With that, he headed back to the car and William trailed after him. Rowan didn't look pleased at the doctor's invitation, but he just fell in alongside William.

William hesitated for a moment and turned back to Frank and me. "Coming?"

Rowan added, "There's no room up front but you can ride in the back."

Frank frowned and shook his head. "No. Thank you."

I wasn't sure why he turned him down, but I decided to walk back with him. I wanted some more time to mull the situation over, so I could talk intelligently to him, when I rejoined him at the castle. "I'll walk with Frank."

William gave me a curious look, and just nodded and continued on.

Rowan shrugged, "Suit yourself."

As they walked away, I heard Rowan say to my Uncle. "You'll be eating crow by the end of the day Gillette!"

"Ha!" he replied, "It is you that shall dine on humble pie for your supper!"

Quiet you two!" Doctor Blum admonished. "I'm not listening to you two bicker the whole ride…"

As they piled into the car, I turned to Frank, curious. "You don't fancy a ride in a paddy-wagon?"

"White man cages have sticky locks." he said defiantly.

I clicked my teeth and grinned. "That's what my gypsy Ma always said!"

8

Frank and I looked at each other and laughed.

"I think a walk would be much more peaceful anyways, eh?" I quipped.

"Usually is." Frank responded, and we headed out ourselves.

Lost in my thoughts about the dead infant I had unanswered questions. Where it came from and why it ended up here? If it was abandoned-why? Why here, on William's property? Who were the parents?

It was all a bit much. To be honest, I couldn't garner much empathy for the infant. I understood William's point of view, but I also agreed with the Chief Inspector. If it wasn't one of the town's residents, why lose any sleep over it? Babies die all the time.

I turned to my Indian escort after a while and asked him, "What do you think of all this, Frank?"

.."Mr. Gillette should bury the child, say a prayer to his God and forget about it."

"Well, you can't give her a Christian burial. She was probably too young to baptize."

He shrugged, "It doesn't matter. The newly born is nothing more than flesh. It has no spirit."

That was interesting. "Funny you should say that. Ozaki once told me that Japanese people don't name their children for thirty days, because that's when a spirit will inhabit the body. He says a lot of babies die soon after they're born, but they're not really considered a person yet according to their Shinto religion."

Frank made a thoughtful face. "I will ask Mr. Ozaki of this. It sounds like something I could believe in."

That struck me as odd. "I'm not sure you can decide to believe in something. Either you believe, or you don't!"

"What's the difference?"

I wasn't about to start waxing philosophies with an Indian! I got enough of that from Ozaki. We reached a small meadow when my tongue broke loose.

"William says you're the best tracker in these parts. Who taught you?"

"My father, uncles, and mostly my grand-father."

I wondered whether his grandfather was as much a brutal taskmaster as my 'Pop-Pop'. "I learned a lot from my Grandpa too. Only about the sea. I never spent much time in the woods."

"It's all about reading the world," he replied. "The land, the sea, and the sky just have different languages."

Good Lord! This man was a Native American Confucius! "Read the world, eh? I like that!" I stopped and motioned for him to do the same. "What do you read right now?"

He smiled and said in a low voice. "A menu. If I had my rifle, I would get my dinner."

I raised my eyebrows and looked around. There wasn't any movement for as far as I could see. I whispered back "Just what were you planning on shooting?"

In one swift motion, Frank stooped and plucked a rock off the ground. Sidearm, he whipped the rock across the meadow to land in a thicket of grass. Instantly, there was an explosion of grass and feathers as a large bird, spooked by the stone, burst out, wings flapping hard for freedom. In one smooth motion, I slid my pistol out, aimed and hit it with my first shot. The bird instantly began to tumble to the ground not twenty feet in front of us. We walked up and found a fat, female pheasant, with its head blown off.

"Dinner's on me." I told him, as I holstered my piece.

William must have seen us walking across the lawn, as he came out to greet us from the veranda. They came down the steps, around to the front and crossed the small bridge to the road by the time we walked up.

"That's a nice hen you have there, Frank," he commented. "What happened to its head?"

Then he looked at me and barked a short laugh. "I heard the shot. My nephew has been showing off, hasn't he?"

"I have never seen such and expert shot from a pistol," Frank replied, "And I doubt I ever will again."

I was a bit embarrassed by the praise, so I pointed out, "Yeah, well, I would have walked right past it if it wasn't for Frank."

"Would you like it Mr. Gillette?" Frank asked, holding it out, the neck still bleeding out a bit. "It was Mr. Frohman's kill."

William held up both hands, looking a bit apprehensive. "Oh, no, Frank. Take it home and enjoy it with your family. Besides, Mrs. Woods would have a fit if I brought that into her kitchen."

"Alright then. Thank you." Frank said, and turning to me he added, "And thank you, Mr. Frohman, for my dinner and the conversation."

I was just as happy William didn't take it. After watching him tote that dead and oozing fowl for the last mile or so, I had no desire to actually eat it!

"The pleasure was all mine," I replied. "Are you sure your wife won't mind you bringing that home?"

He shook his head. "And I'll clean it on the ferry." He had the strangest grin on his face. He turned to William, "Are we working tomorrow?"

William mulled that over for a minute. "Yes, I believe so. There's nothing much else we can learn from the site. Meet Ollie at the usual time. He knows what to do. If you happen to come across anything or even have a new thought on the matter, report it to me as soon as possible. I'll let Ollie know you can do as you see fit."

Frank nodded once. "Goodnight then." Then he simply turned and walked away toward the ferry.

I didn't understand that grin on his face. "What did he mean, 'I'll clean it on the ferry'?"

William laughed, "Just that. Frank likes to clean whatever he had hunted that day on his ferry ride across the river. I think he does it to scare the townsfolk. He'll tear the feathers off and toss them into the water, then he'll disembowel the bird and the offal will join the feathers. That's when the faint hearted will be hanging over the railings. Then he'll tie a rope to the carcass and toss it in the water to clean it. The meat is usually very appetizing looking by the time he pulls it back in. Unless, of course, it's squirrel or possum." He laughed again, "It drives Captain Burke bonkers!"

"I imagine so," I agreed.

When Frank was well on his way, Wiliam turned to me, "Are you ready for some lunch? You must be famished after the walking."

Having gotten up early and having only a muffin for nourishment, he was right! "That'd be great, Uncle Will. Tell me, what did Rowan and the doctor say? I thought you and the Inspector were going to have at it!"

"Bah!" He exclaimed as we walked back to the house. "Chief Inspector Rowan is not convinced of the serious nature of this crime! He seems to view it as if we had found a dead dog in the road. A view I intend to dissuade him of!"

Stepping inside, he called down the side hall, "Mrs. Woods! We are ready for lunch!"

There was a faint undiscernible reply, but it satisfied William. He gestured to one of the couches set into the wall. "Let's sit for a moment. Collin, I can't tell you how much I was looking forward to your visit. I have missed my connection to your family as much as I miss your father. I can't put into words how saddened I am about the child, just when your visit is beginning."

95

I sat up, not liking where this was going. I tried to derail him by saying, "Are you sure you are not taking this a little too hard, Uncle? After all, anyone in the world could have left that child there. It has nothing to do with you personally! Unless… you think it may have been Roy or one of his gang? Trying to scare you...or send you a message?"

"He laughed and clapped me on the knee. "Don't be so melodramatic, Collin. Of course not! Though, to be frank, the thought did cross my mind, but a murdered child has no significance to our relationship.. After all, if not for my railroad whims the baby may have just decomposed into the forest with no one the wiser."

"Even so," I conceded. "That still doesn't make it your problem, Uncle Will. You're just the guy paying taxes on that tree."

"Ah! But that is exactly the point, Collin! Call it fate or providence, or just dumb luck, that poor baby girl was left on MY property!" A deeply sadden look came over his face, "And the one thought that keeps rolling about my mind is- Why did they have to let the child die out on the middle of nowhere. Whoever did it must have been able to see my home. Why did they choose death for the baby instead of simply leaving it on my doorstep?

I didn't know what to say to that, really, but I blurted out, "What would you do with a baby?"

He looked surprised at the question, "Why, raise her, of course. With the help of Ozaki and Mrs. Woods, I'm sure I could have raised a fine young lady."

That statement rocked me on my heels. I never really thought of Uncle Will with a child of his own but judging from the love he showed me and my siblings, well, it shows he had the heart for it. Growing up in a castle with a rich and indulgent caretaker would have made a great life -for anyone!

96

"I imagine so," I said softly.

William gathered himself. In any case, this is my problem. I'm sorry I won't have time to spend with you now, Collin, perhaps, when I have…"

I jumped up and whirled to face him, before I was even thinking of it. My mouth just started going before my brain could catch up. "Don't say it! Don't even think it! We're going to have plenty of time together because I'm not going anywhere until this is settled, see?" Before I could stop myself, I poked him in the chest.

"Now, Collin," he began as he rubbed where I jabbed him, "There is no need for you to put any more on your plate…"

"Stop!" I cut him off again. "I was here when it started, and I'll be here when we get to the bottom of this! I'm not going anywhere! Besides, after that little chat we had this morning, I'll stay right by your side until I'm sure you are safe." I patted my revolver under my coat. "Consider me your armed shadow!"

Looking both pleased and satisfied, he jumped to his feet and placed his hands on both my shoulders. "Excellent! I was hoping you'd feel that way!" He barked a short laugh, "I always think better when there is a Frohman around!"

In short order, we were seated at a narrow table that graced the only window in the kitchen, eating cold chicken and salad. Mrs. Woods had laid out a basket of biscuits and Catty was kind enough to scrounge me a pint of cold ale. I stuffed some chicken in the biscuit, took a bite and asked, around a mouthful, "So, what's our next move?"

"We," He stressed in a teasing way, "shall have to wait a bit longer before we proceed. I have already made two telephone calls. The first to my older brother, George, who, as you know, is in the State Senate. He was not in his office, but I shall try him again later."

"Who was the second call to?"

"The Agent in charge of the nearest Pinkerton office. There is one in New London."

"Pinkertons? If you have the State Police asking around, why do you need to pay those guys?"

"Two sides of a coin, Frohman! The State officers will ask politely, within the law and most likely to law abiding folk. The Pinkertons, however, have a vast network of sources in the criminal and seedier side of our society. If the child was a victim or a casualty of a criminal act-they will know.

"Gosh, Uncle Will, we just found the baby this morning and you already have half the state working on this!"

He laughed, "Think of them as my Irregulars! If in fact, the child originated from outside this county, between the two, I should dare to hope they would discover something."

"And if they both come up blank?"

"Then, as I suspect, our answers will be local. Now, finish up and get ready for a ride. The good Doctor assured me that he would make the autopsy a priority as soon as he returned to his office. He should have started at least an hour ago and it will take us three-quarters of an hour to reach his office. Two hours is certainly enough to discern some answers from a body that small!"

In short order, we were back in the kitchen, this time wearing our leathers and jack boots. Taking a staircase at the back, we descended into the lower part of the castle. I surmised it was his work room as we passed a long trestle like table that had a scattering of tools and bits of wood strewn across it. Here the unique hinges and closers were created.

But that took up only half the space. Around the corner was a rather cavernous, open room with a stone roof and sides. The floor wasn't solid, rather a layer of gravel that glowed softly in the light coming from under the two miniature barn doors on one side. The only things that occupied the room was my Harley Davidson motorcycle, an Indian Chief I knew to be William's, and a tarp covered machine.

"This is the garage?" I asked, skeptically. The doors were awfully low and there was no real room for a lift or chain pull, items you had to have if you owned an automobile and wanted to keep it running.

"Oh No!" he replied. "This is really just storage and receiving area. I have no desire to own an automobile. Ozaki refuses to drive one and my Indian Chief is all the transportation I need."

William had donned his gloves and goggles by then and straddled his machine. I followed suit and right before he kicked the engine into life, he said, "Follow me. It is a short ride down to the ferry landing."

"We're taking the ferry?" I had hoped for a longer ride.

He nodded. "It will be much faster than riding all the way up to the train bridge and back to town. There is something else I wish to show you."

Having said his piece, he started his bike and shot out the door onto the driveway, spraying gravel behind him. I had to laugh and let my bike idle for an extra moment, just to give him a head start.

Of course, I caught him before he was halfway down the hill and the rest of the ride was short. As we passed a half-built home with a donkey tied up out front, William took a hand from his bike and pointed to it. I slowed and gave it a good look- over, but it seemed to be nothing more than middle-class dwelling, though I thought it was in an odd spot. I thought William had told me his property ran right up to the ferry landing.

The ferry was still in the middle of the river and we would have to wait until it docked and unloaded before we would get on. We parked the bikes and when we got off, I asked my uncle, "What's with the house you pointed at? Isn't that your property?"

He nodded. "Ozaki is building a house of his own."

I raised my eyebrows at him but said nothing. Ozaki had been by William's side my entire life. They lived together on the Aunt Polly for years and years and I assumed he would bunk in the castle until they put him in the ground.

William gave a little shrug. "Ozaki and I have been in each other's shadow for many years Collin. Though I treat him less and less like a servant, we are getting older and surlier with each passing year. We need to spend some time apart or we will turn into an old married couple, sniping at each other constantly."

He shrugged and added, "If he was willing to spend his own money building the house, I was more than happy to give him the land."

"His own money? You pay Ozaki a salary?"

William looked at me like I had two heads, "Of course I do. A generous one, I might add. What did you think?"

"Well, I don't know. I just never really thought of you paying Ozaki. I thought you just kind of kept him."

He furled his eyebrows at me. "You will need to rid yourself of those romantic notions when you go to work, Collin. Yours is a business of negotiations and any naiveté will cost you dearly!"

Upon reflection, I knew he was right, but I didn't want to hear a lecture on fantasy from a man who lived in a castle and was building his own toy railroad. I almost said as much when my attention was suddenly pulled to the far side of the ferry lane.

A gaggle of seven young women were gathered in a tight circle next to a pile of bags. They kept their voices low, and there were at several conversations going on at once, punctuated by a group giggle. Every few seconds, one or more would throw a quick glance in our direction, though they tried hard to act nonchalant about it, and that would spur another round of titters. It was obvious that they recognized William and they were local, because a few of them called out greetings, of which, William nodded and waved in return. I of course, affected a disinterested manner, though they were all close to my age and a shapely lot. Two were a cut above the rest and the better of those glided across the lane to greet William.

"Good Afternoon, Mr. Gillette."

William gave her his most charming smile, "Good afternoon to you, Miss Scott." With a smirk, he glanced over at me, "May I introduce my…houseguest, Mr. Collin Frohman?

"Collin, this is Miss Irene Scott."

She was a petite thing, but with a good and ample figure. The cut of her dress and the great plume in her hat was of the latest fashion, though her travel boots were stained and dusty. Her face was beautiful but her most striking feature was her long, dark lashes that framed blue-green eyes. She held out her hand and I took it with a slight bow.

"Enchant'e," I said, giving her fingers the slightest squeeze as I released her hand.

By then, she had gleaned me head to toe and I'm sure she could have told you what my boots cost within the dollar. She must have liked what she saw, or at least the appraisal, because she gave me quite the steamy smile under half lidded eyes.

She looked up at William and said coyly, "You could never guess what my friends and I have been up to!"

Obviously, she was trying to lead into a story, but William took it as a challenge.

"Aside from the fact that you and your friends just returned from an overnight trip, where you attended the Prohibition rally yesterday… I'm glad you managed to get in a little shopping on top of your civic duties and had a pleasant stay at the Montfort. That is one of my favorite places to lodge when I am in Boston. How was the train ride home, this afternoon? Pleasant views from your window seat, I hope?"

Both the girl and I were standing there with our mouths hanging open. The girl stamped her foot, in mock frustration, and gave William her best pout.

"Well! At least you missed one thing!" she hesitated for dramatics, "We also went to see the *USS Delaware* steam into Boston Harbor. They say she's back in America for a refitting, whatever that may mean, and then she's headed right back to the war! Though," she added, "it didn't seem like much of a refitting to us!" She looked back over her shoulder to the other girls she was with. "Poor Monica. Do you know her, Mr. Gillette? Monica Lewiston?"

"I believe I met her parents at church." William replied. "Why would such a lovely young lady be the object of pity?"

After another glance at her friends, she turned an answered in a conspiratorial low tone. "You see, Monica has a beau on the *Deleware*. A junior officer and she was hoping to spend the afternoon with him. But she was turned away at the dock! No one got liberty at all! A few gentlemen, definitely not naval, disembarked along with a squad of Marines carrying a steel box, but there were the only ones. A crane lifted a few pallets of supplies, and she sailed right back out to sea! Poor Angela never even caught a glimpse of her beau!"

"Geez, that's too bad. I guess she needed to get back on station." I observed. "If the war breaks out, she'll be needed on the other side of the Atlantic."

She nodded sagely, and then addressed my Uncle. "But, however did you know all the rest? Everything you said was true!" she simpered.

"Simple logic, really. There is an overnight bag for each of you in that mound over there, which told me you, had all been on a trip together. The bags are big enough to hold a lady's necessities, but not large enough to satisfy her needs for more than overnight. That you came from the train station I know, because only the transport that services the station could hold all of you and you are all energetic to have made the walk from there. It is no secret that there was a grand march in favor of prohibition in Boston yesterday and the stains above the soles of your shoes are definitely the result of the copious amount of beer, wine, and spirits that were poured in the streets."

"I know." The pout was back, "These shoes are ruined! They are all I had for travel until I get home. How did you know what hotel? Or that we went shopping?"

"Why, that gorgeous new hat, and its magnificent feather never came from a haberdashery in these parts!" Uncle Will was really laying it on now. "As for your accommodations..."

As they were talking, I took a closer look at the scene and saw something. "The location of your lodging was perhaps the simplest observation. There is a tag from the Hotel on each of the handles of the bags." I could not read the tags from here, but obviously William could or he recognized the color pattern of them.

Wiliam arched his eyebrows and said nothing. The girl gave me a quizzical look and purred, "Are you a sleuth also?"

I flashed my best smile, "I'm in training."

"And where do you stand on Prohibition?"

I placed a hand over my heart, "Lips that touch liquor shall never touch mine!" I said with conviction. Then I quickly added in a rush, "Unless they are attached to a beautiful woman!"

William bit his lip and looked away, but I could tell the girl didn't quite catch what I said. I'm sure she only heard the last two words clearly, so she brought just enough color in her cheeks to acknowledge.

"Why thank you, Mr. Frohman. I'm glad you took the pledge. Drinking is such an awful vice!" She hesitated for a moment then went into a coy act. "Well, I should be getting back to my friends. Perhaps we shall meet again. Will you be staying long?"

I took her hand and kissed it again, "Long enough, I hope. Good day to you, Miss Scott."

She nodded and gave me the look again before she glided back to her friends.

"You have so much of your father in you." He said between chuckles.

9

Only a few passengers and no vehicles got off the ferry, so William and I each took our motorcycles by the handlebars and pushed them onto the ferry and to the front where we could get off quickly. The small crowd streaming onto the ferry either waved or called out a greeting to my uncle. I was afraid he would have to hold court the entire ride as he often did when he was spied out in public. Yet everyone just acknowledged him and took up a position around the perimeter of the boat, leaving the middle and the two of us alone. I was surprised at first. I had never been out with Wiliam Gillette when he wasn't swarmed by fans. Yet, I supposed that, having lived here for a few years now, the locals were used to him. I was happy to see him fitting into the community as I know he always wished to do.

But the passengers' actions puzzled me for another reason. They lined the gunnels like sentries waiting for an attack, peering out over the water. Every single one of them had their backs to us.

"What's going on, Uncle Will? What are those people looking at?"

He heaved a great sigh. "Not 'at', Frohman. They are all seeking a glimpse of the elusive 'River Monster'!"

No sooner had he spoken, when one of the girls in Miss Scott's' party, screamed as she pointed out. "There! Right there! I see it! The Monster!"

Another of the girls let out a short scream and instantly they were all squealing like a pen full of hungry piglets. Then, to cap off their commotion, the rest of the passengers rushed to that side, causing the small ferry to tilt slightly to port.

Above us, a man stepped out from the wheelhouse and snapped a spyglass open. He scanned the area she pointed to then closed it shut in disgust.

"That's a mooring, you damn fools! Now you people get back to your places!" He glared at the crowd until they sheepishly went back to their original positions. Then he pointed a finger at the group of indignant looking women. "You lot! Stop making a ruckus on my boat or I'll take you back-and leave you!" With that, he stepped back into the wheelhouse.

"Funny to find Captain Bligh on the Had-Lyme Ferry!" I joked.

William barked a short laugh. "Captain Burke is really quite a pleasant person, He simply brooks no nonsense on his boat." as he shook his head in disgust. "Look at these sap-heads! They are right back at it."

It was true. Most folks had drifted back to their original positions but they still all scanned the river's surface. It was obvious enough to me as an outsider, that they believed something was in their river. "When did the River Monster rumors start?"

"I am not quite sure of when," William answered. "I was too busy to hear about it until the entire town was in its thrall. But I can tell you who started it. Catherine's brother, Marquis. He has been regaling anyone he sees, and drinking for free on the tale of how he saw a mysterious shape in the water as he was heading back to his dock one evening. Something big and fearsome bumped his boat a few times until he managed to navigate away from it. He tells it well but offers no tangible

106

proof. So, now, every shadow, every shape in the dimming light, is a monster-looking for prey! Observe these people carefully, Frohman. It is a classic example of mass hysteria. The kind of thing that will either scatter them like sheep with a wolf in the fold, or mold them into a destructive force or the kind that tries to burn the world or lynches a man from the nearest tree."

"Oh, I don't know, Uncle Will." I said looking around at the backs of the passengers. "I think people look for the Monster for the same reason they come to see you at the theater. People, even the happiest, always want just a little more. A little more excitement. A little mystery." I cast an eye at him, "Even a bit of melodrama. The unknown can be a powerful aphrodisiac!"

William looked surprised for a moment, then a sad smile crept across his chin and I thought I saw a tear welling in one eye. I didn't want to embarrass him, so I looked away towards the approaching dock.. It was a few moments before he spoke again.

"Forgive this spate of sentimentality, Frohman." He said softly, "I remember when you took your first steps and now, I see an intelligent, worldly adult man next to me. Perhaps I have no right to say this, yet I am extremely proud of the way you turned out."

I knew I would cry if I looked at him, so I just nodded and mumbled, "My father and YOU were the very best teachers a young buck like me could have. You have my sincere thanks Uncle Will."

Thankfully, our dramatics ended when the crew started walking in front of our bikes in preparation for docking. William placed his hand on my shoulder and broke the mood, saying, "When did you become such the sage?"

I shrugged, "I guess I got more out of all that college than varsity letters, duels, and hang-overs!"

We laughed and hopped on our bikes to ready ourselves for disembarking.

As the crowd started to move forward, in readiness to depart, a few people came up and engaged William. He was polite and charming at first, but when a third person asked him if he had seen anything on the river from his home's vantage, he slapped his helmet on, snapped his googles into place, and then started his engine.

After that, as anyone approached, he pulled back on the throttle to get a respectable engine roar. People tried to holler over the noise so I joined in and soon our two engines were dueling for decibels.

As soon as the rope was dropped over the ramp, William kicked the Indian into gear and he moved off the ferry. I followed so quickly my front tire nearly left the ground. I caught him when he slowed to turn onto Main Street. He motioned for me to keep my speed down as when headed up the main though fare.

Chester was a nice little town. Typical of the kind of towns you found along the coast, the street, though not paved were solid packed from centuries of use and easy on the tires. At one time, the shops and stores, with the exception of a few, had started out as homes. As the population grew and got more affluent, people started building bigger homes on more property. The ones I saw up the side streets leading away from town looked spacious and well kept. I wasn't surprised- This town had probably been here since this land was first settled by white men.

I felt as if I already knew Chester, since I had read its description in my father's journals. To my left was a grassy strip that ran from the ferry landing, along the river and up to Main Street. Smack in the middle was a large, aging gazebo. Then both sides of the street were lined with businesses.

One that stood out was a larger building that had a row of oversized windows facing the street. Inside I could see a few men standing at a bar, behind a hand full of tables, set for food service. This would be the infamous 'Inn' my father described. As we already had eaten lunch, and my uncle wasn't about to agree to an afternoon pick-me-up, I decided to try and make my way there at some point in this visit.

We were about half-way up the main drag, when William pulled his over in front of a Victorian style house and killed the engine. I pulled up alongside him, right under a sign that had two parts. The top read 'John Nelson, MD', the bottom, 'Thomas Blum, MD'. William wasted no time, shedding his riding gear and walking up the steps to the door. I tossed my stuff on the seat of my bike and followed.

The foyer was small, with a staircase that led upstairs, roped off with a red cord and a 'private' sign hanging from its middle. A long hallway ran in front of us, but William opened the first door on our right, and we walked into what must have been the parlor in its residential time.

Now, it was the Doctor's waiting room with a reception desk which was unoccupied for the moment, sat right inside the door to the left. There was a low wooden barrier with a gate dividing the room and the rest of the walls were lined with chairs that were occupied by patients. Most of them knew my uncle and gave him greetings. In return, William walked along the perimeter, shaking hands and listening to their various ailments with compassion. The man knew how to work a room.

A door in the rear of the room opened, and a pert young woman dressed in traditional nurse's garb, hustled out. She set a file on the desk then picked another one from a pile. "Mr. Brown?" she called out.

A large negro man, middle aged, got up carefully from his seat and limped over to the gate. As he walked in front of us, William asked, "Your gout again, Jimmy?"

The man winced and said, "Feels like a weasel chewing on my toes!"

William patted him on the back. "I'm sure Doctor Nelson can help."

He shrugged, "Most likely he will tell me the same thing ole Doc Blum did. No mo' whiskey. No mo' sugar. No mo' greasy food. Ain't any reason to get out of bed without those three!"

William was about to reply when the Nurse said loudly swinging open the gate, "Come along, Mr. Brown. The doctor's waiting."

The man sighed and began to limp along. As the nurse turned to follow him in, William called out to her, "Excuse me, Miss?"

She turned to face him, a cold look on her face. "NURSE. Miss is the girl that comes in and cleans."

William flashed the NURSE his best smile. "Good afternoon. I do not believe we have met. Allow me to introduce myself, I am William Gillette, and this is my colleague…"

"I know who you are, Mr. Gillette. Do you have an appointment?"

"No, I…"

"Unless it's a dire emergency, you'll just have to take a seat and wait. As you can see, Doctor Nelson has a busy afternoon!"

Avoiding a reply, she turned her backs on us and began to head towards the back.

Looking to see William's reaction, I noticed a diploma from a nursing school on the wall next to the desk. I could see my Uncle was starting to look vexed, so I called out loudly, "Excuse me, are they paying you to be the bouncer too? We're not finished here!"

That froze her in her tracks. She turned slowly to face us, cross eyed and flushed with anger. She stomped over to us and opened her mouth to give us the rough side of her tongue, but William held a finger up, just inches from her, and said in a firm voice, "We are not here to see Dr. Nelson. Our business is with Doctor Blum."

That let a little of the steam out of her as she replied defiantly, "Well...he's busy too! Most likely for the rest of the afternoon." She glared at me, "Official police business, if you must know!"

As luck would have it, the door behind the desk swung open, and the elderly Doctor Blum came strolling in. Without a glance in our direction, he called out, "Ernestine! Bring my tea when you get a chance."

"Make sure it's hot, Nurse!" I dead panned- just to tweak her for treating my Uncle so shabbily.

She glared at me, but Doctor Blum noticed us before she could retort.

"Hullo, William. Thought I might see you earlier. Just as well, I only just finished.

Come back to my office."

William stepped forward to open the gate but couldn't because the Nurse was still standing in front of it, glaring at me.

"Excuse me, Nurse. We have some OFFICAL POLICE business with the doctor."

She stepped back, still throwing daggers with her eyes as we passed through to the inner sanctum.

I gave her my best smile, "Remember... Hot Tea!"

The doctor led us down the long hallway to the back of the house, and then, through a mostly unused kitchen. On the opposite wall there was a door, obviously new to the house, which the doctor tried to open but found it locked.

"Damnation! We'll have to go back around the other way. The keys are in my office!"

He headed back out the way we came, and William and I followed. I was starting to wonder about this codger when William spoke.

"It was quite kind of you to give Doctor Nelson your office."

"And look where it got me!" Blum groused as he went through a doorway to a short hallway. Taking a left, we stepped past a few doors until we came to the open one at the end of the hall. Stepping through, he added, "Any further back, I'd be in the garden shed!"

"And I see you have a new girl. What happened with Susan?"

"She's not my girl," He said as he tossed his papers onto an already messy desk." She's John's, though she will steer my last few remaining patients back here to the north forty. As for Susan...well, she left me last-early September if I remember correctly.

I don't know what the devil got into her, she just up and quit on me! Claimed she was going to wait for the husband to come home in the spring. Moved back into her folk's house since them both passed last year, and in with that crack pot 'Marine Engineer' brother of hers. Though, I hear he high-tailed it off to work on another of his so-called inventions! More of those clothes to work under water, I'll wager. Bunch of nonsense!"

William shook his head and asked, "What else did the gossiper's say?" There was a slight mocking edge to the question. Uncle Will never had much good to say about gossiping.

"That she's turned into a mean- spirited recluse over the winter which doesn't surprise me a bit. She always was a bossy, narrow-minded wretch!"

He laughed, "Could you imagine the two of us back here, whiling away the hours? I could hardly stand her ways when she was in the other room! There'd have been another murder to investigate, I tell you!

"But I'm rambling. Make yourselves at home. I don't have any appointments this afternoon."

It was a bit cramped, but it was a pleasant room, with great windows along the wall and a set of French doors that led to a back porch. I assumed that it had started its life as a dining room since it was long and narrow, and I could see where a chandelier once hung and now replaced with an overhead electric light. There was a single bookcase, with a fair- sized desk in front of it, and with two chairs for patients. The opposite wall had a curtain that separated it from the rest of the room, where he must have examined his patients. From the faint, dank death odor in the room I knew the body was behind that cloth.

The doctor turned to us, "Put your things there," gesturing to a hat rack and chair in the corner.

"So, Dr. Blum," William said as he deposited his hat and gloves, "How is semi-retirement treating you so far?"

"About the same as you William. Now I have the time to do all the things I've wanted to when I retired and I can't fit them all in!"

"So true!" William said with a chuckle. "When I am focused on a production, my mind is organized and relaxed. But without that stimulus, well, life has a way of pulling your attention in all directions!"

"Or, in your case- death," Blum countered. "Now, I can tell you everything I know about that child, but I'm sure you're going to want a look see for yourself. Am I right?"

William nodded. "I am sure you are aware of the utter confidence I have of your professional opinion, Doctor, yet a prior examination may help me focus any questions I may have."

He sighed, "As you wish, William, but I must warn you-it's not a pretty sight!"

I supposed it was just nerves, but I blurted out, "Have you ever seen any pretty corpses?"

That set the old sawbones back on his heels, but he recovered quickly and gave me a smile. "You are Charles's boy-no doubt about it."

I regretted my flippancy as soon as he pulled the curtain open. On a clean sheeted gurney, looking miniscule on the seven foot table lay a dissected baby. Quickly I looked away from the gruesome sight, focusing instead on a side table where the baby's clothes and wrappings were piled. Most of that was a depressing filthy gray, except for a pair of knitted booties that stood out with their deep dark red coloring. It was hard to imagine such well-crafted footwear gracing what looked like a butchered piglet on the big table.

She was surgically split from throat to belly button and the skin of her torso was peeled back. What lay in the cavity

114

looked like dried sausage and chum. The fingers and toes were blackened and looked like burnt match sticks that were stuck on rotting turkey legs.

The tiny face, with its distorted features, looked as it did when we found her. Now that she was bare, I saw some moss growing at the base of her neck and her skull was wildly distorted. It stuck up in three peaks with a coating of hair on each. Queasy but still curious, I stepped around William's back to get a better look at the top of her head.

My stomach fluttered and my mouth began to fill with my previous meal, partially digested, when I saw that the doctor had cut a large X in the top of her head and peeled her skull back like a banana to expose the brain.

William, not seeing my pale face, pointed out, like I wanted a lesson, "As you can see Frohman, there is no need to saw into a newborn's bony skull to open it up. The three bones that make up the skull have not yet, and will not for some months, fuse together. This allows the brain to grow without constriction."

Uncle Will bent in for a closer look and I was about to coat the top of my boots, and his, with my stomach's contents, when the doctor came to my rescue.

"Collin!" he said jovially, "Why don't we let William get a closer look." He put an arm around me and gently pulled me away from the table. "Come on over to my desk for a moment. I was a great admirer of your father."

I was still a little numb, but my stomach stopped churning as I sank down into one of the chairs across the desk from him. As soon as he settled into his seat, he opened a top drawer of his desk and pulled out a bottle of bourbon. He rummaged around some more and pulled out two glasses, which he held up with a question in his eye, "I hope the apple hasn't fallen too far from the tree?"

I laughed, "Thank you. I'll have them both. Find yourself another glass and join me."

He chuckled as he poured the two shots and handed me one. "Afraid you'll have to settle for a refill, I only have two."

We saluted each other and downed them neatly. Pouring us another, he said, "I am sorry to hear of your family's troubles, Collin. First your father and then your brother. Must have been hard on all of you. Your poor mother! Tending to a comatose patient is extremely taxing."

I shrugged. "We had two around the clock nurses to take care of my brother. "Mom's a strong old gal. She keeps busy. My sister and her child take up a lot of her time and my younger brother is still in school 'til the end of this year." Then a thought struck me, "How did you know about Michael?"

"Oh! Well…" he stammered, looking a bit sheepish, "William had me make a few calls to some friends of mine in the city who specialize in paralysis."

"Which I assumed would be kept in confidentiality, Doctor!" William said sharply, suddenly appearing next to me. He took the other chair and crossed his legs, "I would hope for more discretion from a man of medicine."

I reached over and patted his arm, wanting to shield the doctor from his ire. "Forget it, Uncle Will. Thank you. I appreciate your efforts on Mike's behalf."

He seemed mollified and the doctor quickly changed the subject. "Well, William? Any deductions on the death of the tiny baby?"

William frowned a bit, "Not really, Doctor. I admit I could glean little from the body, though I will maintain the child was alive when abandoned."

116

Blum slapped the desktop, "And you would be right. I'm certain of that also."

Then Doctor Blum clasped his hands and leaned forward on his desk. In a somber voice, he gave his report.

"First, I'd like to point out that this is the first and only autopsy I have ever done on a newborn. With that being said, there is little I can tell you. Though emaciated, I see no signs of disease or birth defects in the internal organs or brain. An infant's internal systems develop over time. My best guess is the child was one month to six weeks old when it died. You have to take into account that it would mean the child was abandoned somewhere in early January and it must have quickly frozen, obscuring any estimations. I do believe the decay is about six weeks to two months old."

"Which would coincide with our winter thaw," William pointed out. "Why do you say the child was abandoned?"

Doctor Blum leaned back in his chair and sighed sadly, "A few things. First, I believe the child had not one but two bowl movements."

"Couldn't that have happened when she died?" I interjected. "Doesn't the body expel its waste upon death?"

"Once maybe, Frohman, not twice" William answered. "Judging from whoever careful swaddled of the child, I doubt they would leave the child in its own mess."

Now, I almost called him on that. He had no children, but I have seen first- hand from my nephew just how many times a baby could mess itself!

"The clincher" the doctor started up again, "was the frostbite. A baby has no real regulation of its body temperature, so the fingers, toes, and even the nose had severe frostbite."

117

"Yeah, but you said the child froze in the cold temperatures." I reminded him. I'm not sure why I played the devil's advocate; I suppose I didn't want to really believe someone would leave the child to die on its own.

Doctor Blum just took a sip of bourbon and looked at my Uncle. Who nodded slowly and said, "Only the living can suffer frost bite. Dead flesh simply hardens.

"Is there nothing more you can tell us, Doctor?"

He spread his hands apart, "I'm sorry I can't tell you more William, but there was really not much to work with. A newborn is but a few opening notes of a symphony."

"Which should have grown into a beautiful song," William countered as he stood. "Thank you for your efforts, Doctor. Please send me a bill for your time and if you would- contact the undertaker and have him pick up the child and prepare it for burial."

"I can do the latter." he said as we stood. "As for my time-I'll bill the county." He winked at me, "Only way I get some of my taxes back!"

William stuck out his hand and Doctor Blum shook it. As I grabbed our stuff, William said to him,

"If you think of something else-inform me immediately." He turned to walk away, but stopped, "Oh, and could you have the child's things sent to my home. We came on motorbikes."

Doctor Blum shook his head, "You're going to kill yourself on that contraption. I'll send them over first thing tomorrow."

William nodded, and we made our way back to the waiting room, where we found the Nurse in a conversation with a guy about my age. He recognized my uncle and broke off his story-which did not make the nurse any happier with us!

118

"Hello, Mr. Gillette. Feeling O.K.?"

"I am fine, Marquis. I came to see Doctor Blum on another matter."

"Oh!" Marquis snapped his fingers. "I meant to tell you-I've put the same kind of system on my boat as you have on the Aunt Polly! You know, the one that pumps air in and water out of the bilge."

"I remember discussing it with you. How is it working out?"

"It's not hooked up yet. I just got the pump machinery and secured it to the deck."

"Well let me know how it works out." He looked about the room then leaned in and asked in a low voice, "Tell me, are you making a run upriver soon?"

Marquis beamed, "This afternoon, as a matter of fact. Want some more of that…special delivery? He winked. The usual six cases, if you would be so kind. Any chance you can procure more?"

Marquis shook his head. "Six is the limit they'll give me, for now anyways. Next month I think I can bump that up a couple of cases, though."

"Excellent. I'll expect you the day after tomorrow then." With that, William touched his forehead and headed out the door.

The nurse and Catty's brother Marquis, turned their eyes to me, but I felt a bit awkward, as William failed to introduce us, so I just nodded at them and followed my uncle out.

As I was walking out the door, Marquis said in an exaggerated tone, "My, he's young and pretty, ain't he?" The nurse squealed with amusement. I hesitated at the door, knowing full well what he was implying about my relationship

119

with my Uncle. Back in my college days, I would have challenged him to a duel and took an inch off one of his earlobes for an insult like that. Instead, I swallowed my pride and kept facing forward as I went out the door. I was determined not to make trouble for my uncle.

So deep in thought was Uncle Will that he seemed surprised when I stepped up to his side. He looked at me out of the corner of his eye and said, "Forgive me for not introducing you to Catherine's brother. I would not have hesitated if I thought you two had anything at all in common. Knowing you both, I doubt very much that you would get along."

"How right you are," I replied.

William gave me the raised eyebrows, but I didn't elaborate.

10

We walked about a block when we came upon a two storied brick building, as wide as three houses with driveways on both sides. Wide steps ran the length of the front of the building that led to twin doors, set into the center. The doors opened as we walked up and two cops in uniform came out. When the doors shut behind them, the word '*POLICE*', was painted across the top.

"Hullo, Mr. Gillette," one of the men called out in greeting as he took the steps down to us quickly.

"Good Afternoon, Sargent," William held out his hand. "My congratulations on your promotion."

The man stopped a step above William's, making him the same height, and took the proffered hand. "Well, I have you to thank for some of that." He turned and looked at me, "You must be Charlie Frohman's boy. I hear you made quite an entrance at the station yesterday." His eyes narrowed and his visage grew stern which is another way of putting 'Being a public nuisance!

Before I could respond, he turned his attention back to my uncle and said in a low voice. "I'm sorry to hear of your troubles this morning Mr. Gillette. Terrible to come across such a thing on your property. Let me know if I can do anything for you."

"There is something Sargent if you can spare the time in your new duties. I would appreciate it if you or anyone learns anything about the child's identity to please let me know. I will not bury that child without a name."

The Sargent was surprised by his vehement statement, but he didn't hesitate when he replied, "I'll set the boys on it right away. If there are any missing babies, we should know it in a couple of days. I'll ring your house if I learn anything sooner."

"Excellent. May I also trouble you for a list of any and all mid-wives in the area? Or any woman capable of assisting in a birthing?"

He laughed, "Almost every woman knows how to birth a child! Remember, up 'til recently, we only had one doctor. Old Doctor Blum couldn't make it to every birth!"

"Most gals go at it on their own, with the family women helping out. Some of the more timid ones, or the ones Doctor Blum said may have a difficult time, would ask Auntie Hope to tend them when their time came, but she's the only one I know of. Tell you what though, the shift changes in ten minutes. I'll ask the boys coming and going if they know any-along with what they heard about the child. Are you here to see the Chief?"

"More like 'light a match under his rear'! I fear the Chief Inspector does not place the same emphasis on finding the little girl's identity and her killer as an agent of justice as I do, as a mere citizen! That is why I'm counting on you and the men to keep an ear to the ground for me. I will have answers, despite his apathy!"

The Sargent grimaced, "Well, we'll be glad to help, Mr. Gillette. Don't be too hard on the boss. He's been in a tizzy, what with this 'River Monster' and being smothered by a bunch of government people. In fact, he's been on the phone with one folk or another from the state all afternoon, since he got back from your place."

"Really? What is going on? What agency are the government agents from?"

He shook his head and said in a near whisper. "I don't know. It's all 'mums the word'." He shrugged, "I'm sure we'll know soon enough. Whatever it is they're planning they'll need us for the doing! Anyways, I have to go round up a posse! I'll let you know what I found out as soon as I can."

William nodded, "I shall do the same for you after I've talked to the Chief Inspector. It may be that he will let something slip while I badger him."

The Sargent laughed, "Wish I could be a fly on the wall! See you in a bit, then." With that, he cut around us and went down the stairs.

As we went up the stairs towards the doors I said, "Geez, Uncle Will. I guess we can add the cops to your baker Street Irregulars!"

He laughed as he skipped up the granite steps. "Like the Sargent pointed out, Frohman, you get a lot of talk from the planners." He reached the door and grabbed the pull, and then he paused and said to me, "Information and action comes from the doers!"

He pushed the doors open and strode in like he was doing an opening act. I was surprised to see we were in a rather small foyer that was dominated by a six foot high desk. Other than the desk, the only breaks in the bare gray walls were three doors. One on either end of the facing wall and one directly behind the desk. A youngish looking man in a cop's uniform was just hanging up a telephone when William started to walk past the desk to the door on the left.

"Good Afternoon, Andy." he called out with a wave as he reached for the doorknob.

123

The cop looked somewhere between startled and offended, so I kept my head down as he barked, "What can we do for you, Mr. Gillette?"

William just opened the door and gently pushed me through ahead of him. "We are going to see the Chief Inspector."

He tried to shut the door, but the cop was persistent, "Do you have an appointment. He'll take a piece of my hide if you don't and I let you through."

William flashed him his best smile, "Let him know we are on our way-if it eases your mind. I promise to assure him of your due diligence."

Before the cop could figure out that one, William shut the door and gestured for me to follow as he entered the big room.

It was as big as any prescient I had been in, on the few occasions in my college years that got out of hand. There was a long row of filing cabinets and desks along left wall that were occupied by men in plain clothing and women typing away and bustling around the room with stacks of papers in their hands. The room was divided down the center by a low wood railing from the open spaces on the right that held a few benches and three separate hallways leading off further to the right.

William didn't hesitate as everyone looked up and gave us a glance. A few of the men called out to him and he touched his cane to the brim of his hat without breaking stride. He broke right into the nearest hallway and it was deserted until we got about four feet from a door that had 'Chief Inspector' written on a large glass pane. Suddenly, the flatfoot who was at the front desk popped up in front of us. He must have come through the other door to cut us off. I started to wonder if Uncle Will over played his hand.

"I'm going to assume you didn't hear me earlier," he said, with a mean glint in his eye, "when I explained that you need an appointment! The Chief is busy today!"

"The Chief Inspector is expecting me, Corporal." William replied simply.

The Corporal put his hands on his hips and replied in a sarcastic tone, "Every time something out of the ordinary happens around here, the Chief is expecting you!"

William stared at him for a moment then just stepped to the left and rapped the wooden part of the door twice with the head of his cane.

"Chief Inspector Rowan!", he called out in a loud voice.

There was a long moment when no one spoke, and the Corporal was starting to look smug, when a muffled, 'Come in William' came through the door.

William stepped smartly around the stunned copper and went right through the door, leaving me to face the red faced man in uniform. At least I was smart enough this time to keep my mouth shut as I quickly stepped into William's shadow.

He followed us in, and we all found the Chief, sitting at his desk and talking on a telephone.

"Yes sir!" he said loudly into the mouthpiece. "Of course, sir…. No sir…I won't let you down, sir…Thank you, sir…Good-bye, sir."

As soon as he hung up the talking end, the Corporal said quickly, "I'm sorry, sir! I explained to these gentlemen that they need to make an appointment, but…"

"That's alright, Andy," Rowan said calmly. "Go on back to the desk."

Andy nodded and with a quick dirty glance in our direction, went out the door, shutting it hard enough to let us know his feelings.

Rowan deliberately ignored us for a moment as he pretended to ponder a map that covered half his desk. Even I could see it was a map of the town and surrounding area. I could clearly see the river and the train tracks that crossed through the county. When William craned his neck to get a better look at it, Rowan quickly folded it over. He sat back and gave my uncle a cool look.

"Well, Mr. Gillette! I guess I can deduce why you're here. You even brought young Watson along. You can't possibly believe I've cracked the case already? I haven't even heard from Tom yet."

I'd have slapped him silly for his tone of voice, if he wasn't the law in these parts. I saw a muscle twitch in my Uncle's jaw, but he stayed composed. "There is no need to be flippant, Chief Inspector. I am here to assure myself that you will give this crime the gravity it deserves."

Rowan clasped his hands and lowered his head, as if he had to control himself, He looked my way and suddenly, his head snapped up. He tilted it sideways and then got up and walked around the desk to me. Chief Inspector Rowan reached out and pulled my jacket back to reveal my sidearm. I resisted the urge to slap his hand away and he quickly let my lapel go to settle back on my chest.

"Pretty fancy rig you got there, Watson. Just why are you toting that peashooter?"

"Frohman has offered his protection, which I accepted. I assure you he is proficient with a pistol." William put in for me.

126

Rowan looked stern and pointed a finger at my nose. "If that piece clears your little leather pouch, you'd better have a good reason! And if it goes off, unless it's in protection of William's life or yours, you'll find yourself looking out the bars of my holding cell! Got that, Watson?"

"Anything you say, Lestrade!" I snapped back, tired of his pompous attitude. If he was going to keep calling me Watson, he could take the mantle of the thick, bumbling Scotland Yard Inspector.

That put some flush in his pasty face. "Don't you crack wise with me! I don't care who your father was, I..."

"Gentlemen!" William barked, cutting off the Chief's tirade. "This animosity is unseemly and unnecessary! Could we please dispense with the posturing and address the matter at hand?"

I was about to wise off again, but William gave me the look and I snapped my jaw shut. Rowan was on the same track, but he let it go after giving me one last warning look. He hitched up his pants and flopped back into his chair.

"Look, William. I promise I'll read the Doctor Blum's report the second it hits my desk. Then, we'll take it from there. Good enough?"

"Hardly. I have already seen the doctor and he has little to tell us that would lead to the child's identity."

"Then, I don't know what else you expect me to do. I already had Andy double check the birth records and they show no babies unaccounted for. And before you ask again, there were no missing persons reports filed for a newborn."

"Then you shall need to approach this enigma from another angle."

He sighed and leaned back in his seat, "And I will, William. As soon as I get the time. I promise. But, right now, I have too much on my plate. First, I have to deal with this 'River Monster' hysteria. The whole town has gone mad over it and someone is going to get hurt, or worse, if I don't put an end to it real soon!"

"Bah! 'River Monster'! You talk to me about fantasies and yet you call my quest for justice a 'wild goose chase'?

"Believe it or not, William, I still have to deal with the hunters and the frightened. Besides, now, well you heard the Lieutenant Governor's call. Something important is happening and I'm going to need every man in this department to be detailed for a special assignment I've been given."

William tilted his head and asked, "What is so important it needs all your manpower?"

Rowan leaned back in his chair and put his hands behind his head. With a sly look he said, "Oh no, my friend! Not this time! This operation is hush-hush from the very top! Even I don't know the half of it and it'll be my job if word leaks out, so don't think I'm going to say anything more about it. You're not going to pry it out of me this time!"

William just stared at him for a moment, his patented smirk playing on his lips. Then he said, "Very well, Chief Inspector. Since, you deem your other duties more important, I will just have to take matters into my own hand!"

Rowan put his hands up in surrender. "If you feel so strongly about it then be my guest! Hell, I'll even deputize you and Watson if you'd like."

I had to bite my tongue as I stood, for William lifted a finger off his cane to signal me to silence.

"That won't be necessary. I only require a free hand and perhaps your influence, should I meet opposition."

128

Rowan stood as if the meeting was over. I nodded to him and headed for the door. I had to smile as I heard William say to Rowan in a soft voice, "Frohman is a good man, Kevin. But I must warn you- bait him at your own peril!"

I'm not sure how Rowan reacted to that, but William was right behind me as I opened the door and went out. William walked at a furious pace as we retraced our steps through the station. I don't know if it was due to irritation or purpose, but I had to double time it to stay on his heels. We went through the foyer without a glance in the desk's direction and out the doors down the stone stairway. I nearly slammed into my uncle's back when he came to a stop as soon as we reached the street. He turned and looked over my shoulder and his face lit up with some discovery. I turned to see what he was gawking at and saw the Sargent we spoke to on our way in, barking directions at six of his men who were just mounting horses.

After watching for a few moments, something struck me as odd. "I thought the force was mechanized, Uncle Will. Why the Wild West routine?"

He didn't answer me for a moment, and then he just beamed at me. "That is an interesting question, Collin. I suggest we head over to the Inn for tea, where we can put our thinking caps on."

I shrugged, "Sure thing." I readily agreed although my tea would have a foaming head on it.

11

The Inn apparently hadn't changed much since my father's journal description of it, so I felt like I already knew the place. Directly ahead was the front desk, with its usual ledger on the counter and rows of keys and room boxes. To our left was the bar area, with a few older men having a beer at the bar and a few tables that were empty. The room looked old and well used. My kind of place and I renewed my vow to return some night soon.

To our right was the dining area. Only one of the tables was occupied by a couple of older gals, but William waited just off the carpet. I walked up and stood next to him, pointedly looking at all the empty tables.

"They got a strict Matre'D here?" I quipped. William just gave me a sly glance out of the corner of his eye. "Worse. You put one toe on that rug before you're invited, and we'll be tossed out on our ears!"

I didn't see the sense of waiting to be seated in an empty dining room when there was an operating bar just across the way, but I was curious as to why my Uncle was deferential to an eatery in a one- horse town as this. Jeepers! The man had dined with the Queen of England.

It was a solid three minutes before the door that led to the kitchen in the back swung open and a thick-set, white haired woman came bustling out. She was carrying a small tray with a piece of paper on it, but she saw William and changed direction immediately.

"Mr. Gillette! How are you? Come in, come in. Sit anywhere you'd like. I'll be right with you." She hustled off to give the ladies their bill and William led me over to a table on the far side of the massive fireplace that dominated the inside wall. It was a decent sized table, set for two, occupying the farthest point from the entry and the windows on the street side. The sun had passed over by then and it was still too early to light the lamps, so it was dim, yet comfortably private.

"Hello, Kitty." William greeted her. "How is George these days?"

"Just like our clamming boat -- leaky but still reliable!"

We all laughed, and she looked at me, her face turning sad, "And you must be Collin Frohman. Do you mind?"

Before I could ask her how she knew my name or what I minded, she threw her arms around me and gave me a fierce hug. She stepped back and I was touched to see a tear in her eye.

"I was so sorry to hear, dearie. We all were. You father was a kind and generous man!"

"Thank you, Ma'am." I replied. "That's very kind of you to say."

She patted me on the arm. "Sit, Gents, sit! Are you hungry? Jimmy's on his break right now, but he left some venison stew on the stove."

"Just tea for me, Kitty." William replied with a smile, as we each took a seat.

"Alrighty!" She looked at me and must have seen the disappointment on my face. "How about you Mr. Frohman? I

131

never knew a strapping lad who couldn't find room for a bowl of stew." Then she winked at me, "Of course, tea won't go well with that, so how about a pint of our best draft alongside it?"

I wasn't all that hungry, but I remembered Pop raving about the food here and a beer appealed to me far more than a cup of tea, so I beamed at her.

"That would be great."

"Coming right up," she assured us as she hustled off through the kitchen door.

"A bowl of stew, Collin?" William asked with a glint in his eye, "Did I not feed you enough at the lunch we just ate two hours ago?"

I shrugged, "I'm mostly just curious. Dad said he had one of the best meals of his life here, and that's saying a lot for a man that ate like he did!"

William nodded in acquiescence, "Jimmy, the chef here, does have a deft hand in the kitchen. He's not too fancy, not like those high-brow chefs in a city's restaurant, but everything he makes is delicious!" He paused and gave me a sly look, "Though I rather think it was the beer that accompanied it that caught your fancy."

"Well," I tried to be flippant, "I never knew you for an afternoon tea kind of guy! I thought I'd try something new myself." I rolled my eyes in a theatrical way.

He laughed, "Fair enough! No, I never adopted that British custom. I wanted to come here to sit and ponder our next move. I have found the Inn conducive to that." He winked at me, "Though I wish they served the Coca-Cola here."

We sat in silence, not because I didn't want conversation, but because my uncle immediately fell into one of his pensive trances. I didn't have a clue about how to proceed. We had no way to identify the baby, no way to track whoever left her, and little chance someone would step forward and confess! Wild thoughts and implausible theories swam around my head until I gave up. Uncle Will would have to be even more clever than dad made him out to be if he was going to fulfill his oath of justice. The minutes stretched out, so I finally spoke.

"So, what is our next move, Uncle Will? All I see are dead ends."

"Nonsense! Our next step will present herself shortly."

A few seconds later, the door to the kitchen opened and Kitty came bustling in, carrying a tray. She set it on the table next to us and in a jiff had William's tea laid out and a whopping bowl of steaming stew in front of me. I had to suffer a small delay as she added a napkin, spoon, and a hunk of bread to my setting.

Only then did she place a tall stein in front of me, with condensation on the outside and a light amber liquid on the inside. I was just reaching for that goblet of heaven when William suddenly stood and pulled another chair closer to our table. He shot me a look, and I stood also.

Bowing slightly to Kitty he asked, "Would you be so kind as to join us for a few moments, Katherine? I should like to speak with you, if I may."

Kitty looked a bit nervous as she glanced between the two of us, but she quickly recovered and beamed. "Of course Mr. Gillette. I'd be delighted."

When she was settled, her demeanor grew serious. "Would this talk be about the poor babe you found on your property today?"

William sat back with a satisfied look on his face. "Well. I was certain word would get out quickly, even so, I am astounded."

"Why, dearie? You sent the crew home early. Didn't you think a few of them might have stopped for a drink?" She smirked, "On a busman's holiday? With pay?"

William chuckled. "I see your point, but I had hoped the men would be a bit more discreet than to wag their tongues at the first opportunity."

She reached over and patted him on the arm. "Don't be too hard on the lads, Dearie. It was bound to come out sooner than later."

"Any idea whose it was?"

"None. At this late stage, there is little evidence to be gleaned from the child's corpse.

"That is why I wish to talk to you. I asked the Sargent to provide me with a list of midwives in the area, in the off chance that the child was not delivered by the doctors in town. Yet, we both know that there are those who won't speak freely to the police... you though; well... everyone talks to you."

The woman actually blushed a little. "Pshaw, Mr. Gillette. It's the whiskey and wine that does all the talking- I just listen! But give me a minute...let me put my thinking cap on."

William dutifully kept his mouth shut and sipped his tea and I, mostly ignored so far, dug a little deeper into my stew. I was never a fan of game meat, however this was the best bowl of stew I ever saw on a spoon of mine! The meat was plentiful and tender, suspended at all depths by rich, mild gravy, and it had a large variety of root vegetables that were each cooked carefully to preserve the individuality. I tasted turnip, sweet potato, butternut squash, and other root vegetables, along with the usual celery, carrots, and onions. I started toying with the idea of offering the chef a job!

I must have groaned with ecstasy, because the woman gave me a sharp look and lightly slapped me on the arm. Sticking a

134

meaty finger in my face, she warned, "I know that look, exactly like your father's! So, I'll tell you the same thing I told him when he was last here -- If someone hires Jimmy away from me and I have to cook, the first stew I make will be out of your family jewels!"

That hit my funny bone with a ten-pound hammer, and I had to pull my napkin up to my lips, lest I spew food across the table. William roared with laughter. Looking smug, Kitty made a show of hard thinking, while we settled down. Finally, she answered.

"I only know of two women in these parts you could name a Mid-wife. Martha that retired Pinkerton's wife or old Mother Celeste. They belong to my church, so I see them quite often. But, neither of them ever talked about caring for anyone this winter.

Course, it could have been an Indian baby. Those squaws all bear their own at home."

"No," William shook his head, "The doctor was adamant the child was Caucasian." Kitty looked a little confused and he added, "White. The parents were white."

"Oh!" Kitty twittered. "I thought you meant another kind of Indian! Mohegan, Caucasian. Sounded like another tribe."

I put my spoon down for a minute. "It may be that it's both. I mean, what if a girl got in trouble…or a woman got pregnant from another man than her husband. Might she have gone to the Indian woman for help and discretion?"

Kitty snorted and gave me a look. "Not likely, dearie! Those Mohegans may be poor and down-trodden, but they are far from stupid!"

Now, besides hatting to be talked down to, the fact is that I have a sister who bore a child out of wedlock, so I knew of the pressures involved. I was about to snap back at her when William spoke first.

"I'm sad to say, Frohman, that Kitty is right. Even in this 'age of enlightenment' we live in, there are those who would cause the local tribe no measure of trouble if they thought the Indians had anything to do with a white woman."

Kitty sat back and slapped her hands on her thighs. "I guess that's about all I can tell you, Mr. Gillette. Your welcome to talk to the women I mentioned- but I think they'll tell you the same. I'll keep an ear to the wall for you, but I don't think you'll find your answers easily."

William nodded his head slowly then tilted it to one side. "What about Susan Wallace, Dr. Blum's old nurse. She has the medical training and has completely disassociated herself from the doctor. Do you think she might be of some help?"

Kitty looked uncomfortable, and then shook her head. "I doubt it, Dearie. From what I gather, she's 'disassociated' herself from everything and everyone. I hate to speak ill of anyone, but I think that woman's gone a bit around the bend."

William's eyebrows drew together, "How so?"

Kitty leaned forward in anticipation of revealing some significant gossip. "She hasn't been seen in public since she left the doctor! She's holed up in her parent's old house and cut her ties to everyone. Hasn't been to church service since last fall, hasn't come to town, and the only ones that laid eyes on her were a few folks sailing past her house. One saw her hanging some laundry and another saw her walking back from the outhouse. Other than that-she's been a hermit."

. I shrugged. "That doesn't make her mad," I suggested. "Some people enjoy their solitude." That last part was a mild dig at my Uncle.

She just gave me a flat stare. "I've known the girl most of her life. I tell you she was off, and it got worse, I think, after her brother left town. This winter, after a bad storm, her closest neighbor and his son trucked over a mile in deep snow to check on her and she wouldn't even invite them in to warm up a moment! Told them she was fine and to leave her be. Them boys were damn near frozen before they made it back home. No sane person acts that way!"

I looked to William, who shrugged slightly. "She was always a bit...high strung."

Kitty glanced over her shoulder and stood suddenly. "I'm sorry I couldn't be of more help, Mr. Gillette. I'll send word if I hear of anything.

"If you'll excuse me, I think I need to heat up some more stew."

She turned and headed towards the foyer, where the Chief Inspector was standing. He was obviously not pleased to see us or perhaps that we had seen him, and William ignored the look and then raised his hand as if he was in a crowded Bistro. "Hullo, Chief Inspector. Join us-please!"

Rowan looked left then right, but he was trapped. Either he joined us or insulted us. Hat in hand, he shuffled over to our table after talking to Kitty for a second. William stood as he approached and pulled out the chair that Kitty had just vacated, offering it to the Chief Inspector. Rowan sighed and took the seat. He nodded to me and asked, "How's the stew?"

"Best I ever had," I replied.

"Always is," he said with a smile. Then he looked to William, "I was surprised to see you here, William. I saw your motorbikes over at Doc's and I figured you went back to grill him some more."

137

William smiled. "I'm not sure there is too much more the good doctor can expound on, Chief Inspector. We must approach this enigma from another angle. 'Early days' as the English say."

Before Rowan could reply, Kitty burst back into the room and brought an identical serving of mine to the table, minus the ale. Rowan tucked a napkin into his shirt and began to plow into it. William watched him with a hint of amusement on his face as he polished off the bowl with gusto. Suddenly, Rowan swallowed then put his spoon down and looked up at my Uncle.

"See here, William," he spoke with exasperation, "I came here for something to eat, not to be dragged into another discussion about…your problem."

William looked shocked, with a tint of righteous anger. "My dear Inspector!" He snapped, "I did not broach the subject! As I just said, it is too early to make any conclusions. I need more data to proceed. Then-and only then- will I 'drag you into another discussion'!"

Rowan looked abashed, as he picked his spoon back up. "Sorry, William. I suppose I'm just a little on edge. Let's talk about something else, shall we?"

"Of course," William gave him a regal nod. "Let us see…oh, yes. I introduced Miss Scott to Collin on the ferry today. She and a group of young ladies were returning from a trip to Boston."

Rowan snorted. "Right! I heard they were going up to Boston to march for prohibition." He shook his head. "Women these days! Always looking for another way to make our life harder!"

'Only if you let them!', I thought to myself. But Rowan was married, and William was practically a monk-so what would they know about women. I kept quiet as I finished my bowl.

William laughed, "Perhaps, yet she did mention an interesting fact, when she was not mooning over young Frohman here."

Rowan raised his eyebrows at me with a smirk, "Best watch yourself, Frohman. That girl is looking to move upwards in life."

"Not on this ladder," I replied as I sopped up the remnants with my last piece of bread. "What 'fact' were you talking about?" I asked my Uncle.

Rowan had gone back to eating, as William replied. "That the *Delaware* had streamed into Boston harbor. One does not see the flagship of the Atlantic Fleet so close up very often."

"Oh, yeah! She said she was there for a refitting."

Rowan shook his head absently, and without looking up, mumbled, "Resupply."

"What was that, Chief?" William asked, feigning misunderstanding.

Rowan swallowed and cleared his mouth, "Resupply- not a refit. She'll be back on her way in a few days."

"Far sooner than that, according to the lovely Miss Scott. Several officials disembarked with a strong box and she was on her way back to the front!"

Rowan shrugged and purposely went back to his meal, and William gave me a satisfied smirk, and then winked. In a bored tone, he mused, "I wonder...just what is in that box they are shipping by rail to Washington?"

Not even catching on, Rowan said, "Haven't the foggiest and I don't want to know! I..."

He stopped in mid-sentence and dropped his spoon to clatter off the bowl and onto the tablecloth. Hands curled into fists, he pounded the table hard enough to make the bowl jump and glared at my uncle.

"Why must you do that?" His face alternated from furious to awe. "Why must you put me in this position?" He was about to explode, but he caught himself and took a deep breath. Heaving a great sigh, he asked, "How in the world did you figure this one out?"

William shrugged, but I could tell he was delighted with himself. "It is really very rudimentary, Chief Inspector. While in your office earlier, you said you had an important assignment that covered your entire jurisdiction. I couldn't help but notice the map on your desk or the clear outlines of the railroad tracks. There was a Leigh and New England Railroad company seal on the map, so it was an easy conclusion that you were concentrating on the routes. This implies an important shipment that needed extra security. As we were leaving, I observed the Sargent supervising a squad of men who were going horseback. Horses can go where motorcars are not accessible and the only area of any importance in this county that cannot be reached by automobile-and run the length of your territory, is the train tracks. Thus, someone must fear robbery or sabotage along the way."

Rowan looked more annoyed than impressed, but I was thrilled to see my uncle's talent at work.

"Now," he continued. "Does it not seem odd that the Navy would take such an important ship off the front lines-in these critical times, and sail her across the ocean-just to restock their beans or whatever? It makes more sense to believe she was dispatched to deliver something of grave importance to

140

America. The *Delaware* may not be the largest in the fleet, but she is the swiftest for a long journey. I thought I saw a hole in my Uncle's reasoning. "Then why wouldn't they just sail to Washington and skip the rail trip?"

"For the reasons your uncle just mentioned." Rowan explained, "That would add three days to their journey each way. The Navy can't have her separated from her group any longer than absolutely necessary."

"So, what do you think it is, Chief?" William asked. "Perhaps war plans or a treaty?"

Rowan threw his hands in the air. "William, I don't know, and you don't know, and we don't WANT to know! The orders for secrecy came from as high up as you can go! If I didn't trust you so, I'd be holding you in a cell until the train went past." He gave me a steely look, "I'll trust your behavior to William."

I was about to tell him what I thought of that, but William gave a slight shake of his head so, I just nodded.

"In any case, Chief." William went on. "As I see it, your only real point of concern is the bridge. A train would be most vulnerable there."

"Not really," Rowan replied in a condescending tone. "No room to mount an attack and even if someone sabotaged the trestle-it would only cause the train to drop in the river, losing them their prize. Besides, there is still that railroad barge working on the rock footings. I went out and talked to them myself. They are a motley bunch, but they are armed and keeping a watch out for suspicious activities." He looked well pleased with himself.

"I told them there was a gang of river pirates in the area. That'll keep them on their toes!"

I thought it was kind of funny, but William seemed less than impressed. "From what little activity I have seen from that operation, I have no doubt they could find the time to guard the river for you!"

"Just what are they supposed to be doing," I asked.

"They're here to inspect and repair if needed, the footings around the train bridge's trestles in the river. The barge has several cranes and if they find an area that may have been weakened or washed away, they shift the rocks or add fill. They have been here two weeks already, William said, "How much longer are they contracted for?"

Rowan shrugged, "I dunno. Have Catty ask Marquis. He's been quite chummy with them, I hear. Takes supplies out to them almost every day."

William shook his head quickly. "It is of no importance." He then drank the last of his tea and reached for his hat and goggles. He stood and offered a hand to Rowan.

"Well, Chief Inspector. Thank you for joining us. We shall leave you to finish your lunch in peace." Rowan shook his hand and William said to me, "Come along Frohman. I wish to give you the nickel tour of the county before it grows dark."

I got up and nodded to the copper. The book was still out on him, so I said nothing.

Rowan shook William's hand and pointed a finger at him with a squint. "You be careful if you take the bridge home, William. I keep telling you it's not safe!"

William just nodded in acknowledgement, and as we started to go, Rowan put a hand on William's arm and gave us both a hard look, "And remember to keep your observations to yourself. Loose lips sink ships!"

I'm not sure if he even realized what an offensive remark that was to us. William stiffened, but managed a smile as he nodded and turned to go.

I rolled my eyes and followed him.

12

The houses thinned out as we headed up the river. The road was dirt but fairly level and wide enough for us to ride side by side. The train bridge spanned the river to our right and it loomed larger as we approached it. Soon we came to a steep rise where the road crossed over the railroad tracks.

To my surprise, and despite the No Trespassing signs, William slowed then turned on to the trestle! I stopped to watch him as he bounced along the center of the bridge between the two tracks. There was, of course, no solid ground beneath him, just the beams that were spaced apart. The tires on William's Chief were big enough to traverse the railroad ties, and his tires dipped between each one. He was rattling along like a cocktail shaker.

I had a better idea and I lined my tires up on the outer rail, and then gunned the throttle. Between my speed and balance, my tires rode smoothly along the metal rail.

I had an unobstructed view of the river, as there was no fencing on this trestle. I could see William's castle clearly in the distance and the town across the river from it. The ferry was plying its course across the river in its slow and steady fashion. The Connecticut River itself looked like a streak of blue paint, splitting the lush green forests on either side. It was a spectacular view-not as good as the one from Uncle Will's, but grand nonetheless.

In moments, I passed William bouncing along. I wanted to tip my hat to him, but I had to keep both hands on the bars, lest the bike slip off I would tumbl into the water, far below. I had to settle for a nod.

I reached the other side way ahead of him and stopped my bike at a road that crossed the tracks on that side. William pulled up next to me. I thought he would be amused, but he looked a bit stern. He shut off his motor and put his kickstand down and I followed suit.

Pulling off his googles, he growled, "Though I commend you for you riding skills Collin, that was a foolish thing to attempt! If your bike had slipped off or hit an oil patch-you would have gone for a swim!"

I laughed. "Not on your nelly, Uncle. Besides, you know I swim like a fish."

"You would not have survived the fall! The river here is notoriously shallow. Except for the very center of the channel, it is no more than twelve feet or so."

He pointed a long finger at me and said earnestly, "You are a man of responsibilities now. Your family and your company are counting on you. It is far past the time for you to disengage from these unnecessary stunts!"

I should have just nodded, but then again, I never could do the easy thing. "You tell me to be armed in case a thug with a grudge comes after us, but you're worried I might fall off my bike?"

His eyes flashed, but he simply said in a sarcastic tone. "Is this the benefits from seven years of college? A higher form of sass?"

I threw up my hands in surrender and tried to look contrite. "You're right. I'll be more careful."

145

He merely grunted in response then stared down at the river. His face grew long and his ears began to jut out. In the space of less than a minute, he looked gaunter with more prominent cheek bones. I was marveling at the change in his appearance when he reached into his saddle bag and pulled out a spyglass. He put it to his eye and after a moment, simply hummed and handed me the eye piece.

"Tell me what you see, Frohman."

Curious, I put the glass to my eye and focused. After a moment, I began my narrative.

"I see your run of the mill railroad river barge. I'd say she was twenty by forty, with a low bow and double stacked structure on the stern. Most likely it's the crew quarters with the wheelhouse on top. There are rows of windows on all sides and a walkway with a door on one side. In front of the box is a large metal crane, in the upright position, that I'd guess to be thirty-five feet. On port bow is another, smaller, crane of about fifteen feet in length.

There are barrels and timber on the deck, all stacked neatly perfectly wound coils of rope on all four corners." I lowered the glass and a thought occurred to me. The deck and structure were pristine. 'Ship shape and Bristol fashion', as they say. I put the piece to my eye again and looked but I could not see one thing out of place, nor any signs of rust or stain. I had never seen a ship, outside the *Aunt Polly*, that was so well maintained. The captain must be a hard case." I observed to my Uncle. "He runs a tight ship!"

William looked down at me and replied, "Or an idle one. You missed the anomaly, Frohman. Look again and this time, concentrate!"

I sighed and did as he asked. Nothing had changed in the last thirty seconds, except that when I focused on the wheelhouse, I could see the shadows of all three men moving about. I said as much to my Uncle. He sighed theatrically and took the glass from me to stow it away. He shook his head and looked at me as if I had the sense of a mule.

"I did not ask you for a census, Frohman! I asked you to find what was missing."

I took a bit of umbrage at that. "How would I know what was missing? I'm no expert on railroad barges!"

"Irrelevant! You have spent a good portion of your life around boats. The missing piece is obvious!"

I just stared at him, not wanting to give him the opportunity to belittle whatever I said next.

He gave me that sly grin and said, "A boat. There is not so much as a dingy tied up to the barge. All three men are aboard and there is no way for them to get to shore, or do you think they spent twenty-four hours a day, seven days a week on board? There certainly does not look as if a great deal of work is being done, for such vigilance!"

That did strike me as odd. Any watercraft that was moored usually had some type of transport to get back and forth to shore. Still, he was talking down to me again, so I played the devil's advocate.

"Yeah, well, doesn't Marquis bring them supplies regularly? Perhaps he brings them to town from time to time. And I doubt that they're just sitting around day after day. You know the railroad — they don't pay for idleness!"

That sparked some reaction in him. He looked pensive for a minute then broke out in a big smile. "Frohman — you are a diamond in the rough!" He pulled on his helmet and googles and got back on his machine. "That is enough sightseeing for one day! I need to make use of that marvelous telephone!"

I was relieved when he let it drop and we were on our bikes returning to the castle. The day's events and my Uncle's inquisition had put me through the wringer. I figured a nice stiff drink to soak up all the stew in my stomach was in order for the afternoon.

We rode a short way along the road, and then William turned onto a well-worn path that wound through the woods and took a sharp turn upwards. Suddenly, we at the entrance to the road that led to the castle.

I found myself, not forty minutes later, lounging on William's over-sized sofa with a Presbyterian in my hand. Uncle Will had dumped me here as he dashed about between the telephone and his study. He made several calls and though I could not hear distinct words, William's tone was somewhere between disgusted and cajoling.

For myself, I was quite content to sip my drink and contemplate the morning. I was in the perfect spot for it. I'm not sure what Uncle was thinking when he installed this particular piece of furniture. It wasn't a sofa by any standards I knew. It extended out from the windowsill by a good six feet and the walls on either side wrapped around it. It was more like a king- sized bed with curved edges. Not five feet from the bar! I felt like a small prince when I sat upon it. I kicked off my shoes and propped my back up against the wall opposite the bar and stretched my legs out on the soft surface. A small comfy cushion at the small of my back and I was comfortable for the afternoon, providing I could get a refill from time to time. For that, I fell short on my first two attempts. Ozaki walked past and I raised my empty glass to him and grinned. He glared at me for a moment then swore in Japanese and stomped off. I was equally unsuccessful when Mrs. Woods came into the pantry. She gave me such a look that I dared not even try to finagle another cocktail out of her! I was resigned to breaking my comfortable repose to fend for myself, when Catty suddenly rounded the corner from the conservatory with a cleaning bucket in her hand. I flashed my best smile and she came over to stand at the edge of the sofa.

"My, don't we look content?" She cooed. "Are you as comfortable as you look?"

"Not really," I replied wistfully. "I was getting lonely, waiting for a hooch fairy to flitter by."

She gave me a stern look, but there was a twinkle in her eye when she said, "Hooch fairy! What a lovely term! What girl wouldn't be proud to wear that name? Hooch fairy!"

I set my near empty glass on the cloth carefully and put both my hands up in a placating manner. "That's just a short version. I meant to say, an ethereal beauty whose comeliness is only surpassed by her grace, intelligence, and compassion for the thirsty."

She grinned and nodded as she plucked the glass off the seat. "That'll get you a snort!" She sniffed the glass as she stepped over to the bar, sniffed my empty glass again and asked over her shoulder, "Scotch and Ginger ale?"

"Please," I answered. "Your nose is as accurate as it is cute."

She quickly fixed the drink and walked it over to me. As she was handing it off, she asked, "Are you planning on sitting there all day, swilling Presbyterians?"

I couldn't be certain by her expression if she was disgusted or amused, so I chose a light-hearted response. "Why not? I have a comfy roost, a cold drink, and a panoramic view of some of God's best work! I may just stay here until dinner."

She raised her eyebrows and crossed her arms over her ample bosom. "Oh really? Well, you'll have to find yourself another 'Hooch Fairy'! This one's got work to do!"

I didn't want to put her off, so I said seriously, "Actually, I'm just waiting for my uncle to get off the phone. Then we'll see. He's pretty bent out of shape over this…morning."

"I know." she replied, semi-sarcastically, "Us 'Hooch Fairies' keep our ear to the ground." Before I could come back, she went on, "Listen, I'll be done in a half hour or so. If you'd like, I could show you a part of the castle you haven't seen yet." She gave me a steely eye, "Unless, of course, you'd rather lay here swilling booze for the rest of the day?"

I wasn't really sure how to reply, because I wasn't sure of her intentions nor how I wanted to respond due to our positions. I was a guest and she was the help and any chumminess --no matter how platonic -- was frowned upon in our society. Yet, Catty was more like a ward to my uncle and I found her company more than pleasing. A thousand thoughts whirled in my head while I just stared at her like a jackass. Thankfully, I was saved when my Uncle's booming voice filled the small room,

"What are you two scheming?"

Catty and I both jumped. She snatched up her cleaning bucket and I leaned forward to see my Uncle come out of the hallway with a big grin on his face.

Catty caught her breath and wheeled to face him, "There's more sneaking than scheming going on! "She caught herself and went on in a calm voice, "I was simply offering Mr. Frohman a full tour of your home- if he wished to crawl out of his glass anytime soon." She looked over her shoulder and winked at me. I could love her for that alone.

William's eyebrows shot up and he made an O with his mouth. "Why Catherine! That is a capital idea! I'm sure he'd much rather see it with you than his old curmudgeon uncle." He grinned slyly and checked his pocket watch. "I fact, I'll tell

Ozaki to serve dinner at 8:30. That will give you plenty of time for the good part."

"Very good, Sir," She replied politely, yet almost mockingly. She turned back to me, "I just get dinner in a low oven and you can come and find me when you're ready." She flashed me that magnificent smile and went off.

"What are we having?" I called out.

"Chicken and dumplings." was the faint reply.

"Excellent!" William said as he sat on the edge of the sofa, crossing his legs and rubbing his hands together. "If you like Mrs. Wood's biscuits-wait until you taste her dumplings!"

William went silent after that, with a thoughtful look on his face. I was about to ask him what was on his mind, but Ozaki appeared out of the conservatory and asked William if he could get him anything in a respectful, servant-like tone. It was just his way of rubbing it in my face.

William just heled two fingers, one above the other, about six inches apart. Ozaki nodded and stepped over to the ice box and withdrew one of those Coca-Cola's. He levered the top off and brought it over to his employer, giving it to him with a small bow.

I stuck my tongue out at him. Ozaki gave me a smirk and moved off, but I noticed he went no farther than the pantry. Well within earshot.

William looked as if he had something to say but was reluctant to speak. He took out his case and offered me a smoke. I accepted and he lit us both up.

"So, what's the buzz, Unc?" I asked just to break the ice. "You were on the telephone for quite a while."

"Yes, and I'm sorry to abandon you so long. Though, I dare say, you seemed to have made yourself quite comfortable."

I laughed. "I'm like one of your cats, Uncle Will. I can find a way to lounge anywhere, anytime. Though, I'll admit the view from here makes it a whole lot easier."

Speak of the devil, I had no sooner spoken when an orange cat jumped onto William's lap and another black and white came out of thin air to land on the sofa, to prowl about. I had a feeling more would show up, so I held my glass high.

"Yes, and I'm sorry that I won't have the time to share it with you. There was so much I wanted to show and do with you." He paused and drank a good third of his soda pop down, as if it were courage, "I'm afraid this matter with the child will have to be the focus of my attention until it is resolved…I had hoped to discover something by now, but all of my inquiries have met with dead ends. " He looked more crestfallen than when we found the child.

"Hey, Uncle Will, don't worry about it. I understand. Then I added to show my solidarity, "It's like Pop always said- 'nothing costs a penny and nothing takes a minute!' It could be a while before this gets sorted out."

He brightened up a little. "I'm glad you understand, Collin. It does help to assuage my guilt a little.

Now, there is no service for the rest of the day and tonight, but we can get you on the first train tomorrow. I wish we could have had more time…"

The rest of his spiel was lost on me as outrage filled my chest. Here I was, pledging my allegiance and he was talking about shipping me home. I set my drink down and pulled myself as upright as I could. Then I let him have it with both barrels, talking right over his monologue.

"I don't give a fat rat's ass when the next train is, because I won't be on it! I am not going anywhere!

"I told you last night that I would stick by you-even before we found the child! And remember-I was there when we discovered the child! I have just as much right to see justice done for that poor infant as you do!

"I may not be my father, but I am a grown man more than capable of being some assistance to you! We're in this together!"

Out of the corner of my eye, I could see Ozaki scowling at me from across the room. With a shake of his head, he stomped off, leaving me to wonder what his anger was about. I thought to get more of an argument from him, but Uncle Will look stunned by my firmness. After a long pause, he sighed and took another plug on his soda. When he took the bottle from his lips he was smiling.

"Excellent! Like I said before-I always think better when there is a Frohman about!"

"Good, that's settled then." I said, with a smile of my own. "So, what's our next move?"

He took the cat in his lap off and dropped her to the floor. "For the present, I will rest before dinner and you shall take the final leg of your tour with Miss Catherine."

"That's it?"

He shrugged. "We have gone as far as we can with the information we have, Frohman. I telephoned my contact with the Pinkertons, then I placed a call to my brother George, the senator, and he gave me the name and number for the commissioner of the state police. One Michael O'Hare. I rang him up and explained the situation and he offered to have his men in the area ask about. Perhaps they will provide a lead."

"*State* Police?" I asked. "I've never heard of a State Police."

"They are newly formed. No more than a year or two old. Their purpose is to keep the peace in the rural areas of the state, like Chester, that aren't populated enough to support their own force. It is also in their charter to provide support for any and all precincts when needed."

"Oh," I nodded. "Like the Texas Rangers- only without the Comanches."

William barked a laugh. "Quite so. We are fortunate that our Indians are more civilized."

"So, what did the Pinkies have to say?"

He looked troubled as he mumbled. "Nothing new to report, I'm afraid. Though they beat around the bush, they offer no real evidence of his whereabouts! I fear they have lost complete track of Roy since Washington."

Our earlier conversation made sense then. "I see, so you're afraid he may show up! That's why you brought up sending me on my way—again! Well, I hope he does. With the chief's men on high alert and us on our toes—he won't stand a chance of sneaking up on us. And if he does…" I said nothing more but patted the revolver under my jacket.

Uncle Will grew deadly serious and glared at me. "Do not let your confidence in that weapon give you a sense of false security. Roy is a dangerous man. Part of me still rebels in allowing you to be involved with a dispute that is Ozaki's and mine alone."

"Maybe." I conceded. "but who's going to watch out for Mrs. Woods…or Catty?"

He looked a bit poleaxed for a moment. I'm not sure my Uncle could fathom the depth of some men's evil. I'm not sure that someone hurting the girls had ever crossed his mind.

"I'm staying." I said firmly.

He patted me on the knee and stood. "I shall see you at dinner." He turned and walked away, calling over his shoulder, "Eight-thirty sharp!"

13

I finished my drink then swung off the sofa and put my boots back on. I could hear Catty banging around in the kitchen, so I headed through the pantry to find her. When I rounded the corner, I found her bent over in front of the stove, carefully centering a cast iron Dutch oven on the rack. The thing looked like it weighed a ton.

"Need some help with that?" I asked.

"Not likely." she replied as she removed her hands and shut the oven door. Straightening up, she grinned and added. "I've got three brothers who can't fry an egg. I don't trust men in a kitchen."

"Hey," I protested, placing my spayed fingertips on my chest, "I'll have you know I was the frat house chef in my college years! The boys would swoon for my Viand Porcine Cassoulet!" Which was just the French way of saying pig and whistle berries.

She shook her head and laughed, "I'm not surprised a bunch of college boys would go for pork and beans."

This girl was always surprising me. Plucking off her apron, she beamed. "Are you ready to see the rest of the castle?"

"Absolutely! I'm refreshed and rehydrated."

She paused for a moment and looked me in the eyes. "You haven't had too much to drink, have you? You need some balance for this."

Now I was intrigued. I smiled. "No, I'm fine." She still looked skeptical, so I added, "I shared the drink you poured me with a cat."

She laughed. "That-I can believe. We can't leave anything on the counter around here without needing a broom to keep the devils at bay! Alright then, up the stairs we go."

She led me across the kitchen, and we went up the back staircase. We went right past the second level with the bedrooms and up to the third floor, where the art gallery was. Off the landing there was a short walkway that ended at the wall. Two other hallways jutted out at right angles. One that led to the gallery and one that led past a few doors, then on to another stairway that went down to the second floor. Nowhere I hadn't already been.

Catty just stood behind me but didn't offer an explanation. Apparently, she had picked up some bad habits from my uncle. Still, I was more than curious by then, so I asked. "Where do those two doors lead?" I asked, pointing down the hall.

"The one on the right is a closet and the left is a guest bedroom. That's where I sleep when I stay over."

I'll admit now, that I felt a storm of butterflies in my stomach. Surely, that wasn't the place she wanted to show me! I turned to see what kind of expression she had on her face, when she suddenly curtsied and put her hand to the wall next to her. As she slid her arm back, a section of the paneling slid with it to reveal a shallow closet that was filled with crooked shelves.

I couldn't for the life of me, see what they were designed for and was doubly shocked when Catty got a grip on them and pulled them out of the wall. Attached at the floor, they turned out to be a set of stairs that neatly fell forward to rest against the opposite wall. My eyes followed the stairs up to a wooden hatch, set into the ceiling!

157

Catty was delighted at the dumbstruck look on my face. I stared at it for a moment, suddenly realizing how the uppermost balcony was accessed. "Wow! That's the cat's a-...meow."

"That's nothing," She said, waggling her eyebrows. "The best part is still ahead. Come on!"

She quickly scampered up the stairs and easily pushed the trap door up. I waited a moment for decency's sake and followed her. It was dim where the hatch went through the floor to reveal another room, but sunlight was streaming in towards the front and Catty was moving in that direction. I realized that this was the room at the very top of the castle with the highest set balcony.

I rose from my knees and looked around. It was really more like a cave than a room, as the front was completely open with railings that curved out into the air with a slight arch encircling a small balcony. The floor, walls, and ceiling were bare castle stone. No bigger than fifteen by fifteen, I let my imagination run wild and envisioned it as a cell. I laughed when I looked at Catty and thought of the fair maiden locked in the tower.

For herself, she was grunting as she pulled a large, wide, and segmented board from along one wall and tried to muscle it out into the center of the balcony. "A gentleman would give me a hand rather than laugh at me," she snipped.

Not wanting to explain myself, lest I sound like a sap-head, I leapt forward and grabbed the top of the board to help support it. I was caught off guard by how heavy it was, until I realized that it wasn't a single- it was a number of boards attached together in a strange pattern. Before I could ask her what it was, she lifted her knee and pushed the board at a certain point so I could not see from behind.

I nearly let go as the board. Catty pushed down on the top railing and the entire structure collapsed, and then snapped into place. Just like that, I was resting my hand on the back of a bench seat! I just shook my head and smiled.

Folding her skirt under her legs, Catty sat down and patted the bench next to her. I came around and took a seat with a respectful distance between us. "This is amazing," I said, leaning back against the seat. "I always knew my Uncle was a clever man- I've seen countless set designs and special effects he designed, but I never realized he was so handy with his hands."

Catty nodded. "I guess I'm just used to it. It seems that he comes up with something more exiting each week. If you could have seen this place when it wasn't more than stone and bare beams, you would be overwhelmed by the transformation."

"I can believe that. Even my father's descriptions didn't do it justice." I got up and walked over to the balcony. Up this high, there was a stiff breeze and I put both hands on the railing to steady myself. Views from here were spectacular. I knew logically that Long Island sound was too far south to see, but I swear my eyes could almost make out its big blue expanse. To my left was beautiful rolling hills and down below, I could easily make out Ozaki's house and the ferry landing. For that matter, I could see the ferry landing on the other side and the full vision of the town that stretched out and away from it. In fact, I could see well past the buildings and into the countryside behind it. To the right of that was more land and the railroad bridge that spanned the river. The big barge dotted the water below it and there were a few other crafts plying the river as dusk approached.

Looking further right, I could see the trail being made in the woods, for Uncle Will's miniature train tracks, up to the spot where our mystery began. I was awed by the vista. A pair of eagles glided over the river in front of us and I swear I was looking down on them.

I turned to Catty, "This must be the highest spot along the coast! Would you mind pointing out some landmarks for me? I know I've been around on the ground, but it all looks so different from up here."

Catty got up and joined me at the railing. She pointed out various spots along both sides of the river and gave me a general overview of the town. Shoulder to shoulder, I enjoyed her voice and her enthusiasm.

"Where do you live?" I asked.

She pointed to a place past the town. "It's hard to see from here. Open that chest over there and take out the smaller bag."

I hadn't noticed the wooden chest that sat against the wall, my attention being on the bench. On closer inspection, I was impressed that it was cedar lined and tightly fitted against the elements. There were a variety of objects laid out neatly inside, each wrapped in its own cloth bag. There was a long tube shaped article on the bottom and a smaller bag next to it. I took the small one as Catty instructed and set it on the seat of the bench to open it. I was delighted to find a set of fairly large Binoculars.

"Outstanding!" I said to Catty as I brought them over to her. "I suppose the other thing is a telescope."

She nodded and put the glasses to her face. "Last month, Mr. Gillette brought us all up here one night to watch a meteor shower. It was amazing!"

After a moment, she found what she was looking for. She put her elbow on the railing to keep the glasses steady and motioned for me to look through them. I slipped in next to her, enjoying the closeness, and after a few prompts I located her family's home; a typical New England salt box, but it sat on a large wooded plot. Having always lived on the move, it looked like a nice place to grow up.

After a minute, she left the glasses with me and returned to the bench. I was fascinated by the powerful focus of the glasses, so I spent a few more minutes looking around.

I was drawn to movement on the water and saw a small sloop pull away from the barge and headed for the town. Though I had never seen it, there was something familiar…

"Hey Catty, is that your brother's boat?" I asked.

She got up again and leaned against my back and looked over my shoulder so she could track my line of sight. "I think so. Here, let me have those." She reached around, and I relinquished them to her. "Yep! That's him. Looks like he's got a couple of those barge rats with him. Mangy curs!" She handed the glasses back shaking her head in obvious disgust.

"You don't seem too impressed with the Railroad engineers," I commented dryly.

She snorted. "Some engineers! They've been here nearly a month and they haven't so much as moved a rock! Everybody in town is laughing about it. Lazy bums if you ask me! I don't know why my brother caters to them so much. Always taking them supplies and ferrying them back and forth to town. He's at their beck and call all hours of the day and night. Which is strange because all they must do is lounge around."

While she went on her soft rant, I refocused on Marquis's boat. My blood boiled when I saw Marquis clearly, but I kept it to myself for Catty's sake. There were two other men with him on deck. A tall, older man, who appeared to be giving orders, gesturing at both Marquis who was at the wheel, and the other man who was gripping a line that went over the side. As the boat chugged slowly along, the second man would raise a knotted line and the older man would write something in a book."

161

I took the glasses from my eyes and turned my head to face her. "Well, I hate to tell you this, Catty, but they are not lounging now. They're plumbing the depth of the river. Makes sense in their line of work."

"Well…there's a first time for everything, I suppose!" She walked back over and sat on the bench. I thought she was even more interesting when she was miffed, so I joined her on the seat.

"Besides," I pointed out. "I'm sure they have a fat contract with the railroad company. Probably get paid by the day, so I'm sure they're taking their time and most likely they're paying Marquis a pretty penny under expenses. Don't worry about those railroad kings -- they can afford it."

She gave me an arched eyebrow. "Would you accept that from your employees?"

"No," I conceded. "My theater syndicate doesn't import Chinese or exploit negros for our hard labor. My Father taught me that if you paid a man a pittance, they rarely met expectations but if you paid a good wage to a good man, they always exceeded them."

She laughed, "Well, Mr. Gillette pays us fairly well, I guess. Still, he's got more money than anyone I know, and he spends every cent like it he was giving blood!"

I had five times Uncle Will's assets, but I was too embarrassed to tell her that. She must have seen something on my face, because she laughed again and patted me on the thigh.

"Never mind", she said absently as she looked out over the horizon. "It's almost time." She turned to me and gave me that beautiful smile, "You're about to see something that money can't buy."

I tore my eyes off her face and looked out over railing. What I saw was akin to a religious revelation! The sky began to dim

162

as the sun was sinking over the trees in the distance. Slowly edging downwards, we could actually follow the motion. Yellow rays of the sun began to turn into reds, purples, oranges, and every shade in between illuminated the clouds and landscape as if it were a giant painting being brushed into life before our very eyes. Neither Catty nor I looked away or even spoke for the next ten minutes until the sun had dropped below the horizon. When I looked over at her, she had her hands pressed together in front of her and her head bowed. After she opened her eyes and looked up, she saw me staring at her.

With a sheepish smile, she explained. "My grandma always said that if you sent a prayer with the sunset, it goes straight to God as he takes back the light."

"Beautiful place to pray Catty."

She shrugged, "I think she made it up, but I've been doing it since I was a little girl."

"What were you praying for?"

She looked at me for a moment then laughed and poked me in the arm, "Everything you take for granted, I'll wager." She stood and smoothed out her dress.

"Gees Louise, Catty!" I protested. "That's not fair! I know-"

She cut me off by bending over and placing a finger softly against my lips. "We can discuss that another time if you wish," She said teasingly, "But the sun is down, and I have to get supper out of the oven before the chicken is mush and the dumplings are lumps of coal!"

"We don't want that!" I said as I got to my feet.

"Here, help me with the bench," Catty said.

"Could we just leave it?" I asked. "I'd like to come back up here tomorrow, I mean, if you want to."

She gave me a long look, but smiled and said coquettishly, "We'll see."

She did fold up the bench and we stored it against the wall. This one would keep her cards close to her chest.

Dinner was better than I could have hoped for. Never in my life had I enjoyed such a simple meal. The stew was perfect and Mrs. Woods's dumpling rivaled, perhaps even surpassed, her biscuits. It was so good, I settled for cider to wash it down. To my delight, Catty ate with us and Ozaki too which made the meal all the more relaxing, with idle chatter and great food. I was starting to feel like this was a second family to me.

"So, Collin," William asked. "How did you like the rest of the tour?"

"It was great, Uncle Will, I responded." That is a neat spot! And the sunset! I don't think I have the words to describe it."

"Try anyways," he said with a twinkle in his eye.

After a moment, I gave Catty a sly wink and said, "Uncle Will, it was so beautiful, I think I saw God himself as he pulled back the light of day."

"Excellent." Then he laughed, "Though it does sound a bit familiar. Don't you think so, Catherine?"

"Extremely," she replied, staring right at me.

"OK, OK, you got me! Paraphrasing aside, it was the most beautiful sun set I have ever seen."

William beamed. "I'm so glad you enjoyed it. I had a feeling it might be spectacular tonight. After a year here, I get a feel for the atmospheric conditions."

164

"Well, we saw something even more unusual that that," Catty piped up.

William looked to me, but I just shrugged as I didn't realize what she was referring to.

"What would that be, Catherine?" William asked.

"Those barge rats were actually doing some work."

"Oh, Yea!" I remembered. "Catty recognized two of the men from the barge on Marquis' boat. They were plumbing the area around the barge."

Though I think catty had just made a half-hearted remark, William seemed to take it seriously. He spoke to Catty.

"Are you sure they were men from the barge? I myself have never seen them."

"Pretty sure. I saw them through the binoculars. I met them once when Marquis had brought them to town. You know he supplies them with just about everything."

He switched his gaze to me. "You are certain they were plumbing?"

I gave my uncle a look. "I know what plumbing is. One man was dropping a weighted, knotted line over the side and marking the waterline and the other was recording it. What's so strange about that, Uncle? I would think it to be a prerequisite for that kind of work."

William put his fork down and sat back in his seat. He slowly steepled his fingers in front of his chest then lowered his head until his lower lip rested on them. Just like that, the Sherlock Holmes detective was back.

"Do you not think it strange that after a month on station, they are just now preforming a task that should have been foremost on their itinerary? Given the fact that they could just

165

as easy go to the harbor masters office and request an updated chart of the river's depth for mere pennies. Why pay Marquis far more for his services."

I didn't reply because I thought he was being a bit screwy over nothing. No one spoke for a long minute and William picked up his fork and took another bite. We all went back to our bowls for a few minutes in silence when I saw Ozaki catch William's eye. Facing his employer, he flicked his eyes in my direction then rolled his eyes towards Catty. Having been together for longer than a lot of married couples, William knew exactly what the little man meant.

"Oh, yes." William said, and then turned to me. "Collin, I wonder if I might ask a favor of you? Usually, when Catherine works into the evening and is going home, either Ozaki or I will accompany her- at least as far as the ferry. Tonight, however, there are some matters I would like to attend to after dinner and I need Ozaki's assistance. Would you mind terribly, if I asked you to see her home safely?"

A plan popped into my head and I replied, "Of course. I'd be happy to." I turned my head towards Catty, "If you don't mind riding on the back of my motorcycle."

She looked a little hesitant. "Are you sure it's safe to ride one of those things at night?"

"No different than the day," I winked. "I always ride with my eyes closed anyways."

14

Everyone pitched in on clean-up and soon Catty was seated behind me as I kick started the bike and we headed down the steep path to the ferry landing. Catty was an old hand at riding shotgun on a motorcycle from her many trips home on the back of Uncle Wills' and knew how to stay balanced. I let her wear my leather jacket and she had a shawl to drape over her legs, so decorum was kept.

Our ferry ride was pleasant. The river was moving slowly and there was no wind to put a chop on the water. A half-moon gave everything a soft glow and the stars were on parade on this warm spring night.

Being the last ferry trip at eleven o'clock at night, there were few other passengers and one model T, besides us and my Harley. The ferry's engines were flat out as they made a beeline for the town dock.

Of course, a few the walk-ons were staring out over the river and studying everything they saw out in the distance. I stayed seated on my bike, but Catty got off to stretch her legs. She stayed close by and we looked at the stars and talked about getting the telescope out tomorrow night. Everything was Jim dandy until I noticed a man at the railing was giving us a hard look. He was about my age and wore working man's clothes. I watched his out of the corner of my eye for a moment and I could feel the loathing emanating off him towards us. I met his eyes with mine and he sneered.

My first thought was to casually pull back my vest to show him the grip of my Colt .45, in its docker rig, but I didn't want Catty to think I was a thug. Instead, I looked at Catty and jerked my chin in his direction.

"Who is that guy at the railing? Do you know him, cuz, he's looking at me like I just slapped his Mama!"

Catty turned to look, and the coward turned away quickly to look out over the water. Catty turned back to me and sighed. "Yes, I know him. Matt Rainer. I went to school with him. He's friends with my brothers."

"Is he an old boyfriend or something?"

"Hell NO! EEWW!" She said with grimace. Then she saddened and murmured. "Don't get all riled up, he was probably glaring at me. I...I had a bad year last year."

She tried to smile as she said it as if it were a joke, but I could see the deep hurt in her eyes, and I was moved. I reached over and took her hand in mine.

"So did I, Catty. So did I."

The ferry was already about to dock, so the moment passed, and we got ourselves situated to ride off. As we got to the road, Catty put her lips behind my ear and said loudly over the engine noise, "It's the third street on the right. Stop at the corner."

I heard her loud and clear, but I had other plans. As soon as we reached the town, I turned onto Main Street and gunned it a little. Catty cuffed me lightly in the side and shouted, "Where are you going? I said, The third left!"

I slowed the bike to a crawl and turned my head. "I know, but I thought I'd treat you to a drink at the Inn."

She cuffed me again, a little harder this time. "Stop!"

I brought the bike to a stop and half twisted in my seat to face her. "Christ! You're not a prohibitionist are you?"

She frowned. "Hardly. But if you think that I am going into a bar with you- or any other man- at nearly midnight-you are out of your mind! By morning, half the town's tongues would be wagging, and I've had enough of that kind of talk to last me a lifetime."

'And it probably will as long as you stay in this town', I thought to myself. Still, I wasn't really thinking of the ramifications. I simply found myself enjoying her company and I wanted to stretch our time out a bit longer. The drink was an enticement also.

I realized I owed her an apology. "I'm truly sorry, Catty. I wasn't thinking." I shrugged, "I...just like talking to you, I guess."

She smiled shyly at me. "I know. I'd like that too. But it's late." She gave my shoulder a gentle nudge to turn me then she put her arms around me and whispered in my ear, "Now, take me home. Let's get out of here, before someone sees us canoodling out here!"

I laughed and dropped the bike into gear. Holding the right front brake in and gunning the engine, the back of the bike swung around quickly, making Catty hug me tighter. I took off and soon turned the corner. A minute later I was on the corner of her street and I remembered her original instructions. I stopped the bike and she hopped off. Her house was still not in sight.

"Are you sure you don't want me to take you the rest of the way?"

She shook her head. "Thank you, but no. I'm sure someone has already heard the motorcycle and they'll think it was Mr. Gillette that dropped me off like he always does. If they see a strong, handsome man escorting me home-I'll hear no end of it!"

I could see that. "Fair enough. See you tomorrow?"

"Most likely. Thank you for the ride," She hesitated for a moment then began to walk away. Over her shoulder, she added, "and the thought."

I turned the bike around and headed back to the ferry, smiling. She thought I was strong and handsome!

My good mood suddenly died when I got to the ferry slip and all I saw was the dim lights of it across the river. I realized that I had missed my trip back and I was out of luck until the morning. Cursing myself, I headed back towards town. I was going to have to ride the long way home, the way I went with Wiliam earlier, and I wasn't happy about having a forty-minute ride ahead of me. Nor, truth be known, that I would have to cross the railroad bridge in the dark. I hoped I had enough petrol.

As I turned onto Main Street, I figured I could use a bracer for the road, so I pulled up next to the Inn and went in for a drink.

From the foyer, I could hear the low murmur of at least a few people in the bar. I shed my riding gear, though I kept my jacket on, and went to the left towards the sounds. The room was brightly lit despite the late hour. A long bar, with brass foot- and arm-railings, took up the right side, complete with a barkeep polishing a glass in front of a mirrored back, lined with three shelves of bottles. There was a smattering of tables, scattered about, eight or nine, but only two were occupied. One had a few men, more or less my age, that all looked oddly similar. It was the other table that drew my attention. Catty's brother, the smart aleck, Marquis sat at the other with two older, scruffy men and my old pal from the ferry, Matt. Everyone immediately quieted down and stared at me as I threaded my way to the bar. I could feel their eyes on me, but that wasn't unusual for small town patrons. Strangers always drew attention. I made as if I didn't notice as I set my gear on an empty table next to the bar and took up a position near the middle. I was alone except for an older couple that sat at the far end, obviously well into their cups. I decided to buy them a drink after I got one. It was always smart to get in good with the local bar flies.

The barkeep ambled over and grunted a greeting at me. "What'll you have?"

"Evening," I replied as I looked over the selection. The bar was set up like any other, with the gut rot on the lowest shelf, the mid-range on the second, and the best hooch on the top shelf. I spied a bottle of Bombay Gin, that looked quite dusty.

"Bombay. Neat."

With a look of surprise, the keep looked up at the bottle and back to me, "That's six bits a drink."

I fished a gold eagle out of my vest and tossed it in front of him. "Double."

"Yes sir, "He piped up and fetched down the blue bottle. He dusted off the cap and poured me a three-quarter full glass. Setting it down with a flourish, he picked up the coin. "I'll be right back with your change. I'll have to get it from the office."

"Don't bother," I told him. "Hang on to it. I may stay awhile."

He drifted down to his other customers to converse with them in a whisper. I just looked straight ahead and watched everyone in the mirror. They all were doing their best not to seem like they were looking at me, but I could feel their eyes on me. Three men behind me to the left were just curious, but the other table was going to be trouble.

171

My pal, Matt, was talking low to Marquis who in turn stared at my back with daggers in his eyes. I don't know what manure he was shoveling at Marquis, but I knew it was about me and Catty. Whatever it was, the older two fueled the fire when one made some sort of joke and they both laughed out loud. That's what set Marquis off.

Inwardly, I heaved a sigh and briefly thought about leaving when Marquis rose to his feet. I could tell from his jerky, slightly clumsy, movements that he had put away some drink before I arrived. As he ambled over to the bar, about three feet from me, I knew I should have left right then and there before there was trouble. I wasn't afraid for my safety, but of bad feelings from Catty or embarrassment to my uncle. If only he hadn't made those remarks at the doctor's office.

Gripping the brass with his right arm, he turned to face my direction. I didn't even move my head, but I kept my eyes on him in the mirror-after making sure no one else was getting up.

"Well, well. If it isn't Dandy Boy himself." he said loudly.

I didn't expect that angle, but I didn't react except to put a bored look on my face.

"Marquis!" The oldest man from the other table cried out. "Don't start with him!"

"No, No," Marquis returned. Pointing at me, he said, "I went up to the castle today to make a delivery and I saw this," He paused to look at me, and continued in a contempt filled tone, "*Man*, lying about on a big sofa in his stocking feet, swilling booze like he had nothing better to do." He turned back to face me, with a sneer on his face. "Of course, I guess he can now that he's got daddy's money!"

He turned back to his friends, "Guess he's lucky his old man couldn't swim too good!" My glass was just touching my lips and I froze, a little of the gin sloshing onto my lower lip. Time

172

seemed to stand still. In the mirror, I saw the three guys at the table recoil in shock. The older one who gave Marquis a warning looked furious. Matt, knowing that Marquis had crossed the line past bad talk, guzzled his beer down and slipped away. The other two looked faintly amused but had the good luck not to laugh out loud.

I didn't dare move, because I thought I might just kill the fool if I did. Unbelievably, he started in again. Glaring at me, he took a step forward, pointing a finger, "You think you can ride into town on your fancy two-wheeler, throw your money around, and MESS WITH MY SISTER!" He slapped the bar for emphasis.

I had heard enough. Over the years, Ozaki has taught me how to channel my anger. When I'm truly vexed, I don't shout or swear, I just focus my energy into preparing for an action to resolve the situation. When I'm calm, that's when I'm dangerous. Still, for Catty's sake, I needed to give him one more chance, though I prayed he wouldn't. I set my glass down, pushing it forward to keep it out of harm's way, and then I turned to face the jerk.

"You are an insect," I explained in a low steady voice. "This is the second time today I have had to endure your pesky buzzing. Now, go sit with your friends and keep still like a good bug or you might just get swatted."

Marquis's sneer turned into a snarl, "I'll give you 'swatted'!" Then he stepped towards me and put all his weight into a great looping punch, aimed at my jaw. It was child's play.

Hardly seeming to move, I pulled my head back as my right hand connected with his left bicep and I easily pushed the strike past me. The momentum carried him over the bar and as he was already bent over, I took the back of his head and bounced it off the bar top. Not hard enough to put him out, but it should have knocked some sense into him.

His eyes crossed and he began to slide down the bar, but he managed to grab the railing in both hands and pulled himself up right. He shook his head to clear it and I was convinced I was going to have to strike him after all. Even though I was ready, I was nearly caught off guard when he suddenly grabbed his beer bottle and smashed it on the railing, before thrusting the broken shards directly at my eyes!

I barely leaned back and got my hands up in time. My right hand grabbed his wrist and my left found a grip behind his elbow. With a hard squeeze on several pressure points and a slight twist, the bottle neck dropped harmlessly onto the floor. Marquis would have no use of his arm for a while. I released him and he took a half step away from me before he turned to face me. His right arm hanging useless, nonetheless, he balled up his left fist.

I really wanted to break his neck, but instead my right hand flew out and over to connect with the side of his face in a resounding open-handed slap that sounded like someone cracked a bullwhip. The blow spun him halfway around until he was facing the tables again, and I lifted my leg and stomped on the back of his knees, causing him to drop like a stone. I didn't let him fall forward, though. I brought my left hand up and caught him under the chin. I put a finger and thumb on his carotid arteries and squeezed. With his right arm still useless, all he could do was squirm and slap at my hand with his left. I could feel the strength draining from him as the blood flow was cut off to his brain. I didn't intend to kill him, but I wanted him to think he was dying, just to teach him a lesson. I didn't want to go through this every time I talked to his sister!

I leaned over to put a warning in his ear, but before I could open my mouth, the three men at the table jumped up.

Their glasses went flying, but one of them managed to grab the table before it went over. They started to move, so I let go of Marquis, who grabbed a chair next to him to stay somewhat upright and pulled my colt.

Time stood still for the second time that night. The three men froze. The younger ones looked like they were going to wet their pants. The older one was wary, but I saw no fear in his eyes, nor any threat. Out of the corner of my eye, I could see the older man who was sitting with Marquis, toss some coin on the table and jerk his head at the other man. Without a glance in our direction, they slipped out to the foyer and the front door could be heard opening in the stillness. I turned my attention back to the three I had covered.

"I have taken all the guff I'm going to for one night." I jerked the barrel of the gun towards the door. "You finished your drinks. Now go home." I figured I'd have to pay the barkeep off for some lost business, but I was still hoping I could have a drink in peace before I went home.

The younger two were nodding like a feeding chicken, but the oldest took a deep breath and held up his hands where I could see them.

"Look Mister, we don't want any trouble. Now I know Marquis was way out of line and you don't know how grateful I am that you didn't plug him! He deserves a bigger whupping than you gave him, for sure, but please don't hurt him. You see…well… the thing is- he's our brother!"

I didn't see that coming! First, I thrashed one of them, and then I pulled a gun on the others! Catty -- or Uncle Will -- wasn't going to appreciate this! Speechless, I quickly stuffed the .45 back into its holster and stepped away from Marquis.

The man wasted no time in sending his siblings to collect their brother. "Put him on his boat and make sure he stays there!" He instructed. "Then go home. I'll see you there-and don't say a word to Ma or Da!" I was impressed how they obeyed him without question. They each took one of Marquis'

175

arms and pulled him to his feet while keeping a wary eye on me. One even mumbled, "Thanks, Mister", as they half walked, half dragged him out to the door.

The man watched until the door shut then he turned back to me, hands up by his chest. "Thank you again. Mind if I ask you a question?"

I wasn't sure where this was heading, but the barkeep was quietly cleaning up the mess Marquis made on the bar, so I figured I wasn't getting tossed out right away.

"Sure."

He lowered his hands, "You said this was the second time Marquis was at you. Where did you see him before?"

"I was at Doc Blum's office with my uncle and he came into the office to make a delivery. Your brother has a smart mouth."

He shook his head and grimaced. "Me and Da both have pummeled him for it, but he just can't keep a civil tongue in his mouth." Then he looked me square in the eye and said, "And, believe me, as soon as he sobers up, I'm going to slap him around for that remark he made about your father! I met your Dad…he was a good man."

He seemed to run out of steam a little. After a moment's hesitation, he added, "I'm Tom, by the way. The other two with me were my other brothers, Luke and Cody.'"

"Damn! How many are you?"

He smiled a bit. "Just the four of us and our sister, but you know Catty."

I held up my hands in a 'whoa' manner. "Look, I just gave her a ride home because my uncle asked me to."

He laughed. "I didn't mean it like that. In fact, I'm grateful you brought her home. I know now she was in good hands."

176

Now, I could have responded to that in a number of ways, but I really just wanted to get back to my gin at that point. "Join me for a drink? I think I still have some change on my tab."

He looked at me thoughtfully for a minute and nodded. "I'd be happy to."

I picked up my glass as he walked up. Pouring the rest down my throat, I signaled the Barkeep. He threw down his rag and gave me a steely look as he walked over.

"Could I get a drink for me and Tom here?"

He planted both hands on the bar and dead panned, "Are you planning on pulling that pistol again?"

I made a show of looking around the empty bar and cracked, "There's no one left to shoot!"

I could see he was a breath away from tossing me out. "Absolutely not!" I assured him. "Tell you what... why don't we call my first tab closed," I fished another twenty- dollar piece out of my vest and tossed it in front of him. "And I'll start another."

His eyes lit up and he agreed. Twenty dollars was probably more than he made in tips for the week with his usual crowd. He reached up and grabbed the bottle. When he was finished pouring for me, he looked to Tom. "The usual, Tom?"

"Nah. I'll have what he's having."

And so, our night began. I figured he'd had a few beers before I came in, so I didn't expect him to match me drink for drink-but he did. After an awkward start, our conversation came naturally. We had enough in common to get connected, but there were enough differences to keep it interesting.

We told each other a bit about our families and our lives, and then the conversation drifted into my uncle and the castle. He

177

had me laughing over the rumors when he first started saying that William was a warlock or a devil worshiper. Not only did I dispel those notions, I went on to tell him a great many of my uncle's talents and abilities. I knew Uncle Will would hate me talking about him so, but I have always been proud to know him and wanted everyone to know how great a man he really was.

By the time we hit the quarter mark on the bottle, the barkeep, Fast Eddie –that's who Tom introduced him as -- had joined us. I wondered if he was charging me for his drinks, but I was mellow enough not to really care.

I asked Tom about the two men who were with his brother.

To grimaced. "Barge rats! Least that's what most folk call them. Showed up about a month ago on that big work barge. I figured they were here to shore up the rock around the trestle, but they haven't done much of anything-that I can see!

Older one's the boss…forget his name, the other was just one of the crew." He snorted. "They sure scooted when you pulled your 45 on us!"

The conversation quickly turned to the 'River Monster' saga, and they both had a lot of wild stories they had heard. We kicked a few theories back and forth but soon lost interest and went on to solve the rest of the world's problems. We were a third of the way into the second bottle, when our talked turned to the baby we had found. Eddie had heard a little about it, but Tom was totally ignorant of the affair. I'm afraid I let my tongue run away – like I always did when I had an audience -- and I told them everything I knew about it. Neither one had anything coherent to add to the situation, so we toasted the child and left it at that.

Last I remember the conversation turned to Catty. Fast Eddie mentioned her, and I just had to pipe up.

"Catty is a fine woman," I announced. Tom arched an eyebrow at me, so I quickly amended that, "she's a great person."

Tom chuckled and replied, "I'm glad you think so. You seem like the decent sort, Collin, and Catty is a grown woman, but she's been through a lot this year."

Eddie pointed an unsteady finger at me and said loudly, "So keep your hands in your pockets when you're around her!"

"What?" I replied, indignant.

"Well, you wouldn't be the first rich man to have the maid turn down the bed --while you were in it!"

Both Tom and I gave him a hard look. Eddie threw up his hands in surrender. Tom turned back to me and, in a drunken, dramatic manner said, "All I wanted to say was, even though Catty acts all tough…she's going to be a bit fragile for a while." He turned back to his drink, embarrassed by what he said.

I clapped him on the shoulder. "I know," I assured him. "When a person's fiancé turns out to be a thief and a murderer, that will leave a mark!"

Tom was shocked. "You know about that! She told you?"

Even in my drunken stupor, I realized that I had said too much. I flapped my arm like a wounded duck and slurred, "Nah! Just a lucky guess."

15

One minute I was draining my glass and the next I heard a familiar voice say, "What a mess!", and the next I was lying in bed, staring at Catty's cleavage.

She gave a short scream, and I leapt off the opposite side to stand there- not really knowing where I was for a moment. My sudden motion set off a chain reaction in my body. My head felt like it cracked open and my stomach wanted to turn itself inside out. I was chilled from head to toe. Yet, it wasn't until Catty put a hand over her eyes and turned her back to me that I fully realized my situation.

I was standing in my bedroom at Uncle Will's. Naked as a jaybird! I hopped quickly back in bed and pulled the blankets up to my neck. My embarrassment gave heat to my words.

"What are you doing? Are you in the habit of ambushing people in bed?"

Her back stiffened and she started to turn back towards me. She lowered her hand to peek and when she saw me covered, she spoke. "I should say not! I didn't even know you were in here. I always make the beds this time of day. Most folk are up and dressed long before 11 o'clock! I saw a lump of bedding and I pulled it back to straighten it and there you were! Then you started jumping around like one of Mr. Gillette's frogs!"

Since the last thing I remembered, before I woke, was having a drink on the other side of the river, I reasoned that I couldn't be mad she woke me, even if every sound she made was like a kick in the temple to me. I was as hung over as I have ever been, and I couldn't piece together my night before after a certain point. The memories were like bubbles in a pool of water that were slowly rising but hadn't burst on the surface yet. Eleven o'clock! Good thing I was on vacation.

"You're right. I'm sorry…and I'm sorry I… exposed myself. I was startled. I…I didn't really know where I was at first." The effort of talking made me groan.

Catty stepped over to me with a look of concern on her face. She put a hand to my forehead gently and asked, "Are you sick, Collin? Is that why you're still in bed?"

I smiled weakly, "Oh, I'm sick all right, but I know what ails me. Last thing I remember was having a drink at the inn with…" I stopped short as that part of the evening snapped into clarity.

"With who?" Catty asked.

I looked up and squinted when the sunlight pierced my eyeballs. "Shut those curtains and I'll tell you a sad story. Maybe you'd better sit down."

I thought she would pull over a chair, but she just waved me over to the other side of the bed and sat down next to me. I was a little uncomfortable, but the door was wide open and what I had to tell her seemed to overshadow any decorum.

I started slowly but gathered steam and I told her everything that occurred after the time I dropped her off until when she woke me up. Of course, I tried to show my actions in a better light, but I didn't have to exaggerate Marquis' meanness. Her eyes crossed when I told her what he said about my father. Of course, I left out any discussions about her, but I was honest about the rest. She seemed to take it mostly in stride, so I finished up with, "I'm truly sorry if this causes you any grief. If

I knew they were all your brothers, I would have just walked away when Marquis started on me. I have a sister too."

She hadn't said anything up to that point and I was worried about what was going to come out of her mouth. She took a deep breath and said, "So let me get this straight --you beat up one of my brothers, pull a gun on the others, and then end up drinking yourself into oblivion with the oldest."

"More or less," I replied sheepishly.

She started laughing. "Well, you know just how to get along with my family!" That wasn't the reaction I thought I'd get, but I loved her for it.

She patted me on the leg. "You don't need to apologize, Collin. I know what my brothers are like. "As for Marquis, he's one to talk! He's either dallied with or tried to seduce every girl in the county! He doesn't care about my virtue; he just likes to make trouble. And I'm sorry for what he said about your dad. That smart mouth of his is going to get him an early grave." She shook her head angrily, "When I see him next...I'll give him a piece of my mind he'll never forget!"

We were quiet momentarily, and then something came to me. "Well, maybe you shouldn't be too hard on him. It's that Matt that I'll have words with if he crosses my path again!"

"Matt Rainer? What's he got to do with it?"

I sat up straighter in bed. "You remember how he was hawking us on the ferry? Well, when I walked into the bar, he was sitting with Marquis and his friends and his jaw was flapping hard! I'll bet he was filling your brother's head with all kinds of garbage about us! He's the one who got him riled up, I know it! And those two barge rats didn't help either, I'll wager."

"That trash!" She sneered. "Marquis told me once that they were going to be his ticket to the big time. I don't see how, as

182

they never seem to do a lick of work. Ever since he chummed up with those men, he's been even more arrogant than ever! As for that Matt, I'll slap his face when I see him next!"

We were quiet again for a moment, until I said, "I hope my Uncle won't be upset with me. I think I may have embarrassed him."

"You needn't worry about that, Collin." His voice came from just outside my door. Then, he stepped in with a grin across his face. Boy, he liked to make an entrance.

"If Catherine is satisfied with your actions, who am I to take offence?"

Both Catty and I froze at his appearance. "I pulled the blanket up to my neck and stammered, "Uncle Will! How long have you been standing out there?"

He smirked. "Shortly after Catherine arrived. In fact, I was trying to head her off, as she didn't know about your late, very adventurous night!"

Before I could reply, Ozaki stormed in behind William. He stopped and planted his hands on his hips. "Catherine! Why are you in Master Corrin's bed? Now is not the time for this! Get about your work!" Catty jumped up and glared back at the little man.

"I was not IN his bed, I was ON it!"

"What the difference?"

She picked up the basket she brought in and stepped up to stare down at Ozaki.

"The difference IS, if I was IN his bed, the door would have been locked!" With that, she stormed out of the room. The three of us looked at each other with stunned silence, and then we burst out laughing.

William turned to Ozaki, "Remind me to remove the lock from that door."

"Aw, Geez Louise, Uncle Will," I protested. "It isn't like that. You heard what happened."

"More than I wished for, you scamp! Must you make a scene everywhere you go! I dare say I'll be hearing from Rowan before long!"

Now, I loved and respected the man, but I was not about to be lectured like a schoolboy. "Listen, I'm sorry it happened but none of it was my fault. I just wanted a little nightcap before I rode home. Besides, it all turned out OK. Marquis will live to mouth off to someone else and Tom and I became pretty good friends. All in all, things evened out for the better!"

William grunted. "In so far as you remember! Tell me-do you have any recollections about your movements after you left the bar?"

I tried to concentrate but with my pounding head I was drawing a blank.

"Like I told Catty, one minute I was drinking with Tom and Fast Eddie, the next I was lying buck naked in this bed."

Ozaki and William looked at each other and laughed. William shook his head in mock despair. "Well, I am grateful that you weren't hurt, and that you didn't maim Marquis and you made a drinking buddy of Tom. Yet, your adventures weren't over just yet."

I had a sinking feeling to add to my other miseries. "Oh, No," I whimpered, "I didn't do anything stupid, did I?"

Ozaki and William looked at each other and grinned. "More foorish than stupid." Ozaki judged.

184

I could see that Uncle Will was trying to hold back a laugh while maintaining a stern face. "Apparently, our milkman found you, just before daybreak, out in front of the Inn. You were on your motorcycle, with the engine ignited, but the kickstand was still down."

It seemed incredible that I had no memory of it, but I asked, "So, I rode my bike back here?"

This time, he couldn't hold it back any longer and he barked a laugh. "Oh, No. The motor was running, but you were slumped over the handlebars, dead to the world. He tried to rouse you, but you didn't stir, so he panicked and fetched the police officers on duty. They came and, after determining you weren't dead. they loaded you into their car."

"So, they brought me home?"

"Yes, it was very kind of them." Then his face went serious. "Of course, that was AFTER they called the Chief Inspector and woke him from a sound sleep. Inspector Rowan directed the officers to bring you here rather than jail. Ozaki got up and dragged you to your room."

I clutched my head to keep it from exploding with the next pulse beat. "I'm sorry, Uncle, Ozaki, for being such a pain. I must have drunk a lot more than I thought."

Thankfully, before I had to grovel anymore, Catty called up from the great room.

"Mr. Gillette! Telephone! It's Chief Inspector Rowan!"

"William pulled out his watch and looked at it with a sigh and a smug look. It was before noon. He gave me a look and left to get the phone.

Ozaki just stood there, grinning at me, like I was a vaudeville act.

"Thank you for putting me to bed, Ozaki." Then I cracked, "I don't mind you undressing me-but do you think you could have put some pajamas on me?"

The smile slid off his face. "What am I-your mother?"

Before I could retort, William strode back into the room. "Get dressed, Collin. The Chief Inspector wants me to meet him at the Police dock as soon as possible."

Sounded interesting but I wasn't sure I could make it to the toilet, much less back to town. "You go on, Uncle. I'll catch up with you later when I'm alive again."

He shook his head. "Sorry, but he specifically directed me to bring you along!"

Groaning, I swung my legs off the edge of the bed and waited a moment until the room stopped spinning. "Bet he said, 'bring Watson with you!'" I growled.

He chuckled. "Good guess! Now, hurry along. The Inspector has piqued my interest!" He bolted back out of the room. Ozaki shook his head and laughed, then followed him out.

I guess my interest was roused also because my curiosity overcame my revulsion of moving as I completed my waking rituals and dressed quickly. I was down in the kitchen, where Uncle Will was already dressing for the road. He gestured to a plate on the counter that had a muffin on it and a bottle of Coca-Cola next to it.

"Drink that down and eat the muffin if you think you can keep it down. I don't want you throwing up on me or my motorcycle! Regardless whether you eat, drink the Coca-Cola."

I drank about half the bottle at once, as I was desperately thirsty. In a moment I felt well enough to try the muffin, so I broke it in half and wolfed it down. I followed that with the second half of the bottle, and I was ready to go. A thought occurred to me.

"Why are we riding? Why don't we just take the Helena over?"

He gave me that look that made me feel like a moron. "Then how, pray tell, will we retrieve your motorcycle?

I slapped my forehead. "That's right! Holly Moly! Where is it?"

"At the station, I imagine. We'll fetch it before we go to the docks. Besides, I am beginning to see a thread that we may wish to follow. Who knows Frohman, perhaps it will lead us through this mystery!"

I didn't have a clue as what he was talking about as I was more concerned with staying on the back of his bike and not puking on the way.

Uncle Will and I were both experienced riders, so the trip down to the ferry landing was short and sweet. About halfway across the river on the ferry, I was feeling much better. That Coca-Cola was wonderment for hang-overs! As the name suggest, there is a small dose of cocaine with every bottle and probably why Uncle Will is so fond of it.

Again, the crowds were lined along the railing, peering outwards and pointing. They seemed a bit more animated this morning and I commented that to my Uncle.

He was disgusted. "Bah, Frohman! Most likely another sighting- or at least someone heard of one from their cousin who talked to a friend of whoever made the sighting! Blithering Sapheads!"

I let the subject drop and kept one eye on the water when Wiliam was looking elsewhere. I didn't see anything but a small chop and the channel markers.

We were first off the ferry with me clutching the seat below my rear rather than putting my arms around my uncle. I managed to stay on though it was a challenge on the cobblestone leading up to the Police station. We pulled up and I hopped off the Chief, as Wiliam killed the engine. My bike was nowhere in sight, but I could still hear a motorcycle engine, when the Chief went quiet. I looked behind me and there was my motorcycle, with some man in a uniform tooling along towards us!

To think someone had the gall to take my new Harley for a spin without my permission infuriated me. Copper or not, I was going to call him on it!

He pulled up to us, with a big grin on his face. He shut the engine off and set the stand before he dismounted.

"Afternoon, Mr. Gillette." All I got was a nod. He gestured towards the bike. Magnificent machine! Hope we can get something like it for patrolling someday!"

Afternoon, Jack" William replied. He saw the look on my face and quickly put in, "Of course, you already met Collin." He turned to me. "Jack is one of the men who brought you home this morning."

Embarrassment quickly drowned my rage and I stuck out my hand, "Thank you. I...I don't remember what happened.

He laughed. "I can tell you that you tried to go drink for drink with Tom Alexander! Bad idea. No harm done, except to the Chief Inspector's sleep. I got an earful for that!" Then he simply dismissed me and turned back to my Uncle. "The Sargent wanted me to let you know that there has been no luck with our inquires. No unaccounted-for babies or pregnancies anywhere in the county. Must have been outsiders."

William didn't look like he agreed, but he just replied, "Thank the Sargent, and the rest of the men for your efforts. Even so, I would ask that you all keep an ear to the ground."

"Always do, sir." he answered, then turned to go back in.

I felt like I should say more. "I'm sorry I was such a bother, Officer."

He looked back over his shoulder. "You weren't a bother, Lad. In fact, you were quite funny and had us laughing all the way to the castle!"

"What'd I say?" I asked, but he just started up the steps, chuckling to himself until he disappeared back inside.

When I looked to my Uncle in misgiving, he shrugged and said with a straight face, "You come from a long line of droll fellows, Frohman. Now! Start your engine and let us mount up! The Chief Inspector awaits!"

16

We traveled down Main Street a few blocks, and then cut
down an alleyway that led to a road parallel to the river. Not a
minute later, we were pulling into an open area that led to some
docks. The area was swarming with men in uniforms. Most of
the activity was around a damaged boat they had up on cradles
lying on its port side. Uncle Will and I had barely dismounted
and took off our gear, when Rowan came strolling up.

"Hullo William! Have I got something to show you! But first,
I need to settle with young Mr. Frohman here."

I managed not to heave a great sigh, as he hitched up his
pants and stomped the few steps over to me. Trying to look
stern, he pointed a finger in my face and snarled, "I don't
appreciate having my house woken in the middle of the night.
If you can't hold your liquor, STAY HOME! Next time it
happens, you'll wake up in the drunk tank and face a judge in
the morning! Understand?"

He was really rubbing me the wrong way, but I caught a look
at my uncle's face out of the corner of my eye and just ate the
crow. "Understood, Chief Inspector. I'm truly sorry I disturbed
your family. I was in a sorry state for sure. It won't happen
again."

He gave me the eye and a hard probably thinking I would
wise off, but I just stood quietly, looking as contrite as I could.

After a moment he turned back to my uncle. "Well William,
let's see if we can make a believer out of you!" He waved us

onward and we followed him over to where all the activity was. Stopping, he asked my uncle. "Would you care to examine the boat first or talk with the eye witness?"

William thought about that for a moment. "The boat, I think. Let us see if the evidence bears out his narrative."

"Excellent choice!" Rowan replied with a grin. You'd think he was the wine steward or something. "Come right over here."

Rowan led us over to the craft that was up on the cradle. At first glance, I opened my mouth to say something, but William held up a finger to forestall me. So, I dogged him silently as we made a slow circuit around the boat.

There was nothing special about the design of the boat. It was a plain utility craft with a shallow draft and three foot gunnels. Square on the stern and pointed at the bow, it was completely unadorned. The only features that separated it from a big rowboat was a covered box at the stern that probably house the diesel engine and a center console with a small wheel and a simply control panel. There wasn't even a chair for the pilot. There appeared to be another storage unit in front of the pilot box. Just another twenty-one foot boat you might find on a river or coast line; something you might use for light fishing or clamming. The only thing that set this boat apart is that it looked like it had been in a bar fight!

After making a full circle, William first bent down to study the severe damage to the bow. Starting at the waterline, there were two long, deep gashes on each side of the hull that led to large holes where the planking had been pulled out. Even the keel was cracked in half, a foot-long piece jutting out like a figurehead only below the waterline!

"I guess we can rule out hitting a rock." I observed. "That hull was stove out not in."

191

"Obviously." He took a closer look then straightened and headed towards the middle of the boat. Whatever was in front of the pilot box looked like a tornado hit it. The battered top and one side hung at an angle, a huge padlock still hanging on a hasp with twisted ends. It was still in a locked position. Another side was completely missing.

We continued our survey. The pilot box was relatively intact as was the cover to the engine. The rest of the real damage was on the stern.

The port stern gunnel was gouged, and even had a few wood chunks missing. Oddest part was that the prop shaft was bent. So much so, that the blade of the prop had dug into the wood of the stern. I bent low to examine the length of the hull, but no scrapes that would have indicated they drove over a rock. This was a screwy as it gets. I turned to my Uncle to express that, but he cut me off quick. "Please refrain from further remarks until we have all the data. It serves no purpose and, quite frankly, it is distracting." He was in full character now.

He turned to the Chief Inspector. "Could we talk to your eyewitness if you please? Rowan led us over to an overturned skiff on which a man was perched, slumped over and clutching a wad of bandages to his crown and sopping wet. He was a big man, rotund but solid. You might have thought him a bruiser until you saw his bright eyes and kindly features behind a long flowing beard that nearly reached his stomach. He sat up and winced as we approached.

"Can I go and find a telephone, now, Chief? I need to find a way home."

"Soon Francais", Rowan replied, taking a seat next to him on the boat. "First I'd like you to tell your story to these gentlemen."

Francais didn't even look our way before he turned to Rowan. "I'd rather not, Chief. I already told you everything and I really just want to go home."

"I know Frank, but I'd appreciate it if you'd tell Mr. Gillette exactly what you told me."

The man's head slowly turned and he stared up at my Uncle. "Gillette? William Gillette?" His eyes widened and a grin split his round face. "I'm a fan of yours! Went to see you in Norwich a few years back." He stuck out his hand, "I'm Francais Larabino. Find something to sit on and I'll tell you a story stranger than anything you put on a stage!"

There was an old wire spool near us, so I dragged it out and rolled it up in front of the man. I was about to brush it off for William, but he plopped right down. Steepling his fingers, he closed his eyes and after a brief moment, made a twirling gesture with one hand; clearly indicating that Larabino should get on with it.

Larabino clicked his teeth and grinned. "Ain't this a thing? Can't wait to tell the missus." The big man cleared his throat and smoothed out his features.

"I work for Ewing Seafoods -- maybe you've had some of our products or heard of us? Been with them for thirty-two years, the last fifteen in payroll security. Good company to work for..."

William's eyes popped open and Larabino's blathering stopped in mid- sentence. He clapped his hands together like a teacher trying to settle her classroom. "The facts, Mr. Larabino! Start from the beginning. Tell me everything that occurred. Leave no detail out. Concisely and quickly, if you please!"

Frank was a little stunned, but when William closed his eyes again, he dutifully told his tale.

"We were making our usual Thursday run down to the plant in Essex. Mike Schultz and I and Mike was driving and I was riding shotgun. We left at ten in the morning, like we always do. The weather was nice, no wind with the water flat as a skinny girl's bottom. Along with a good current we had a quick, easy trip until the train bridge was ten minutes behind us.

"We always stay in the channel, but on our last few trips we've made a little detour into a small inlet about a half mile up from here. Mike is getting ready to do his shad fishing when they run, so we run over to an old dock where Mike has his bait pots tied.

"Only this time, we're about thirty feet or so from the dock when all of a sudden all hell breaks loose. The boat came to a sudden stop. Mike is slammed into the pilot box and I'm knocked right off the motor covers onto my rear end! The engine is still running so the stern swings around quickly, cuz, whatever had a hold of the bow was keeping it fixed in place!

"Before I could even get to my feet, Mike had killed the throttle, but the bow kept bobbing up and down with the water frothing and a'churning all around it! We heard a crack in the wood that I could feel through the soles of my boots, and I finally stood and could see water coming up through the floor planking. I started forward to see what I could to do to plug it. Whatever hit us on the bow, now moved to the stern.

"Again, we could feel banging through the deck. We were taking on water, so Mike tries to get us moving towards the dock but we didn't move. Something was binding up the drive shaft.

"Then the stern starts to bob up and down and the boat's rocking for all git out! I was trying to hold on to the pilot box to steady myself, but Mike, God rest his soul, must have seen something in the water. He pulled his revolver and emptied it into the water, but that didn't stop it, nor slow it down, as far as I could tell. Then the last thing I would have suspected, the crazy fool pulled out a knife and leapt over the side!

"I couldn't believe my eyes and I tried to pull myself to the rear to see what was happening, but I was on the starboard side and when Mike's weight left the port side.–Our boat flipped and I went right into the water! When I came up for air, the boat was capsized. I was going to make my way to it, but there was some kind of commotion… a shape in the shallows and the water was frothing all around…and turning pinkish. My survival instincts took over and I headed for the dock instead."

"Now, I'm not much of a swimmer and had to dog paddle, its the best I can do. Finally I managed to make it to the dock before I went under or something got me! I held on to the piling for a moment to catch my breath, and then made my way to the bank. From there, I ran out onto the dock to see what happened to Mike. The boat was just drifting along, upside down." Frank hesitated and went on in a sad voice with his eyes cast down, "Then I saw Mike's body surface, face down and the water pink all around him." Tears began to leak from his eyes.

With a glazed look in his eyes, he mumbled, "I…there was no way I could bring myself to go back in that water…something was still out there." He shook his head and went on. "That's all I know, Sir. I walked out to the road, and a couple in a buggy was kind enough to bring me to the police station."

William turned a flinty gaze at Rowan. "You did not tell me there was a fatality."

Rowan shrugged, "I thought you would rather hear it first-hand. Besides, you don't believe in the monster story; or do you now?"

195

Before William could answer, two men walked up to our little group. One was a uniformed officer and the other was a short solid-looking man, about my age, who sported a short beard and long hair, tied back behind his head. He was dressed like an average working man in Levi pants, boots, and a homespun shirt and was carrying a shotgun.

Rowan leapt to his feet. "Well? Did you find it? Did you see anything?"

The man ignored the chief and addressed my uncle. "Hello, Mr. Gillette!"

"Afternoon, Gordon," William replied. He gestured at me, "This is Collin Frohman. Collin, this is Gordon Steele- our harbormaster as of last year."

We nodded to each other, however Rowan couldn't be ignored any longer. Gordon turned to him. "Nothing, Chief Inspector. Used a ten-foot rake and went over the area a few times, but all we got was some rocks and this shotgun. I assume it's yours, Sir." He stepped over to Frank and handed it to him.

Rowan shook his head. "Go back, widen the area. It has got to be there!"

Francais groaned and dropped his face into his hands again. "That it. I'll get the boot for sure! The company will never believe that a fish ate their money! I'll be lucky if I don't end up in jail!" He started to cry again, so I looked to my uncle, who was rising to his feet.

"What, exactly, are you searching for, Chief?" he asked Rowan in a cold voice.

"A locked box. Iron. It was locked in the cabinet in front of the pilot's box. Must have fallen out when the boat capsized."

"And what was in the box?"

196

"The weekly payroll for the factory in Essex."

William stared at Rowan with his teeth clenched, then turned to address Francais. "I am sorry for your troubles Mr. Larabino. I'm sure the Inspector will shine the best light he can on your actions. Please give my regards to your wife. Good day!" With that said, he started walking towards the motorcycles. I stood confused for a moment, and then followed after him, with Rowan hot on my heels.

William was already putting on his gear when we caught up to him. Rowan strode right up to William's side and started right in. "William, you are as stubborn as a blind mule! After what you just saw and heard—how can you still be skeptical? Does something need to bite you on the backside before you believe in it?"

"Spare me your insane delusions!"

"What put the bee in your bonnet?" Rowan demanded to know. "Are you mad because you were wrong about the Monster? Don't you want to find this thing-before it strikes again?"

"BAH!" William snarled as he kicked over his engine. "Find the payroll and you will find your 'River Monster!"

Then he just sped away. A minute later, I was after him, leaving Rowan to glare at our backs.

17

I finally caught up to him when he turned onto Main Street and had to slow down for a freight wagon plodding along. He waved to me and then I followed him over to the Inn.

"I am sorry to pull you away so quickly Collin, but I could not endure another agonizing moment of that 'River Monster' foolishness!" He opened his saddle bag and removed a bottle of Coca-Cola. "Shall we go inside? Perhaps you could stomach some solid food by now."

Connecticut River boating accidents, River Monsters, and Mike's drowning had made me forget I was hungover. However, I was looking at his bottle of soda pop and wondering why he brought it to a bar.

"They do not carry Coca-Cola yet. It helps me think." he explained, as if he was reading my mind. He hesitated and offered as sip half-heartedly. "I only brought two, Frohman…but if you would like the other…"

"No, that's alright, Uncle Will. I'll have a little hair of the dog."

"As you wish." Obviously relieved, he grinned and made a half bow as he gestured towards the door. "After you, my good man."

A bit perplexed by his attitude towards the soda pop, I went in, crossed the foyer, and stepped into the empty bar. The only soul in there was the barkeep who was polishing bottles. Uncle

Will went straight to the farthest table, and then instructed me. "With whatever you are having, Frohman, please include a glass and some ice for me." I nodded and headed over to the bar with vague memories of last night's debacle. I looked up and stopped short. The man putting ice into a tall glass in front of me was one of Catty's brothers!

I caught him staring at the bulge in my jacket, so I knew he was aware I was armed. I had the feeling he would have bolted for the door if I had so much as grimaced. I didn't want any more trouble with Catty's family. I put my best smile on and stuck out my hand, "I don't think we were really properly introduced last night. "I'm Collin Frohman and you're ...Cody, Right?"

Wide eyed he nodded, then blurted out, "There's no hard feelings about last night, are there?"

"No, of course not. I owe you the apology. I would have never pulled on you guys if I knew what was happening. Please try to see it from my viewpoint- I'm a stranger in town, just looking for a night cap, and some guy insults my family then tries to carve out my eyeball with a broken bottle! When you guys jumped up, I figured I had to level the playing field."

He thought it over for a second and then shook my hand. "I know. Tom said the same thing this morning. Sorry about Marquis. He naturally has a hot head and then add the liquor on and he is like a stick of dynamite ."

"He always was the wild one, and lately I swear, he's gotten worse."

"Was he alright after?"

He shrugged. "He was coming around. He could move his arm and we put him in his bunk to sleep it off."

"And what of the men he was with?" William asked from the table

Cody looked confused. "The barge rats? I never saw them." He shrugged. "I guess they went back to their nest."

"That is interesting, Frohman." William pronounced from the far table, and then fell silent.

I had no idea what he was talking about and the last thing I wanted to do was rehash what I remembered of last night. Why he would chime in on such a trivial point was beyond me. We had just heard a bizarre tale of murder, monsters, and robbery, which he just sped away from!

To change the subject, I turned to Catty's youngest brother and asked, "You work here?"

He shrugged again. "Just on Fast Eddie's day off, or days when he can't answer the rooster! I crew full time on the ferry in the busy season, but I'm just a weekend deck hand for now until folk get to moving about more."

"Well," I observed. "I'm not surprised Fast Eddie laid low today. We were at it until the wee hours of the morning."

He laughed. "I guess so! Tom said you kept up drinkin' pretty well, for a dandy!" His eyes flew wide and he clamped his lips shut when he realized what he just said.

I wasn't insulted, my boots cost more than these men made in a month. "Oh, he did, did he? Tell him this 'dandy' is up and moving while he's still under the covers. Your brother has a wooden leg!"

He laughed nervously. "Both of them! So, what can I get for you?"

"A glass with ice for my uncle." I gestured to the one in front of me. Cody' nodded and called out over my shoulder. "Afternoon, Mr. Gillette."

"Good afternoon, Cody'. How are your parents these days?"

"Fine, sir. I'll tell them you were askin'?"

"Excellent! Now, could I get that ice before it's a half a glass of water?"

Cody let the rebuke roll over him and he winked at me. "He must be detecting."

I shook my head in mock despair. "You have no idea. I'll have a beer." I took a five- dollar piece out of my pocket and tossed it on the bar. "We'll run a tab."

He gave me a look. "That's a hundred beers!"

"I was hoping to have something to eat, if it's not too late for lunch."

"Sure. Jimmy made pork chops today."

Pork chops weren't my favorite. I was hoping for some beef, but it was apparent I would have to settle, and I just nodded in acceptance. I wasn't totally sure I could keep anything down anyways.

I turned and called over to William. "Would you like something to eat?"

He was staring at his bottle Coca-Cola and didn't look up. "No, just the ice please!"

I winked to Cody, who answered back. "On its way, Mr. Gillette!" He poured me a quick beer and I carried it over to the table.

William produced a slim piece of metal from his pocket and quickly uncapped the bottle and slowly poured the dark amber liquid over the ice. When the foam settled, he took a long drink and smiled. "Nectar of the Gods."

I lifted my glass and pulled half the beer of it out then clicked my tongue, "Depends on which Gods you worship."

201

He took another long pull from his glass and announced, "Now, no more distractions, Frohman! I need to think." He sat back, put his fingertips together in front of his face and closed his eyes.

I knew I was going to have to amuse myself for a while, so I got another beer and wandered around the bar for a bit admiring the memorabilia. Once a place has been around for a while, like the Inn, it usually collects some pretty nifty history. My visual jaunt was interrupted when Cody brought lunch to the table. With one look at William's closed eyes, he rolled his and walked away.

I went back to my seat and was pleasantly surprised to find some first-class looking fare before me. The chops were thick and nicely brown with crispy fat. There was a tan sauce with tiny strings of onion across the top and a mound of fluffy mashed potatoes with a pat of butter melting on top. The aroma alone quashed what was left of my hang-over and I was suddenly famished. I took my first bite and was amazed. It was as good as anything I had ever eaten. The meat was tender and juicy, and the potatoes were like thickened air. I attacked with gusto and didn't slow until I was scraping the plate with my fork for the last scraps of potatoes.

Uncle Will finally came out of his trance. "My word, Frohman! You are eating like a condemned man! You are feeling better, I trust?"

"Much better." I replied as I laid down my tableware. I had to resist the urge to pick up the bones and gnaw on them. "I'm ready to find Tom for a rematch."

William rolled his eyes. "I would avoid imbibing with Tom for a while, Frohman. The Chief Inspector obviously needs his sleep."

"Seriously, Uncle Will, what riled you up so much at the docks?"

He took a cigarette out of his case and offered me one. We lit up and he turned in his chair to face me. "Rowan was wasting my time with fish tales."

"Gee...you have to admit that something strange happened this morning...and a man is dead!"

He heaved a sigh and said gravely, "The murder was a tragedy, Frohman but the simple facts are these -- the boat was attacked, and the money is missing. Those are not the actions of any creature but those that walk on two feet! Mysterious as the method may be-it is no more than piracy."

"Piracy? There weren't any other boats involved! In fact, if I remember correctly, that Larabino fellow didn't see anyone at all!"

"We don't have enough data to make a cohesive theory." He paused, and then snorted. "And I wouldn't put too much stock in Mr. Larabino's testimony, Frohman. He did not strike me as the overly vigilant type. A man like Frank sees his worst fears in times of duress.

"No, it was the pilot, Michael Shultz who could have cleared the matter up. Unfortunately, he took what he saw to the grave."

"Jeepers, Uncle Will, that's cold fish."

He rolled his eyes at me again. "Emotion has no place in an investigation, Frohman. I seek solutions, not absolution!"

"Then you're going to look into it?" I asked. The way we left, I assumed he had no interest.

He gave me a long look and replied, "Perhaps. But first, there is the matter of the child. That is my priority for now. Though," he tapped his lower lip with a long forefinger, "I have a vague notion that one may lead into the other."

If there was a connection between an abandoned child and a river heist that took place months apart, it eluded me. Still, my Uncle had amazed me more than once these past few days, so I kept my opinion to myself.

William slapped the table lightly. "Now, if you are sated, I would like to attend to a few matters before we return home."

I drained my beer. "Ready when you are."

"Excellent! Our next stop is my church, up a few streets."

"Is there a service today?" I asked. I knew nothing of the Episcopal practices.

He laughed. "No, of course not, Frohman. I need to make arrangements for the child's burial. She has been with Doctor Blum long enough."

Cody was nowhere to be seen, but I had given him more than enough for the lunch fare and a generous tip already, so we left and mounted up again.

It was a quick ride with a few turns, and we were soon pulling up in front of a typical New England church. White clapboard, stained glass, and a steeple. William indicated I should remain with the bikes as a tall gaunt man, in a dark frock coat, came out of the front doors and down the steps to greet him..

They talked for a few minutes and their discussion grew heated. The Minister or whatever they called their Shaman in these parts had an apologetic cast to his face as he shook his head. I could see my uncle stiffen with tension and replied in a stern voice, that I just couldn't hear. There was a little more back and forth, then they came to some sort of agreement and shook hands. The man went inside, and William walked back down, not looking altogether happy.

"What was that about, Uncle Will? You looked fit to be tied for a moment."

"I was making arrangements for the child's burial. At first, the good Reverend refused to officiate as the child was never baptized.

That was what I was taught by the Catholics but it still peeved me. "As if it were the child's fault? Is that it?"

"Precisely, Frohman. I pointed out that when an innocent babe was murdered, I doubted very much that our lord looked the other way."

"Good for you. That convince him?"

William hesitated, and then half smirked, "The good reverend capitulated, swayed by my logic of course... and a sizable donation.

"In any case he has agreed to arrange the site and perform the ceremony however it will not be on consecrated ground. We agreed on the old Common Cemetery. Our babe will rest in nice spot on the river, just down from the train trestle. It will be held the day after tomorrow, Friday, at nine o'clock."

"In the morning? That's a bit early for you," I teased, trying to lighten the mood.

"Best be done quickly," he replied as he donned his riding cap. "It is three months overdue."

I had no retort for that as we started our bikes and headed off. William led me down some back streets and we met up with the same road we had taken out of town yesterday. We were tooling along the winding road when William suddenly slowed and pointed to the river with his right arm.

I slowed down to a crawl and looked over the vista and saw nothing of interest. There was no traffic on the river, or breaks in the calm flowing river, or anything else out of place. I looked back to William about to ask him what he was pointing at, but he poked his arm out again more vigorously. I slowed the Harley and looked again, as William rounded a bend before us where I lost sight of him.

I jumped when I heard the sound of metal scraping and a sharp yelp of pain. Kicking back into gear, I gunned the throttle and sped forward. I rounded the corner to see my Uncle's Indian Chief lying on its side, with my Uncle's right leg pinned beneath it! I was relieved to see that he was already sitting up and was trying to move the machine off his limb, but his face wore a rictus of pain.

I stopped as fast as I could and leaped off to grab his Chief by the handle bars and pull it upright. I set the kick stand then helped my Uncle. Uncle Will was sitting up and clutching his right leg below the knee. I gave him a quick look over, and could see no obvious damage, except for the dirt that stained his right side. His pants leg wasn't torn and when I gently pulled it back, there were no scrapes or bruises on the outside of his calf. I began to fear he may have broken some bone, but I was reluctant to prod it, as I know nothing about first aid.

"Please try to move your foot," I commanded.

He waggled his foot up and down and that was a relief. My Uncle was sitting up, alert, without a head injury, and moving his foot. I was impressed he could lay his bike down so smoothly.

"What the hell happened?" I demanded.

"As I pulled off the road, my back tire slipped in a gravel rut as I was pointing" His lips pulled back in a grimace of pain.

"You were lucky you didn't get scraped to the bone," I admonished him. "What the hell were you pointing at anyways?"

He was annoyed. "Could you please dispense with the questions and help me to my feet?"

When we rose up and I stepped in front of him, I could see what was giving him so much pain. There was an ugly red strip burned into the inside of his calf about three inches above his sock. The red hot exhaust pipe had gotten him good! I kept his arm around my shoulder and we took a few tentative steps. I walked, and he limped badly.

He stopped and smiled at me and looked over to a house. "Perhaps we should go prevail upon that household for some ice before we continue our ride home."

I hadn't noticed the small, one-story dwelling that sat down a slight hill on the river bank. I didn't see the point.

"How about we get you on the back of my bike and take you to the doctors? We can come back for yours later."

He gave me a mocking look of horror. "Surely you jest! I wouldn't be caught dead on a Harley-Davidson!"

"This isn't a joke, Uncle Will. You need to get your leg looked at."

He patted my shoulder. "Excuse me, Collin. I do not mean to make light of your concern. I think we can find what we need at that house."

That seemed a little crazy to me and he seemed alert and confident so I just shrugged and started lugging him .down the pathway.

18

We followed the rutted path that served for a driveway --
though it looked as if it hadn't seen any traffic in a long while –
which passed through a thicket of trees and bittersweet that
made the property nearly impossible to see from the roadway.
We hesitated at the very top of the path to see what the
property revealed.

The path led down to a mostly level plot, about an acre that
sat right against the river. There was a modest one- story house
with lattice a few feet high, surrounding the base. I assumed the
house was built on pilings to minimize the damage done from
rising waters that must happen from time to time. It sat at a
fortyfive degree angle to the river, with a full-length front
porch. Weathered shingles, with faded white trim, gave it a
slight look of neglect, yet it was in pretty good shape. Not
twenty yards from the house was a high, sturdy pier that
extended some fifteen yards into the river. It was much bigger
than most private docks I had seen and could berth a good-
sized boat.

Besides an old outhouse behind the home, there was a large
shed set on the riverbank nearby and, higher up on the left was
a small barn. As we started to hobble forward again and got
closer, I could see the shed was really a boat house that could
be accessed from either the river or land.

A few steps out the back door there was a large patch of bare
earth with a low fence around it. Soon it would be filled with
growing vegetables and, perhaps, a flower or two. Up from

that, at the edge of the lawn, was a stone lined garbage pit, which was half full of table scraps, wrappings, unrecognizable bits of trash, and a few cracked or broken Coca-Cola bottles. All heaped upon a fair amount of brush and leaves, to help it burn. The smell made me grateful that our garbage was hauled away to be burned. In many ways it reminded me of some property in and around where my mother's family was from on the South Fork of Long Island. Cozy, yet functional for a family that made its living on the water.

As I looked around, I noticed additional small signs of neglect. A few shingles hung loose on the roof and a broken shutter hung askew on one of the side windows. Not that the place looked trashy, but just a bit lacking in upkeep. Uncle Will had said it was a harsh winter. Maybe they hadn't gotten around to the repairs yet.

A curtain flashed from inside the far left window. From the stove pipes that came through the roof above it, I surmised it was the kitchen area. I expected someone to come out of the house after seeing a man being carried towards the house.

I was wrong. We had to walk around to the front of the house and stumble our way up the few stairs to reach the porch and front door. I waited a moment, but still there was no acknowledgement of our presence. The hair on the back of my neck started to rise as I said to my Uncle,

"I know somebody's home! I saw the curtains move in the kitchen, so they know we are here. Are people around here so unfriendly? This place is giving me the willies!"

William, who looked like the cat who ate the canary, replied in a low voice, "Easy, young Frohman. Do not be alarmed. I believe the occupant of this house is simply being...cautious. Perhaps with good reason. Let us show a bit of courtesy. Knock on the door."

I did a lot more than that! I ignored the brass knocker and pounded the wood panels with the side of my fist.

"Hello?"I bellowed. "We need some help here! There has been an accident! Hello in there!"

I was about to start thumping the door again when a voice off to the side brought me up short.

"STOP that caterwauling and leave off on my door! Just what is the problem here?"

Startled, I swung around, still supporting William, to find a visibly angry woman, with her hands on her hips, standing on the end of the porch. She must have come out another door and came up behind us. Before I could answer, she recognized my uncle. Her eyes narrowed and she stalked across the porch, not looking pleased at all. She looked down and saw the torn pants leg, then looked up and snapped.

"Mr. Gillette. What's this all about?"

William took off his hat and nodded the very picture of civility. "Susan. Good afternoon. I seemed to have stumbled onto a bit of unfortunate happenstance."

She snorted and then bent at the waist to look closer. "I doubt it will prove fatal." She turned her cold look to me, "And who is your two-legged crutch? The one bent on breaking down my door and yelling to wake the devil?"

William replied calmly, "This is Collin Frohman."

Her eyebrows went up, "Your friend Charles' son?"

"I'm afraid so," I answered for him, "Pleased to meet you."

She looked me up and down, then reached out with a slender finger and tapped the pocket in my jacket that bulged with the outline of my flask. My gun she either ignored or didn't notice. "I see you inherited his love of spirits. One can only pray you didn't get his penchant for foolishness!" Before I could come back to that, she went on. "Well, you might as well drag him inside. I'll see what I can do for him."

With that she opened the front door and walked inside, holding it open for us to enter. Once inside, she closed the door behind us and pointed to a rocking chair that sat in front of the hearth, a large ball of crimson yarn, stuck through with knitting needles, sat in a basket besides it. She made it sound like a sigh when she said, "I'll get some things" Then she bustled off into the bedroom as William settled into the chair.

I looked around as we waited for her return and was impressed with the home's design. It was a charming one-level, with an enormously long hearth that split the house in two. We were in the living room with a table and some sturdy chairs. The doorway to the right led to a bedroom and on the opposite corner, an area was set up as a parlor, with nice furniture and well carved side tables draped with lace. The back left was walled off for the kitchen and on the other side of the hearth was the dining room. Each room had ample windows and each had a view of the river.

Mostly though, my attention was drawn to a harpoon that was hanging above the fireplace and the various carvings and knick-knacks that lined the mantle. There were scrimshaw pieces, some quite good, and a variety of small carved figures of strange looking animals, all in bone. It suddenly occurred to me who the woman was.

Making sure she was still out of the room, I leaned over uncle and said softly, "This is the woman who used to work for that old sawbones, isn't it?"

He looked up at me and grinned, "Excellent Frohman. There is hope for you yet!"

I let that pass. "Then you knew she lived here." He looked like he was about to protest, so I cut him off. "Don't try to deny it! She was twice as surprised to see you as you were to see her!"

He gave me a bored look. "Obviously."

I would have carried on, but the woman suddenly appeared carrying a bowl of water and a satchel. I stepped aside as she nudged a hassock forward with her foot and sat before my uncle. She put her knees together and gestured for him to raise his leg.

William did so with a minimum of theatrics and she began to probe the wound with her hands.

"How did this happen?"

William winced as she squeezed the flesh around the burn and answered through clenched teeth, "My rear tire hit a patch of sand and the bike went out from under me."

"Ouch!" She grunted. "You men and your contraptions! They're bad enough with four wheels-never mind two. You're lucky you didn't crack your head open!" she had the bit between her teeth now. "Faster! Higher! Deeper! Why can't you men ever be satisfied?"

William nodded, as if he agreed she had a point. "Speaking of deeper, I understand your brother has taken his work to Long Island sound."

She gave him a look. "Yes, he did. Picked up at the beginning of last summer and told me he was going to work on some new designs, and he'd be gone the better part of a year or more. Left half his junk in the shed and boathouse and off he went, leaving me to keep this place up all on my own!"

William tried a little sympathy. "It must be very hard for you, Susan. Please, feel free to ask me for help. I would be happy to send some men over to do any repairs you need."

She waved the offer away. "There's no need, Mr. Gillette. I manage just fine, and my husband is due home at the end of next week."

"Ah! Well, you must be excited!"

She ignored the statement and picked up the cloth, dipping it into the bowl of water. "Well, it doesn't look too serious," she assured us as she rinsed the area of dirt. "Nothing's broken and the burn looks like a second degree. Just keep it clean and cooled. It may be tender for a day or so, but you'll be fine. Just like any other child who stumbles and falls.

Let me bandage it up," she said as she reached into her bag.

William held up a hand to stop her. "There is no need to trouble yourself further, Susan; Ozaki can dress the burn when I return home."

She gave him a flat stare, "So your heathen is a nurse too? I'll just put something over it, so you don't coat it with dirt or rub it with your pants." She fished around in her bag and pulled out a white linen cloth. When she held it up to fold, you could see the beautiful laced edging.

"Susan," William protested. "You should not waste such a fine napkin on my old leg."

Susan sighed and replied, "It WAS a fine set at one time, straight from the old country, but others got ruined, so you needn't worry about it."

As she wrapped the cloth around his leg, she advised, "If you have any ice at that fancy castle of yours, apply it until it melts before you cover it up again. That's about all you can do. Maybe some aloe, if you can find any this time of year."

William leaned forward. "I thank you for your care Susan. You have been very kind." He lowered his foot to the floor and slowly pulled his pant leg over the bandage. I could feel the air

213

in the room change as he looked her straight in the eye and asked, "I wonder if I might impose on you just a little further?"

She leaned back at his intensity, to sit stiffly. "In what way?" she asked with wariness in her eyes.

"Oh, just a question. Nothing more."

She didn't answer him, but it was obvious she was waiting for it. William stared at her intently. "I was wondering whether you had known of or participated in any births this year. Around the first of the year?" His gaze became even more focused, "One, perhaps, that might not have been recorded?"

Her eyes popped open in surprise at the question but quickly narrowed to slits that screamed of suspicion. "My, how quickly you go from patient to policeman, Mr. Gillette!" She stared at him for a minute, and then answered, "I have kept to myself since I left the doctor's employ, Mr. Gillette. I have not left this property and don't intend to until my husband returns from Iceland later next week. Why would you ask me such a question?"

William sat back and folded his hands in his lap. "To be blunt Susan, out of desperation. This morning, some workers of mine found an abandoned baby on my property, some distance from my home."

Her face flushed and she made the sign of the cross. "Is the child safe now?"

William shook his head sadly, "I'm afraid not. The baby had been dead for some time. I have no clue to the identity of the child and so far no one knows who she could be. You seemed to be a logical ..."

The woman suddenly jumped to her feet and snapped at him, her eyes ablaze. Logical what? How dare you ask me if I had anything to do with the mistreatment of any child! I am a trained nurse and have taken the same medical oath as a doctor!"

"Susan," William tried to speak reasonably, "Your training is why I …"

"Stop!" She nearly screamed. "Not another word! Your wound is tended! Now leave my house and take that fool's git with you! Immediately!"

I wanted to say something to her, puzzled by the venom in her voice, but she stared at the ceiling and began to tap her foot.

I put an arm out for my uncle and between that and the cane, he got to his feet. He looked down at Susan.

"I am sorry if I have given offence." He started calmly.

Her head snapped down and she spoke over him, "You don't give offence-you bring it! The last time I saw you, a horribly mutilated man was brought to the office and another young man had been murdered and now…now a dead baby! These tidings are exactly why I keep to myself! You are a harbinger of death! Leave my house!" She pointed to the door, shaking like a leaf. I couldn't believe how angry she was! I was afraid we might have to shoot our way out.

She kept pointing at the door and throwing daggers with her eyes. William, who had walked away without saying another word to her, turned at the entry and said in a strong, but serene tone, "I will find justice for that little girl, Susan."

The whole scene was getting too macabre for me, so I pulled William through the door and slammed it shut. I could hear her sobbing as we crossed the porch. We made it down the steps and halfway across the yard when I said, "Gee, Uncle Will! You sure got a smooth way with women!"

215

He gave me a smirk, "Yes, well, Harbingers of death are rarely suave, Frohman."

Quickly we reached the top of the hill and William took his arm off my shoulder and limped the rest of the way to his Chief. I stood there, dumbfounded, until it came to me.

"You faked the accident! Or, at the very least, you caused it on purpose JUST so you could talk to her!"

He tilted his head at me, "Did this just occur to you? Of course, I did. Nothing less than a play on her medical ethics would have gotten us an interview. Of course, I had not planned on setting the exhaust pipe across my leg. The bike was heavier than I calculated. Careless on my part, but it was quite convincing, don't you think?"

"Right now, the only thing I'm convinced of is that you are acting crazy! If all this was just a sham, why didn't you let me in on it?"

He gave me a big grin as he suited up and straddled his bike. "I have found that most people are better actors if they are not aware they are playing a role."

I was a bit put off and didn't like to be a stooge. "So we came all the way out here, so you could burn a leg and I could break a leg? Still got us nowhere. It was a waste of an afternoon."

"Was it?" He kicked over the engine and dropped it into gear, cutting off any more discussion.

19

To my surprise, instead of heading up the road towards home, William turned his machine around and took off like the devil towards town. I was a little miffed at his disregard for his wound but was satisfied when he led me straight through the burg to Dr. Blum's office. Instead of dealing with the surly nurse, we went around to the back and directly to the doctor's cubby hole.

When we walked through his door, the doctor was sitting behind his desk, or rather, lounging there. He had his legs crossed and up on the desk as he leaned back in his chair and sipped amber liquid from a low tumbler. My first thought was to join him, but the smell of the room made me a trifle queasy.

"Well, hello boys!" He raised his glass in salute. "I figured you'd be by. Thought you'd be here an hour ago. 'Spect you want to hear about the pilot, Mike, they brought in today."

William pulled off his gloves and sat in the visitor's chair. "Actually, we just spent a rather unpleasant half hour with your ex-nurse, Susan."

The doctor pulled his legs down and sat forward. "Susan? What the devil did you want with that nag?"

William shrugged. "She fits the criteria. I thought she might have some insight into the babe."

Dr. Blum snorted loudly then laughed. "I'll admit she's still on the tail end of her childbearing years, but who would want

217

to put up with her long enough to impregnate her? Even her husband is happier beating baby seals to death in the frozen Artic than warming her bed!"

Uncle Will rolled his eyes and sighed. "Given her training and profession, I had thought she might have had some involvement in a mid-wife capacity."

"And did she?"

"Never found out," I chimed in. "Called Uncle Will a 'harbinger of death' and threw us out."

William gave me a sharp look, but Blum laughed. "She's right, you know, William. Every time you show up here there's a fresh corpse." He drained his glass.

Uncle Will was annoyed. "How very amusing, Doctor. Now, if you can give that bottle a rest for a moment, perhaps we can return to the business at hand."

"First," I said loudly. "My uncle needs some medical attention."

William stiffened but said nothing as the doctor put his glass down on the desk. He looked William in the eye. "What's this?"

"It is nothing, Doctor. Frohman is just being a mother hen."

I shook my head behind his back, "He's got a bad burn on the inside of his right calf from his motorcycle's exhaust pipe."

William went to protest, but Blum was having none of his objections. He got up from his desk and walked around to stand over my uncle.

Looking resigned and irritated, William pulled up his pant leg and propped his foot up on the desk. Blum put on a pair of glasses and bent close to look it over carefully. He peeled back a portion of the cloth wrap, grunted after a moment, and then replaced the bandage.

"Not too bad. Susan do this?" William nodded and he went on, "I think I'll just let it be. Put some ice on it when you get home and keep it clean." He looked at William and smiled, "No charge for the examination."

William shot him a look as he rolled down his pantleg and put his foot back on the floor.

"Now," William said in a voice that brooked no nonsense. "If you and my nanny are satisfied, could we please hear the findings of Mike's autopsy?"

Dr, Blum grew serious. "Be better if I show you, William. There are a few things I don't understand."

William immediately popped to his feet and I reluctantly followed him as Blum pulled back the curtain that separated his work station from his office. In the center of the area, on the same table we'd examined the baby, was a bloody sheet outlining the shape of a man. When Blum stepped up and pulled back the sheet, I wished that I had insisted on a drink earlier.

He had been an older man with salt and pepper hair and a neatly trimmed beard that stood out in stark contrast to his bleached-out skin. There was a long gash down the center of his chest that had been loosely stitched back together. His right arm was fairly well mangled, and his head was a bloody mess on the left side, his left ear dangling by a few shreds of skin and his lower jaw was out of whack. I stayed back and tried to close my nostrils to the stench of wet death as my uncle and the doctor began to discuss his wounds with meticulous detail. After a moment, William straightened up.

"Cause of death?"

"Oh, he drowned alright." Blum replied. "Lungs were full of water and there were burst capillaries from his esophagus to his tonsils. Though I suspect he would have died from the blunt force trauma to his head, had he not drown."

"Then he was knocked unconscious and drowned as the result?"

"Most likely, but I think whatever got him, grabbed him by the arm and held him under until he sucked a good part of the river into his chest."

Uncle Will was disgusted. "Bah! Do not waste my time with drivel, Doctor! You cannot have possibly joined the rest of those blithering sapheads who lay these events on the door of a mythical sea monster?"

Blum looked at him like he had three heads. "For argument's, we'll put aside the extreme tearing of the scapula and glenoid and ignore the fact that the arm was wrenched so hard that it's only attached by a few stubborn tendons and skin and we'll focus on the wrist.

"Whatever got him, crushed a four inch strip of flesh and bone so hard it was nearly severed in two!"

I looked down at the wound in question and I saw that the doctor was right. A whole section of his wrist and forearm was flattened to less than a few inches that formed a perfect rectangle. Summering in Amagansett when I was growing up, I had seen the results of a great white shark's attack and I couldn't imagine a creature having such a powerful bite.

William rolled his eyes and replied through clenched teeth. "Yet, there is no puncture mark on the wound, or anywhere else for that matter. Predators have sharp teeth, Doctor. Would you not expect to find bitemarks where something clamped down so hard?

"Or do you think your 'Nessie" is an herbivore. A mad sea cow, perhaps?"

Blum had nothing to reply to that and I couldn't explain it myself. I might have pointed out that there were many species in this world we knew little or nothing about, but I thought my opinon would just get me another of my uncle's 'slap downs'. Instead, I put the burden of proof on him.

"What do you think happened to him, Uncle Will? I mean, if he wasn't attacked by some freak of nature…well, I doubt he fell into a laundry mangler running on the bottom of the river under eight feet of water!"

Dr, Blum huffed and nodded his head once, but William looked like he was about to dress me down properly for a second or two. Then he slowly relaxed a bit as he got that concentrated look on his face. He didn't speak for a few moments, but just stared up at the ceiling and taped a finger to his lower lip.

Suddenly, he came alive and clapped me on the shoulder. "What would I do without a Frohman around."

Before I could question his comment, he wheeled about and said to the doctor. "Thank you, Doctor. I think I have all I need for now. Will I see you at the babe's funeral? It's set for the day after tomorrow. At eight a.m."

Blum was obviously used to my uncle's quirks, so he just sighed. "I'll be there."

"Then good day." He gestured to me, "Come along, Frohman. The chase is on and we are still behind!"

Uncle Will decided to forgo the ferry for our return trip, so we sped up the road to the train bridge. There was one disconcerting moment, while we were half-way across the

221

span, when I saw smoke from an oncoming train headed in our direction. My heart skipped a beat at the thought of trying to share the space with a locomotive, but we were off the bridge long before the train reached the trestle. I realize there was no reason to panic because the train was moving at a pace slower than a running man. I thought it odd as it was a passenger train rather than a freight. The train I took here had sped right along.

When we reached Uncle Will's home, I asked why the train was traveling so slowly.

"Geography, Collin." He pointed out to the front of his property. "As you can see, the land slopes down and away. There is a fairly steep grade a southbound locomotive has to traverse until the tracks level out before the bridge. That's why they only get up to speed after they have crossed the river."

I took that in and commented. "I hope the Chief Inspector takes that into consideration. It's a lot easier to jump on a train when it's going six miles an hour, than when it's going sixty!"

Uncle William looked impressed. "That is solid thinking, Collin! You would make a fine Jesse James!" He laughed.

Uncle Will went off to his study, excusing himself saying he wanted to spend some time 'delving'. I had no idea what he meant, but it had been a long day, so I poured myself a tall one, including a refill of my flask, and took it up to the library. As I had hoped, Uncle Will had a few books on astronomy, one that even showed the stars' positions at various times of the year in this hemisphere. I was going to awe Catty with my knowledge of the universe! Ozaki came and we talked of my family, the folks we knew from my childhood, and life in general. I spilled a little about my misgivings at heading the production company and he gave me a few sensible pointers. Not about how to run a business but how to handle myself while leading the company. I'd forgotten how much I missed his insight and sage advice.

After he left to check on Uncle Will, Catty came to see if I needed anything and we chatted for a while. I casually mentioned that it was supposed to be a clear night, great for using a telescope, and we made plans to do some star gazing after dark. When she left to finish preparing dinner, I was feeling pleased with myself and had a couple more gulps from my flask. When the sun started to get low in the sky, I got up and went to my room to freshen up for dinner.

At the dinner bell, I went downstairs and headed for the dining room. Uncle Will was still in his study, just rising from his chair when the telephone rang. Uncle Will saw me and waved me inside as he picked up the receiver.

"Hello. Yes, it's me. Of course, please put him through."

I realized he was talking with an operator, but when I got close; he reached out and pulled me next to him. He angled the ear piece out so I could hear what was said.

"Hello William. It's Kevin Rowan here."

"Good evening Chief Inspector. It is a bit late, are you working still?"

"Oh, I'll be working straight through until the day after tomorrow. Have to keep a tight rein on security along the tracks until then. Thank the saints that it's due through here early in the morning. We can all get back to our routines after that.

"But that's not why I rang you William. I have an interesting tid-bit to share with you. Guess what showed up this evening, about a half hour ago?"

Even through the tinny sound of the wire, Rowan sounded like the cat who ate the canary."

"I have no idea, Chief. Do tell."

223

"Well, Gordon Steele was locking up the harbormaster office for the night when he saw something sitting at the end of the dock."

There was a long hesitation. I think Rowan expected Uncle Will to take the bait but he misjudged. Finally, he said, "The missing payroll box! Still locked and full of cash."

I wouldn't say William was confused but he did look concerned. "And what do you discern from that Chief?"

"Why, the obvious of course. There was no robbery! No self-respecting criminal would kill a man and sink a boat, just to return the money!"

Uncle Will smirked and winked at me. "So, you think that your sea monster, after realizing the box was not nutritious, conveniently spit it out on the dock so Gordon Steele could return it?"

There was a dead silence and Rowan responded in a tight voice. "No, of course not. I think a good samaritan came across it left it for us to find. There are some good people in this town William, people who do the right thing and don't want any credit for it."

"They have a lot of faith in this Steele too." I mumbled.

"What was that?" Rowan asked over the wire.

"A valid point Chief Inspector. Whoever left the box must know the harbormaster, or at least of his reputation for honesty. Many men would not be inclined to give up such a windfall."

Rowan heaved an audible sigh. "Then what do you think is going on?"

"I can't say, but I'm sure it will be clear to us soon. Thank you for the call. I'm sure we shall see each other tomorrow. Goodnight."

224

He set the phone back on its cradle and shook his head. "Ninny!"

He didn't elaborate as we headed for the dinner table.

20

Since Catty was staying for the astronomy lesson, Mrs. Wood could take the night off after our dinner. To my delight, she joined us as well. Near the end of the meal, as we were savoring our rice pudding, Catty broached the subject of the infamous 'River Monster'.

"Well, sir, are you beginning to rethink your denial of the creature."

William's spoon stopped in midair. "Why ever would I do that, dear Catherine?"

Catty looked at him like he was mad. "Why, because of the attack today! There was a victim! I heard the poor man's head was torn off and his arm was eaten!"

"Catherine!" Ozaki was appalled. "That is certainry not appropriate dinner conversation."

William put his spoon down. "No, No, Ozaki. It is quite alright. This is a valuable lesson in life for our next generation." He gestured at Catty and I, then began his lecture.

"This is exactly why I do not listen to gossip! Everything you just said was a gross distortion of the facts. Neither the men nor the boat was the focus of the attack. The strong box was the target and the former were nothing more than collateral damage. Second, though he suffered a blow to the head and a severe wound to his right wrist, no part of him was bitten, much less devoured! The official cause of death was drowning.

In fact," he sat back and drummed his fingers on the tabletop, "evidence suggests the wounds were not the result of an offence."

Catty looked at him like his train had jumped the rails, but I thought about what he just said, and it came to me.

"The knife! That fat guy said the pilot pulled a knife with his right hand and dove into the river. So ...whatever... grabbed his arm did it in defense!"

"Excellent, Frohman! Now, what does that infer?"

I thought about it for a second then replied carefully, "Whatever it is, it's smarter than a fish!"

William laughed and slapped the table. "Eloquently put, Collin! Enough of that monster fairy tale for one night. Just remember, children, gossip is nothing more than vague sources spreading misinformation to the bored and petty."

I wanted to get back to the knife, but I knew by the look on his face that my uncle would not be forthcoming, so I let it lie.

Wiliam smiled and announced. "I suppose we shall forgo the after-dinner smoke tonight Colin, as you and Catherine are planning on stargazing tonight."

"With your permission, of course, Sir." Catty put in quickly.

"How'd you know we were thinking about it?"

He laughed and replied. "Ozaki told me you were pouring over the astronomy books in the library. It was a logical deduction."

Catty whirled to face me looking half outraged and half amused. "So you were planning on dazzling me with your knowledge of the stars?" She had seen right through me.

"I was just boning up." I blustered. "I know enough about the stars to steer a boat by-day or night!"

"That much is true." Ozaki put in.

"It's just as well you are occupied tonight," William said as he tapped the floor switch and rolled the table away from us. "I have a great deal of correspondence to deal with before I retire. You'll see Catherine home, I presume?"

As it turned out, we did have time for smoke as I had to wait for Catty to tidy up after dinner. I was dying to ask him for his thoughts on the day's events, but I sensed he was through discussing it for now. Instead, he gave me instructions on how to set up the tripod for the telescope. Then he said something cryptic.

"Don't just look up with the instrument, Frohman. There may be just as many interesting points down here on earth."

Catty appeared before I could ask him what the hell he was talking about and we said goodnight.

I ducked into the library on our way up to the third floor to grab the book with the star maps. The cat was out of the bag anyways and everything I had read this afternoon was pushed out of my head. We pulled out the secret staircase and had the telescope set up and pointed skyward in a flash.

We had a grand time. The air was crisp but still retained some of the day's warmth. There wasn't a cloud in the sky, and I don't remember ever seeing as many stars so clearly before. I would pick out a star in the book and Caty would find it. Then I would tell made up stories about the constellations and she would laugh. I loved her laugh. It was rich and throaty and came straight from her heart.

I took out my flask and to my surprise she took a long pull before letting me have it. I was impressed as it was straight gin and she didn't even wince. I remembered my experience with her brother, so I decided to watch myself in case it was a family trait. Over the next couple of hours, she matched me snort for snort and showed no outward signs. When it was my turn to man the instrument, I remembered Uncle Will's advice and turned the lens at the town and the river. There wasn't much to see in the darkness. There were lights in town, but I couldn't make out any movement. There was some activity on the barge, some powerful lights shining on its deck and men moving about, though I couldn't discern what they we about. Then I saw Marquis's boat, drifting down the river. It was hardly moving and canted at a strange angle, so I knew it wasn't under power.

"Hey Cat," I said. "I think I see your brother's boat drifting on the river. What's that all about?"

She got up and positioned herself on the eyepiece, then shrugged. "Probably passed out, the damn fool, and forgot to set the anchor."

"He'd better be careful," I joked, "or he's going to wake up off Long Island. Does he live on the boat?"

"Not really. He still has a room at our house. Funny thing is he's been spending more nights home this past month than he did all winter. I wonder how he didn't freeze to death all those nights he spent out."

I didn't really want to talk about him at the time, so I let the subject drop and we talked about anything else. We were having so much fun, I nearly forgot about the time. I pulled out my watch and my heart sank a little. "Damn! The last ferry leaves in forty-five minutes. We'd better pack it up and head down."

I was pleased to see she seemed disappointed as well, but she was more pragmatic, as women are prone to be. We stowed the telescope and returned the book to the library then headed down to the river. When I went to get my motorcycle, Catty

229

suggested we leave it and walk, as it was a lovely spring evening. I was just as happy since we'd have more time to talk. Besides, I was feeling the effects of the day's drinking and didn't want to spill us both on the road.

As we walked down the hill towards the landing, I could see the ferry was still out on the river and there were just a few folks milling about, waiting to take the last run as we were. We were just about abreast of what would be Ozaki's new home and I was regaling Catty with some of my college day's antics when I realized I was walking alone. I stopped, mid punch line and looked back to see Catty standing still with a big grin on her face. I knew she was feeling the Gin also.

"I want another drink." She announced. I almost laughed, but I could see she was earnest.

"Well, we drank all my gin; I suppose we could stop at the inn for a nightcap."

She shook head and the grin never left her face. I was beginning to think she was far drunker than I thought.

"That's our only option at this time of night, Catty."

"Actually, it isn't." She said slyly. She jerked her head over her shoulder. "Your Uncle keeps a well- stocked cabinet on the Aunt Polly."

"Girl...you're a genius!"

Catty led me down a path that followed the river bank between the trees and boulders, and we soon came to the dock. As we went up the gang plank to the aft deck, I was thinking how I could break in without causing any damage. Catty walked right over to the French doors that led to the salon and reached into her purse to take out a set of keys.

"You have a key?" I asked.

"Of course," she replied as she opened the door. "Who do you think cleans Aunt Polly once a week?"

Once inside, I sent Catty to fetch a bottle and a couple of glasses, while I pulled the blinds before lighting a lamp. Both my Uncle and Ozaki had sharp eyes and I didn't want any light showing.

I plopped down on one of the sofas and Catty returned quickly with what I sent her for. She poured us each a stiff one then curled her legs up under her and draped an arm on the back of the sofa behind my head as she sat down next to me. Very close to me.

I clutched my glass with both hands in my lap, trying to understand what was happening. Funny, at any other time with any other girl, I would have called on every bit of my charm, however with Catty, I was as flummoxed as an adolescent.

My discomfort was obviously amusing to her. "Something wrong, Collin? You seem a tad nervous."

I started to stammer like a schoolboy. "No...I mean...well, I'm not sure we...I mean...are you sure?" I knocked back my drink to calm my nerves.

She laughed softly and put a hand on the back of my neck. Collin, you are no monk and I am certainly no blushing maiden and neither of us are virgins." Then she leaned in a kissed me long and hard.

Before I knew it, she had me by the hand and was leading me to the hallway that led to the bedrooms. Any doubt or reservations I may have had dropped right out of my head.

The night was more wonderful than I could have imagined.

And then some...

21

We awoke as the first rays of morning light spilled through the windows and washed over the bed. I opened my eyes to find Catty, lying on her side next to me, staring at my face. I smiled and rolled over to put my arms around her.

"Now, where were we?" I asked.

She laughed and pushed me away. "None of that now, my bucko! I have to get to work. Sweet Christmas! Wasn't last night enough for you?"

"I'm not sure I could ever get enough of you, Catty."

She wore a sad smile when she said, "Don't be starting with all of that! We both know what last night was."

Never had I gotten off the hook with a girl so easily, yet, I found myself not wanting that. "Hey now!" I protested. "I'm not saying that a part of me didn't want this to happen, but you were the one doing most of the seducing."

She laughed out loud. "I practically had to hit you over the head and drag you in here!" Then she settled down and said seriously. "Look, I now you were trying to be a gentleman. That only made me want you more, but we both know you'll go home soon and someday you'll find a girl from your station in life. Last night was deliciously wicked and I will treasure it always, but I knew this was just a ...tryst. You don't have to pretend it was more, not for my sake."

I sat up a bit to levy another protest, but she put a finger to my lip. Then she kissed me long and hard. Before I could put my arms around her, she shifted her legs off the bed and sat up. She jumped up before I could lunge for her and she started to put her under things on. I laid back in the bed and started wondering how we were going to keep this from Uncle Will and Ozaki. Not that I was ashamed, but they would definitely not be pleased with me if they found out I was slept with their maid.

I looked over and Catty was riffling through the closet. We were in the second suite, where William's guest usually stayed. "What are you looking for?" I asked her.

She turned and gave me an annoyed look. Hands on her hips, she groused, "Well I can't very well go to work today in the same dress I wore yesterday, can I? Your Uncle would see right through that! Miss Barrymore keeps some spare clothes here for when she visits. We're the same size so no one will notice."

"You're lucky she's a …busty one herself."

She crinkled her nose at me then stepped into a blue dress that fit her to perfection. She was just slipping on her shoes when there was a loud meowing at the door. She hopped over one on foot and opened the door. An orange blur streaked past her and leapt up onto the bed with me.

"That's Maurice." she informed me as she twisted her hair into a bun and started to strategically stab it with bobby pins.

Maurice didn't seem very happy to make my acquaintance. He paced back and forth on the bed but hissed when I went to pet him. I was about to swat him off the bed, before he settled at the end, atop my trousers, and stared at me. By the time we had made our truce, Catty was ready to go. I was hoping for a good-bye kiss and was sadly mistaken. She was all business now that she was dressed.

234

"I'm going to walk back the way we came last night then walk up to the castle. Wait awhile before you make an appearance."

"Tell you what; I'll walk up the long way from the boat shed. I'll probably be there before Uncle Will gets up, but if he asks—I'll tell him I took a walk."

"Thank you. I'd rather no one knew about us. I've had enough gossiping to last me a lifetime already."

I nodded. "I understand, Catty. Well…I hope we can spend some more time together while I'm here."

Bless her heart, she gave me a seductive smile and replied. "Oh, you can count on that, me bucko! We'll just have to be sneaky." Then she grinned ear to ear. "That's what makes it so fun! I'll talk to you later." With that, she went out of the room. "Make sure everything is put back and locked up when you leave!" She called out from the hallway and then I heard her go out the door.

I laid half under the covers for a while, just feeling swell.

I followed my end of the plan and walked through the front door just as Uncle Will was coming down, I assumed, for coffee. As fortune would have it, Catty came from the hallway to the kitchen bearing a steaming cup of coffee on a silver tray."

"Morning Mr. Gillette. Morning Mr. Frohman." She greeted us cheerily. She held the tray out to my Uncle who took the offered cup with thanks. Then she turned to me. "How was your walk?"

"Fine, Catty. It's a beautiful day."

"Would you care for a cup of coffee?"

"Love one. Thanks." I replied nonchalantly. I was quite proud of the way we were pulling it off.

"Coming right up," She replied and headed back to the kitchen.

As soon as she was out of sight, William reached over with his free hand and clamped down on my ear. Pulling me close, and nearly tearing my earlobe off, he hissed in a low voice, "WHAT DID YOU DO?!"

I pulled his fingers off my ear and tried my best to look indignant. I might have pulled it off if I hadn't answered in a low voice so Catty wouldn't hear. "What is the matter with you? What are you talking about?"

"Don't act the fool with me, Collin. You know very well what I'm talking about! Your pants are covered with orange cat hairs!"

I tried to look at him like he was crazy. "So what? There are dozens of the little beast around! What do you expect?"

He narrowed his eyes at me. "That is true, but I have only one orange tabby. A tom called Maurice—who stays on the Aunt Polly and favors the guest suite to sleep in! That and the fact that Catherine is wearing a dress that would cost her well over two month's salary and she's still wearing the same shoes as she did yesterday --that do not match the dress -- leads me to a very disturbing conclusion!"

As my luck would have it, Ozaki came trotting over just then. He glared at me too.

"What is the matter with you? You no come here to sreep last night? You get drunk and pass out again? Maybe you no take Catrine home no more. You no can get past the bar!" He giggled.

"That would be quite a feat," William growled, "since his motorcycle is parked exactly where he left it yesterday!"

I knew I had been made, but William shushed Ozaki and was all smiles when Catty brought me my cup of coffee. I thanked her and Ozaki said to her. "I put vases in pantry. They need a good cleaning. Do now, prease."

"Right away, Mr. Ozaki." She replied sunnily, as she turned to go do his bidding.

Ozaki looked up at uncle with wide eyes. "She is some happy today!"

Uncle Will, tilting his head, growled through clenched teeth. "We will continue this discussion in the study!" It felt like it did when I was at boarding school and was summoned to the head master's office for disciplinary action. I knew I was caught, but I didn't think William would disown me, or even toss me out. I decided then not to defend myself, as I didn't want to discuss my mixed feelings for Catty with the two of them. At least, not until I had a chance to talk to Catty about them. I'd take my tongue lashing and keep my trap shut.

Uncle Will wasted no time. As soon as Ozaki pulled the door shut behind us, he lit into me. Striking his most imposing stances, he glared down at me and slapped a hand on his desk hard enough to make me wince.

"Collin Thomas Frohman! Of all the despicable acts! Your mother would be appalled. Even your father would never be so crass! Not only is that girl in my employ, she is very special to us and I will not see her treated in such a callous manner. That young woman has suffered enough at the hands of an unscrupulous man and deserves better. How dare you bring your bachelor debauchery into my household!"

I know I said I was going to keep my mouth shut and take it like a man, but this was too much. Even before I thought it, I barked, "Shut up!"

So violent was my outburst that Uncle will's eye flew wide open and Ozaki even dropped into a position to defend himself. I took a deep breath and said, in a stern voice, "It wasn't like that at all…"

Suddenly, the telephone on the desk trilled, cutting me off mid-sentence. We all looked at it and when it rang a second time, William went to reach for it. Before he could pick it up, it stopped. We stood staring at it for a moment then heard Catty's voice calling my uncle's name from the great room.

We walked over and opened the door and I heard Catty say, "There is a telephone call for you, sir. It's Chief Inspector Rowan."

"Thank you, Catherine." He replied and closed the door. Striding over to the desk, he picked up the devise. "Hello, Chief Inspector. Have you any news?"

The smile slid off my uncle's face and he paled. "Oh, no…where…when did this happen? Have you determined a cause of death?"

I knew then that things went from bad to worse. Uncle Will listened for a few minutes, and then exploded into the mouthpiece. " Then it was foul play! Will you kindly dispense with that nonsense! Push those childish fairy tales from your head and THINK man! There is no monster!" He listened some more, all the while tapping his fingers on the desk and rolling his eyes. Finally, in exasperation, he said, "Very well, Chief. Where is he now? Excellent, I will meet you there as soon as possible. Good-bye." I could hear the phone click from the other end, but there was still noise coming out of the receiver. Instinctually, I knew it was the sound of Catty crying, and I was out the door before the other two reacted.

238

I dashed through the hallway next to the staircase and found Catty slumped on the floor next to the hutch, crying her eyes out and wailing like it was the end of the world. She didn't even seem to notice me as I knelt down next to her and put a hand on her shoulder. Uncle Will came up behind me and set the telephone receiver back in its cradle. I realized that she must have dropped the phone when she heard what Uncle Will and the inspector were talking about. She knew and cared for, whoever they had been discussing.

Uncle Will shouldered me aside and gently lifted Catty to her feet, whispering soothing words to her the entire time. She collapsed in his arms and sobbed her heart out. I look to Ozaki, who mouthed the word 'Marquis' and slid a finger across his throat.

Mrs. Wood, having heard the commotion, hustled out of the kitchen with motherly concern on her face. She looked to my Uncle, who said softly over the top of Catty's head, nearly just mouthing the words. "They found Marquis today…he's dead, I'm afraid."

The shock on Mrs. Wood's face was doubled when Catty pushed herself off of William's chest and snarled through her tears. "I heard what the Chief said! He was killed by the river monster; the one you said didn't exist!"

I wanted to put my arms around her and hold her close, but Mrs. Wood beat me to it, taking her by the shoulders and cooing at her to calm her down. After a moment, Catty regained her composure and said to my Uncle.

"Forgive me, Mr. Gillette. I know it wasn't your fault. I…I…just can't believe he's gone. What could have happened?" Again, she broke into tears.

Uncle Will put a gentle hand on her cheek and said, resolutely, "I do not know—yet! But I promise you Catherine, I will get to the bottom of this!"

239

"Come, Catty dear," Mrs. Wood said. "Why don't you sit down for a moment?" She went to lead her off to the kitchen, but Catty stopped and looked at me as if she saw me for the first time. Despite the audience, I took her hand and said gently, "I am so sorry Catty."

She nodded and put her hand on my cheek. "We'll talk later." Her eyes said everything she wanted to say to me. I nodded and Mrs. Wood led her away. I turned to my Uncle, who was looking at me speculatively. I think he was just starting to realize how wrong he was about Catty and me. I wanted to know what happened to her brother.

"Marquis was floating in the current this morning, parallel to the inlet where the pay roll robbery took place. He was dead from a serious wound."

"What kind of wound?" I asked. "Gun shot? Stabbing?"

William heaved a sigh and shook his head. "We will have to rely on Doctor Blum's report for that information." He sighed again, "Though the Inspector insisted that he was chewed on, of all things! Unfortunately, Catherine heard his most gruesome descriptions."

. "Chewed on? As in eaten by the river monster?"

"Do not waste your breath or my time on that drivel, Frohman. We need facts!" He turned Ozaki. "See that Mrs. Wood takes Catty home after she is settled and then meet us at the boat house."

Ozaki put his hand up and waved it in a negative gesture. "No. You two go on. There is much to do here." he hesitated and gave us both a stern look. "Take care of each other. Something very smelly is going on."

I smiled and patted my chest. "Don't worry, Uncle Ozaki, I have my gun."

He snorted. "Three days—three dead. You take two guns."

To make haste, we rode our bikes down to the docking area instead of taking the tram. We quickly readied the *Helena, Uncle Will's smaller boat,* and got underway, with me at the helm. Soon we found ourselves weaving our way through a small flotilla of boats. There were of all sizes and shapes, from rowboats to draggers. Every boat had men at the railings, looking out over the water and ready with everything from spears to shotguns. I even saw one man with a crossbow hiked to his shoulders. The river was so thick with craft, we could hardly go at a quarter throttle. The hunt for the river monster was in full swing!

"Damn, Uncle. Word spreads quickly in this town!" Then a thought occurred to me, though I was a bit embarrassed to voice it, "Why was Catty listening in anyways?"

"That was an accident, I think, Frohman. Catherine must have set the receiver down when she went to tell me of the Chief Inspector's call. I fear she did not replace the receiver when she returned to cleaning the vases on the hutch. She must have heard the Inspector tell me of her brother."

I shook my head and veered starboard to avoid a sailboat heading in our path. "I wonder who told all these men Marquis was killed by the monster!"

William replied, "That is the flaw of the telephone. Though I will attest they are a marvelous convenience, they are hardly private! It is quite possible the operator, herself, was listening in. I imagine most conversations between Rowan and me are prized for their gossip potential.

"I also doubt, very much, that whoever discovered Marquis were very discreet."

241

Just as we tied up at the now empty town dock and stepped onto the pier, shots rang out across the water and we looked over to see a group of boat converging on one spot and firing into the water with great abandon. When the gunfire tapered off, William shook head and turned away.

"Blithering Sapheads!"

22

Walking up from the pier as we rounded a building onto Main Street, we could see a small crowd of people milling about the front of the doctor's office. I recognized Catty's brothers among them, and William pointed out his parents to me. We surmised the family was waiting for the doctor to finish his examination so they could claim the body. No one had noticed us yet, so Uncle Will and I scooted across the street and made our way down the back of the buildings. I thought it unlike my uncle, not to say a word of solace to the family, but when I asked him about it, he muttered something about 'distractions'. I, myself, had no desire to meet Catty's parents just then. Not under these circumstances.

The door to Doctor Blum's office was locked, but, at William's soft knock, it opened a crack to reveal the Chief Inspector. After peering behind us to be sure we were alone, he opened the door enough for William and I to slip through, then locked it.

Again, the room smelled of death and chemicals. Doctor Blum was behind his desk and Rowan had flopped down in the visitor's chair. Each had a drink and I hoped they saved some for me.

I looked over to the curtained off area and saw the soles of Marquis's feet on the table through a gap. Though I can't say I had any fondness for him, I could feel pity for his dying so young and for the effect it would have on Catty and her family.

"Why the tight security?" my Uncle asked the Chief as he shed his gloves and hat. "Is that crowd out front giving you trouble?"

"No, nothing like that. I just want to keep a tight lid on this. Despite your denials, there is a killer in that river!"

I could see a smirk of disgust forming on my Uncle's face, but he said nothing as the Chief rambled on. "The only ones that know he was attacked so far are Gordon, the harbormaster — who saw Marquis floating on the water and fished the body out — and me! Thank God, the man had the sense to call me directly and together we brought the body here. I'm not worried about him, he'll keep his mouth shut if he wants to keep his job! Now, I just have to figure out how to break it to his family without starting a panic."

William kept a straight face, but I had to hide my smile behind my hands. William leaned on the edge of the desk and said, "Hmm...well...of course, you swore the telephone switchboard operator to secrecy. Otherwise..."

Rowan's eyes flew open and he sat up straight. "Oh, No!"

I couldn't resist needling him, "Oh yes! The river's so thick with monster hunters that we could hardly get through on the way over."

"And now the fools are shooting at anything that moves in the water." William added blandly.

"Damn it!" Rowan swore, before tossing back the rest of his drink. He jumped to his feet. "I'd better get out there before it gets another one! All hell will break loose!"

He turned to the doctor, "I want to see a written report on my desk by the end of tomorrow, Doc." He nodded to my uncle, "For once, I'm sorry to see you proven wrong, William."

244

Uncle Will shook his head in disgust, "You are not still going on about a rampant creature, are you?"

"Wait until you see the wounds, William." He looked over to the doctor. "Right, Tom?"

We all looked to him, but he just shrugged and sipped his drink. "I've never seen anything like it."

"Besides," Rowan turned his attention to me. "if he wasn't obviously a victim of some freak of nature, then I'd be pulling you down to the station for a few questions!"

"Me?" I protested, "Why me?"

He looked me straight in the eye. "I heard about your dust-up with him the other night. So, just where were you last night?"

The question caught me off guard and all I could think of was keeping Catty's name out of it. Thankfully, my uncle came to the rescue.

"I can vouch for Frohman. He was at my home until about ten o'clock last night then he spent the night on the *Aunt Polly*."

"How can you be sure he stayed on board?" Rowan asked. I don't think he really doubted my uncle's word, since he was convinced Marquis was killed by the monster, but he wanted to take a jab at me.

William didn't answer him, and the Inspector went on to say. "Doesn't matter. I know I'm right. Have a look and you'll see!" Rowan put his hat on and grabbed his coat, but before he could rush out, William stopped him.

"Where is Marquis's boat? Was it near the body?"

Rowan looked a bit set back, but he replied, "As a matter of fact it wasn't. We recovered the boat near Essex, a few miles down the river. It was drifting. The body was found upriver, about halfway between here and the train bridge. Gordon found him this morning when he was out surveying the moorings. The body... Marquis... was hung up near the shore. I figure he must have been pulled overboard before he could set an anchor...or run."

"So, where is his boat now?"

Rowan shrugged and checked his watch. "Most likely it's at the town dock by now. I sent Gordon to fetch it, so he'd be out of town and less likely to let the cat out of the bag." Then he remembered that the situation had gone way past that point. "I have to go. I'll talk with you later William." He was grimaced. "Last thing I need is trouble on the river tonight! The train is coming through in the wee hours and I need every man I have!"

Doc Blum looked up at my Uncle as soon as the Chief was gone. "Why so concerned about the boat, William?"

"I am not concerned about the boat, per se, but about its position. The fact that it drifted so far south tells me it must have been in the middle of the river, where the current is strongest. The victim, on the other hand, was found in the shallows, where the current is weakest."

I wasn't following his line of reasoning, "Are you saying that Marquis wasn't on his boat when he was killed?"

"Not at all Frohman. There is not enough data to form a hypothesis! Yet it does create a...calculated influence on the circumstances."

The doctor echoed my sentiments when he groused, "Whatever the hell that means!" as he heaved himself out of his seat.

"Let's get this over with!" Blum said gruffly. "Those folks out front are waiting."

"Just a minute!" I blurted out as I remembered something. "We saw his boat last night! It was drifting near sideways on the river about half-way between your place and the train bridge!"

"When?"

"Me and Catty saw it with the telescope just before it got dark. About eight or eight-fifteen."

"And neither of you thought it worth mentioning before now?" William asked, exasperated.

I ignored his tone and shrugged. "Catty didn't seem too worried. She thought Marquis was probably drunk and passed out."

"Did you see him?"

I shook my head. "No, but it was dim light and far from us. I figured he was in the cabin."

William turned to the doctor. "Have you determined a time of death?"

"Hard to say. Being submerged and, well, other factors made that difficult. I'd say he was dead sixteen hours or perhaps a bit more from the time he was brought in at ten this morning."

We all looked at our watches and counted back. Marquis was killed around the time we saw the boat or a little before! Within an hour or so anyway!

"Interesting!" was all William said to that. He looked to Blum. "What did you mean by 'other factors', Doctor?"

"Better if I show you." he replied and stepped over to pull the curtain open. I shuffled in after uncle and when I looked at the body, I wanted to run right back out. In fact, I wanted to run to the train station and go home to my mother! I won't be a hypocrite and say I cared one whit for the arrogant sod

247

stretched out on the slab, but I wouldn't wish to see any human in this shape. I couldn't make my feet carry any further than the end of the table. Not that it helped my stomach; I could see him clearly in his entirety.

He was bloated, as corpses will be after being in the water for a long time, but his skin was soft and doughy. It was an extremely pale gray in color, and it sagged to form creases that made it seem like it was melting. The only color was the darkened skin of his face and hands and the mop of wet black hair plastered to his skull. I was grateful the doctor had draped a sheet across his privates. I was trying to keep my gaze averted from his major wound until I could get my stomach to settle enough, and that's when I noticed the numerous marks all over his skin. I looked closer and saw the tiny divots taken out of his flesh. I knew what caused these, because I had seen them before, on chicken legs when I crabbed as a kid.

"Minnows"

Uncle Will glanced at me and the doctor said. "Exactly. Not bad for a city boy."

He pointed to the place I didn't want to look and said, "And those are nothing to what they did to the soft tissue of the wound."

Uncle Will walked around the head of the slab to get a better look but my legs turned to lead, and my bowels were following suit! I had seen a man gutted in a bar fight and that hadn't been half as gory as this.

On his left side, just above his waist and inches from his side was a gaping wound. It was at least twelve inches long and seven wide, with thin strips of shredded skin draped about it like a drunken bakers icing. Everything was exposed but I couldn't tell you what was intestine or what was organ. The only thing that kept the whole mess from spilling onto the table was a strip of intact skin that ran directly along his side. It all

248

looked like it went through a grinder. Marquis's body seemed to have a coating of fur on it. I knew it wasn't hair, but the fine shredding from a multitude of tiny mouths feeding on the soft innards.

"Gordon said he never saw so many minnows feeding in one spot." Blum said sadly. "I hate to turn him over to his folks like this." He sighed and shook his head.

William didn't respond to him, for of course, he had his trusty pocket magnifier out and was going over every inch. There was nothing to do but wait for him to finish. Blum and I looked at each other and we both rolled our eyes, but we stayed silent. After a long few minutes, William stood and addressed the Doctor.

"It does not appear that you probed too deeply into the wound, Doctor."

Blum was slightly offended. "No need. Whatever got him before the minnows chewed him up enough to kill him, but that's not what he died of! He drowned, just like the other fellow, the pilot. Lungs were intact and full of water."

My uncle didn't say anything, so I chimed in. "Gee, Doc, if he was floating around dead for half a day, why wouldn't he be full of water?"

"Incorrect." William said. "If you were to toss a corpse into water, the air in the lungs would be trapped because there would be no breathing cycle. One must physically suck in water to fill the lungs." He turned to the doctor. "Is your theory that something bit down on him and held him under until he drowned?"

Blum squared his shoulders and gave my uncle a withering look. "I am saying that he drowned." He pointed at the wound, "But something turned his side into a mince pie! There are pieces of his kidney, stomach, and both large and small intestine severed and mixed together and there is a matching wound on his back! I've never seen such damage to the human body! Even a deer is dressed out with far less damage to the internal organs."

·Uncle Will, true to form, ignored the doctor. I could tell he was restraining himself from blasting Blum for even considering a creature caused the wound. He looked closely again and stood.

"Shall we roll him on his side? I wish to see the damage in its entirety."

The doctor grunted and put a hand under the shoulder next to him as William slid a hand under the thigh. They rolled him in my direction, but the body, in its stiffness, refused to stay in position

"Frohman! Move the left leg away until it touches the table."

The last thing I wanted to do was touch that cold dead flesh, but I managed to find the gumption to reach over and grasp him by the left ankle. It felt like a raw chicken in my hand, but I did as I was asked, and the body settled in place.

The back looked worse than the front. There was an exit wound, even bigger in diameter. I could only image one thing that could have wrought such mayhem.

"Must have gotten caught in his prop." I observed, trying to sound as sage-like as possible.

My smugness vanished immediately as my uncle replied in less than a heartbeat.

"Rubbish! A craft of Marquis's size would have an engine with the horsepower to turn a propeller of at least eighteen inches! Much too large for this opening and not nearly long enough!" He turned his head and gave me a withering look, "Do try to think things through before you speak, Frohman."

He turned back to his examination before I could retort.

Uncle Will; with magnifier in hand, he bent over to examine that side as he did the first. Without looking up, he held out a hand. "Might I borrow two of your probes, Doctor?"

Blum hesitated. "I'm not so sure that would be ethical, William. I owe it to his folks to see he's treated with respect."

William kept his gaze on the wound and flexed his hand. "Come now, Doctor, matters have progressed far past the delicate stage."

Blum sighed and fished about on his tray to find two long metal sticks that he slapped into William's hand. Uncle Will put his glass down and, with rods in both hands, proceeded to root about.

Some blood slowly oozed out and bit and pieces of undistinguishable anatomy plopped onto the table. Blum winced and I had to swallow down some bile that rose into my throat. William dug deeper and deeper and spread the probes farther and farther apart until, thank the stars, he was satisfied. He left the probes deep inside the wound but straightened and addressed the doctor. "Ha! Your monster must be somewhat civilized. He appears to have used a knife and fork!" William picked up his magnifier and held it a few inches away from the probes, gesturing for the doctor to take a look.

Blum recoiled in surprise then quickly bent over to look. Holding the glass with his left, he manipulated a probe with his right. Suddenly he gasped after a few more moments of study. It was obvious that he ignored the gloating look on my Uncle's face and said to me, "He's right. There are cuts deeper, sheer and straight — definitely from a sharp edge!" He pondered the discovery for a moment, and then turned to my uncle. "But that doesn't make sense! If it were a blade that did this, it would not have caused all that damage. I've seen a few knife wounds, even stitched up a farmer who fell on his aerator! He was all cut up inside, but his innards stayed in place!"

Uncle Will didn't respond right away. Finally, he spoke. "I shall have to consider the matter." He got that faraway look again then shook his head and got back to business. "Where are his personal effects?"

"There wasn't anything but what he had on." Blum replied. "They're over on that counter. "William walked over and plucked a swath of white cloth off the surface and shook it out. He found himself holding a pair of thick long johns with a red rimmed tear in the left side.

"Is there nothing else?"

Blum shrugged and shook his head. "All he was wearing was those and a pair of woolen socks when he was brought in." He looked dumbfounded for a moment. "Didn't think much of it at the time, but it's strange that's all he had on …kind of warm for long johns and woolen socks, isn't it?"

William tossed the clothing back on the counter and said to Blum. "We shall let you get on with your duties, Doctor. We shall see you tomorrow at the funeral. Nine a.m. sharp!"

I barely had time to say good-bye to Doctor Blum before following my uncle out.

23

"Where to now?" I asked my uncle as we struck out, keeping behind the buildings to stay out of sight. I was hoping he would say 'The Inn'. I was in desperate need of a double after that ordeal. Alas, I had to suffer a little disappointment. Little, because I still had my flask, which I took out and upended.

"To the town dock, Frohman. I wish to examine Marquis's boat, if it is there."

Still a hundred yards away we see the dock was empty with two boats approaching about thirty yards out. By the time we stepped off the shore, Marquis's boat was pulling up alongside the pier. The man piloting her had a rope in one hand and was angling to one of the pylons. I ran over and gestured for him to toss me the line, which I caught and tied off. Then I ran to the bow and jumped aboard grabbing the bow line and leapt back onto the dock to secure it. The Pilot shut down the engine and stepped onto the dock. He checked the aft line and was satisfied it was right. He smiled and nodded as I stepped up to him. "You know your way around boats."

I shrugged. "I spent my summers on South Fork growing up."

The man talking was about my age with a somewhat weathered complexion. He was solidly built with longish hair and a closely cropped beard. He also looked amused. "Sailing? Yachting?"

"I wish!" I sniggered. "Trap fishing, but mostly cutting bait and sorting catches."

He smiled even wider as he looked my hundred dollar suit up and down. "Fishing must be good lately!"

I liked him on the spot. I stuck out my hand, "Collin Frohman."

"Gordon Steele. I'm the harbor master here. I think we may have met once before briefly"

"Could be," I started.

"NOW that we are all good friends," William nearly barked from our side. "perhaps we can get down to brass tacks! I understand you recovered the vessel in Essex. Did it get there under its own power?"

The Harbormaster thought about it for a moment and replied. "No, I don't think so. The current would have taken her that far. She'd have been in the sound if she was underway. The engines were dead cold when I started her up to bring her back."

My uncle nodded. "I wish to examine the boat."

Gordon looked up and squinted in the afternoon sun. "Did Rowan send you down here?"

There was something perfunctory about the way he asked, and I countered, "Do you really care?"

"Not in the least."

William snorted, and looking exasperated, stepped past us and onto the boat. Gordon looked at me as if expecting me to follow, but I reached into my jacket and took out my flask. I knew my uncle would want a moment to look about alone. Besides, I owed Gordon something for my uncle's abruptness.

"Snort?" I offered.

"Thank you," he replied as he took the flask. "It was a long trip to Essex and back.." He took a long pull and sighed with satisfaction. "That's good hooch! Thanks again." He handed it back to me.

I took a pull myself and capped it. I gestured with my head towards my Uncle who was busy roaming around the boat. "Sorry if my William was rude."

Gordon leaned in and said from the corner of his mouth so William couldn't hear. "I have seen him this way before. It's kind of neato. Like seeing him in a play for free!"

"Let's go then." I winked. "We have front row seats today!"

When we stepped onto the aft deck, William was below in the cabin, rummaging around. Looking around, I could see that Marquis kept his boat in good shape. The lines were coiled neatly, the deck free of debris, and, if not gleaming, the brass was clean. I turned my attention to the small derrick, mounted at the very stern.

It was a simple structure of three steel poles that formed a pyramid about seven feet off the deck. At the top was attached an arm on a large swivel. In its former life, it was used to haul up traps or nets and if you ever had to do it by hand over hand for a hundred feet of line — as my grandfather made me do — you could appreciate its usefulness. I'm sure it saved a lot of back breaking work for Marquis and allowed him to work alone and keep all the profits. My estimation of him went up a notch and again when I saw a clever little trick he had employed. I picked up a thin line that led me to the lever that activated the gears that drove the winch. I imagined that it allowed him to start the lifting process from almost anywhere on the boat. Handy if you had to work the engines to parlay the weight of wherever you were loading.

255

"Ha!" William barked as he climbed out of the cabin and saw me. "You have found it for yourself, Frohman! Excellent. Be sure to make a mental note of that line."

I tried to work out its importance on my own but was stymied. I turned to ask my uncle for and explanation, but he was already across the deck, sitting on his heels and examining a length of chain. When I came up behind him, I saw that he was holding up and end of a chain with a yoke like piece of metal welded to it. On each tip of the prongs a hole was drilled that aligned with the other. I had seen a fastener like it before. You slipped the yoke over a pipe or dowel and slipped a pin through the holes to keep it in place. It didn't seem out of place, especially since the length of chain it was attached to a three-pronged anchor on the other end. Marquis probably used it on the bow or stern, depending on the current while he was moored. Then I looked a little harder and saw some red streaks on the tips of the anchor.

"God damn! Is that blood on the anchor?" I pointed, wondering if that's what killed Marquis.

William rose to his full height, still holding the chain and scowled down at me. "I never broke your father of the habit, but YOU, young Frohman, will not blaspheme in my presence!"

I held up my hands in surrender and mumbled an apology.

He frowned and said, "Of course it is not blood. Blood does not dry to such a bright shade of red."

I didn't have time to ask him more, since he wheeled and addressed Gordon. "Before matters progress any father, I intend to immediately claim my property." He gestured to the inside of the cabin and me and the Harbormaster both looked. Stacked neatly to one side of the room lay stacked eight cases of Coca-Cola. Even though I remembered my Uncle and Marquis discussing the deal at the doctor's office, I was

256

surprised he would bring it up now. Gordon looked uncomfortable and dubious.

"You'll have to take that up with the Chief Inspector, Mr. Gillette."

"You can take it up with the Chief Inspector, if you feel you must. I shall take the Coca-Cola when I leave." He replied firmly. Then he simply dismissed the discussion and walked over to a large box that sat alongside the port rail and asked Gordon, "What might you know about this?"

Gordon and I ambled over to join him. It was a square box, about three feet by two feet, and three feet tall. Three holes drilled into the top, two were a few inches in diameter and the last a full six. Hasps mounted to the deck on all four sides to keep it in place. I was sure it was obviously an engine cover, but I was mistaken.

"That's a pump under the cover. I helped Marquis get it onboard about two months ago. Damn thing weighed a ton!" He squinted at my Uncle, "He told me he got the idea from you. Said he was going to use it to pump air into the bilges if the hull was ever breeched. I thought it pretty clever."

William tapped the top. "Open it."

Gordon bristled at being ordered about so, and I just shrugged and winked at him, patting my flask inside my Jacket pocket. Together, we each unlatched two sides and lifted the cover. Then we nearly dropped it.

There was nothing there but an outline with a hole at each corner. We stepped towards the starboard and set the cover down. I was surprised to see it was lined with blankets, held in place by strips of wood. Gordon was staring at the empty space and scratching his head.

William said, in a bland voice. "You were saying?"

257

Gordon looked like he was kicked by a mule. "I don't know what to say. I can't think of a reason why Marquis would get rid of it after all the trouble to buy it and put it on board!"

"Marquis could not have removed it. He didn't have the time." William stated, as if it were gospel.

"You think somebody stole it?" I asked, not sure what he meant by his last comment.

"Even if somebody wanted to steal it...How?" Gordon blurted out. "Sweet Christmas! Even his dragger couldn't lift it! We had to slide it down thick planks and even then, we used the dragger to take off some weight and keep it level. Then we lag bolted it to the deck! I can't fathom how he got it off! He'd need ten men!"

"When was the last time you were SURE it was on board?" William asked.

Gordon mulled that over. "I'd say…about four days ago. Yes! That's right. I came out of my office one day and he was tied up at the dock and was tinkering with it. He had a couple of those barge rats with him, so I just left him to it."

"Folks around here don't seem to like the barge crew much, do they?" I observed. "No one's got anything nice to say about them."

Gordon shrugged. "They're a rude lot and none to friendly themselves. Keep to themselves on their little steel island. Though, I have to admit, the boss is better. He was polite to me anyways when he came and bought some sounding charts. He looked like a bum, but he spoke like a gentleman."

William was silent for a moment then came alive. "I have seen enough. Thank you for your time Gordon. I will collect my property and be on my way. Come Collin, lend me some of that youthful vigor!"

He went right to the hatchway and descended. I could see Gordon struggling with his conscience, but I went to help my uncle anyways. William grabbed a case and handed it up to me, then got another for himself and brought it up on deck. I thought for a moment that Gordon was going to protest, but he just sighed as William walked past him and climbed up onto the dock. He looked to me and I gave him a face that said, 'What's a fella to do?' Gordon grabbed two cases and followed us to the launch.

By the time we made our second trip for the rest, I was grousing in my head that we should have been concentrating on whoever—or whatever—killed Marquis instead of worrying about a bottled drink that wasn't even alcoholic!

When we were loaded, I took out my flask and Gordon and I drained it while saying our good-byes. William didn't partake, but instead saw to starting the *Helena* and making ready to get under way. As soon as I tossed the lines aboard and stepped on the deck, he shoved the throttles forward and we headed out. The Chief Inspector must have sent out a squad, because most of the traffic was gone and nobody was shooting at minnows with a shotgun.

I walked over to stand next to my uncle. He looked very pleased with himself as he steered the boat with one hand and rested his other arm on a stack of Coca-Cola."

"You know, you never paid for that soda, so they are not really yours." I observed, just to tease him.

"Ha!" He replied grandly. "I'll see to it that his family receives payment!" He looked up at me from his seat and grinned. "It would have been a shame to waste it on the Chief Inspector and his men!"

24

Uncle Will was silent for the rest of the trip. I knew by then he was in one of his thinking moods, so I let him be. Even after we got to the castle, he excused himself and went to his study alone. After, of course, he saw to his precious drink.

I made my way to the bar and had a drink, refilling my flask while I was there. Mrs. Wood had not returned from taking Catty home and Ozaki had made himself scarce, so I just sat in the conservatory and sipped the rest of the afternoon away. Brooding mostly, as I railed against the circumstances that kept Catty away. I was surprised at how much I missed her company. After a few hours, I realized I was almost three sheets to the wind so I made my way to my room and took a nap. The dinner bell pulled me out of a groggy slumber.

Ozaki prepared and served us dinner around eight o'clock that night, as was the custom here. It was simple fare but filling and just what I needed to get back to an even keel. When I brought up the mysteries all around us, William delayed any discussion until after dinner. In fact, he was silent for most of the meal. I almost thought he might have a glass when Ozaki put the opened wine bottle on the table. He didn't and someone had to be polite so I took wine with dinner, but just one glass, as I wanted to be alert when we discussed the day's event over brandy and a smoke.

With the girls gone, it fell to us to carry our own plates and utensils to the washing sink. I would have washed them, but

Ozaki told us to leave them to soak and shooed us out of the kitchen so he could put the rest away.

William led me out to the great room where we settled into a pair of wing back chairs that generally faced the great fireplace. I had a cigarette but was delighted to see William amble over to the stone wall and pull a curved briar pipe from between two of the stones. There wasn't a tobacco filled slipper to go with it, but I chuckled when he produced a sock stuffed with his favorite brand. I waited until he took his seat and had a good head on his bowl before I asked,

"So, what's our next move, Uncle?"

He blew a few more thick clouds of smoke before he answered. "Patience, Frohman. Our next move is to exercise patience. There are several points I am still considering, but I am fairly confident I know how the murder and robbery of the payroll was committed and by whom. But there are still a few threads in this tapestry we need to unravel."

I wanted to pounce on his theory, but I knew he wouldn't be any more forthcoming. I decided to try another track. "Any revelations about the baby?"

"None, save the fact that I believe that both crimes are connected in a way, though I confess that I am not sure how."

That statement, I thought, was a bit far-fetched. "C'mon now, Uncle Will! How could they possibly be related?"

He puffed away and gave me a sly smile as he answered. "Such negativity will never do! You will never see a solution unless you keep an open mind, Frohman."

I thought about that while I smoked and took a long pull on my drink. "That's a load of manure, William."

He barked a laugh and sat forward. "Very well then, Frohman. I will give you four points to ponder between now

261

and until after the child's funeral tomorrow, at which point, we will follow a few threads until we arrive at an answer. Though I fear, we have not seen the rest of this play unfolding about us. There is still another act, unknown in nature, which worries me!"

I knew it was the most I would get out of him until tomorrow and his enthusiasm was contagious, so I agreed.

"Excellent! Now, point number one—Marquis was wearing nothing but long johns and woolen socks when he was pulled from the river. Number two—the payroll was returned untouched. Number three—the missing machinery from Marquis's boat. Last, but not least, number four—there were eight cases of Coca-Cola in his hold." He sat back with that smug look my father described as his 'spit-in-your-eye' smirk.

I was too mellow for the complexities of the first three points, but the last stuck a chord. I remembered something Marquis said, and Catty echoed earlier at lunch. "Eight cases? I thought Marquis could only get six at a time?"

William's eyes flew open, and he plucked the pipe from his mouth as he broke out with a great grin. "Bully for you, Frohman!"

"Marquis was always adamant that six cases were all he was allowed out of the warehouse per visit."

"Then what did he do with the other two? Catty said he hated the stuff!"

I never got my answer because suddenly Ozaki appeared like a wraith to stand between uncle and me, at the edge of the gaslight. He was rigid in his stance, with arms crossed over his chest and a scowl on his face that made him demonic looking in the dancing shadows. "Enough talk of murder and mayhem! We have famiry business to discuss!"

William suddenly looked stern and pulled the pipe from his mouth. Pointing the stem at me, he said in a lecturing tone, "I am very disappointed at your behavior towards Catherine, Collin. She is very special to us and has been through great personal drama this past year. I realize that you are both consenting adults and have seen this type of thing happen countless times in my career, but she deserves better than being seduced and eventually left behind when you leave.

"I thought better of your morals and your common sense. Your little tet-e-tet is going to have an effect us all for the worse in the end!"

I sat there stunned. I didn't know whether to squat or wind my watch, as my father used to say. He was so far off base it was laughable. I felt my temper starting to flare and I groped around my head for the words to explain what really happened in a good light, "Look, Uncle Will, I'm sorry if you think I was out of line with Catty but the truth is…"

Ozaki didn't let me finish. He planted his hands on his hips and glared down at me. "No buts! You have disgraced yourseve, your famiry, your uncle…and your father's memory!"

I snapped. It was bad enough they were forcing me to say things I didn't want to reveal before I could tell them to Catty, but I wasn't about to be berated for them. And he should have never brought my father up!I leapt to my feet and squared off with Ozaki. "SHUT UP!" I hollered at the top of my lungs. When William went to protest, I snarled at him. "Both of you! Neither one of you know what the hell you're talking about, so, listen and listen good! Whatever has occurred between Catty and me…is occurring…or will occur is nobody's business but our own and it's going to stay that way until, if and when, WE decide to share it! Got that?"

Both were too stunned to reply to my outburst and the looks of hurt and confusion on their faces drained the anger from me like pulling the plug on the bathtub. Only anger drains slower than water. This conversation had gone badly, and I needed to get away.

Between clenched teeth I said, "I'm tired, I think I'll retire now. Goodnight."

I turned and quickly walked to the staircase. Neither one of them said a word. There was dead silence as I walked to the second story balcony to my room. I snuck a peek at them from the corner of my eye and they were both staring at me, slack jawed, until I went into my room and shut the door behind me.

I was still angry and I began stuffing my things into my valise, sure that I was no longer welcome at my uncle's home. But as I went along, I thought of Catty and her grief, the baby's funeral, and the cases we were working on. My thoughts got so clogged; I finally put my flask on the nightstand and got undressed to hop between the sheets.

25

I was up early enough to wash up and dress before there was
a gentle knock on my door. I called out for whoever to enter
and the door opened to reveal my Uncle.

"Oh, good. I see that you're almost ready."

None of last night's harshness showed in his manner, but I
reminded myself that he was an actor. He stepped inside and
gently shut the door. I had but to look at him and I felt a bit
ashamed over my behavior the night before. "I'm sorry I
shouted at you and Uncle Ozaki last night, Uncle Will. I... I
wish I could make you understand…"

"No, Collin," He waved a hand in a negative gesture. "It is I
who owe you an apology. I let my emotions cloud my
judgement and I made rash statements with no basis in fact.

"I am fond of Catherine, yes, but no fonder than I am of you.
You are both sensible adults and it shall be as you said last
night. You shall have your privacy." He glanced over and saw
my overflowing valise and he looked crestfallen. "Are you
leaving us, Collin? Did we anger you so much? I had hoped
you would at least stay and accompany me to Marquis's
funeral, the day after tomorrow."

"Of course, I'll stay Uncle Will." I wanted to say more, but
tears were welling in my eyes and I threw my arms around him.
He hugged me back then pushed me out to arm's length. He
was grinning from ear to ear. "That's settled then! Since you're

ready, I suggest we grab a cup of coffee before we head to the cemetery."

As we walked towards the stairs, a thought occurred to me. "You said you would give us our privacy...what about Ozaki?"

William smirked and replied. "Him...you may have to fight him!" He laughed at the look on my face and added, "Just don't shoot him! He's vital to my day to day operations."

Reconciliation with Ozaki would be a longer road. When we came face to face, no matter how I apologized and despite my assurances that I had no intentions of disgracing anyone, his only response was a hard look and him muttering something about, "See what the future brings." At least he gave me a cup of coffee. Halfway through a second cup, William checked his watch and declared it was time to make our way down to the *Helena*.

Because of Ozaki's aversion to motorized vehicles, we rode the tram down to the dock. As soon as we began our decent, the old machinery began to buck, as if the gears were slipping and catching out of sync.

"Ozaki," William proclaimed loudly patting the railing in front of us, "I think it may be time to retire the old girl!", as if it were a living entity. We dropped a good foot or so just then, before the gears engaged and steadied descent. He said to me over Ozaki's head, "She hasn't been the same since she crashed last year."

I knew my Uncle was just trying to get a rise out of me, as he loved to do to my father, but I wouldn't take the bait. I acted totally unconcerned though I did make sure I could reach one of the guide ropes in case the bottom dropped out from under us.

The river was flat as glass this early morning and the warm spring air caused a mist to rise that made me think of the River

Styx. Ozaki drove the boat while Uncle Will and I sat on the side benches and looked out over the river. There was no other boat traffic, but the air was so still, we could hear some machinery working on the barge downriver. A funny thought popped into my head as I gazed at the water and I half chuckled to myself.

"Something amusing, Collin?" William asked me, with a little chiding in his tone.

I shrugged, "I just thought how ironic it would be if some great beast surfaced right now."

William sniffed. "It will be so good to dispel the Chief Inspector of that ridiculous notion!" he grinned mischievously, "I can't wait to see the look on his face when I present him with some hard facts to ponder."

"Facts? Not a solution?"

He shook his head firmly. "That, I will not hand him on a silver platter. Not after the way he has clung to his fantasies!"

That said, he looked away and stared off into space. I knew I'd have to wait again. In the silence, I started to review the four points my Uncle had challenged me with before our argument, or rather, my outburst last night. I hadn't made any progress with even the first one when the sound of our motor changed, and we began to slow down.

Ozaki shifted the boat into neutral and Uncle Will and I stood to find the *Helena* gliding up to a rickety dock. I saw rows of head stones behind the sparsely leafed bushes that grew in a rough hedge along the riverbank. Uncle Will got the stern line and I the bow. We tied her off and I was waiting for Ozaki to join us, but Uncle Will took me by the arm gently and led me down the dock.

267

"Ozaki won't come. He's staying with the boat." He didn't offer any further explanation, but I knew the old man had his own set of ethics he rigidly adhered to.

About a hundred yards from where we stepped onto the turf, there was parked a hearse, it's all black team contentedly munching on the spring grass. Next to the back stood a distinguished looking gentleman, also in black, and a workman holding a spade in front of him. Ten yards closer to us and to the right stood the Doctor and the preacher. A small box lay at their feet, next to a small hole in the ground.

It was a well-kept resting place, the ground free of sticks and leaves. The budding Oaks, Elms, and Maples were straight and spaced nicely. The property bordered the river for a half mile and was flat as a flap jack.

We arrived at the grave and shook hands all around. After a moment of awkward silence, the Reverend asked, "Would anyone like to say a word before I perform the ceremony?"

William cleared his throat and stepped forward. When he bowed his head, we all followed suit.

"We beseech you, o' lord, to take this child into your grace. She never had the chance to grow…to be loved…or even, perhaps have a child of her own to love one day. Her sole purpose on this earth was to show us all; the gravity of life. May she rest in your arms."

We all said 'amen' and looked to the preacher, who seemed a bit flustered. Uncle Will was a hard act to follow.

The preacher opened his bible to a marked passage and began to drone on in scripture. As he went on and on in a low monotone, I began to hear wailing in the distance that seemed to grow louder by the second. When it was loud enough, the horses behind us began to prance nervously, shaking the glass of the hearse. I looked over my shoulder to see the undertaker using his considerable weight to keep his horses from rearing and bolting as the noise got loud enough to drown out the preacher's voice.

We were all looking at the road and the gospel had dried up altogether when a police sedan passed through the gates, lights flashing and siren at full blast. It screeched to a stop in front of the hearse and the passenger door opened and the Chief Inspector walked as fast as dignity would allow toward us.

Uncle Will, obviously vexed, turned to face him, feet planted firmly and leaning on the cane in front of him with both hands. "What is the meaning of this? We are trying to bury this child!"

Rowan had the good grace to go red-faced at the rebuke. "I'm sorry, William." He looked around at all of us and stammered, "It's important...something has happened and I need to speak to you about it...I mean...I'd like your advice..."

William sighed and replied, "Calm yourself, Chief Inspector. Organize your thoughts and we will speak as soon as we are finished here." Without waiting for a reply, he turned back to the grave and said, "Reverend?"

I guess he wasn't used to interruptions. He fumbled with his bible for a moment, and then gave up. "Um...ashes to ashes, dust to dust. Amen."

We all echoed them then gathered around the Chief in anticipation. William posed the question, "Now, what is so important you felt the need to interrupt this ceremony?"

"The train was robbed! Somewhere between New London and Chester the strong box disappeared!" He pulled off his hat and ran a hand through his hair. "That stretch was my responsibility, William! I'll be lucky if they let me be a janitor on the force after this!"

"Tell me everything you know quickly and concisely. What was stolen, where it was kept, and when it was discovered missing."

The chief seemed to find some reassurance in my Uncle's manner and he answered in a calm, professional voice. "I was never told the contents, but they were locked in a steel case, three feet by two feet and eight inches deep. As you already know, it was being transported from Boston to Washington. The case was locked in the conductor's office car with two Federal agents on guard. The passenger cars on both sides of the office car were each filled with a squad of marines.

"The train stopped in New London, where two more federal agents boarded the train. They had the proper identification and they offered to take a watch. The first set of Agents from Boston took the opportunity to have dinner in the club car. When train reached the Chester Station, the train made a scheduled stop for water and coal. The original set of Agents, having finished their supper, returned to the conductor's office—to find their relief Agents missing, and the box was gone!"

We opened our mouths to state the obvious, but Rowan held up a hand to forestall us. "It must have been perfect timing because the first set of agents came out the door towards the rear of the train, just before the second set entered from the front. They told the officer in charge of the soldiers that they relieved and were going to stretch their legs. "He paused and spoke slowly, so there was no misunderstanding.

"Neither man was carrying anything, and they weren't wearing overcoats they could have concealed under -- if that's even possible with a three- foot steel box! It must have weighed a ton!

"By the time the theft was discovered, the first two agents had disappeared. One eyewitness said they may have seen the two walking down to the road and get into a waiting automobile. In any case, they have vanished." He sighed and looked somber. "I just got word before I came to find you, that the two real Federals were found in New London–murdered and stuffed under a blanket in the back seat of a car at the train station there."

A thought came to my mind, one I thought was clever. "Maybe…" I drew it out for dramatics, "it never left the train. Perhaps they hid it somewhere and planned on coming back for it later!"

I was pleased to see my Uncle raise his eyebrows in admiration of my logic, but Rowan quickly shot me down.

"Not a chance, Watson! They near tore that train down to its frame by now and the case hasn't turned up!"

I was about to snap a jibe back at the chief for the 'Watson', but William patted me on the back and murmured; "It was a clever thought, Frohman."

William gave the chief a hard look and said. "Of course, you must have considered that they could have passed the case off to someone else."

Rowan shook his head emphatically. "I already thought of that! I had men stationed on both sides of the tracks at Chester and there were a lot of soldiers walking about, stretching their legs. It couldn't have happened while the train was stopped."

That didn't leave much. So, I put in, "They must have tossed it to someone on the way."

"A heavy black box? Tossed off a speeding train in darkness? Why would someone go to all the trouble and risk of murdering, then impersonating Federal agents, stroll through twenty-five armed soldiers, just to take a chance like that? It was too well planned to culminate in a random act." Rowan responded, and then sighed.

"Besides, I had men patrolling the tracks on horseback while the train was passing through my jurisdiction. Each one saw the train pass at some point, and none saw anyone near the tracks. When I first got the news, a few hours ago, I sent for and deputized Frank Chapman. He and a couple of my men examined both sides of the track from New London to Chester. He just reported to me before I came here. He found no sign of anyone but my men for as far out as he looked on either side!"

That did it for me. I was confident that if Frank said no one else approached the tracks, I would take it for gospel! I was completely baffled, and I turned to my uncle to get his reaction. I didn't bother to open my mouth.

Uncle Will was staring out into the sky as if the world had faded away for him. I expected the Chief Inspector or the doctor to say something, but they were a tight lipped as I was, each knowing about William's way when he pondered a problem. I stepped away from the group and lit a cigarette. I puffed away watching my uncle until I tossed the butt on the grass and ground it in with the heel of my boot.

Suddenly, William came alive like a drowning man finally getting a breath of air. You could feel his intensity like the air before a lightning strike.

"Frohman! Run ahead to the dock. Have Ozaki get us underway as soon as possible. Chief Inspector—to the *Helena*!"

Rowan obeyed without question, so much was his faith in my Uncle, and I couldn't do less than follow suit, so I turned and bolted towards the river. The doctor made like he was to join us, but William took his arm to stop him. "Doctor, I need you to go back with the police car and tell the Sargent to send the launch."

"Tell him not to dawdle," he called out over his shoulder at the dazed Doctor as he broke into a trot. "and tell the Sargent to bring as many men as he can!"

26

With me undoing the lines and Ozaki starting up the engine, the *Helena* was roaring across the water, at full throttle. William leaned over to give Ozaki directions above the noise of the engines and pointed towards the train bridge. Rowan, clutching the side of the wind screen, looked uncertain about the situation and was bursting for an explanation of our impromptu departure.

"What are you about, Gillette?" He shouted above the din. "Why are we heading for the bridge?"

"Not the bridge, Inspector — the barge! If I'm right, we may be in time to recover the stolen item and," he smirked smugly, "find the answer to Marquis's demise!"

That brought on another slew of questions from the Chief, but William ignored him, concentrating on the barge. The first thing I noticed was that it wasn't at its usual mooring. The engines were chugging loudly, black smoke belching from its exhaust ports, as it slowly moved towards the center of the river, almost directly under the bridge.

Around four hundred yards out, I could see two men on the deck. One was standing next to a piece of machinery that was putting along for all it was worth, while the second, older man stood near a crane. I recognized the two as the men who were at the Inn with Marquis on the night I trounced him.

When we were two hundred yards out, the older man by the crane, saw us approaching and shouted to the second man as he stepped towards the cabin. The man crouched down behind the machine and when he rose, he was pointing a rifle at us. I saw the puff of smoke from the barrel but could hear no report over the roar of the *Helena's* engines at full throttle. I only heard the ugly whine of the bullet pass over our heads –uncomfortable close.

Ozaki cut the throttle immediately, and as we slowed the Chief Inspector rose to his full height and growled, "How dare he fire a warning shot at us! He'll regret that!"

He cupped his hands around his mouth and shouted at the top of his lungs, "Cease firing! This is the police! Prepare to be boarded!" He turned to us with a half a grin on his lips, "I've always wanted to say that!"

The grin dropped off his mug when William shouted a warning and another shot rang out. This slug smashed right through the center pane of the wind screen and passed between me and my Uncle. The glass exploded everywhere, but luckily, only Ozaki got a small cut on his ear before he slid out of the seat to crouch behind the wheel. The man who shot at us ducked behind the machine again and I could see the barrel was sticking up. I knew he would be reloading.

Rowan, to his credit, wasn't going to let that happen. He pulled his thirty-eight from its holster and started blasting away in a measured staccato. It was too far for him to do any damage, but it did keep the man down. When the hammer clicked on an empty chamber, Rowan immediately ducked down to reload, but that was what the man was waiting for. When the echo from the last shot faded, the man rose and took aim once more.

William barked. "Frohman!" but I had already pulled my piece. Steadying my right hand with my left, I judged the roll of the boat and sighted at the tip of the rifle barrel pointed at us.

275

I squeezed the trigger and the man snapped backwards then crumbled to the deck like a sack of dropped potatoes.

We were no more than twenty yards away by then and I swung my gun at the older man. Rowan reloaded by then and had his weapon at the ready.

"Put your hands up and stay where you are!" he ordered.

The Captain looked over at his downed companion, then back to us before darting to the cabin. He pulled open a door and quickly disappeared inside.

Rowan looked over at us and asked, "Where does he think he's going to hide?"

Ozaki expertly pulled alongside the barge and Rowan leapt off to rush to the door the man had disappeared into. I grabbed a stern line and looped it over a cleat on the deck then made sure my uncle wasn't injured. We made a quick check on Ozaki, who waved us off with a grunt. The three of us stepped onto the gunnel then leapt onto the barge.

Rowan was pounding away on the door of the cabin, demanding that whoever was inside to come out with their hands up. His words were lost on me as I approached the still chugging machinery with my pistol ready. Every part of me was focused on the man lying behind it. I saw his feet first and hesitated, but nothing moved so I walked in a wide circle around the machine until I could see him entirely. As I got nearer, I realized that my pistol was no longer necessary. He was lying on his back, staring sightlessly into the bright spring sunshine. Standing over him, I saw a ragged hole in his head, just above his left eye, and a fast spreading pool of blood on the deck beneath his head. My mouth went dry and my heart hammered in my chest when I realized what I had done. I stiffened from head to toe and I could see the barrel of my pistol bob up and down as I began to tremble. It was Ozaki who brought me to my senses. He stepped between me and the body and gave me a slight bow. "Thank you. You saved our rives."

Suddenly, I felt no real remorse. When I thought of either of my uncles taking a bullet from his rifle, I was glad my aim was true. I had no more time to dwell on it then, as the Chief had given up on yelling and was trying to kick the door in. Uncle Will stood still, taking it all in. His gaze went from the machinery to the crane and then out onto the water.

Rowan gave up trying to muscle the door and put three shots into the lock to blow the handle off. Suddenly, a sound of an engine erupted from within the cabin and William shouted a warning and pointed to the front of the barge. I rushed around the side to the gangway in time to see hidden doors open and the bow of a boat appear from within cabin area. Soon it was ten yards out and was picking up speed when I reached the bow. I lined up a shot and could have plugged the Captain easily, but there was nothing to hit but the back of his head.

Rowan ran up next to me and started shooting away, but the boat was fast and began to weave after the first pop. It was a thin, low draft boat about fifteen feet long, the last ten feet of the back was an open engine big enough to push a vessel four times its size, the front was little more than a wind screen and a sunken cockpit. In a couple of minutes, it was nearly out of sight.

Rowan disgustedly holstered his weapon and wheeled on me. "Why didn't you shoot?"

I shoved the forty-five back in my docker's rig and replied. "I already got my quota today." Then I walked back to join my Uncle and Ozaki. Rowan was incensed when he joined us.

He snatched his hat off and slapped it on his thigh. "Well...if you think they had the box—it's gone now!"

"Perhaps not, Chief Inspector." William relied calmly. He turned and addressed me, "That explains why we never saw a boat tied up to the barge—besides Marquis's, that is."

"I expect so, "I allowed.

It was Ozaki who pointed at the crane and brought our attention to it.

I hadn't noticed before, over the din of the machinery, but the crane's motor was running also with its gears in neutral. There were ropes lines leading from the tip of the cranes into the water. One, which ran down the length of the arm to coil around a drum at the base, was quite large, more than an inch thick. The smaller line was attached to a box at the tip of the crane and had enough slack to flitter in the breeze. Suddenly the smaller line went taut and a bell chimed. It went slack then taut again and the bell chimed a second time. Uncle Will began to issue orders.

"Collin, get to the pump and find the off switch. Stand by. Chief, ready your weapon." He nodded to Ozaki, and then took the controls for the crane.

I have no idea where he learned to handle heavy equipment, but he began to pull levers with familiarity. The crane's motor kicked into gear and went up several pitches as the thick line went taut. All eyes were glued to the spot where the line entered the river, as the rest of the rope slowly began to build layers on the drum at the base of the crane.

There was an eerie glow coming from beneath the surface getting larger and brighter as whatever William was raising came closer to the surface. A Large hook was the first to break the surface, followed by an odd glass bubble reinforced with brass strips. Like a hooked fish breaching, the man shaped object popped from the water's surface. Before my mind could register it, my eyes were staring at a nearly seven-foot tall mannequin made of canvas, brass, steel, and glass. There were brass fittings around the knees, elbows, shoulders, hips, and the neck to which a glass bubble was secured by large ring-tipped screws. From somewhere on its back, the same tubing trailed into the water as was attached to the pump I was now controlling. The feet were shod with calf-high boots that had several inches of steel for the soles. Even more menacing were the steel pinchers that sat at the end of the arms. The right held a lantern, still glowing in the sunshine. From the left dangled a large steel strong box.

A bearded man's face was visible inside the helmet, close enough for us to see his eyes widen in shock when he saw the four of us. His mouth moved with silent curses when he saw the Chief pointing a gun at him. Something started to whirl in the apparatus clutching the strong box, and it was becoming obvious he intended to drop the box back into the river. Rowan shouted a warning and cocked his revolver, but William was quick to act.

He slammed one lever forward and yanked back on another at the same time. The arm of the crane swung towards us and the man in the diving suit swung over the deck before he could react. Rowan barely had time to leap aside as it swung between us. William halted the crane's movement and the man continued on in an arc until he was four feet off the deck and twisted around to face us. It was then that my uncle released the brake on the rope. He yelled to me, "Shut off the pump, Frohman!" When I did as he asked, the world went silent.

It took a few seconds for the tension in the rope to slacken, and then the man dropped to the deck like a rock. When his steel shod boots hit the steel deck, it sounded like a blacksmith's hammer on an anvil. Unbelievably, the man kept his balance and stood there swaying like a drunken bear. The lantern dropped to his feet and shattered. He was visibly panting under the glass plates, now that he was running out of oxygen since I had shut off his air supply. He managed to raise his arm and the now empty claw began to snap open and shut. I was about to pull my piece to back up the inspector with his gun pointing out in front of him, when I guess Ozaki had seen enough.

Ozaki charged at the suit and when he was six feet away, launched himself into the air and planted both feet in the direct center of the suit's chest with a force that would have tipped a buffalo! The weighted boots wouldn't allow the man to fly backwards, however his body snapped back and downwards. He hit the deck so hard that you could hear the thick glass plates in his helmet crack. Ozaki managed to keep his balance and he landed on his feet a few feet past the helmet.

Rowan rushed forward and straddled the nearly unconscious man with his right foot planted on the diver's free arm, holding his gun in both hands and pointing it right at the man's face. He turned his head to me and barked, "Quickly Collin! Get his helmet off before we kill him!"

I ran over and dropped to my knees at the top of the helmet. I noticed Ozaki out of the corner of my eye as he sidled past us towards the feet. There were eight screws clamping the helmet in place. I grabbed one with my bare hand and could hardly get it to move it was so tight. I started to panic, knowing I could never get all eight off before the diver suffocated. Then, like manna from heaven, a wrench appeared in front of my face. Looking up I saw my uncle holding it out with a smug look on his face. "I believe you could use one of these."

I snatched it out of his hand and attacked the screw again. I had it off in no time and went for the second.

.Time sort of stood still then. The Chief kept pointing his weapon while I moved from one screw to the next. After the fourth one, I glanced up to see William and Ozaki removing the strong box from the pincher. Rowan was completely unaware of what was happening behind him. Ozaki, with great effort, picked up the box and scurried towards the *Helena* with it on his shoulder. Once again, I was amazed at the strength of the old man. He looked like Atlas carrying the world as he scooted away from us.

Uncle Will took up a position to block his movements in case Rowan looked over his shoulder. I caught William's eye and he put a finger to his closed lips. He was going to clip it! I was all for that! On top of all the other things I wanted to know, I was hoping my Uncle was finally going to reveal what was in that box!

I doubled my efforts after that and soon was lifting the helmet away from the man's head. I thought maybe I was too late, but his eye lids started to flutter and a loud moan escaped from his lips. Rowan still hadn't changed position when I got to my feet. He looked up long enough to nod his thanks to me then resumed his vigil on the beaten barge rat, who was starting to come around. Rowan immediately started in on him with a barrage of questions and threats.

I looked to William, who waved me over frantically. I stepped past Rowan and William flicked his eyes and turned his head towards the *Helena*. We were going to make our break. I walked as fast as I could without causing Rowan to look up and boarded Uncle Will's launch. I could see the police launch coming towards us and I was relieved. For a moment, I thought that William had intended to run off and leave the Chief with that monster.

William, edging backwards to us, called out. "That is it, then, Chief Inspector. We shall leave you to your duties. Congratulations!"

He leapt aboard the *Helena* and Ozaki fired up the engines. As we shot away from the barge he called out, "Telephone me at my home when you are finished with the arrest and interrogation!"

The Chief was screaming bloody murder as his voice faded away in our wake.

Uncle Will looked at me, smiling to beat the band. I think he expected praised, but I was giddy with our success. I scowled up at him and groused, "I guess you'll be eating crow tonight, Uncle Will!"

I laughed at the indignant look on his face and explained, "Rowan finally caught the River Monster!"

27

William laughed. "Well, one of them anyways. Though I fear the biggest fish eluded our grasp."

"You could say that again!" I exclaimed. "That was some boat! I guess he planned for every contingency.

"I see now why you were wondering about the barge having no other transportation."

"Every rat has a bolt hole," William observed. "Though I was a fool not to see his earlier. I should have deduced its presence! A drydock hidden in the bowels of the barge speaks of an especially sharp mind! Then he looked solemnly into my eyes and added, "You could have stopped him. That shot would not have been beyond your skill."

I knew he wasn't trying to chide me. He was just looking for my reaction, trying to see how I was feeling about killing that other man.

I stared straight ahead and replied. "If I could have winged the captain—I would have, but all I could see was the back of his head. I'm not about to kill a man in cold blood while he is running away. The one by the pump…well, he would have killed us all if I had given him the chance." I shrugged. "I don't think I had a choice."

My uncle nodded sagely and clasped my shoulder. "You certainly did not, Frohman. Undoubtably, we owe you our lives." He gave my shoulder a squeeze before his hand dropped away. "So, as the Scots are fond of saying—'Dinna fash yourself, Laddie!'" he added in a good imitation of a Scottish burr.

That brought a smile to my face. I was touched by his concern, but I knew of someone who would see it differently. "I doubt Rowan would agree with you on the subject. He was pretty mad the Captain got away!" Then I stole a glance at the strong box and added, "But not as mad as he's going to be over you making off with that box, Uncle Will!"

"Bah!" Ozaki snorted from the pilot's seat. "If not for your Uncre, those scums would have got away with it!"

"Just so." Uncle Will said, smugly. He popped his eyebrows at me. "I am sure the Chief Inspector will come around—once I explain my reasoning."

I wanted to ask him what reasons they were, but there was so much more I wanted filled in first. "Uncle Will, I have a pretty good idea how the box got stolen and the method of recovery, but how did Marquis tie into all this? Did they kill him to steal the pump off his boat?"

He didn't reply right away, and my question seemed to make him melancholy. He reached over and patted me on the shoulder again. "Patience, Frohman. I would rather not have to go over everything again and again. I am sure the Inspector will ring me shorty after we get home -- if he does not show up on my doorstep before! You will have all your answers then. Now, perhaps you would give me a hand cleaning this mess up."

I wasn't happy with that option, but I knew well enough, by now, to accept his decision. We spent the rest of the trip tossing splintered wood and broken glass over the side. Before I knew it, Ozaki had cut the engines to a near idle and we slipped into the boathouse.

Ozaki killed the engines and I tied us off. Uncle Will gestured at the strong box and asked me. "Could you carry this please?"

I grabbed the handle and lifted and nearly yanked my arm out of its socket. It was a heavy piece of luggage! I managed to muscle it up the few steps and out the door, but it was so heavy it banged off my legs, making me take tiny mincing steps.

Ozaki laughed. "You walk like a geisha!"

I set the box down and took off my jacket. I folded it over a few times and laid it over my right shoulder. I jerked the box up and settled it on my shoulder. It was easier going, but the tram still looked a long way off.

"Tell me again," I said sarcastically, "Why did we take this?"

William smirked. "Bait. There are still a few monsters out there."

I stopped and put the box on the ground. I transferred the jacket to my left shoulder and hoisted the box up onto that side. Best to keep my gun hand free.

William's prediction was right on the money. Not five minutes after we had gotten in the castle and brought the box into the study, the phone on the desk begin to ring. William motioned to Ozaki in some form of unspoken communication and the little man left the room. He let the telephone chime for another minute as he sat behind his desk and composed himself, then picked up the receiver and put it to his ear.

"The Gillette residence," he said in a neutral voice. I couldn't make out the words going into Uncle's ear, but the tone and the volume were enough to know it was the Chief Inspector on the other end. Rowan sounded like one of the Banshees of legend.

William listened patiently for a moment, rolling his eyes once, and then replied calmly. "Yes, of course I did. There is no need to thank me though…why, for removing it from that maelstrom. After being nearly killed and the master mind behind it all escaping, who knows what other attacks we were vulnerable to…I am sorry you feel that way…yes…I understand that…but not yet…calm yourself, Inspector. Hysterics will get us nowhere…because we have a chance to end this once and for all…"

He looked at me watching him intently and made a drinking motion with his hand. I knew he meant that he wished a drink for himself, and I was happy to take him up on his suggestion. William focused back to his call and the last thing I heard him say, as I headed out to the bar, was, "You should come before dusk, Inspector and this is what you will bring with you…"

I had the secret bar panel open and passed right over the sherry and gin to settle with some aged brandy. I poured myself a good jot and threw it back all at once, letting it burn my throat, warm my chest, and numb my nerves. I poured another and sipped at it more moderately when I realized Ozaki was standing just to the right of me holding a bottle of Coca-Cola for Uncle Will. He was in a fresh suit, and there was an orange stain over the thin red line on his earlobe. I managed not to jump out of my underwear as I turned to face him, resigned to a lecture on my drinking habits.

Instead, he put his left hand over his clenched right fist and bowed to me. I was staring in disbelief when he straightened and said to me formally. "You were a warrior today. Thank you for protecting your uncre." Then he reached up and patted me gently on my cheek before walking towards the kitchen door. After a few steps, he hesitated. "One more!", he said over his shoulder. "You drink too much!"

I chuckled to myself, pleased beyond words at his praise. Topping off the glass, reluctantly stowed the bottle before heading back to the study. Uncle Will was just hanging up the earpiece when I entered the room. He sat back in his chair and rubbed his eyes as I walked up to the desk. The strong box sat on the desk between us. The brandy had oiled my tongue.

"So, I take it the Chief was none too happy with you absconding with the evidence."

He peered up at me, under half lidded eyes and a grin slowly spread across his face. "That would be an understatement, Frohman! It took all my powers of persuasion to convince him to hold off reporting it to the Federal agents for a bit."

"How long is a bit?"

"Midnight. I told the Chief Inspector he could report to the Federal authorities then."

I set my drink on the desk and pulled up a chair. "Are you sure that's a god idea, Uncle Will? If what's in that box is so important, maybe you should get yourself out of harm's way. Get rid of it!" One look at his face told me that wasn't going to happen." You really think they will try to retrieve it tonight?"

"I am sure of it. Stay alert, Frohman—and armed!"

I patted my jacket where the gun rested under my arm. "I'll be ready!"

"Good man". He looked past me and stood. I followed his gaze and Ozaki entered the room, carrying a hammer and chisel. This, I thought, was a bad idea. I took a swig of brandy and said,

"I'm pretty sure the Chief also told you not to open it!"

"Of course, he did," William replied as he took the tools from Ozaki. He set the chisel and smacked it once with the hammer. The lock popped open and he pulled it out of the loops. "But he knows me better than that."

287

My curiosity overcame my foreboding and I walked around the desk next to his side to see what lay within. He slowly lifted the lid, and a small trickle of river water dripped out of the edges. Inside, filling the entire space was a watertight bag! My heart was beating rapidly with anticipation. Was it packed with money? Jewels?

William slowly opened the sealed top and reached inside. I must confess to utter disappointment as he pulled out a packet of official-looking documents. There were two sets. One with the British seal and one with France's. They hardly looked worth all the blood that was shed for them.

Ozaki looked at me and shrugged. He tottered off, muttering under his breath and I returned to my seat and brandy. William sat down and began to read, his face a mask of concentration. I lit up a cigarette and watched him read as I smoked. After a few minutes, he looked up at me, obviously uncomfortable with me watching him while he read. "You can read these after me, if you like Frohman. Perhaps you should take this opportunity to freshen up."

I knew he was trying to get some privacy, so he could study the documents in peace, but I was in a teasing mood.

"I don't think I should leave you unprotected, Uncle Will. Those hooligans could be back any minute."

He gave me a level glare. "I am sure we shall be unmolested for the next few hours. Even such a well-organized cabal, as we face, will need some time to formulate a plan of attack! Now, go wash up and let me read! You shall get your turn when I am finished."

I laughed and stood up. "If it's alright with you, Uncle Will. I'll just take a synopsis from you!" I picked up my drink and saluted him, but he had already forgotten I was there as he buried his nose once again.

I was feeling a little grubby, so I went to my room and got some fresh clothes before heading to the bathroom. Filling the big tub with steaming hot water while I undressed, I hung my holster on a towel rack nearby and slipped into the water. Between it's hot embrace and the brandy, I was afraid I might drift off, but my mind wouldn't let me relax completely. I began to run the events of the last few days in my head to try and make some sense of it all, but it only left me with more questions. I could reasonably construct the train robbery, and when I took that a step further, I could apply the same methods to the payroll robbery the day before. What I wasn't sure about was how Marquis fit into the picture. Was he forced to participate? Did they kill him and take the pump from his boat? No, that couldn't be right. The barge was a good half mile from where the payroll was stolen. Much too far to pump air to a diver. Yet, it was hard to think of Marquis as such a cold-blooded killer. A hustler and a rake, certainly, but I would hate to have to tell Catty her brother was the 'River Monster'!

Then again, if he was — why return the money after killing a man for it?

And what about the baby? We seemed to have lost track of our original investigation. We buried the child—Lord, that seemed like it was last week rather than this morning—and we were still no closer to her identity, not to mention, whoever had abandoned her!

This and a thousand other details swirled in my head, while the hot water seeped into my bones, until my brain just shut itself off. I woke, disoriented, when the now cold water made me shiver. I stood and shook myself awake like a dog would and got out of the tub.

The cooling evening air made my skin tingle after the hot bath and I was feeling refreshed. Returning to my room, I dug out some fresh clothes, casual and loose in anticipation of some action to come, I dressed quickly, ready to see if my Uncle's predictions were right.

As I was stepping out onto the balcony, I heard a rap on the front door downstairs and it slowly opened.

"Gillette?" a voice called out from the shadows of the foyer. I recognized Rowan's voice, then another -- the old Doctor Blums', "William? Are you here?"

"Good evening Gentlemen. So good of you to come! Come in, come in. Make yourself at home." I heard my uncle call out, but I could not see him from where I was standing. I happened to look up and saw him in one of his mirrors. He was seated on a semi-circular couch along the wall, newspaper in one hand and a coca cola in the other. Rowan ran up the steps from the foyer and rushed across the room to face him, the doctor trying to keep up with him and failing. To be fair, he was carrying a medium sized box. Rowan put his hands on his hips and snarled, "This isn't a social visit, Gillette! Where is the box?"

William set his paper down and looked up at the Chief, his face serene, "Safe. Did you do as I asked?"

I stayed where I was because I saw Ozaki slip up behind our two visitors unnoticed. Ozaki was as silent and stealthy as a cat.

"Everything's set, though for the life of me, I don't know why I just don't haul you down to the station instead! Of all the irresponsible things—" Rowan squawked, and the doctor jumped when Ozaki interjected loudly from behind them. "Would you Gentlemen care for a drink?"

I nearly bust a gut keeping my laughter inside. Ozaki just stood quietly, a toothy grin on his face, as he waited for the men to recover. Rowan shook his head, but the doctor said he would accept a glass of sherry. Ozaki bowed and went off, leaving the group in an awkward silence. Rowan was still mad, but Ozaki had taken the wind out of his sails.

"I still say the box would be safer at the station." Rowan groused.

"I disagree, Inspector. It would take ten average men a week to discover where I placed it!"

"This lot is anything but average, Gillette." Rowan argued.

"Bah!" Uncle Will countered, "Aside from their leader, they are nothing more than run of the mill criminals!"

"What are you basing that on, William?" Blum asked. Then he suddenly noticed the box in his arms and walked it over to put it on the table. On his way back, he added, "I've known some pretty smart criminals in my day."

William looked up, like he was asking for strength from heaven, and sighed theatrically. "I beg to differ, Doctor. If one knows about them, they are not good criminals. The first precept of crime is to remain undetected! It is the unforeseen, the unknown in the shadows we should fear."

If this were a play, the curtain would have fallen. I decided it was time to make a grand entrance and I called out a greeting as I skipped down the stairs to join them. After I shook hands with the doctor, the Chief stepped up to me. I tensed up, thinking I was in for another verbal drubbing over not shooting the fleeing suspect. I was ready to rip into him and was looking forward to pointing out that I had more lawyers at my disposal as he did constables. I was through being talked down to.

He gave me a hard look, which I returned, and then he suddenly grinned and stuck out his hand. "Thank you for your assistance today. You did good work out there. We were lucky to have you with us."

Stunned, but a little suspicious, I took his hand and asked, "You sure you're not sore about the second guy?"

He shrugged. "Nah! It would be better if we caught him. There are a lot of people who want to talk to him. There's a massive dragnet going out in all directions to find him. I'd be surprised if he isn't in custody by tomorrow." He nodded and turned to William. "So, what was in the box?"

It was a crude attempt to catch my uncle off guard, but William laughed and replied, "Papers."

"Papers? What kind of pap -- No! Don't tell me! I don't want to know!" He shook his head, "But you can be damn sure you'll be in Dutch with the Feds!"

William laughed and clapped him on the shoulder. "Calm yourself, Chief. Everything has been repackaged exactly as the original!" Then, to change the subject, he said to Blum, "So, Doctor, I see you brought another mystery box with you."

Blum, who had been sipping his sherry and watching the exchanges, came back into the moment. "Oh, yes. I did indeed. They are the babe's clothes and swaddling. When I saw they hadn't been picked up yet, I thought I would just bring them over."

William's eyes lit up. "Excellent Doctor! Perhaps they will reveal a clue of some sort."

"Oh, William!" Rowan exclaimed. "Are you still on that? You're wasting your time, my friend, that's a dead end!"

William sniffed and walked over to the table, proclaiming, "If you conduct your investigations with that attitude, they will all be dead ends."

We all gathered around as William opened the box and began extracting the items. First came tattered blanket that was wrapped around the girl. A second, finer and cleaner wrap was next, and then the one piece suit the child was wearing. Next was that pair of tiny dark red booties that made me sad to look at. They were so small, their deep crimson color a stark contrast to the graying material next to them. It all highlighted the infancy of the child.

Last, was a square cloth with fancy lace around the edges. It was stained but it was obviously a cut above the rest of the material that dressed the babe. William stared at it for a moment, then laid it on the table and excused himself. He dashed up the stairs and into his room. After a moment, he came out with something in his hand. He made his way stately down the steps, no doubt to make us wait in confusion just a bit longer. He walked over and laid the object down on the table. It was a twin to the last item he pulled out of the box.

Blum broke the silence, "Where—"

"FIRE!" Ozaki yelled at the top of his lungs.

28

We all nearly jumped out of our skins as we looked up to see Ozaki pointing out a window off the upstairs hallway. "Fire at the dock!" He screamed.

Being the youngest and fastest, I was across the room and out the French doors to the terrace before the others got a few steps. I dashed to the edge of the low wall that faced the river and saw a faint orange glow, towards the stern of the *Polly*. I turned in panic to face my Uncle who had come up behind me, feeling like I was going to lose control. Uncle Will, though, was a rock! He was concerned, of course, but he took control of the situation as if it was all in a day's work.

He turned to Rowan. "You can ride with me." Then he turned to the Doctor. "Go to my study and use the telephone to report the fire — then barricade yourself in!"

I wasn't sure what was going on, but I couldn't stand there any longer, while the boat burned. Ignoring my Uncle's cries to hold up, I dashed back into the house and saw Ozaki across the room, waving me on frantically. We dashed through the kitchen and down the stairs to where the bikes were stowed. Ozaki ran over to open the doors and I jumped on my machine. Not bothering with the hat and gloves, I flipped the ignition and kicked her into life. I eased towards the door and when Ozaki jumped on behind me and wrapped his arms around my waist, I hauled back on the throttle and we roared out of there like a train coming out of a tunnel. I left a rooster tail of gravel as we shot up the rampway and onto the drive.

Between trying to keep one eye on the road and one on the ever-growing flames on the Polly's aft cabin area, and hearing a steady stream of Japanese obscenities in my ear, in no time I was pulling up to a screeching halt on the dock next to the stern gangway.

I hit the front brakes hard and the rear tire fish tailed to a stop. I couldn't tell whether Ozaki was tossed from the back on the bike or he leapt, but he hit the boards running and flew up the gangway. As soon as he was aboard, he ignored the flames that had engulfed the salon and bolted towards the wheelhouse. I knew what he was after.

I killed the engine, dropped the stand, and dismounted in one motion. Ozaki didn't need me up front, so I jumped down onto the stern deck to see how bad it was. I heard a rumble and I could feel the *Aunt Polly's* engines begin to cycle.

Relieved, I ran from the port side to the starboard, but saw no flames on the outside of the ship and realized the fire was contained to the interior, with luck, just in the salon. The curtains were burned away from the windows and the French doors, but there was too much smoke and fire for me to see much. I edged up and reached for the door handle, to maybe get a better look, but I could feel the heat coming off it from a foot away. I had stepped back and taken off my jacket off to wrap around my hands when there was a great roar and the flames were dramatically reduced under a great hissing cloud of steam.

Ozaki had activated the fire suppression system.

Water, pumped up from the bilges, sprayed in a steady flow until the flames had all but died. I peeked around the corner, but Ozaki hadn't reappeared, so I used my padded hand to open one of the French doors. A great cloud of black smoke washed across me. It was so thick, I couldn't help but take a great lungful of it and I fell back, choking for air. I staggered over to the gunnel and leaned against it to get my breath back. I saw then that Uncle Will was pulling onto the dock, with the chief sitting behind them. I waved and was about to call out to them, but the smoke billowed, and I lost sight of them.

The wind was blowing towards the dock, causing the billows of thick smoke top obscure my view of the bow. I still hadn't seen Ozaki, so I fumbled around in my jacket until I found my handkerchief and wrapped it around my face. Able to breathe a little, I plunged through the smoke to the port gangway to find Ozaki. I didn't have to look hard, for he came out of the wheelhouse and headed towards me. I was about to call out to him, when suddenly, the side door to the master suite opened hard, knocking Ozaki sideways into the gunnel. I saw something like a striking snake and Ozaki grunted, and then toppled over the side into the water. A puff of breeze stirred just then, clearing a patch of smoke and I saw the man who escaped from the barge clearly, one hand on the door and the other holding what looked like a marlin spike. I snatched my gun from its holster, this time intending to shoot him dead!

But he stepped backwards, quick as a mongoose, and my bullet only took off the middle hinge of the door at the frame. I cursed, wanting to chase him down and end it, but I looked over the side and Ozaki had disappeared.

I threw my gun on the deck, picked my spot, and dove into the cold water. I hit my mark perfectly and when I turned upwards towards the surface, Ozaki was directly above me. He was slowly sinking when I slammed into his chest with my shoulder and drove him to the surface. I went to suck in some air, but just sucked the water out of the cloth around my mouth. I was choking and clawing at the kerchief and trying to get Ozaki onto his back. Uncle Will and Rowan had run to the side of the dock, next to a ladder that led to the water, and were shouting instructions and encouragement—just to add to the mayhem!

I splashed my way over to the ladder like a wounded duck and grabbed it with one hand. At the top, Rowan had gotten to a prone position on one side of the ladder and stretched his arms down as far as he could. William got to one knee on the other side and lowered his cane. I grabbed it with my free hand and William pulled me close enough to the ladder for me to get a foot on the bottom rung, below the surface. I let go of the cane and grabbed a rung, then I heaved us both up until Rowan could put a hand under my arm and help. William reached down with his long arms and got a double grip on Ozaki's jacket. Suddenly the weight was off me and he was pulled to safety. Rowan gave me a hand and I collapsed on the dock.

Uncle Will straddled Ozaki, after laying him face down, and heaved up until he looked like he was holding an inverted 'V'. After a couple of lifts, a stream of water rushed out of the little man's mouth and he started heaving with great racking coughs. Uncle Will rolled him over and I half crawled over and got onto one knee near his head. Uncle Will pulled him into a sitting position, and I propped him up against my leg.

There was a growing goose egg on the crown of his forehead, but no blood. His chest heaved and his eyes fluttered but he made no sound except the wheezing in his throat. Uncle Will was calling his name and looking him over when I caught a glimpse of a shape moving quickly across the stern deck towards the gangway. It must have been the man I missed, Ozaki's would-be killer!

Without hesitation, I turned to the inspector, who was standing behind my uncle, watching the scene and I shouted, "Rowan! Watch out! On the boat!"

Rowan stood and wheeled about to face the Aunt Polly. Past him, great swaths of black smoke still poured from the salon across the water to docks. His eyes swept the boat from bow to stern and he saw nothing to react to.

"Watch out for what?" he asked, frantically.

"Me!" a gravelly voice said.

Uncle Will, Rowan, and I all swung our heads at the sound to see a figure step out of the smoke, like a wraith from hell. I instinctively reached for my gun, but of course, all I grabbed was the leather of the holster. I had dropped my gun on the Aunt Polly before I dove in after Ozaki.

Rowan had the same idea and I could see him begin to reach for his weapon, but he wasn't fast enough. Our sight blocked by the inspector, I couldn't see who spoke, but there was no mistaking the shape of my pistol that swung in an arc to smash Rowan across the face. Rowan valiantly tried to keep his feet, swaying like a reed in the wind, but he lost the contest and he staggered six or seven steps to his right before he collapsed in a heap.

Standing where the chief started from was the captain of the barge, smirking and pointing my gun right at us!

William, to my surprise, seemed to pay no heed to our assailant and moved to check on Rowan.

"Leave him!" The Captain commanded. "Stay where you are!" William froze, and then slowly started to turn towards him.

Ozaki groaned then and opened his eyes. His weight came off my leg as he sat up on his own, one hand clutching his head and the other spayed on the dock to keep his balance. I slowly stood.

"You too, Master Frohman. Leave that little monkey where he lay. I owe him that much, and more!" The captain warned. "Take one step and I'll put a bullet in Gillette's head!" Then he grinned like Satan at a lynching and added. "Nice gun, by the way. Semi-automatic. Saves me having to cock it every time I shoot one of you!"

298

William planted his feet and stood his full height, with one hand behind his back, holding his cane.

"Captain Roy. We meet again." William said calmly, as if they had just run into each other at a local restaurant. The name hit me square between the eyes and my jaw dropped. Even the Captain was surprised by his naming, the way his eyebrows shot up.

Roy chuckled, and then shrugged. "I wasn't certain that losing thirty pounds and shaving would be enough to fool a man of your intelligence, so I kept out of your view. Still, I give you kudos for recognizing me."

"I recognized you on the barge, before you fled." William replied blandly. "Yet, I must offer my own applause for your ability to elude the consequences of your actions. For the second time—that I know of."

The smirk dropped off the captain's face at the taunt and the gun came up an inch. I was afraid he was going to shoot my Uncle right then and there, when Uncle Will added, "Still, I must admit that, although I stopped you, I was remiss in this whole affair. I failed to see the most important aspect."

"And that being?" Roy asked. I was a hair relieved to see the pressure coming off the trigger. I also noticed that he hadn't pulled back the hammer. That might give me a chance at the right moment.

William acted surprised at the question, but I knew he was just taunting the Captain in his own way. "Why, your hand in all this, of course! The corruption of a young man, the underwater element to your crimes, and the combination of inside information and prior planning—those are all trademarks of your work!"

Roy nodded and smiled. "I'll accept that from you, Gillette. It's all true, though I wouldn't say I corrupted Marquis. In fact,

I never thought of him as more than a delivery boy until he told one of my men where he could lay his hands on a diving suit. Then he was worthy of attention."

It helped that the boy was a bad egg to begin with. A couple of drinks, a few slaps on the back, and he jumped in with both feet." He barked an evil laugh, "You could even say he went overboard!"

"I imagine you were madder than a wet hen when Marquis brought his spoils to your barge." William observed. "Increased attention and patrols in your area could have put a serious dent in your plans. Which is why you returned the money; to divert the authorities' attention."

Roy dipped his head in acknowledgement of my Uncle's reasoning. "I had Marquis and my men practice in the waters closer to the town. It kept prying eyes off me and gave the unwashed another legend to crow about!" A dark cloud passed over his face and he snarled, "Then that pissant had to go and show off!"

The smirk returned to his mouth as he went on. "Well, what's done is done," he waxed philosophically. "I did admire his initiative and his plan was very clever. I was especially proud of the fact he left no witnesses."

The calm cool way he spoke of a man's murder made me shiver. "Then why'd you kill him?" I blurted out. I was trying to stall him, with my eyes fixed on the hammer of my pistol.

Roy tossed me a contemptuous look and snarled. "Shut up, boy! The adults are talking now." He turned his gaze back to William. "In four bullets, it won't matter anymore."

He raised the pistol an extended it closer to my Uncle's head. "Gillette, I once warned you to stay from my ken. You will now pay the price for your failure to heed me."

I coiled, ready to spring into a suicidal attempt to stop him, but froze when my uncle said loudly, "Shoot us and you'll never get your hands on that strong box!"

Roy chuckled and shook his head, but he still had not pulled the hammer back on the pistol. "Oh, Gillette. You disappoint me! After making your fortune and fame on the Sherlock Holmes name—haven't you even read Doyle?"

"You are of course referring to 'A Scandal in Bohemia'. Yes, it is one of my favorites."

"Then you know now this fire was a diversion. I knew you'd all come running when you saw your precious boat on fire. It broke my heart to put the torch to the old girl after all the time and work I put into her while I worked for you and captained your precious *Aunt Polly*." He sighed theatrically, "Still it had to be done. It gives my men the chance to retrieve the box— and me the chance to balance the scales and settle up with you."

William shook his head sadly. "I'm afraid your masters will not be pleased if you let those papers slip through your fingers. Germans are not known for their forgiveness."

A look of uncertainty crossed Roy's face and he hesitated long enough for me to spit out." You're a dirty Hun?"

He swung the gun in my direction and sneered. "No one is my master! My only loyalty is to profit, and the Kaiser pays top dollar right now."

He dropped the jovial façade and sneered in a manner as evil as I had ever witnessed. "For instance, like he did when I told them the *Lusitania* was carrying armaments. They would have sunk any ship I pointed at, but I knew your father was sailing on her that trip."

I couldn't believe what I was hearing. "You sank that ship just to get back at my father?"

He shrugged and gave me and evil smirk. "Two birds with one stone." He swung the barrel back at William, who wore a mask of rage and then Roy proclaimed. "Now that you know—you can all die"

I was so focused; even in the dim light I could see his finger go white on the trigger. When nothing happened, he hesitated, and I realized I might get the few precious seconds I needed to act. I sprang to make my charge.

Uncle Will was faster. A twist in his cane's handle and a flip of the wrist saw the sheath of his 'cane' flying into the river. I saw a glint of steel from Uncle Will's cane just before he shoved all two feet of the sword through Roy's heart. I stopped short as William put his face to Roy's, almost close enough to kiss and said. "Though you deserve much more than this—that was for Charlie!" Roy began to sink slowly to his knees and William lowered himself to keep eye contact.

"You have failed," he intoned at the wide eyed and grimacing Captain. "I have bested you again. This time will be the last."

Rage flooded the dying man's face, but before he could scream his rage, William yanked the blade back and Roy toppled over, all life departing him. William stood slowly and turned to me. Our eyes met for a long moment then I nodded my approval. He tossed the cane out into the river where its false cover went and brushed past me to the inspector.

Rowan was just beginning to stir, and I thought my Uncle was going to his aid, but he reached into the Chief's jacket and pulled out his service revolver. He walked back over to straddle the dying Captain Roy. Pointing the gun down at the blood stain on Roy's chest, he cocked the pistol and fired. Twice. Then for a third time.

I just stood like a statue as he calmly stepped over the body and went back to Rowan, who was just starting to come around. I jumped a foot off the deck when Ozaki, who had somehow found the strength to grab my ankle, said, "Three is a good number."

Still trying to decipher that, I watched Uncle Will get down to one knee next to the Chief and gently lift him into a sitting position as his eyes began to fully open. Then Uncle Will quickly put the revolver in Rowan's right hand. After a few seconds, we could see his fingers tighten on the familiar grip. He came awake and looked around, surprised to see his gun in his hand. "What…what's going on?" He asked groggily.

William beamed at him and said in his best stage voice," You got him, Chief Inspector! You saved us all!"

29

I could see what my uncle was doing, and I thought I knew why. Covering up the stab wound with bullet holes and giving the Chief all the credit would save him a lot of press and all the other invasiveness that comes with killing a man, especially if you're William Gillette! In the middle of my gloating over how clever my uncle was, a thought broke through and I panicked. Dashing over, I grabbed my gun from where Roy had dropped it and looked at my motorbike. Deciding in a flash that it would only announce my arrival, I bolted for the tramway across the clearing. I managed to say, "The doctor", as I passed William before breaking into a full run. I heard him calling at me to wait, but I knew Doctor Blum was up at the castle alone and those men of Roy's would kill him with no remorse. It was time for me to be the hero!

I started the tram and leapt aboard. On the trip up, I heard a siren and saw a police car heading down the road towards the dock. Satisfied that Ozaki and Chief Rowan would get the attention they needed, I steeled myself for the task ahead. I figured I was sitting in the cat bird seat for now. I hoped that Roy's men, if they were still inside the castle, would hear the siren and see the police heading to the docks, giving them more time to search. They wouldn't be expecting me, or my forty-five!

It seemed like an eternity until the tram got me to the top. My wet clothes were sucking the heat out of my body and were sticking to me. I was just as glad I left my jacket on Ozaki as it would have restricted my movements.

As soon as I was level with the landing, I killed the power and set the brake. Dashing in a crouch, pistol at the ready, I crossed the driveway and went up on the porch and walkway encircling the castle. There were some lights on in the great room, so I stayed low, so as not to be seen from anyone inside and did the same when I came to the lit kitchen windows. I decided to go in the door to the conservatory because it was dark and I thought the plants would cover my entrance. Once inside, the faint light from the moon shining through the glass of the conservatory was enough to make my way into the pantry on tip-toe. I could hear noises from in the great room, so I flattened myself against the wall next to the hallway leading to the interior of the castle. I was just about to edge forward when I heard footsteps behind me. Turning about, I heard the hammer click of my .45. I froze and found myself staring straight down the barrel at a very stunned Catty!

Dazed, I dropped the gun and whispered, "Catty! What the hell are you doing here?"

The shocked look dropped off her face, and she scowled like a she-wolf. She planted a hand on her hip and stuck her face out. "Well, it's nice to see you too!" Then she stamped her foot and stormed off into the kitchen leaving me standing there with egg on my face!

"HO! You sure ruffled her feathers, young feller!" I turned to the voice, still confounded, to see Doctor Blum standing across the room with one hand in his pocket and the other holding a drink. "I see you're back. Is the fire under control?" He looked around, "Where are the others? We had a bit of excitement of our own up here!"

"The fire was nothing but a red herring. Roy- the boss of the gang, who robbed the train said he sent a couple of men to steal the box back! I thought you were in danger!"

Blum was touched, and maybe a little embarrassed by my concern. I could tell he was trying to save my pride when he walked over and put a hand on my shoulder. Still, I could see he was holding some laughter back. "You're a good man, Collin. Your father would be proud of you...but you needn't have worried about us. Your Uncle William and Chief Rowan had cooked up a little scheme. C'mon, I'll show you."

I started to follow him into the hallway to the great room but stopped. "Where was Catty in all this?" I asked him. She was the last person I expected to see this night.

"I wasn't here yet," Catty replied from behind me. She must have come out of the kitchen and fell in behind us.

I nearly jumped out of my skin. "Sweet Christmas, Catty!" I yelped. She laughed, put a hand on my arm, and apologized. Then she asked, "Why are you all wet?" Her eyes went wide. "Did the *Aunt Polly* sink?"

I put a hand over hers and asked calmly, after remembering my earlier blunder. "You know I'm happy to see you Catty, — but how...why are you here? Shouldn't you be home with your family?"

She stepped back and crossed her arms over her chest. "I was! All day long. The wake started at noon and by the time I left for the last ferry, the men were near passed out and the women were drunker—and everyone was crying. I had to get out of there. I didn't think Mr. Gillette would mind if I used my room tonight. I...I need to get some rest before the funeral tomorrow."

I stepped forward and put my palm on the side of her face. "I'm sure he won't mind. Catty...I never really got the chance to tell you how sorry I am about everything."

She smiled and whispered softly, "Everything?"

I smiled back. "No, of course not. I meant everything but that."

We gazed at each other like a couple of moon-struck calves when the doctor cleared his throat. We quickly stepped away from each other, blushing as she turned to him.

"Come along children. You can do your canoodling later!"

We followed him into the great room where there was quite a sight.

Next to the semi-circular couch, where William had been perched when the Chief and the Doctor first arrived stood a flatfoot, calmly tapping a nightstick on his open palm. It was the Sargent I met out front of the station a few days ago. Two feet from him sprawled on the couch, were two men in rumpled suits laying slumped against the wall. Neither was moving and I have no doubt that they would have tumbled onto the floor if not for the fact that each of them had an arm outstretched above them that was handcuffed to the wall sconce. Both of them were pie eyed, slightly grinning, and drooling like starving dogs. They didn't so much as bat an eye as I walked up to get a closer look at them.

I looked to the copper and asked, "What the hell happened to them?"

The man in uniform smiled and nodded towards the doctor. I looked to him and he waggled his eyes as he took a sip of his drink.

"Oh, I just gave them a little something to keep them calm until William and Chief Rowan get back."

I looked at the loopy grins on the two men and asked the Doctor, "Do you have any more of that stuff?" I felt like I could use a shot of it myself.

He grinned but didn't reply, so I turned to the Sargent. "So, spill already. What's the story with these two?"

He grinned and replied, "Not much to tell really. The Chief pulled the four of us from our regular duties and brought us up here with him. He told us to stay out of sight and keep a close eye on the doors and windows. He also told us not to leave the grounds under any circumstances. So, when we heard the commotion in the house and saw the boat was on fire, we stayed out of sight when you and Ozaki tore off like bats out of hell and then the Chief went with Mr. Gillette. Believe me, we weren't happy about having to hide in the bushes all night, but as soon as you four were out of sight, Frank Chapman appears, and tells us that these two gents were coming up the drive. Then he disappeared into the night and we saw them run up the steps and break in through the terrace doors. I signaled the boys and we snuck up after them. We watched from the windows as they bee lined for the study. Doctor Blum had just managed to get inside and lock the doors before they could get in. Old Doc here kept them outside and they didn't have a clue we were coming up behind them. They tried to bust the huge oak doors down but they were too sturdy for that. When they drew their guns to shoot off the lock, we jumped them! They put up a hell of a fight, but we managed to cuff them.

Once the situation was under control we were trying to decide how many of us could go and help at the fire. I didn't want to underman myself, with these two. These are a couple of dangerous men, if I know anything at all! Then the doctor came up with the idea of drugging them. Wish we could do this with everybody we pinch. They are so sedated that my grandmother could keep them two under wraps!"

The grin slid from his face and he asked. "How bad was the fire? Was it still burning when you left the dock?"

"Just like here, everything's under control. The fire's out and Ozaki and Inspector Rowan were back on their feet when I left to come up." Then I added as an afterthought, "Captain Roy is dead."

The Sargent's eyes flew open wide and he sputtered. "Roy? THE Captain Roy? He's behind this?"

Catty, who was silent up until now snarled, "That devil!" Then she stepped up and slapped my arm hard enough to make me flinch, then latched on, digging her fingers into my forearm. "What do you mean, 'Back on their feet'? Are Ozaki and the Chief Inspector alright?"

Before I could open my mouth, Doctor Blum set his drink on the table and grabbed my other arm. "Do they need medical ATTENTION?"

"No, No," I stammered feeling like I was caught in a vise. "I mean...well ...I suppose you should have a look at them, Doc. Both took a nasty whack to the head and Ozaki near drowned, but they'll live."

The Sargent stepped up and took his turn at me. "Where did Roy come into all this? Sweet Marie! Half the country's lawmen have been looking for him! What happened, who killed him? Not that you'll see any tears from me! I'm just sorry I didn't get to see that SOB hang!"

Before I could even answer one of his questions, Catty and the Doctor each began peppering me with more questions, so fast that I couldn't have answered fast enough if there was two of me.

I was about to explode. I was wet, tired, cold, and now that it was truly over and everyone who mattered to me was safe, I just wanted to grab a bottle and crawl inside. Their three voices had blended into a buzzing in my ears and I nearly wept with relief when the front door opened, and Rowan called from the foyer. "Sargent! Is everything secure?"

Everyone let go of me and turned to face the crowd coming into the great room. Rowan and my Uncle were supporting Ozaki between them. Three uniforms brought up the rear. Catty and the Doctor rushed towards them. I made tracks for the bar.

30

I drank one and poured another before I returned to the commotion. The two would be thieves were being dragged out to the police car, while the doctor started fussing over Ozaki, who was having none of his ministrations. The Chief Inspector, who looked worse than Ozaki, with a gash across the bridge of his nose and one eye nearly swollen shut, was being clucked over by his men until he brought them up short. Holding a wet cloth from Catty on his face, he began spitting orders.

"Enough! I'm alright! Sargent—you and the men take the prisoners right to the station. I want them each in a separate cell from the first one we brought in! Keep the fourth one ready in case someone else pops up! No one is to see or talk to them until I get there."

"You're not coming with us, Sir?" The Sargent asked as he pointed to the box on the coffee table. "What about that?"

"That stays in my sight until the Feds come to pick it up. I'll call them from here when I'm ready to head back to the station."

"The hell you are!" Blum interjected, as he wrapped a bandage around the head of Ozaki. "Kevin — we are going straight to my office so I can look you over. You probably have a concussion, at the very least!"

"In a pig's eye, Tom!" Rowan retorted. "I'm not going anywhere until we get this sordid mess straightened out!" He looked at William. "I have no intentions of looking like the village idiot when they start asking me for explanations."

Everyone started objecting at once until Uncle Will threw up his hands and cut them off. "Settle down, Gentlemen." He turned to the Sargent. "Get the prisoners to the station and carry out your orders, Sargent. When that is done, send a car back for the Chief Inspector. That should give us ample time to…clear the air."

Then he turned to the Doctor. "Doctor, if you would be so kind, please take Ozaki up to my room and put him to bed."

"Baka on that!" Ozaki snarled as he got to his feet. I do not need any of your western medicine!" he paused and gave a slight bow to the Doctor, "No offence." He turned back to William. "All I need is some tea and peace and quiet! I go to my own bed, thank you very much!"

William obviously didn't agree with that decision, but he also knew that his man could teach stubborn lessons to a mule. He sighed and said, gently. "If you are sure, old friend. At least let the Sargent drop you off on the way to the Ferry. It's late and we're all tired." Then he reached out a put a hand on his shoulder. "I am so sorry, Ozaki. We nearly lost you tonight. I should have seen that coming!"

Ozaki shook his head. "Karma, Wirriam-san. Our enemy is dead, and we have peace — that is what matters."

William nodded sagely. "you be sure to sleep in tomorrow. We will be back by the afternoon and you can come up then— if you are up to it!"

Ozaki nodded and turned to follow the Sargent out to the car. He was stiff back and shuffling slowly and even with the loose end of the bandage wafting out behind him, he was a paragon of dignity. William looked to me and jerked his head slightly. I nodded and walked out the front door and up the drive. Not one

312

word did we exchange before Ozaki climbed into the crowded Police car, where he stopped and faced me. Deeply, from the waist, he bowed solemnly to me. I returned it and held it until he got in the car and shut the door behind him.

When I returned to the great room the Inspector had gone to make his telephone call, and Catty was squaring off with Uncle Will with Blum looking on in concern.

"Catherine, of course you are welcome to stay here tonight. I do feel, however, that you should retire to your room soon. There are things you should not hear that will be said tonight."

Catty stood firm with arms across her chest and staring up at him defiantly. "If it has anything to do with Marquis' death, then I want to know! You've never kept the truth from me before, Mr. Gillette! You know I can take it!"

William looked to me for support, but he wasn't going to get any from me! I had my own bone to pick with him. He looked to the doctor, who just lowered his eyes and sipped his drink. After a few moments, he sighed again. "It seems that no one will listen to me tonight...so be it." He clasped his hands together. "If you are going to stay Catherine, might I impose on you for some light refreshments? I, for one, am famished."

She agreed and the doctor seeing the thundercloud on my face beat a hasty retreat with her. "Let me give you a hand," he called out as he followed her off.

William's smile dropped off his mug when he looked at me. His eyebrow shot up and he asked, "Is something on your mind, Frohman?"

"You might say that," I snapped back. "Like why you didn't feel you could trust me with your plan! I looked like a fool running up here—like Don Quixote at a misshapen stone windmill!"

313

He returned my glare with an admonishing look. "Of course, I trust you, Frohman. If not for you, Ozaki would be dead. I am extremely grateful for your actions tonight. If you recall, there was never a chance to fill you in on plan. You did not join us until the Doctor and the Chief Inspector arrived and there certainly was not a moment to explain after that."

I grudgingly had to accept that. Everything had transpired in a whirlwind afterwards.

"And, you will remember, I did try to stop you as you ran for the tramway. You were off like a hare and I certainly could not leave the Chief Inspector and Ozaki in their state."

"Yeah, I guess you're right, Uncle Will. I guess I just feel a bit stupid."

"Never feel foolish for trying to do the right thing! You were brave and resourceful tonight, and I could not be more proud of you."

I felt my eyes well up with his praise. "Well, I'm just as proud of you, Uncle Will. If not for you, we'd all be dead!"

He stepped closer and lowered his voice. "On that subject—I am sure that you agree that the 'official' version of tonight's events are that Roy struck Rowan and the Chief Inspector shot him as he fell. That ending is best for all involved."

I nodded. "I understand. My lips are sealed."

"Good man!" He clapped me on the shoulder. "Now, perhaps you should get into some dry clothes before we wrap this up." He looked over my shoulder and amended, "Perhaps you might first find the Chief Inspector a comfortable chair."

I turned to see Rowan gingerly stepping through the doorway of the study, the bloody rag he held over his nose was dripping and he could barely stay upright. I helped him over to a padded chair, switched his rag for a clean one and gave him my drink.

"Did you reach the authorities?" William asked as Rowan.

"I told them I'd telephone and tell them when to meet me at the station. But they're chomping at the bit, William. I won't be able to stall them for long." he replied, looking a bit more alert. "We only have enough time for you to fill me in."

"Not before I fix you up." Doctor Blum informed him as he walked over to join us. He said to my Uncle, "Catherine will be bringing some food and drink in a minute."

"Then I'll go and change quickly," I said. Pointing a finger at my Uncle, I warned, "Don't you start without me!"

William laughed, "I would not dream of it!"

I decided against getting fully dressed again, rather I opted for pants, shirt, slippers, and a dressing gown. As I joined the gathering at the table in front of the fireplace, It struck me that I was dressed like my uncle would be if he were in costume for one of his Holmes plays. Uncle Will saw the likeness too and laughed.

"My word, Frohman, perhaps you should take center stage for this final act!"

"I would, if I knew what the hell was going on!" I retorted, with a grin, as I picked up a plate. "As it is, I'll just have to eat, drink, and listen carefully as you talk!"

Dr. Blum snorted and said loudly, "If we're going to be here until William talks himself out, we'd better freshen our drinks and fill our plates!"

"We need to get this show on the road!" Rowan put in. "I have to be at the station when they show up to get their box, and I need a bit more on how we got it!"

"Do not worry, Inspector," William assured him. "All will be revealed — almost all anyway. Now fill your plates,

315

gentlemen, it would not do to let Catherine's efforts go unappreciated! You have outdone yourself, young lady!"

Catty blushed and gave a little curtsy at our murmurs of approval. She really had earned the praise! There were plates sliced cheese and smoked meats. Sandwiches, pickles, and even some of Mrs. Wood's biscuits warmed up. I hadn't eaten since breakfast, so I heaped my plate well past the point of gluttony. When I finished piling it on, everyone was staring at me.

"What? I'm a growing boy!"

We juggled our plates and drinks as we crossed over to the nearby sofa and chairs. The inspector and the doctor both took chairs, leaving me to settle on the short sofa --what my mother would call a loveseat. William set his plate on the coffee table between us all and held his Coca-Cola bottle on his knee. While we were getting situated, he pulled Catty aside and spoke to her in a low voice. He was obviously trying once more to talk her out of hearing what would be said, but she set her face in defiance, shook her head fiercely, and joined me on the sofa. I leaned into her and was going to add my voice to uncle's, but she just cast an evil eye on me and mumbled softly, "Don't you dare say it Collin Frohman!"

I looked at her and I know she could see the pity in my eyes. "Alright then — but, it's not going to be pretty."

She looked a little scared then, but she held her head high and announced, "Whenever you're ready, Mr. Gillette."

Uncle Will grimaced in resignation and gave her a slight bow. Mostly for dramatics, William slowly set his drink next to his plate and rose up. Walking over to the massive fireplace, he reached into a gap, to fetch a sock from between its massive stones. Armed with his pipe and tobacco, he flowed back into the chair and languidly crossed his legs, moving all the while like one of his cats. He didn't even look at us until he had filled his bowl and struck a match.

Blandly, he asked. "Just what is it you wish to know, Inspector?"

31

Rowan rolled his eyes. "Very well, William. We'll do it your way. I can tell you what I know and you can fill in the blanks…

"The strongbox was sent to Boston where Federal Agents took possession of it and arranged for a train to transport it to Washington DC with an Army escort. The Federal Agents were going to work in shifts. The first two would ride along until New London, where they would be joined by another two. The four of them would stay with the box until it was delivered to the State department in Washington.

"Everyone with me so far?"

All of us nodded—except William, who looked at the ceiling with a smirk and quietly sipped his Coca-Cola.

Rowan went on. "The two agents who got on in New London were imposters. Earlier that day, they had killed the two real Agents and, with their I.D. cards and credentials, assumed their identities. Neither of the sets of agents had met before, so it was a snap to get past their counterparts and into the office where the box was held. They waited until the train was over the bridge and tossed it out the window to the river below. It was still dark then, so no one witnessed its fall into the water below.

"Then, when the train got to Chester, they simply avoided the next set of Agents, by going out the opposite end of the car. Cool as cucumbers, they strolled right off the train and made their getaway in a car that was waiting for them." He paused and looked to William. "How am I doing so far?"

Wiliam raised his bottle in salute. "As I was not privy to that information, we shall have to take your word for its accuracy. Still, I am fairly confident that you have laid that aspect of this affair out in good order. Please, continue."

Rowan sat back, looking pleased at the compliment and continued. "As we all know now, Captain Roy had planned this with meticulous care. I made a telephone call to a railroad administrator this afternoon and his description of the real Captain of the barge bore no resemblance to Roy! I'm sure there are more bodies out there somewhere. Roy and his crew have lain in wait these past weeks, planning this heist all along." Rowan paused and took a sip then continued. "As we all know, he used a deep-sea diver's rig to recover the box and had done so right before we came across him. Between William's insight and Collin's good shot, we managed to thwart them. Though I still say we could have saved a lot of time and injury if you had shot him when he was escaping."

I shrugged. "If I knew then what I know now, I might have! But tell me this — Roy was halfway to the sound before we took the box and came back to the castle. How did he know we had it in the first place?"

Rowan looked at me in surprise and sat back in his chair. My query seemed to knock some of the wind out of his sails.

"I...I don't know, Collin. I never even thought about it." He looked to my uncle, but before he could weigh in, Catty spoke up.

"How does Marquis fit in all this?"

The Inspector was a bit sheepish in his answer. "That I'm not sure of either, Catherine. Apparently, at the very least, he supplied them with the air pump to operate the underwater suit."

"You mean, they killed him and took the machinery off his boat, wouldn't you say?" I pointed out. "Marquis was already...gone before the robbery."

"Yes" he countered, "But not before the payroll job, which, I have to believe, was the work of Roy and his gang! The method was all too similar. Wouldn't you agree William?"

My uncle didn't answer for a long minute. He set his bottle of soda on the floor next to his chair and calmly repacked his pipe with tobacco. Setting it between his teeth, he struck a match and took several long pulls until it was burning evenly. He sat back and blew a great cloud of blue haze into the open air above us, before he spoke.

"If you are all through with your idle speculations, I will endeavor to give an accurate account of the very complex situation that has played out these past few weeks."

I think we all rolled our eyes and the doctor even snorted and shook his head, but William took no notice and continued.

"The first fact which is crucial to understanding is that this was no ordinary crime -- either for profit or emotion. It was purely a matter of espionage!"

"Espionage? As in spying or sabotage?" The Doctor blurted out. "By whom?"

"By the world's current aggressor, Doctor. Germany and Kaiser Wilhelm. Roy admitted as much to us before his...demise."

"When did he admit that?" Rowan asked, rising painfully his chair. "I don't remember that!"

There was an awkward pause at that point. The Inspector was out like a light when Roy and my uncle was going back and forth, but William couldn't admit that without letting on what really happened. The doctor, bless his heart, came to our aid unwittingly. Uncle William reached over and put a hand on the Inspector's arm. "Calm yourself, Kevin. It often happens that a person will lose some memory when he suffers a blunt force trauma. You may remember some or all of it as you recover, but, on the other hand, there may be a permanent gap in your memories."

Rowan was uneasy with the explanation but seemed to accept it. He looked to my Uncle. "I guess you should fill me in. I don't even remember shooting him!"

William smiled at him and said, "You're just too modest, Chief Inspector!" He threw a sideways glance at me and I gave him a wink in return.

He took a few more puffs on his pipe then returned to his narrative. "As I was saying, this nasty business was all on the behalf of the Kaiser. Captain Roy was expecting a large reward for stealing the box and getting it into German hands."

"Just what was in the box?" he began to silently tick off a list on his fingers. "What was so important that four men had to die for it?"

"Five," I corrected him as I glance at Catty. "Don't forget Marquis in your count."

"Four." William corrected me but said nothing more by way of explanation. He turned to Blum, "I am sorry to be so unforthcoming, Doctor, yet I will not reveal the contents to you or anyone else." he pointed to the case that rested on the table. "The documents in that satchel are of an extremely sensitive nature and, I am ashamed to say, they do not shed a very good light on our great nation."

Now, that really piqued our curiosity, but William took it even a step further. "In fact, now that I have more data, I believe the theft and murder last year was an earlier plot by Germany to throw our country into turmoil and prevent the United States from entering the war."

Before I thought about my words, I blurted out. "Well, I imagine stealing the treasury plates might just have had that effect!"

Uncle Will's eyes flew open and he jabbed his pipe stem in my direction. "Ha! I knew it! Your father did write it all down!"

Everyone's eyes turned to me, so I quickly picked up my drink and took a long draught to cover my slip of the tongue. I could feel Catty's eyes boring into the back of my head, but when I stole a glance at her face, she didn't seem angry.

Thankfully, Rowan diverted my Uncle's attention. "We could discuss this at some point in the future William. Be that as it may, my time is limited tonight. Let's pass on that subject for now and get back on track."

Uncle Will gave me a look, then nodded and went on. "Roy revealed much, with a bit of prompting on my part. Luckily, men with that caliber of ego tend to boast of their prowess."

I had to hide a smile behind another pull on my glass, but both the Inspector and doctor rolled their eyes. Roy was not the only one with an oversized ego in this scenario.

"Before you go on," I said, trying to keep the train on the tracks, "with Roy's appearance, can you answer my previous question to the Inspector? How did Roy know you had the steel box?"

William tapped the ashes from his pipe and began to reload it. "Of course, I cannot say with absolute certainty, but I

322

believe that we were observed by the very same two men the Chief took into custody tonight.

I would make sense that they were to meet back with Roy after they had thrown the case from the train and made their escape. They must have been nearby when we stormed the barge and thwarted their plans. When Roy made his escape, they must have watched and waited. When they saw Osaki put the box on *Helena,* it was reported to their leader."

"How did they find Roy?" The doctor asked.

"I am sure they had a contingency plan Doctor Blum, or at the very least, a location where they would meet up after retrieving the case. I am sure that Roy rubbed his hands in glee when he found out that I, not the Inspector had taken the case."

"I'm sure you're right, William." Rowan exclaimed. "He knew that if I had taken it to the station, there would be little to no chance he could make another play for it. But, if it were here, at the castle..." He let the thought trail off.

William flashed a quick self-satisfied smirk. "I was counting on him making another grab for it and after I had read the documents, I was sure he would!"

"So, you knew Roy was behind it?" Catty asked. "You just let him burn the *Aunt Polly?"*

William frowned and shook his head. "Of course not! If I had the slightest inkling that Roy was within a hundred miles of here, I would have turned the case over to the Inspector immediately! For my oversight, I had my yacht nearly burned to the waterline and almost lost two of the dearest people in my life!

"No, I failed to make the connection. I should have seen his pattern in all this, but I underestimated him again! I did not consider the chance that he might return to this area and set up shop again. I worried he might reappear for revenge, but never for another crime! I cannot say I was shocked to see him step out of the smoke on the dock, but I was as surprised as anyone."

"So, what was all that, *A Scandal in Bohemia* stuff about?" I asked. "I remember reading the story when I was the lad, but I don't recall the plot."

"Oh!" Blum spoke, "I know that one! It's where Irene Adler gets the best of Holmes."

William smiled in his condescending way, "Yes, that is how the story ends, but that is not what Roy was referring to. In the story, Holmes sets a fire at the residence where Irene Adler is staying to draw her into revealing the hiding spot of the damaging letters.

"Roy's variation on the theme was to set fire to the *Aunt Polly* to draw us out of my home so he could have his men ransack my castle for the case."

"Well, why the boat? Why not set a fire at your house?"

"For two reasons, Doctor. First, because we were here, and I am certain they had a healthy respect for Collin's talent with a firearm and second...stone does not burn easily." He took a few puffs on his pipe and added, "I imagine he was delighted to set the *Aunt Polly* on fire, either to draw us into his net, or if for nothing more than revenge upon me." He looked a bit glum as he added, "Had I realized who our adversary was, I would have set a guard on the old girl."

"Even so, your Uncle was one step ahead of them. It was his idea to secretly put men around the grounds tonight, Collin." Rowan said to me. "It was his plan that saved this day!" He looked at my Uncle and beamed, "and bringing Frank Chapman in for support was sheer genius!"

"Yes, and a plan he could have shared with me!" I looked right at my Uncle. "It may have saved us all a lot of pain!"

324

As soon as the words were out of my mouth, I regretted them. It wasn't my intention to accuse him of nearly getting Ozaki killed. He met my eyes with a level look and said seriously,

"Had you not jack rabbited off with Ozaki, I might have done so. At the very least I would have put you on guard. If you recall, I did try to stop you, as I did when you hared off from the docks earlier. You are brave and you are fast, Frohman, but you are far too impetuous for prudence's sake! You always have been."

Of course, he was right, so I kept my mouth shut and tried to look sheepish.

"Still", he went on, "it was your heroic act that saved Ozaki's life. Had you not dove in after him...well, I shudder to think what my life would be now."

Catty put her hand on the back of my neck, and I felt much better. "Yeah...well...I was still dumb enough to drop my gun for Roy to pick up!"

"Actually Frohman, that too was a bit of good luck. You see, we found another pistol on Roy. One that he brought with him. Had he not picked up your gun—he would have used his own. Thank the stars; he wasn't familiar with that model. That split second of hesitation was all...the Inspector needed."

"What caused the hesitation?" Blum asked, though I could see that everyone but Wiliam was wondering the same thing. I took out the pistol and showed them. "This is a semi-automatic pistol, you see. It will fire as fast as I can pull the trigger. But! Only after it's manually cocked for the first shot. After that, I can blast away until the magazine is empty.

"Luckily, Roy didn't know that. When he went to shoot Uncle Will, the trigger wouldn't budge and that gave..."

"Giving the Chief Inspector," William put in quickly, "the chance to draw and put that monster in his grave!"

Rowan shook his head, obviously still having a hard time remembering or believing in our version. "I don't remember shooting him at all. And three times at that!"

"Well, the three of us are grateful that you did, Chief." I said, hoping to shore up our story.

"That was quite some shooting," I added in a joking tone. "Great grouping! Well done"

"Hear, Hear!" William cheered to our laughter.

To all our surprise, Catty rose off the couch next to me and leaned over to kiss the Chief Inspector tenderly on the temple. She sat back down next to me and said, "Thank you"

Rowan looked a bit embarrassed. "No need to thank me for saving their lives, they would have done the same for me."

'And did!', I thought to myself.

Catty smoothed the skirt over her lap and said, "Of course, I'm grateful that they weren't shot, but that's not what the kiss was for." She paused, "It was for killing that bastard."

As we all stare at her in stunned silence, she turned to my Uncle with a glint in her eyes. "Now Mr. Gillette, if you would, please tell me how my brother fit into all this."

32

William met her gaze with an intensity of his own. He was still in character and I was sure he would stay that way for now. I realized it was easier for him to deal with emotional matters as Sherlock Holmes. William Gillette was far too good a man to say these truths to someone he cared about.

"Catherine. I will give you one more chance to retire…no? Very well then-- prepare yourself." He relit his pipe and began, "Marquis, in many ways, is the lynch pin of this whole affair."

He looked to me and Catty. "Frohman, Catherine, do you remember what was unusual about the entries in Marquis' logbook? The one Frohman picked up off the floor of the Inn after the fight?"

I had to think about it and the answer he was looking for tickled the back of my mind, but it was Catty who came up with it first.

"All the deliveries to the mysterious 'S'. That and the barge were his two most frequent spots."

"Excellent, Catherine. I wasn't sure at the time, but I came to realize that the 'S' stood for Susan Wallace."

"Susan," The Doctor blurted out in disbelief. "My old nurse? What could she possible have to do with…" his voice trailed off then he sat up and cried out, "Oh! I think I know where you are going with this."

Rowan looked annoyed. "Well, I don't! That woman is practically a hermit! You think she was one of the gang? Susan Wallace?"

William sighed. "Do not be ridiculous, Chief Inspector! Susan Wallace was merely a pawn in the robbery and an indirect one at that! What you must consider is that Wallace is her married name. Her maiden name is Macduffee and she still lives in the house her parents built, and until last summer, one she shared with her brother, Chester E Macduffee.

"If you do not know the name, Chester Macduffee was one of the foremost marine engineers in the country. His work in undersea salvage suits was ground-breaking! And, I believe, if we were to take a look inside the boat house at the back of Susan's property—where her brother did much of his work— we would find a deep-sea diving suit or two. I would also wager there was one missing, which Marquis took and put to use. The fact that Marquis was wearing nothing but long-johns and woolen socks when he was found told me the extent of his involvement."

"Of course!" I slapped my forehead. "He wasn't dressed because he was in the suit, but he would need some protection from the water. It's still pretty cold this time of year!"

Catty, her lower lip trembling as she fought back tears, asked, "So, are you saying my brother was behind all this?"

William gave her an exaggerated skeptical frown. "Marquis? Behind a plot by a foreign government to steal top secret documents? I think not! The train robbery was certainly the work of our Captain Roy. It started months ago when Marquis began making bi-weekly deliveries to Susan. As he was her only contact with the outside world and she was dependent on the supplies he brought her and, considering Marquis's well-known charm, she gradually opened up to him. At some point in her conversations with him, she must have told him about her brother and the suits that were still in his workshop." At this point my uncle paused to take a few puffs.

"Later on, when the barge was stationed at the train bridge, Marquis started delivering supplies there also. With, as Roy put it, 'a few slaps on the back and a lot of drinks', Marquis soon succumbed to the false comradery of the barge crew and it's Captain. He must have told them about the suits and Roy saw an opportunity to put them to use. He convinced Marquis to procure one.

"It must have been Captain Row who put up the money for the air pump Marquis installed on his boat-... Why do you think Roy ponied up?" Rowan asked.

"Because air compressors of that size and power, are a specialized piece of machinery and it would have cost more than Marquis made in a year. I know, for a fact, from the bill Roy presented me with for the one he and Nickolas installed on the *Aunt Polly* last year!"

"Well, it paid for itself tonight," Rowan said off-handedly.

William, seeing the confused look on my face, explained. "Last year I had the system converted to a fire suppression system. Luckily, Ozaki activated it before he was attacked, or the old girl would be sitting on the bottom of the river now for sure!"

He paused to reach for another bottle of soda, opened it, then he gave Blum and Rowan a smirk. "That, gentlemen, was the start of the 'River Monster' episodes.

"Marquis, Roy, and some of the crew took the suit out onto the river to practice with it. Therein lays the basis for all the mysterious bubbles and underwater damages discovered. The mechanical grips, used as hands on the suits, are extremely powerful and more than capable of crushing bait traps or scoring the keels of boats.

329

"Working at night, with the sound of the compressor muffled by the padded box built around the unit, they were neither seen nor heard. I'm sure if we were to interview some of the more adamant witnesses to the mysterious events, we would find that they recalled seeing Marquis' boat in the area, although they would not have made special note of it as he was a common sight on the river at any times of the day or night.

"When Roy was sure they could handle the recovery, he set the other half of his plans in motion at the right time. His henchmen killed the two agents in Providence and took their place. The rest you already know."

Something occurred to me. "But the compressor wasn't on Marquis' boat-- It was on the barge. Why would they go to the trouble of moving it?"

"And you're leaving out a big part, Gillette," Rowan announced. "You surely haven't forgotten the payroll robbery. From what you told me, it was obviously pulled off with the new underwater skillset Roy and his gang had. And why would they kill a man and take a safe—just to return it within twelve hours?

Uncle Will was dreading the answer he had to give. In a sad voice, he said, "The answers to both your questions stem from the same source. Marquis acted alone when he attacked that boat."

Blum and Rowan both gasped and Catty made a strangled moan. I turned my head to see tears streaming down her cheeks but was proud when she said in a level voice "My brother killed that man…"

William sighed. "If it is any consolation, Catherine, I do not believe that Marquis acted with any real malice. I want to believe he started out by simply trying to show off to his new friends; the barge gang. I know he could be wild and sometimes reckless, but I do not think he was evil at heart."

Rowan look as if he was about to dispute that observation. I'm sure the police tendencies in him would see the murder and the payroll robbery in a much harsher light. Doctor Blum seemed more concerned for Catty's feelings as he watched her closely. As a guy who did a lot of dumb things in his life, I could see where things got out of hand once it started, but I had my doubts also.

"Are you sure he did the job all by himself Uncle Will. I mean, that suit weighs a ton and there was a lot of equipment to handle. I don't see how he could have managed stopping a boat dead in the water, capsized it, and then smashed through the bulk heads to tear the payroll safe off its mount and carry it off."

Uncle Will said nothing as he sipped his drink, so the Chief piped up. "He makes a lot of sense, William. I think he has torn some considerable holes in your theory."

Uncle Will looked up sharply, his face blank. "Then consider this, Inspector. Aside from the two men on the boat, Marquis was the only person who knew they would layover at the spot. It would be a fairly simple task to tie up on the riverbank or in one of the nearby estuaries and hide it == perhaps making use of one of the existing duck blinds that riddle that side of the river. He then donned the suit and turned on the compressor before slipping over the side in the shallows and walking out into deeper waters. The suit, while cumbersome on land, would be buoyant in the water and easier to handle. Then he only had to wait for the boat to come along."

"That doesn't explain how he stopped it so suddenly. Even if he grabbed the keel, the weight of the boat would have just carried him along!" I argued.

"Do you recall the missing pin, Frohman?"

I took me a moment to remember. "Sure. It was missing from the shackle on the end of the chain attached to the anchor we found lying on the deck of Marquis' boat."

"Excellent! I see you have learned to file information! Marquis came up with clever plan. He must have found a spot in the boat's path that was deep enough to hide, but shallow enough so he could nearly reach the surface. He then drove a spike into the river bottom and attached the anchor and its chain to it. When the boat passed over him, he reached up and smacked the prongs of the anchor into the bow, below the waterline."

I slapped my forehead and groaned. "Of course! That was bottom paint on the anchor, not blood!"

"Correct again, Frohman. The result of the jarring stop was two breeches in the hull. As the boat swung around, Marquis used the mechanical grips on the suit to disable the props and then began to try and capsize the vessel. That's when things took a turn to the worse. As we heard from Mr. Larabino, just before he was tossed overboard, the pilot went to the stern and saw something in the water. He drew a knife and leapt over the back.

"Now, no sane man would have attacked a creature in its own element. Gentlemen, what the pilot saw was neither natural nor supernatural! He saw a man shape and knew what was happening. Sadly, his dedication to his responsibilities cost him his life."

"That poor man." Catty said in a low voice. "My brother murdered him! I can't believe I grew up with that monster!"

After a pause, William shrugged. "Perhaps you should not judge him so harshly, Catherine. Although he was the cause, one could almost make a case for self-defense. After all, if the pilot had succeeded in cutting the hoses to the suit, Marquis would have surely drowned before he could make it to shore. I

332

doubt Marquis had mastered control of the power in the grips on his suit. When he grabbed the arm that was wielding the knife, he nearly tore it off and in the ensuing struggle he fatally wounded his attacker. I am sure he was more scared than vicious."

We all looked to Catty, who mulled it over and replied softly. "Thank you for that. I know Marquis was a bad apple, but I never saw that much meanness in him."

William nodded, the Chief scowled, and the Doctor shrugged.

"In any event," William went on. "As Mr. Larabino was floundering to shore, Marquis managed to turn the boat turtle and then used the grips to smash through the cabin roof and tear the safe from its mount. After removing the shackle to the post in the river bed, he took the anchor and strong box, and then made his way to his own boat to escape."

"Whoa, wait a minute, Uncle Will," I protested. "I can see everything you've said so far, but he must have had help when he got back to his boat! That safe was heavy and there was no way he walked out of the water in that cumbersome suit, carrying it—much less getting it onto his deck, all alone!"

"Ah, Frohman! Two steps forward and one step back! Do you not recall the other point of significance I told you to take note of?"

I thought about it and then let my breath out slowly in a long 'ooooohhhhh', with my eyebrows raised.

"Correct." He looked to Rowan to explain. "We discovered a long cord attached to the engaging lever on the motor that drives the winch on his boat.

Before he set out to trap his quarry, Marquis lowered a harness into the river with his winch and tossed the cord in after it.

"When he got back to a spot below his boat, he simply put the harness on the safe, then pulled the cord to raise it. After that, he walked out of the water and, once on deck, swung his prize onto the deck."

William paused as he reloaded his pipe again. The wait was too much for the doctor.

"What happened then?" Blum demanded.

"Why, he took his ill- gotten gains to the barge," He replied as he lit his pipe.

"Where he did not get the reception he expected!"

33

We all began to ask him what he meant by that, well, everyone except the Chief Inspector. Rowan stared at his feet for a minute then slapped the arm of his chair loud enough to cut us all off in mid-query.

"That's why the money was returned so fast!" He nearly shouted, giving my Uncle a bug-eyed stare.

William looked as proud as a mother hen. In a challenging tone, he said "Tell us what happened then."

Rowan rubbed his hands together briskly, his excitement growing over his epiphany. "Well… I imagine Roy was furious when Marquis showed up with that stolen payroll."

"He was mad?" Catty asked. "Why would he be mad? They were all a bunch of thieves and murderers!"

Still looking to my uncle, he replied, "The last thing Roy would want at that late stage of his plans was attention that could upset the apple cart! As long as that money was still missing, my men would have been all over that area until we figured it out. He knew I'd be all over that barge with a fine-tooth comb. So, he secretly left the money on the dock where someone would be sure to find it." He slapped the arm of his chair again, "And he got just what he wanted! I pulled my men off the river and reassigned them, leaving him a clear field to pull off his train caper!" He stopped there and his eyes flickered towards Catty. He knew the next part of this tale would be hard for her to hear.

Oblivious to the drama, the Doctor blurted out, "Well? What happened then?"

Still keeping his eyes averted from Catty, Rowan replied. "You already know the answer to that, Doctor. In his rage, Roy beat and mutilated Marquis and tossed his body in the river. Then he took the suit and the compressor off Marquis' boat and set it adrift."

I thought about it and couldn't agree. "I don't know about that. Gordon told us he recovered the boat past Essex and that's miles down the river. A boat that size wouldn't drift that far that fast."

Rowan flicked a hand at me in dismissal. "It's the only way it makes sense..." He broke off his explanation when there was a loud knocking at the door. He pulled out his watch and checked the time. "Hm. That was quick." He stood suddenly and said to my Uncle. "That must be my men. They're here to give me a ride back to the station. He called out and two constables hustled in and carried the documents off to the car on his orders

We all stood, and the Doctor gathered his hat and cane. The Chief took a step towards the door then stopped in front of Catty.

"I am going to write a report on your brother. I have to close out the case, or there will be too many questions asked.

But I won't make it public. In light of the outcome, it wouldn't do much good anyways. The only hitch is that the victim's family deserves the truth."

"I understand, Chief Inspector." She leaned up and kissed him on the cheek. "Thank you. I would spare my family if I could."

Rowan nodded and then added one for me as he held out his hand to my Uncle.

336

William took it and clapped him on the shoulder. "Congratulations Inspector—this will be another feather in your cap! Fortune and glory wait!"

Rowan smiled and shook his head slowly. "Again, none of this would have been resolved without your help, William. I am in your debt." My Uncle opened his mouth to protest, but Rowan cut him off. "Never fear, William. I know the routine by now...I will leave the two of you, "He jerked his head in my direction, "out of my official report. I will protect your privacy—as much as I can without committing perjury!"

"That is all I can ask, Chief Inspector. I know you'll do your best."

"Then it's Good night, William." He headed for the door, calling out over his shoulder, "Coming Doctor?"

"Be right with you." Blum replied as he picked up his medical bag. He stopped at Catherine and took her hand. "I'm so sorry, my girl. You should get some rest." He patted his bag. "Do you want something to help you sleep?"

Catty declined his offer and bid him a goodnight and then, I think to hide her tears, Catty began to gather up the empty glasses and took them to the kitchen. The Doctor looked at her glumly as she walked away and came over to my Uncle and me. He looked over to be sure Catty was out of earshot and said. "One thing that doesn't make sense to me William, is the condition we found Marquis in. Why would Roy bother to maul him so? He could have just shot him or tied an anchor to him and toss him in the river! Leaving him around for us to find would just draw the kind of attention he didn't want."

William hesitated, and then shrugged. "Who knows what transpires in the criminal mind, Doctor."

Blum looked him straight in the eye, "You do, usually."

With that, he made an exit as dramatic as any William ever did on stage.

Uncle Will laughed as the Doctor went out the door. I was amazed at how alert he was, but I was grateful. There was still a lot left unanswered. "Uncle Will, there are a few things I still don't understand..."

Just then, Catty came back in the room and William held up a hand to stop my questions. "We will finish this tomorrow, Collin."

Then he stepped around me and took Catty by the shoulders as she bent down to gather another tray of dishes. He gently pulled her upright and said softly. "Leave them, Catherine. It's been a long day for all of us. You need to get some rest young Lady, so march yourself up to your room and get to bed." Then he shocked me, by folding her into his long arms and hugging her fiercely.

When they broke apart, Catty and I stared at each other for a moment, but it was too awkward with my Uncle standing between us. She said her goodnights and headed up the stairs to her room. When we heard the door of her room shut in the stillness, William put a hand on my shoulder and gently shoved me toward the stairs. "Now you, Collin. Get some rest. We have another long day ahead of us tomorrow, I'm afraid."

Later on, as I was lying asleep in bed, I awoke to feel movement next to me. I carefully rolled over to find, Catty snoring softly in a deep slumber.

That was fine with me.

34

Catty was gone when I awoke, but I still wasn't alone in the room. I heard a 'whish, whish' noise as my eyes cracked open, and saw Ozaki standing at the foot of my bed, holding a dark suit up with one hand and brushing it with the other. A bright white bandage encircled his head, but otherwise not a thing about him was out of place.

"Good morning, *vera saku.*" He said cheerfully. "It is good you are awake. Your Uncre is getting dressed. He wants you to meet him in the kitchen for coffee when you are ready." He hung the suit on a hook on the back of the door and said, "You need to pack your crothes better. It took me an hour to get the wrinkres out."

I was amazed at his resiliency. Aside from the bandage that encircled the top of his head, you would never know he nearly died twelve hours earlier.

I swung out of bead and reached for a robe hanging off a chair. "It's not like I can hang a garment bag on my motorcycle, Uncle Ozaki." I quipped as I belted my robe.

He gave me a sly look and smiled as he opened the door to the hallway for me. "Then again, I suppose you will have someone do it for you from now on."

That hit me right between the eyes as I headed for the bathroom. After everything that happened in the last few days, soon I would have to return home to take the mantel of a million-dollar theater business --- that I knew little about. Then, there were the feelings inside of me that were growing for Catty. It was all too much.

At least, I had the ability to push everything else to the back of my mind and concentrate on the here, and now. First, I would get past Marquis' funeral then I could start making plans. After a French bath and a shave, I returned to my room to find Ozaki gone, the bed made, and the suit laid out on it. On the floor next to the bed, were my boots, polished to a high shine. A tie clip, cufflinks, and my father's pocket watch were laid out in a row on the nightstand. From the smell emanating from the kitchen as I approached, I knew the coffee was ready and I was more than ready for it! I found Uncle Will sitting at the counter by the window as Ozaki poured him a steaming cup of the brew. When I entered, Ozaki flipped another mug and filled it.

"Good Morning, Collin," Uncle Will greeted me. He looked me up and down as he reached for the coffee Ozaki held out for him. "I hope you got some sleep last night."

I knew where this was going and decided to nip it in the bud. I took my coffee from Ozaki and took a sip. "It wasn't like that, Uncle Will. Nothing happened between us last night. She just needed some ...human contact. Can you blame her after what she learned last night? When I woke in the middle of the night, she was just there lying next to me in the dark, sawing wood. When I woke the second time, she was gone, the sun was up, and Uncle Ozaki was brushing my suit. That's all."

Ozaki's eyes crinkled over his cup of tea. He took a sip and said in a low voice, "Some Romeo."

I would have retorted but Uncle Will cut me off. "Enough!" He snapped, glaring at both of us. "Catherine is in for a long difficult day and deserves nothing less than your sympathy and compassion for her feelings!"

340

My stomach dropped to my knees. "Gosh, Uncle Will, has she come down yet?" I asked in a panicked voice. I wouldn't be happy if she was listening in right now.

He seemed slightly amused by me trepidation. "Relax Collin. She's long gone for more than an hour. The Doctor picked her up this morning to give her time to be reunited with her family before the Church service."

"Oh," I was relieved she didn't hear me telling William and Ozaki our private business. To change the subject, I asked, "What time does it start? Do I have time to clean up our bikes before we go?"

William shook his head somberly. "No need. We won't be taking our motorcycles."

That was a stunner. "Someone picking us up?"

"No, we'll be taking the *Helena*."

Now, that didn't make sense! If I remembered correctly from our top floor telescopic scan of the town—it seemed like it was a month ago since Catty guided that tour—the church was a good mile from the docks. What if it was a long procession to the graveyard? Not to mention if there was a reception back at the house.

In any case, I wasn't going to argue with him on such a somber day. "Well, I guess we'd better get going then. We have to get over and dock then hoof it up to the Church, if we want to get there before the service begins."

"Finish your coffee, Frohman. We will not be attending the service."

"We're not?"

"No. I told Catherine that we would meet them at the graveside. There is something we must attend to first."

He went back to his coffee, facing the window he greeted a warm spring day outside. His eyes closed and he fell into one of his deep thought trances and I knew I would get no more out of him for now.

I took the last drag off a cigarette and tossed the butt into the water. I had to pull the collar of my coat up over my ears to keep them warm out here on the river. At least Uncle Will, who insisted on driving the *Helena*, kept it at a quarter throttle. There was enough of a breeze to make the river a bit choppy and, going any faster we'd be soaked in spray before we got to the other side.

"So, tell me again Uncle Will, where are we going and why is it so important that we need to skip Marquis' funeral?"

He gave me a sideways look. "You should have figured out our destination by now. I would not have attended his service in any case."

"I thought you liked him?"

He shrugged. "I did, until he showed his real character in these last few days. He had a black heart and, though I may say a prayer for his soul, I will not honor him in a house of the Lord!"

"Jeepers, Uncle Will, you weren't that hard on him last night. You practically told Catty that he was just misguided!"

He stared at me with flint in his eyes. "I lied. I would spare that girl all this grief and pain if only she had let me. She has been through so much." He added, flicking another look at me.

I was afraid I was going to get another lecture about Catty, however William suddenly cut the throttle back, and I looked up to see us approaching a dock that stuck out from a private home. It took me a minute to recognize the place from this angle.

"Why are we stopping here?

He expertly cut the engines and the *Helena* slowly glided sideways to the dock.

"To finish this... Once and for all. Would you mind getting the bow line and tying us off?"

William tied off the stern then walked up the dock towards the house. I quickened my step to catch up as we crossed the lawn to the front steps. I was still confused as to why we were here, of all places.

"Is now the time to confront her about the diving suit? Even if she did know Marquis had it, do you think she was an accomplice?"

Uncle Will stopped dead in his tracks and looked down at me, with that infuriating smirk and said, "You really have not thought this out yet, have you. My word, Frohman! Your mind is like a bog. Every fact you take in is tossed into the muck to sink out of sight."

"So, exactly what should I do with them, the facts?" I asked. I knew I was being petulant, and I really hated being talked down to.

He smiled and answered, "You use them to build a bridge over the mire." He clapped me once on the upper arm and went up the steps to the front door.

Once there, he struck a regal pose, one hand behind his back and one holding his cane planted on the porch floor. In the back of my head, I wondered if this cane had any special features – or if we would need one!

When he was set just right, he looked to me and jutted his chin at the front door. Feeling like a valet, I stepped up and knocked on the door. We heard the distinct scrape of a chair on the wooden floor, but no one acknowledged the knock. After a moment, William boomed out in his stage voice,

"Susan Wallace! Open this door. We must speak." When nothing happened, he indicated I should knock again. This time, I used my fist sideways and rapped as hard as I could. The door frame shook with the blows. The door flew open and I jumped back at the sight that greeted us. Susan had gone quite downhill since we had last seen her. Before, she was a handsome woman for her age, but now she looked the hag. She looked as if she hadn't bathed or changed her clothes in a week. Her sallow face was deeply etched, and her mouth quivered like a dog before it barked.

But it was her eyes that scared me the most. Red-rimmed and blood shot, they never seemed to stop moving, flickering back and forth. Something -- or someone -- had pushed this poor woman over the edge.

A few paces into her home, she turned and snarled at us. Well, William really, she didn't seem to even notice me. As they stared each other down, I took a look around.

The place had become a mess since we had last been here. There were smears of dirt all over the floor and even some on the furniture. The greatest amount was in front of the fireplace and it had that rotting odor of low tide. It looked as if she was burning rags in the hearth, instead of wood or coal. The knick-knacks that had lined the mantle were knocked over, with many strewn about the floor. Even the harpoon hanging above the lintel looked the worse for wear. The polished wooden haft was splintered on the end and had a great crack that split it up to the metal cap, though the shaft and barb gleamed in the sunlight that came in.

344

Wild eyed and disheveled, she slowly stepped backwards until her back bumped into the back of a rocker in front of the fireplace. Uncle Will matched her step for step until he was just a few feet away from her.

"Git! Get back on your boat and be gone, Gillette! I don't want to hear anything you have to say."

William looked down at her sternly. "No, you do not. Yet, better you tell me everything than try and explain yourself to the Chief Inspector."

Her eyes narrowed to thin slits, but still, she didn't reply.

"Very well, Mrs. Wallace." William said in a reasonable tone, "I will make this quick and easy for you." He reached into the pockets of his overcoat and pulled out his fists with two wads of cloth in each hand. Her eyes were glued to his fists as he raised them slightly above his shoulders.

"Explain these and I shall leave you in peace." He opened his hand and twin squares of linen dropped like the curtains on a stage. Both were white with fancy lace and I recognized them at once.

The one in his left hand was the cloth she had wrapped around his leg, when we were here last. The one in his right was wrapped around the dead baby found on Uncle Will's property...

35

The evil grimace dropped from her face and her features softened as she reached up and took the cloth from William's hand and clutched it to her face. After a moment, she lowered her hands and clutched the cloth to her chest. "My Kara." She murmured as the tears rolled down her face. She turned and walked to the front of the rocker and slowly sank into it, her back to us now.

"The child was yours and the father was … Marquis." William said gently.

There was a long pause, where I wished I had brought a flask, and then she finally spoke in a voice that sounded from the grave.

"Aye. He was. What can I say in my defense? That I was lonely? That he was handsome and charming, so eager to be sure I had everything I needed? All of that is true. I was weak. He plied me with attention and…I welcomed it. He sweet talked me, then, despite my marriage vows and my sensibilities…I let him seduce me."

She fell silent and William prompted her. "So, when you became pregnant, you left the doctor's practice before your condition became apparent. Why did you not seek the doctor's assistance?"

"That was Marquis again. He convinced me that we could have the child on our own. After all, I was a trained nurse and he promised to stay by my side. He told me that it was proof of

346

our love and we shouldn't let the town judge us. I…I wanted to believe him. I am a married woman and I didn't want to show the world my letter 'A', that was swelling more in my belly every month! Never-the-less, I was filled with joy on January second, when my time came, and Marquis and I delivered my sweet Kara into this world. We cherished our child."

"Not enough to keep her safe and alive!" I hadn't meant to say it out loud, but the words exploded out of my mouth. She whirled around in her seat and snarled at me with a look that made me wish I had brought my pistol instead of the flask!

"I had nothing to do with that, you heartless twit!" She screamed. Then she turned back to the cold hearth and choked back another sob. Marquis told me that he had an Aunt, who was childless and would be overjoyed to have a baby. He said we could have the best of both worlds. Kara would be loved and cherished and raised in a good home and we would still be able to see here from time to time. He convinced me that someday I might even befriend her and be able to tell her that I was her mother…

So, when she was just a few weeks old, one morning I dressed her warmly and bundled her up for travel…and I gave her to that monster."

Her shoulders shook as the grief overwhelmed her again. After a minute, she spoke. "Then I learned the truth from you."

William took a long deep breath. "Then, when Marquis came to you for help the other day, instead you took that harpoon from its place and ran him through with it. Somehow, you both ended up in the shallows, where you held him under, like a speared fish, until he drowned.

"But after he was dead, you realized that you could not pull the harpoon from his body because of the design. So, you took a rock from the river bottom and pounded the shaft until the tip

347

completely went through him. Then you unscrewed the head and pulled the shaft out of him.

"It was simple enough then to push him out into the current and let him drift away."

She didn't say anything at first, still sobbing quietly, but she regained some of her composure and answered. "My, my, William Gillette. You are as clever as they say.

"When I saw Marquis backing up to the dock, I had a…revelation. I grabbed the harpoon and went out the door. As soon as I was outside, Marquis was calling for me to come and help him. He said he was hurt badly but he had no idea.

"When I reached the dock, he saw the purpose in my stride, and the harpoon in my hands and he tried to escape his due. He pushed the throttle forward, but I was quicker. With a great leap, I landed on his deck and plunged my spear into his side.

The momentum carried us both over the gunnel and we ended up in the shallow water and deep mud of low tide. Still, he tried to escape me, but I held on with both hands, tugging and twisting the shaft with all my might. He finally pitched forward into the water and I held him down with my weight on the shaft. The rest… the rest was as you said. When I saw the wounds I had inflicted on his body, I figured if he were ever found, fools would blame it on that creature everyone was going on about!"

"And his boat?" William asked the back of her head.

"I didn't think about it. It just kept going out into the river and the current turned it downstream. It was still running when I lost sight of it."

William stared at her back for a long moment. He looked like he was done with the whole scenario. Finally, he spoke, gently, but firmly.

"Susan, what Marquis did was inexcusable -- in the eyes of God and man -- but that did not give you the right to take the life of another human being."

Susan didn't answer and I had had enough by this point. I wanted nothing more but to go and get the Chief Inspector and wash my hands of this whole affair. Poor Catty lost a brother and a niece she never knew she had. I was about to tell my Uncle that it was time to go, when Susan drew a great breath and suddenly screamed, causing both of us to jump back.

"It was the will of God!" she shrieked.

She leapt out of her chair and turned to face us. Her teeth were bared, and her eyes nearly rolled back in her head. Raising a fist in the air like a maniacal prohibitionist, she yelled at the top of her lungs, spittle flying from her lips. "When he came back to me, beaten and weak, God showed me what must be done!" She pointed to the harpoon above and behind her, "He gave me his spear and commanded me to smite that evil filth from this earth."

We both stared at her, too stunned to move and she went on, in a milder tone. "God needs a sacrifice...like Abraham of old. He demanded my first born as a sign of obedience. A sacrifice to make room in me for his will...."

William didn't flinch and looked down at her coldly. "Our Lord had nothing to do with this, Susan. There was no sacrifice...She was just a baby girl...Your daughter...Kara was her name."

That was the straw that broke the camel's back. Susan's eyes flew open wide and froth bubbled out from between her lips.

"MY BABY!" she screeched and collapsed on the floor at William's feet. I thought she had a seizure and died, but she

349

was still sobbing and saying her daughter's name over and over.

William looked down at her and said, "We shall never speak of this again. I hope that God grants you peace someday."

He looked at me and we turned and walked out the door. Inside, she began wailing again, that only slightly lowered in volume when I closed the door behind us. I could still hear the shrieks until we started up the Helena and pulled away from her dock.

36

I took the wheel on this leg of our trip. The wind had died off and the water was smoother, so I goosed the *Helena* and took us away from that wretched home as fast as I could. When the dock was well in our wake, I cut the power some so I could speak to my Uncle without shouting over the engines. I swiveled in the pilot's seat to look back at him.

"Shall I take us over to the town dock?" I asked, assuming that was where we were heading.

William, who had stretched out on the bench seat along the side of the deck, looked at me from under half lidded eyes. "You are under the impression I wish to make a report to the Chief Inspector. I do not."

"You don't?"

He tilted his head and asked, "What good would it do? Marquis is beyond the reach of the law now, and Susan…well, I think it best we leave Susan to her demons I fear she shall suffer far more left alone than she would under arrest. Besides, had she not killed Marquis he would surely have hanged for the murder of the payroll guard."

"Gee, Uncle, I never thought of you as an 'eye for an eye' kind of person."

"I am not, Collin. Vengeance is the Lords and the Lord's alone. Yet, I do believe in balance. I have often seen, throughout my life that most situations will even out in the end.

Now, take us to the cemetery where Kara is buried. Marquis will be interned there, in his family's plot.

"And, could we please continue on in silence? I need time to reflect."

His tone was so somber and his face so long, I nodded and turned back to the wheel and steering the boat. For myself, I could applaud his form of justice, and I had no zeal to see that mad woman hanged. But I also knew it would challenge his morality. Evil either thrives or dies – goodness suffers perpetually.

Life was so unfair at times. Where everyone else involved was basking in glory and accolades—we were left with a sour taste of the ugly truth in our mouths...

Despite the peaceful beauty of the river, the rising sun warming the air enough for us to shed our overcoats, and the blooming foliage on both sides, the half hour trip to the cemetery was pure torture for me.

I was still jumping out of my skin with questions I wanted answered. It had been a whirlwind of a week and though I was witness to much of what happened, there were many points that I just couldn't string together! I felt like I had gone to a play and fell asleep after the first act, and only awoke for the finale!

Yet, I had to respect my uncle's wishes, so I kept my tongue behind my teeth. As we approached the dock, I cut the power and spun the wheel, neatly setting the *Helena* on a slowing drift to the dock. I was happy to find uncle more like his usual self as he jumped up right before we kissed the pylons.

"That was excellent seamanship, Collin! You do your forebears proud!" He clapped me on the shoulders with a big smile and took up the stern line. In no time, we had the *Helena* secured and, after straightening our clothes and brushing ourselves off, headed off the dock and into the graveyard.

We only made it as far as the first row of stones when William stopped and pulled out his pocket watch. He grunted and put it away. Looking around, he pointed with his cane to a bench that was set at the edge of the lawn, close to the river. "We may as well have a seat. The procession won't be here for a while yet."

"That's fine with me." I answered. It was a good a time as any to pry some explanations out of him.

Seating ourselves, I was impressed by the beautiful vista that spread out before us. Across the river, the high hills were the perfect backdrop to the flowing blues of the water. One thing struck me as odd.

"Not that it's not a nice view," I commented, "But shouldn't we be facing the graves rather than the river?"

Wiliam chuckled, "I suspect it was put this way for people like us—those that are here out of duty more than compassion or," he paused and gave me a sly look, "love."

I let that pass and didn't reply as I stared out over the river. I let the silence stretch out while I tried to frame my next thought.

"You have questions, Frohman."

I nearly laughed out loud at that understatement! Instead, I took out my flask and took a quick snort.

"One or two, I guess…maybe a hundred in all!"

He laughed like a loon, and then shook his head. "Frohman…you are so much like your father. You have seen all that I have seen and heard all that I have heard. You already know the answers to your questions."

When I just stared back at him, he laughed again and took out his cigarettes. "Still, if I can help clarify a few minor points for you," he lit his smoke and blew out a huge plume. "Ask away!"

"Then let's start at the beginning," I suggested. "What put you on to Susan in the first place."

"Simple really. When I realized that no one in town knew of an unwanted pregnancy or a missing baby, I fell back on the simple rule, written by Sherlock's creator – Conan Doyle. , that applied. 'When all other possibilities have been exhausted...'"

"Whatever remains, no matter how improbable, must be the solution!" I finished for him just like my father would have.

He barked a laugh, delighted by my knowledge. I explained, "My father quoted that to me from the time I was very young."

He shook his head and the smile faded from his face. "Oh, how I miss your father, Collin. He would have been so proud of you."

I didn't want this to turn into a crying fest, so I patted him on the knee and said, "Just go on—I'm sure he's listening too."

Uncle Will brightened at that and came back to life and continued with details about Susan. "She first became a candidate for my investigation when the doctor mentioned her, and her abilities as a midwife at the office, but she became a suspect after our talk with Kitty at the Inn.

"She was a recluse that no one had laid eyes on in months, and she had a strong knowledge of child birthing. The only obstacle was her refusal to have contact with anyone."

"So, you faked that spill outside her home. Which could have caused you considerable harm!" I accused.

He raised an eyebrow at that and gave me his little smirk. "Oh, Frohman. I do so find comfort in your concern.

"Yes, I did. I was counting on her ingrained training as a nurse to overwhelm her desire for seclusion. Of course, I was right."

"You were stupid!" I pointed out. "You gave yourself a nasty burn!"

He wasn't sure how to react to that. I'm sure he was rarely called 'stupid' by anyone.

His smirk became an acquiescent pout. "Perhaps. I laid the bike down gently, but I confess I had forgotten about the hot tail pipe when I slipped my leg beneath it. Still, it only enhanced my deception and served its purpose to gain us access to her."

"Did you know then that she was the mother? I know I didn't make any connection."

"You should have. Though something about the napkin she wrapped around my burn nudged the back of my mind, it was the knitting needles and yarn next to the chair that connected her."

I closed my eyes and thought back to the first time we were in her house and it came to me. "Red! The yarn in the basket next to the rocker and the baby's booties were that same shade of red, almost crimson!"

He smiled and nodded with a slight tilt to his head. "Of course. It was confirmed last night when I received the baby's clothing from the Doctor, and I matched the napkins."

I shook my head slowly in amazement. The answers always seemed so simple when he explained them. "So, when did you peg Marquis for the father? I mean…jeez…she was nearly old enough to be his mother! Who could have imagined that those two would…make a baby?"

355

He snorted. "I found it hard to believe at first myself, Frohman. I thought Susan had far more sense. But remember, Marquis was known for his silver tongue. Truth be told, he was an immoral pig with an insatiable lust! I would not have trusted him alone with my cats!"

I had to laugh. Normally, Uncle would have never made such a ribald joke. He smiled slyly and took another drag off his smoke. "To answer your first question-I had my suspicions before we even got inside her home. I know you glanced at her midden heap, as I did. You saw it too."

I remembered the pit where she burned her trash and I brought the picture to my mind. The oddity struck me right away, but I wasn't sure of its significance. "The empty Coca-Cola bottles?"

He beamed and raised the head of his cane to touch the brim of his hat. I wondered what he had inside this new cane. "Bravo, Frohman. You have got it!"

"Got what? We already knew Marquis made deliveries here. Susan and the barge were his two biggest customers in that log I found."

He sighed in mock exasperation. "Yet there were no Coca-Cola bottles on the barge—were there?

"You have been told repeatably how notoriously tight-fisted Marquis was with that product. He sold the lion's share to me and spared a bit for his immediate family—and then, only on occasion. Bear in mind also that Marquis himself didn't like the stuff.

"That he treated her to the soda was a strong indication that their relationship was more than a business arrangement."

That seemed a little thin to me, but hey, who was I to say? It proved out in the end. "So, why didn't you confront her with it the first time we were there?"

"I could not have accused her—or Marquis—of such a heinous act as infanticide without tangible proof. I wished to confront Marquis before I took my next step, only I never got the opportunity. After he deceived Susan and pried the child from her mother's breast, he crossed the river and then abandoned the child in the woods to die." His face turned hard. "May he burn at Satan's feet for all eternity!"

We sat in silence for a moment then a thought occurred to me. "Do you think Susan knew Marquis had taken a diving suit? Think she gave him one and maybe was in on it?"

William considered the question. "No, I rather think not, Frohman. If she did, she probably thought Marquis was simply playing with it. The old saying of 'Boys must have their toys'."

"Like motorbikes and trains?"

His eyes snapped up, and he grinned. "Touché! Yet, I think that if Captain Roy even suspected that she knew the suit was being used for some other purpose, he would have sent a few men to insure her silence. The stakes were far too high for loose ends.

"If the Captain had known Marquis was going to Susan for help after the robbery, he would have surely stopped him. I suspect that Roy, after having administered a thorough thrashing and a death threat against his family, no doubt, expected Marquis to anchor somewhere out of sight and lick his wounds. He would have been long gone with the documents before Marquis recovered."

That was another bone of contention with me. "I'll give you that. I understand that Roy was angry. He cuts Marquis out of the deal, takes the suit, and uses the crane to take the air compressor from Marquis's boat. I even get returning the money as to avoid having the police swarming the river. Why didn't Roy just beat the hell out of him and send him on his way? Why not shoot him and sink his boat?"

357

He looked at me like I asked him what my name was. "You just answered your own question, Frohman. If Marquis was found dead or gone missing, it may have caused the same activity the stolen payroll would have."

I snorted. "So, how'd that work out for him? Remember that crowd out on the river? Susan using that harpoon on him nearly threw a wrench into his gears!"

William shrugged. "Circumstance has ever impeded genius."

I didn't have the time to tackle that one. I thought I saw movement up the road, though it was hidden by the trees. The funeral procession was coming, so I figured it was now or never. "So, what were those documents?"

He stared at me for a long moment. I had the feeling he was weighing the merits of answering against the nature of my character. He finally spoke.

"They were Treaties, Frohman. Between England, France, and our United States. Well...actually, they were more of a list of demands made by our government. Lower trade tariffs, forcing them to cut ties with some of their colonies, allowing autonomy, and creating new spheres of influence across the globe. Our government was demanding quite a few conditions be met, before we would involve ourselves in the war. Quite likely, and with good reason, many Americans would have seen this as extortion on a global scale. Certainly, the isolationists would have cried foul on moral grounds. Releasing those documents, by the Germans, could have very well kept us out of the war entirely."

That frosted my behind to no end. My father lost his life and my brother had one foot in the grave because of the Huns and here our government was wasting time trying to bend our allies over a barrel. "Maybe we should have just let them take the papers. Wilson and his cronies deserve an undoing for that nonsense!"

"I agree, Collin. But then I think of the sacrifices your family—and others—have already made. Would we want them to be in vain?"

We had let it go at that as the hearse, pulled by six black horses, reached the edge of the cemetery lawn by then.

The graveside service was calm and uneventful. There was a big crowd -- Catty's family was huge -- but, aside from the usual sniffling and the occasional sob, there were no dramatics. The Priest droned on a bit too long, as Catholics were prone to. For those of us in the know, there was more relief than grief when they finally lowered him into the ground.

Yet, the thing I will always remember about that day was how William introduced me to folk. I expected a lot of 'This is Charles son', and the like, but he said every time, "This is my friend, Collin Frohman".

My elation was dampened when William, with me in tow, stepped over to give Marquis's parents his condolences. Catty was standing beside them. When her eyes met mine, she gave a slight shake of her head. It was obvious to me that any further attention would be unwelcome at that time and place. It would have to wait until we could be alone.

When the crowd was back on the road to town, behind the empty hearse, William and I headed back to the *Helena*. Halfway there, William broke to the right and I followed him to the grave of the baby girl named Kara. He stood silently over the tiny patch of bare ground for a minute and then said, "Amen."

For my part, I heaved a great sigh. "Jeepers, what a mess, Uncle Will! Here lies baby Kara while they shovel dirt over the father who killed her, and upriver Kara's murdering mother is ready for a sanitorium! I thought I'd never would understand tall these deaths…it's all so depressing!"

He reached over and patted me on the shoulder. "Sometimes I think that is why I prefer the stage to reality. Under the lights, I can make everything turn out as beautiful as we would wish it to be. Truth is all too often ugly and chaotic."

He changed the tone and the subject, asking, "So, what are your plans now, Collin? Of course, you are welcome to stay as long as you wish—or until you prove to be too much the distraction for my maid."

"Don't worry about that," I assured him, depressing myself with the words coming out of my mouth. "She is going to need some time and I want to steer clear of her until I'm sure I won't spill my guts. I don't want her to think about what her brother did every time I'm around!

Besides, though I'm sorry, I think I have to cut my stay short. I should head home tomorrow if there is a train. If I'm going to run my father's theater syndicate—I might as well be there Monday morning, bright and early."

His face softened and he smiled, "That is very wise, Collin. And I wouldn't worry about Catherine, if I were you. She's as tough as she is sweet and I'm sure you'll say the right thing, at the right time. Besides! You should have no problem acting naturally around her! The theater is in your blood!"

I laughed and nodded. "So, what about you, Uncle Will? You discovered the parents of the child, solved yet another river robbery and murder, and, quite possibly, changed the course of history. What's next?"

William shook his head with a sad smile. "Retirement, Collin. From here on out, I will leave Sherlock Holmes on the stage. I plan on building my railroad, doing some entertaining, and make the occasional appearance on stage- as I promised I would.

"It's the simple life for me now."

I thought about the stack of stories my father had written and were piled on my desk at home. I had my doubts. "Good luck with that, but you better hope Rowan doesn't start asking too many questions. There were a lot of thinking that didn't add up for me, until you explained them, and he's a professional in Law Enforcement."

"Bah! The Chief Inspector will be basking in glory for weeks, possibly months! Police are fond of closing cases in nice, neat little packages. Soon enough, the file will be in the back of the cabinet, all but forgotten.

As for the rest of the populous-in a month it will all be local folklore. Connecticut swamp Yankees tend to move on quickly."

He gave me a straight look. "Only two of us know the entire story and I know you can keep a secret." He laughed. Then he stopped dead in his tracks. Squinting a side look down at me, he warned "And don't you go writing anything down- like your father did!"

I laughed to show him the absurdity of the idea, and we started back to the boat.

Notice--I made no promises......

EPILOGE

Six weeks later, I was just getting up to leave for the day, when the telephone on my desked rang loud enough to stop my heart. I considered not answering it—having already putting out numerous fires throughout the day—but curiosity was always my bane.

"Hello." I said loudly into the mouthpiece as I put the receiver to my ear.

"Working hard, I hope." The voice on the other end was distant and a bit tinny, but I'd know William Gillette's voice anywhere.

"Uncle Will! How are you? To what do I owe this pleasure?"

"I called to ask when you might be planning to return my maid to me."

I laughed. "That's not up to me, Uncle. You'll have to talk to Ma and Arianna about that! They've been monopolizing all her time since she got here." Which was true. After the funeral, Uncle Will and I went to the home of Marquis' family for a gathering. I explained to Catty that I needed to get home and take over the syndicate in my father's place. On a wild hope of, a slim chance, I asked her if she would like to come for a visit to my family's home in New York. To my delight, she accepted. Uncle Will assured her parents that my Mother and my sister Arianna would be adequate chaperones, so last week she took the train down to spend some time with me.

Unfortunately, my mother and sister took an instant shine to her and, with the exceptions of a few late-night visits and some canoodling in the garden, I had seen little of her besides dinner and coffee in the morning. Still, every moment we stole was wonderful.

"I'm glad that everyone is getting along so famously, but, Collin…my home is starting to look a bit…dingy!"

"Then go stay on the *Polly*!" I teased him. "How are the repairs to her going?"

"I heard a big sigh. "Slowly, I'm afraid. The fire caused more damage than we originally thought. I think she may never sail again."

.I could hear the sadness in his voice, and I felt the same way. That ship was a big part of our lives.

"Still," he went on in forced joviality, "I suppose if my home, the Seven Sisters gets too cluttered, I can always book a room at the Inn."

I laughed. "Well, we can't have that, can we? I guess I can bring her back in a while. But Uncle, I have to warn you that you will have to find yourself another girl eventually. Catty's going to have another job."

There was a pause and William asked, "Would you really hire her away from me? Make her a secretary? Or were you planning on putting her on the stage, Hmm?"

"No, No, nothing like that-though she probably could be an actress after being around you for the last year or so, but I have a bigger job for her than that."

"Such as?"

"My wife. I intend to ask for her hand, at least, I will as soon as it's appropriate."

There was the stunned silence that I had hoped for and then his voice boomed in my ear. "That's wonderful news, Collin!

I'm so happy for the both of you! My word! Two of the people I love most in the world getting married!"

"Well…hold your horses, Uncle Will. Let's see if she even says 'yes'"

"Oh, don't be a blithering saphead! Of course, she'll accept. I've seen the way she looks at you, my boy, and I can assure you she's in love. After all that poor girl has been through, I think you're just the man she needs. You'll both be good for each other.

"I know your father would have approved and been over the moon about it."

That touched me. "Thanks, William. I guess something good came out of that mess after all. By the way, were there any other reverberations for what happened? Anybody come at you over it? Has Rowan been on you?"

"The Chief Inspector? I have not heard a peep out of him! As I predicted, he's been showered with accolades and praise. Word around town is that several Federal agencies have made him offers. I'm sure the town of Chester will be looking for a replacement Chief Inspector before long."

"If they only knew." I mused. "Well, that's good, I suppose. Now you can build your railroad in peace."

"That's true, happily my privacy is intact. There is one outcome that is worrisome, though I must ask for your discretion."

"Of course, you have it. What's the problem?"

"It's Ozaki"

My heart skipped. "Ozaki? What's the matter?"

"Well, ever since he took that blow from Roy, he's been doing poorly. He won't admit it, but I can see him struggling to perform his duties and he hasn't been himself at all."

"What's the matter with him?"

"Well, we're not quite sure. Doctor Blum gave him a thorough exam and I even took him up to Hartford to consult with a few specialists. They put him through a slew of tests."

"He must have LOVED that," I said sarcastically.

I could hear his sigh over the line. "Collin, it was like giving a bath to a rabid badger. I feared he would do violence to the doctors a few times!"

"That sounds like him! What did they find out?"

"Nothing conclusive, I'm afraid. The general consensus is that, after getting a concussion from the blow then drowning shortly afterwards, that his brain has been compromised. There is a chance that there is some swelling in his brain. There is no way to determine that without an operation, which would likely just cause more damage...or worse. All we can really do is wait and see what happens. Though, I do think a visit from you would do him a world of good. Catherine too."

That sounded ominous to me to me, so I was already making plans in my head. "Alright, Uncle Will. Let me wrap a few things here and I'll bring Catty home in a few days."

"That would be grand, Collin. I promise you'll have a much more relaxed atmosphere this visit."

"Sure, sure," I replied. "Just don't go changing history until I get there...."

THE END

James Michael Walker

I sincerely hope you enjoyed this William Gillette book who played Sherlock Holmes from 1885 to 1915. Gillette's Castle is located in East Hadlyme, Connecticut, and is open to the public as a State Park.

My other novels are available from Amazon.com and if you have comments please add them to the comment area. Thank you again for all your support.